KINGS
FEAR NO ONE
A FORCED MARRIAGE MC ROMANCE

SIENNE VEGA

STEEL KINGS BOOK 3

CONTENT WARNING

HELLO AND WELCOME!

This book will be a dark forced MC romance following Logan and Teysha as they find love despite the horrific situation they've survived. It *will* have a happy ending, but before we reach that part of the story, there's some themes/topics included that may be upsetting.

I do want to first stress that this book will feature heavy religious themes and varying view points on the subject. I know this can be a deeply sensitive and personal matter for many people, so I just want to make it clear that if this makes you uncomfortable, please feel free to skip this book. Also, please know that I mean no offense to anyone on either side of the spectrum. This is simply how the story appeared to me creatively, and as I do with all of my stories, I followed where it naturally led me.

Below are some other sensitive topics included in this book:

- Graphic violence and sexual situations
- Graphic nonconsensual sexual violence
- Graphic depictions of nonconsensual and dubious consent sexual situations
- Graphic depictions of religious cults and cult-like mania
- Heavy religious themes and topics
- Depictions of mental health struggles, including severe PTSD, self-harm and attempts to take ones life
- Brief mention of abortion

I understand if these topics make you uncomfortable and you decide it is best to forego continuing with this story.

This book is not suitable for readers under the age of eighteen.

<3 Sienne

PROLOGUE - TEYSHA

July 2012

"Teysha Patrice Baxter, get your behind upstairs and go change. Lord knows the last thing I need is for everybody to think I've got a fast one for a daughter."

I glance down at the tank top and shorts I'm wearing. "But, Mama, it's hot out."

"I don't care if it's 200 degrees out. Put on some proper clothes. I raised you to know better."

It takes everything I have not to roll my eyes and stomp my feet. I wait 'til I've turned around and Mama can no longer see me before I make a sour face.

Texas is in the middle of a record-breaking heatwave, but Mama's rules are Mama's rules.

Rain, shine, or unfathomable heat.

It doesn't matter. I'm to be well-behaved and properly covered at all times.

I *should* be used to it by now. Last year, at the middle school dance, Mama made me wear a dress that swallowed me up the way a bedsheet would. The other girls sparkled in their cute dresses they'd bought from the mall while I sat frumpy and ignored in a corner.

Once in my room, I toss the tank top and replace it with the kind of baggy t-shirt that'll get Mama's stamp of approval. My short shorts meet the same fate—I put on a pair of capri pants that go down to my ankles.

"That's better," she says when I show my face down-stairs a second time. She steps forward to smooth down some flyaway hairs on my head. "You might think I'm being harsh, Tey Tey. But people talk. This is the big barbecue fundraiser Pastor James is throwing for the church. We need to make a good impression."

"Yes, Mama."

"And don't you go pushing your chest out trying to show off for them boys."

"I don't push—"

"Do I need to remind you I've got two working eyes, girl?" she interrupts sharply. She tugs on the hem of my baggy t-shirt as if wishing it were a couple sizes larger. "You just had to be big-chested like the women on your father's side."

"What's that about our chests?"

We look up at the sound of Grandma Renae's voice. She enters the living room clutching the aluminum tray of home-baked biscuits she'll be bringing to Pastor James's event.

Mama swats her hand at her. "You know more than anybody. Aren't you the one always complaining about your back aching?"

"Don't make the girl more self-conscious than she already is. You're *adorable*, Tey Tey."

I'm not sure what to say.

The mixed signals are nothing new.

Mama has pure intentions, but she can't seem to follow God's wisdom about judging people. Grandma Renae tries to smooth things over, but she's as much of a gossiper as the rest of the people they're worried about.

And Papa's oblivious either way. He honks the horn from the front drive. His warning that we have a few seconds to make it out to the car or he's leaving without us.

I'm silent the whole car ride over to the park.

Gospel music blasts from the stereos that have been set up. Picnic tables line the grassy space. Some used for seating. Others for the buffet-style food set up. Plenty of people have already arrived, mingling and chitchatting. Children chase each other around, squirting water guns and playing hide-and-seek behind trees.

Papa puts the car in park and announces we've arrived.

My belly gives a flip.

Wallace Scott stands by the drinks table grabbing a can of coke. He's grown even taller since school let out and summer break began. I'm not the only one who's noticed—the other girls in the area are practically his not-so-secret fan club.

I trail behind my parents and Grandma Renae, trying to make up my mind. How can I talk to Wallace without making it so obvious?

"Where do you think you're off to?" Mama snaps suddenly, catching me before I can walk off. "What have I told you about these events?"

"I should say hello to everyone."

"You know better than that. I've raised you to have manners, didn't I?"

"Yes, Mama."

"Patrice, go easy on her," Papa says from her side. While Mama struts, Papa *strolls*, at ease considering the summery occasion. "Tey Tey probably wants to say hi to her friends."

"Say hi to her friends or go off with some boy? You didn't see the outfit she had on. Booty shorts, Reggie."

"You remember how you used to put on those miniskirts and sneak out to see me, right?"

Grandma Renae cackles. "I sure do. Why do you think I always made you two keep the door open? I knew what your fast little behinds were getting up to."

"I was not fast," Mama says quickly, her nose practically in the air. "We were in *love*. And we did things the proper way. We got married so we could be together."

"If that's the story you're sticking with. I found the condom wrappers buried in the trash."

"Renae! Teysha is listening."

"So what? She's getting around that age where she's curious—"

"Not here. Lord knows the last thing we need is for people to overhear us." Mama shakes her head in disapproval, her lips pursed, then she puts an arm around my shoulders. We've ventured into the thick of the park grounds where other church members are mingling. She stops us in front of the pastor's wife. "Edna, what a nice event you've put together. We've brought some of my mother-in-law's home-baked biscuits."

"They were so delicious last time, we'll eat them right up."

I stand by obediently as the two chitchat, and I pretend I'm listening to what's being said. Once the conversation turns to sharing recipes, I'm barely hearing a word.

I'm not alone.

Papa and Grandma Renae wander off to check out the rest of the food tables.

I'm checking out the food tables too—Wallace Scott has grabbed a bag of Doritos to go with his can of coke. I could walk right up to him and ask him how his summer vacation's going.

My belly gives another funny flutter.

The nerves always get to me when I think about talking to him. I always end up chickening out.

It doesn't help that I'm dressed like I'm about to do chores around the house, swallowed up in the baggy t-shirt Mama insisted I wear. The other girls from school look cute in their summer outfits. It's the school dance all over again.

A sigh blows out of me. I slowly back up to go sulk away from everyone else. Someone walks up first and interrupts before I can.

"If there's one rule I have for today, it's that all the pretty young women are supposed to smile," says Pastor James. He's smiling himself, showing off the gap in his front teeth. "What's got Teysha Baxter so down? Turn that frown upside down, young lady."

"Pastor, hello..." I murmur, brushing a loose piece of hair behind my ear. "Thank you for inviting my family and me."

"It wouldn't be a community event without the Baxters." He leans slightly closer 'til only I can hear him. "Between me and you, you're my favorite."

"Um... thank you."

"You're growing up before my eyes. I remember when you were a tiny little thing barely starting school. What grade will you be in?"

"Eighth next year."

He whistles, his hands on his waist. "I bet the boys have taken notice. Has your father had to beat them off with a stick yet?"

"Um... no... not really..."

"He will soon." His smile spreads to go along with the chuckle he lets out and the way his gaze roams over me.

Confusion flickers through me. Suddenly, I'm thankful for my way-too-big t-shirt. I'm wishing Mama would stop yapping with Mrs. James and come rescue me.

"How are your grades in school, Teysha?"

"Very good. I got all As and one B."

"That's my girl. I knew you were a smart cookie. But you haven't been attending my Bible study class that I offer every other Saturday. Can I expect you this summer?"

...no thank you...

"I'm not sure," I say, easing half a step back.

He inches closer, the spice of his cologne tickling my nose. "If you're to grow into a good Christian woman, it's important you take your studies seriously."

"I will try to make it, pastor. But, um, I see one of my friends. Please, excuse me."

I make my exit like I'm a mouse scurrying in a kitchen late at night. The pastor doesn't have a chance to trap me again before somebody else calls out to him. I'm long gone within a matter of seconds, slipping through the crowd.

Maybe this will finally be my chance to talk to Wallace.

Mama's busy chitchatting with Mrs. James. Papa and Grandma Renae are lined up, fixing plates of barbecue. Emerging from the crowd, I spot Wallace toward the back by the trees. My feet move faster, my pace picking up.

I smile, about to call out to him, then I stumble to a stop. The smile drops off my face as my insides twist into a pretzel.

Wallace is off by the trees, but he's not free to talk like I've been hoping.

He's in the middle of kissing another girl from school. Viveca Robinson is one of the prettiest girls in my year. Popular, fashionable, and confident, we couldn't be more different.

Night and day.

It feels like I'm frozen in place. I'm powerless to stop my heart from leaping into my throat and making it impossible to speak.

The two separate to share in a smile, then grab each other's hands to go sit on a picnic table somewhere. I watch them go, feeling foolish for any hope I've had.

How could I think a boy like Wallace would ever want to talk to me?

I'm not the girl boys my age like. I'm not the girl they want to dance with or kiss.

I'm the girl who stands on the sidelines and watches.

"There you are," comes Mrs. James's voice. Her friendly tone from earlier is gone. She blocks Wallace and Viveca from my line of sight by stepping in front of me. "Your mother is looking for you. She says you weren't supposed to go off."

"Oh," I say, forcing an apologetic smile. "I'm sorry. I'll go find—"

"I would appreciate it if you knew your place," she interrupts sharply. "I saw you earlier, and I would prefer if you behaved your age. My husband has a reputation to uphold. One I won't let be tarnished by a girl getting certain ideas."

"But I wasn't—"

"Marriage shall be valued by all," she recites louder than me. "It is an institution that is sacred. I will not tolerate mine being disrespected. Stay away from him."

The woman trudges off with a final judgmental glare.

I've gone from stuttering to speechless all over again, more lost than ever.

It's not long before Mama calls out to me and issues more scolding about how I didn't do what I was told. For the next couple hours, I'm her shadow, going where she goes. Hovering beside her as she chats up everybody in attendance.

Any time I feel Pastor James's eyes on me, I'm looking in the opposite direction, praying his wife won't get mad and tell me off again.

I'm ignoring how Wallace and Viveca seem to be everywhere in the background, still holding hands.

My heart aches inside my chest. I blink trying to fight the itchiness of oncoming tears. I just want to go somewhere... anywhere...

Any place that's not here.

All I've wanted is to be noticed by the boy I like; all I've wished for is a love I've been told exists. The kind of love in the movies or books, where the couple gets married and grows old together.

The kind of love Mama says exists between husband and wife.

But then I realize I'm being silly again. I'm not sure if I'll ever find that special person. Someone to fall in love with and spend the rest of my life with. A happily ever after doesn't seem like it's meant for me...

1

LOGAN

Ten years later...

Day nine hundred and sixty-one of captivity.

I etch a small line on the wooden panel with the dull blade of my knife. It joins the hundreds of other tick marks on the cabin wall.

The sun didn't bother coming out today. Thick storm clouds hide it from view. More rain'll be coming by tonight.

The pots placed around the room need to be emptied. They're still full with the water that leaked in during last night's downpour.

I roll over on the sunken bunkbed 'til I'm sitting up and my bare feet touch the puddles on the ground. We ran out of pots, causing water to pool around the room.

I barely notice the difference—my feet are pruned to the point of numbness.

Some of the others still cry about it.

I rise up off the bunk to the sounds. A skeleton of a woman sits in the corner opposite me, her bony knees drawn up to her chest, sniveling as she checks her toes.

She's one of the newer ones. Still naive. Still delusional with hope.

They're my least favorite types. The ones who think there's still some grand silver lining somewhere.

Relief will have to come eventually...

I make my way across the room and stop in the doorway long enough to take in our surroundings. It's still early enough that the rest of the compound's dead silent. The other cabins bear no sign of life despite the fact that each one has people packed in like sardines in a can.

No different from the cabin I'm in.

My gaze switches out from peering around the grounds to inside the cabin where there's an empty bottom bunk.

Today's the day she arrives. They'll bring her in, and she'll be initiated into the family.

Whoever she is, she probably doesn't know what's in store for her. They're probably still transporting her. Meaning she's probably still knocked out.

In dreamland, clueless to the hell she's about to be put in.

The Leader and his saints have been searching far and wide. They've spoken about the new believer they needed to replace the last one. Not just anybody would do—she had to be of pure faith. She had to have a good heart.

Something the Leader claims is damn near impossible these days.

"Most women are deviants," he'd explained during one of his sermons. "They're dirty, filthy sinners that will burn in hell on judgment day. Our new believer must be worthy of our sacred home."

Never mind that I'm as sinful as sinful gets.

Never mind that he and his saints are the rottenest, evilest people I've ever met.

In their eyes, they're doing the work of some higher power.

None of that matters in this fucked up world we're captive in.

I'm standing so long in the doorway that Brody appears from the large house upfront. He crosses the grassy stretch of land carrying his AR-15 against his shoulder, his expression tight-lipped.

Our eyes lock onto each other.

I don't bother letting him finish his walk toward my cabin. I step forward to meet him damn near halfway. He clamps a hand on my shoulder and shoves me forward as if I wasn't already going voluntarily.

But appearance is everything in the Chosen Saints— Brody's making sure he *looks* like he's in control; he's leading me, not the other way around. Believers aren't supposed to have autonomy.

"You know the rules," he growls low enough for only my ears. "No crossing the threshold on your own unless directed."

I grit my teeth. "I saved you the steps."

"Hurry up." He shoves me again. Harder, so I stumble.

There was a time in the past where I was in good enough shape to take out any of the men in the Chosen Saints. I had the muscle power and the hand-to-hand combat skills to not just kick their ass. I had the ability to snap them like twigs.

Nine hundred and sixty-one days into captivity, things've changed. I'm a shell of what I once was, whittled down from the powerful man I used to be.

Brody pushes and shoves me all the way to the main house. The three-story mini mansion is where the Leader and his most loyal saints sleep. It's night and day between the main house and the cabins the believers are kept in.

Dry. Insulated. Full furnishings. Electricity and running water. Luxuries like TVs and real beds. It couldn't be more different from what we're subjected to out in the cabins.

The only time any of us spend in this house is when we're called upon. When we're needed for what's known as an 'act of service'.

I'm called to the main house almost daily.

The curse of being a saint's favorite. Brody leads me upstairs to the fourth bedroom on the left, then nudges the door open.

She's waiting for me, propped up on her recliner she treats like a throne. Her eyes light up and a smirk twists onto her lips. She flicks her satiny robe open and kicks her legs up onto either side of her footstool. She doesn't care that Brody sees she's wearing nothing underneath.

The concept of modesty doesn't exist in a place like the Chosen Saints's sanctuary.

But that doesn't mean privacy isn't sometimes wanted for these acts of service.

Brody knows to close the door without any questions. I know to step forward and then kneel.

Mandy spreads her legs wider. "I've been dreaming of you, boy. All night I was. Almost had Brody go down and pull you out of your cabin. It couldn't have been earlier than three, four in the morning. Go ahead and have a taste. That tongue of yours..."

She shudders instead of finishing her train of thought.

I urge myself to tune out of the moment like I usually do. Some days it's easier than others.

In the beginning, I fought. I raised hell each and every time. My back bears the lash marks to show for it.

But everybody surrenders eventually; take any person and put them in this situation. They'd eventually tap out and comply.

I kneel between Mandy's legs and press my face to her vagina the way she likes—so that she's basically grinding into my face as my tongue pokes out and licks at her clit.

Her fingers grip my hair, and she sighs in encouragement. Soon her thighs are quivering around my head as I work my lips and tongue the way she likes. I'm checked out of the moment.

So gone I don't taste her. The slick evidence of her arousal doesn't register.

I lick and suck at her while my mind's thousands of miles away.

There was a point in time where I used to laugh and tell my brother Mace and his best friend Cash I hadn't met a pussy I didn't like. Turn off the lights and they were all the same—they all felt pretty damn good wrapped around my dick.

It was a joke. Something dumb we laughed about before getting shitfaced and going home with a different club girl.

I was always in control. I was always in the driver's seat.

Not once did it ever occur to me that it could be different. That there'd come a time I didn't get any say.

Mandy bleats like a fucking goat when she comes. She rifles her fingers through my unkempt hair, then sags against the cushions of her recliner. Her eyelids grow heavy and her eyes hazy.

"You are the best, boy," she purrs, petting me like a dog. With affection that makes my skin crawl. "You like the taste of me, don't you?"

My glare would give me away to a sane person. Somebody not delusional.

Turns out, Mandy and the saints like her are as delusional as the new believers who still have hope—the difference is that the believers tell themselves help is on the way.

Mandy tells herself I'm enjoying this; that she doesn't repulse me on every fucking level.

I give the slightest nod in answer. Because if I didn't, I'd be on the receiving end of a whip. She keeps hers on her end table, within reach. Brody didn't say it, but he's out in the hall. It wouldn't end in my favor even if I did defy her.

It never has in the past.

She strokes my hair again. "Good boy. Have another taste."

Plugging her pussy with two of her fingers, she gathers some of her juices from her orgasm and then slips them past my lips. Her eyes glint as she watches me. She's waiting for me to play along.

I suck on her fingers and will myself to ignore the tart taste of her.

The only pussy I've ever almost retched at tasting.

When she's satisfied with my performance, she sits up straighter and calls for Brody.

I'm collected and escorted back toward the rear exit of the house. Brody's decided he needs to flex even more of his authority by gripping my arm. The urge to crack my elbow into his face and flip him on his ass rises up inside me.

The ceremony room stops me. I catch a glimpse of the inside where saints and believers are setting up for another ceremony, and my stomach roils.

"That for tonight?"

Brody jerks me along faster. "What do you think? She's arriving. You know what you have to do."

I suspected.

It's different hearing it confirmed. Knowing I'm about to be forced to participate in more fucked up depravity I never wanted...

The ceremony begins at sundown. The saints are already seated in the first few pews when the believers are shoved and prodded into the room by the likes of Brody and a few other designated henchmen. None of us fight them. They're well-fed and armed. We're malnourished and barely functioning.

I drop into a seat toward the back, right next to the skeletal woman from my cabin. She hasn't stopped sniveling since this morning, wiggling her toes every so often; apparently she still can't feel them.

Xavier, one of the other armed guards, mutters something in Brody's ear, then points in my direction. Brody nods and comes over to collect me.

"Get up," he says. "We need you up front. You'll be performing your marital duty."

I stand up only after he jams the barrel of his assault rifle into my stomach. I've barely squeezed into the only open space up front when the double doors fly open.

The Leader strides through in his billowing white robe. His sheets of hair sway around his face like white-blond curtains. A few saints follow, their own like-new robes fluttering. The two in the back enter clutching a squirming, shrieking woman.

The new believer.

My stomach muscles clench. I track every movement of hers down the aisle toward the altar up front.

She's a mess. Clothes torn and streaked with dirt. Her hair's a knotted cloud, like a fist's been gripped up in it and disheveled whatever style it had been in. She's got a bruise on her cheek, a plum shade against her brown complexion. Tears brim in her wide, expressive eyes that match the panicked expression etched onto her face.

...but it's a face I could tell would be pretty in less grim circumstances. In a less fucked up moment where she was put together and not covered in bruises and scrapes.

She's on the shorter side. Pear-shaped and curvy in an enticing way.

But there's nothing enticing about this. It can only be described as the depraved fucked up shit that it is.

Yet we believers sit obediently in our pews and pretend we're not disturbed.

The woman's thrown to the floor of the altar. She lands right at the Leader's feet. He peers down at her with his cold, emotionless eyes, then steps over her like she's an inconvenience.

My hands curl into fists in my lap.

"Saints and believers, we have a new companion in our midst," he announces. "We searched far and wide for a woman with the purest heart who would join our mission. Behold—we have found her!"

Everyone rows back cranes their necks for a better look. A few murmurs break out.

The woman has sat up and tried to scoot away. Xavier nudges her with his boot to keep her in line.

"Silence!" the Leader calls. "It is time the ceremony begins. We have gathered today to welcome our new believer to our family, where she will be cherished and loved as we are all cherished and loved by each other. The bond we have formed is only outmatched by the bond we have with our sacred Leader and Lord."

Several of the saints and believers nod and mumble along, drinking in every word he speaks. I'm the only one glaring, fighting off the pulse of anger that throbs inside me.

Me and the woman.

She's looking up at the Leader with tears streaked down her cheeks and horror widening her eyes.

"And now, we will bear witness to another sacred bond," the Leader continues, his slivery voice echoing. "The bonding of a man and a woman. Believer Logan, step forward."

2

LOGAN

"I now pronounce you man and wife," the Leader says to the room full of Chosen Saints. "You will now drink the matrimonial red wine that signifies the family bloodline you will create."

I'm handed a goblet. The woman, whose name I've learned is Teysha, is given one too. She stands opposite me, averting her gaze. She stares anywhere but at me and the Leader and anybody else in the room.

We're the enemy. Her captors.

If she had any idea how wrong she is.

I'm not one of them...

"Drink," the Leader commands.

I blink and realize he's repeated himself twice now. Cause for punishment if he's in a bad enough mood.

I bring the goblet to my lips and swallow down the wine in a few short gulps. It tastes of bitter sour grapes mixed with something chemical. Some ingredient that shouldn't be in wine. A drug to make us more complacent.

It's a taste I've noticed several times before. During past

ceremonies where I'd been forced to consummate a bond with the woman chosen for me.

Teysha's here 'cuz the last bond fell through. Grace hadn't been able to take being captive another second...

I keep my expression neutral while consuming the wine. Teysha makes a face of disgust, stopping after only a mouthful.

"Drink," the Leader repeats. His teeth clench and his eyes flash with warning.

She chokes on the rest of it. A couple droplets slip down her chin and splatter onto her chest. My attention's drawn to the area—she's busty to the point of distraction, and the wine slides down the cleft between her breasts. Breasts that are only halfway visible due to her blouse being torn and muddied.

My gaze lifts a couple inches to her throat. A golden cross pendant dangles from the necklace she wears. Her *real* religion.

No wonder they chose her.

One look at her, and you can tell she's the type to be seated in church every Sunday. Everything from the modest skirt and blouse she's wearing to the horror on her face reveals she's exactly the 'pure heart' type they like to corrupt.

She catches on that I'm studying her and wards me off with a knit of her brows and suspicious bend of her mouth.

"Now for the bonding," the Leader says, stepping aside. His arm sweeps in dramatic fashion as he gestures to the bed that's propped up on the dais.

A bed that I'm more than familiar with. That makes my stomach roil on sight.

"Get started," he prompts.

I take a step toward the bed, then realize I'm alone.

Teysha's stayed put. She makes no attempt to hide her tears or the fact that she's shaking on the spot. Her fingers have clasped around the gold cross like she expects for it to protect her against the evil swallowing her up.

The Leader sighs. "Brody, Xavier. Help our new believer."

Both men stride forward to grab one of her arms and drag her toward the bed. They lift her up and throw her down onto the mattress like they couldn't give less of a shit how much she screams and struggles.

"No... NOOOO!" she screams in sudden wild hysterics, kicking her legs out.

And I stand by and let it happen.

My heart's racing. My fingers twitch and itch. I can barely control my breathing.

The room feels hot and like it's spinning.

My temper pulses, but I tamp it down. I remind myself there's nothing I can do. A lesson I've learned dozens of times over the past nine hundred days.

I can't stop what's about to happen. But I'm maybe the only other person in this room that feels sick from the ceremony we're being forced to participate in.

"The binds," the Leader drawls lazily from the sidelines. "Use the binds if she refuses to lay still."

Brody and Xavier wrap leather binds around her wrists, tethering her to the bed, and then move out of the way.

The silence in the room feels deafening. Disorienting as all attention falls on me.

I swallow down the sick feeling and urge myself to black out. Just like I managed earlier with Mandy.

But blacking out when you're on top of a crying, trembling woman is nowhere near as easy. Flashbacks of my first time with Grace pollute my head. She'd cried too, begged like I had the power to end what was happening to us.

I'd caught her eye, and then she understood. She got that I was just like her. I was forced into this fucked up situation too.

The room watches on in silent interest as I position myself between Teysha's legs. It takes me a moment to get hard, stroking my dick, reminding myself there's no choice. If I can't perform, then I have no use. Then the Leader's going to turn his ire onto me.

Another thing that wouldn't be the first time...

I try to tune out our surroundings. Nobody else is around. Nobody else is watching.

It's just me and this woman on the bed. We'll do what we have to do as quick as possible to get it over with. Then we'll go back to surviving our captivity.

I guide myself to Teysha's entrance and pause for a second. Even if this isn't consensual—*neither* of us want this —I was hoping I'd catch her eye like I caught Grace's.

Make her understand I have to. I'll make this quick and finish in a hurry. But she won't look at me. She's turned her head away, her eyes clenched shut. Her chin quivers as her cries continue, silent and terrified.

It's enough to hollow out my insides. I'm left with a sinking, empty sensation.

My erection twitches in a warning it'll soften if I don't get going.

I take in a breath and push myself inside. The girl bows against me and cries out in agony. By the way her body jerks and the slight resistance I encounter, I understand what's just happened. What I've just taken from her, and I'm sure she'll never forgive me for.

She's outright sobbing now. The horrific sounds chip away at me as I draw my hips back and then thrust into her.

Her walls clamp down on me and the tight heat massages my dick. Soon the beginnings of a climax tickle their way up my spine. I thrust a little faster, chasing the end, wanting for this moment between us to be over.

My gaze remains on her face. Futile hope she'll finally look up at me and I can make her get it. I can promise her it'll be over soon.

But she never acknowledges me in any way beyond her sobs and pained jerks of her body. It's only been a few minutes when I'm able to give in and let go. My release spills from me in a weak pulse of pleasure. I wait for every drop to be spent before withdrawing and tucking myself back into my pants.

Blood coats the head, confirming what I suspected. A detail I've got to bury in an effort to fight off guilt at what I've done.

The Leader's smile takes up half of his face. Several of the saints mirror him, smiling at the two of us on the bed as if we've made them proud.

As if what we've done isn't fucked up and depraved.

In the world of the Chosen Saints, it's simply bonding. Just like I bonded with Mandy earlier. Just like the Leader bonds with any of the female saints and believers on a whim. Just like... Teysha will be made to bond with me and others too.

Free love is a whole different concept in this so-called family.

Teysha's taken away to be cleaned up.

The ceremony ends with a celebration of food and drink. The believers are allowed to stay for the first hour.

Once it's up, we're corralled back to our cabins—unless the Leader or one of his saints have chosen you for the night.

I'm not chosen, so I wind up in the dank cabin, sitting in the dark on my sunken bunkbed. As far as I'm concerned, a better turnout for the night than if Mandy had requested me a second time today.

Teysha's brought in after everybody else in the cabin's gone to sleep. She's deposited onto her bunk by two of the saints who brought her and then left without a word. They shut the door to our cabin and total darkness commences.

I sit still and watch her corner of the cabin. Though shadows blanket the space and I can't see her, I can hear her —she's sobbing herself to sleep. Probably the first night of many where she'll fall asleep like this.

For half a second, I consider getting up and going over. Explaining to her what I did was unavoidable. Telling her I didn't mean to hurt her. Letting her know she's got to toughen up, 'cuz this is the way things are and we're all captives here.

She can't let herself end up like Grace and the other women before her.

It'd be the first real human words I've spoken in days. Maybe weeks.

But I don't. I stay where I am, sitting in the dark, and I listen to her cries without ever saying a comforting word.

Instead, I focus on the anger I've learned to control. I allow myself to think about something I've avoided for months. Something that gives the false hope I hate seeing in others but reminds me there might be a reason to keep holding on.

One day... one day I'm busting the hell out of here. Then... then I'm making every last one of these bastards pay...

3

LOGAN

I etch the mark on the wooden panel with the dull blade of my knife. It joins the hundreds of other tick marks on the cabin wall.

The sun rises by the hour, bathing the landscape in pale morning light. The worst of the storm's yet to come.

This calm is just the lead up. The false silence before the break of thunder. The rain will flood us out. The cold might be too much.

Last year we were made to double up in the cabins still dry enough. An already packed sardine can now fit to burst.

But nobody was under any other false belief. None of us were foolish enough to think our well-being had shit to do with it. We were the minions.

Easily replaced and holding little to no value.

We're too damn beat down to disagree. Too broken and isolated.

I turn away from the cabin door and peer around the tight space. The only other person up is an older man by the name of Hershel. He's quiet and keeps to himself and wakes early most mornings. He likes having time to pray.

Talk to his god before he's sent to hell for the day.

He's been here almost as long as I have, and he's still foolish enough to think it makes a difference.

I shake my head and drag my gaze from where he's kneeling to the bunk below his. My newest wife has spent the last couple days ignoring my existence. She's just about ignored everybody except when forced otherwise.

During mealtimes and chores. When the guards make her.

Luckily, she hasn't been here long enough to be called upon again.

I already know I am before it happens. It's Wednesday morning, which only means one thing. Xavier shows up with his rifle, exhibiting his usual bully tactics. He yells at Hershel and another cabinmate named Isadora. Both Hershel and Isadora scramble to obey his order; they'll be working in the corn fields today.

Xavier pinches her ass on the way out.

I'm collected and sent up to the house.

"Mandy wants to see you. Then you'll be put on laundry."

I comply without giving any reaction. My legs move and I walk up toward the main house escorted by another guard, but I'm not present in the moment. I'm existing in my head only. Compartmentalization I learned even as a kid.

I got better at once it I came to Camp Hell. Once I was 'saved' by the Saints. Now I can check out of anything.

Mandy blows smoke in my face, her lips stretching into a big smile that shows off her chipped front tooth. "There's my boy. Get to it."

She drops backward into her favorite armchair and kicks her legs up onto the armrests. Her robe falls open as her thighs do and her bare pussy glistens up at me. I haven't fully kneeled before she's digging thick fingers into my hair and shoving my face in between.

She groans and rocks against me as I'm buried in her pussy. I'm doing what she's requested—a tongue to work her inside and lick up juices.

I'm thinking about anything else.

I'm wondering about the storm that's migrating in and if the sky will be clouded over by afternoon. I'm imagining the cold drops of rain splattering onto my face as I stand outside the cabins.

Not the drops of cum on my tongue as Mandy cries out her release.

"The bed," she puffs. "C'mon, stallion."

The room fills with more of her bleats. She's shaking on her hands and knees as I give her what she's asked for. I grip her rolls of freckled skin and fuck her from behind. My dick's learned to dissociate too... for the most part.

When fulfilling a role for high-ranking women in the Chosen Saints, like Mandy, there's no other way. If you can't get hard, you're of no use. You don't last long once you've got no use.

"Yes, stallion!" she bleats, her pussy squelching from all the juices. "Yes, yes, yes! Fuck me good! OHHH!"

The whole house has to hear.

Mandy loves when they do. For everybody in the Chosen Saints to know I'm her favorite.

Her stallion.

I'm dripping sweat by the end. She rolls over lazily, smiling up at me, then pulls me down for a kiss. Her breath reeks of cigarettes, and she lets her nails drag appreciatively over my skin.

"You never let me down," she hums. "Now, on about your way."

I get up off the bed and walk toward the chair where my tattered clothes lay.

It's the first time I'm aware we're not alone—the Leader stands in the doorway, leaning against the frame, his arms folded.

I stop where I am. Everybody knows the Leader's married to Mandy. She was his first wife. She's high-ranking, but she still belongs to him. As do all the women in this place.

For a second, he looks me up and down and I stand naked as the day I was born, waiting out the moment. There's no such thing as free movement in this house.

"What a show," he says finally, giving a nod. "It is no wonder Mandy's always calling on your service."

I'm finally present enough for a real reaction. Heated by blood in my veins and the muscles that clench. Compliant as I am, I'll never stop fighting. I'll never let him win.

"I have things to do," I say. "You're going to need to move out of the way."

The Leader's icy eyes light up. "Of course, Believer Logan. Do what you have been instructed to do."

I slide into the workman's pants and hole-riddled t-shirt that are the only clothes I have and stride past him.

Something tells me he watches me on my walk out.

The rest of the morning, I'm under the close surveillance of Brody and another guard named Amos. We're at the back house, far across the property, using the industrial-sized washing machines and dryers.

Doing laundry for dozens of members in the family takes hours.

There are sheets, blankets, towels, clothes to launder.

Brody and Amos watch on from lawn chairs as I haul out bag after bag of laundry and toss it into the pickup truck.

"Faster, boy!" Amos barks, then laughs.

My muscles ache as I sling another bag of blankets over my shoulders and carry four others. It's backbreaking, sweat-inducing work that would go smoother with more people.

But that would be too easy.

And the guards always get a kick out of pushing me to the limit. Most of them are forced to hear Mandy's cries when I pleasure her. Her screams about how satisfied she is. It's created some kind of unspoken resentment between me and the other men in power here.

I'm hauling one of the last bags when I notice the other believers in the distance. Those that have been sent to pick berries and apples from the fruit field. Teysha's among them.

The basket's limp at her side as she wanders like someone too dead to be alive. Her expression's dark and unreadable, her movements sluggish. A strong gust of wind would knock her over.

When a breeze does come through and blows the strap of her tattered potato sack of a dress down, she doesn't bother fixing it. She doesn't bother with anything. Even picking the fruits she should.

The whistle sounds and one of the guards comes over to check their bounty.

"What's this?" he yells at her. "You had an hour and you bring me two?"

SMACK!

His hand crashes down across her cheek and she tumbles to the ground. The basket flies out of her hand, where it lands on its side next to her. Two measly pieces of fruit tumble out and roll away.

An immediate current of rage rushes me. The laundry bag drops from my shoulder and my fists curl. I take a step forward despite the fact that I'm ten yards away.

"Hey, boy!" calls Amos. "Didn't I say hurry the fuck up?"

I'm caught between blinding anger and the sense to move on. It's like standing on the border of two worlds. Two versions of myself.

I stare at the scene far away, where the guard kicks at a collapsed Teysha and grabs a fistful of her hair to yank back her head and scream in her face, and I feel the anger shake in my bones. The dissent that spreads so fast it's taken over me many times before. All the times I've pushed back against the system.

All the times I've gotten my ass knocked right back down.

But I got up.

I always get up.

Teysha does too—she wobbles to her feet and collects her basket and two pieces of fruit. The guard shoves her some more to get her going.

I breathe what feels like fire. I talk myself off the ledge. Remind myself now's not the time.

Now wouldn't make a difference. I can't change anything.

Yet.

"Boy, this is the last time we're telling you!" snaps

Amos. He thrusts a finger at the pickup truck. "Hurry the fuck up!"

The violent screams go mute. The urges melt away. I unclench my fists and pick up the bag of blankets and take them to the truck like I'm told.

Not now. But soon.

"You were right," Hershel says, looking over to me. "A storm's coming."

I grunt in answer, wiping down my workman boots with a rag.

The cabin's lit only by the melted wax candle perched on the windowsill. Shadows cover the rest of the confined space. Several of the others have already crawled into their bunkbeds for the night; it's easier to go to sleep on empty stomachs than stay awake through the evening.

No supper for us tonight.

Not unusual. But no less cruel.

"I wonder if the storm'll make them cancel the celebration," Hershel goes on when I say nothing. He strokes his overgrown beard that resembles a white cloud more than anything. "It could get real nasty for a few days."

Though Hershel's just looking for conversation, I can't bring myself to answer.

My mind's still on earlier. The laundry's been long done. The other chores have been finished up. All believers have been returned to their cabins.

Yet I'm stuck on what I'd witnessed. I'm witnessing more of it as Teysha crawls onto her bottom bunk. Her cheek's swelled up from the hit she took. Her knees are bruised from spending so long bending over in dirt, picking fruit from bushes.

Neither seem to register. Just like the strap of her dress being down hadn't.

She's compartmentalizing, clutching her gold cross pendant and muttering words.

Prayers.

She's not really here right now.

When Grace and I first got married, I was bitter and angry. I still hadn't learned the dynamics of the Chosen Saints. The first few months we were married, we kept our distance. The only time we were together was when we had to perform our marital duty. Usually at the whim of the Leader.

But after a while, some attachment formed. Our marriage had not happened out of love or a desire to spend our lives together. It had been forced under the guise of the Chosen Saints. We were stuck with each other.

We learned to make that enough. We became each other's sanity check.

As fucked up as it is to admit, I could find a crumb of pleasure after that. In the things we were forced to do, I could pretend it was good. I could enjoy Grace and feel no guilt. Come to hate myself less for what I was doing to her. Blame myself less for letting it happen.

The bright spot we found together wasn't enough for Grace.

It couldn't erase the rest of the darkness. It couldn't save her from the nights she was called to the Leader's quarters.

She was found one morning hanging from the tree outside our cabin, a belt wrapped around her neck.

I've wondered if it could've been different. If maybe

there was something I could've done. I should've got in when the Leader called her into his bedroom. I shouldn't've pretended I couldn't hear Brody when he came looking for her in the middle of the night.

Would any of it have mattered?

The questions are still turning in my head when I set aside my workman boots and toss my rag. Hershel interrupts himself in the middle of his sentence as he watches me get up and walk over to the bunk where Teysha's sitting.

She takes her time acknowledging me. Her eyes are cast to the floor. Her ample chest shakes from the deep breath she draws in then releases.

Up close, I notice what I hadn't before—the tiny cut at the corner of her lip and the hints of purple blended into the bruise on her cheek. Her dress is torn and tattered and her nails caked with dirt. She looks like hell like the rest of us.

Except for the gold cross hanging around her neck. Bright and intact more than anything else in the room.

I swallow against the stiffness in my throat and ask, "You alright?"

Her bottom lip quivers and the next breath she takes in sounds torn. She's trying her hardest not to cry.

"Hey," I say. My fingers slip under her chin and tip her head up. "You alright?"

Tears blur her vision. "Y-ye... ye-yes."

"It's going to be alright," I say. "You've just got to count the days."

"For... what?"

"For when we get out of here. You'll escape with me."

I drop my hand from her chin and then return to wiping down my boots. I pick up the rag I've been using and then feel her stare from across the room. The bloodied corner of Teysha's mouth quirks before it's gone. The quickest, smallest hint of a smile I've ever seen.

But damn it. I'll take it.

"What a joyous occasion!" Saint Crystal cries out at the dinner table. She clasps her hands together, eyes shining with tears. "I am grateful for the love our Leader gives us."

The others nod their heads and sip their wine. Those who are allowed seats at the main table.

The rest of us sit in chairs on the outskirts of the room. We've been given paper plates of a single slice of deli ham and American cheese. Otherwise known as the closest thing to a meal most of us have had in forty-eight hours.

But it wouldn't be captivity if we weren't kept down in different ways.

Sometimes that's physical beatings. Other times it's starvation or isolation. It's backbreaking labor and squalid living conditions. It's everything at once.

I got used to the idea my clothes would always hang off me here a long time ago. And though I'm still a man of intimidating stature, I've lost half the power I once had.

Whittled down to the point of going invisible.

It's what we're subjected to as we wipe clean our paper plates. We obediently watch the Leader and his Saints enjoy a long, gut-busting meal. The smells of garlic and butter linger in the air, clawing away at the barren insides of my stomach.

It's past the point of gurgling.

Teysha's on my right. She's hardly touched her ham and

cheese. Her eyes have filled with tears again as she stares ahead at the dinner table. The ceremonial aspect of these dinners seem to bother her most.

Some disturbance to her spirit.

I grit my teeth and turn my head straight too. We're in the front row, and the Leader has been in a mood all day. Several of the Saints, like Crystal, have picked up on it and decided to shower him with praise. Nobody wants to be the one he takes his frustrations out on.

He swirls the wine in his glass, his eyelids low. "Yes, well... you should all be inherently grateful you have been blessed to be part of my family. I have welcomed you with open arms despite your flaws."

Teysha sniffles, then wipes her face with the back of her hand.

"Shhh," I hush.

But her tears can't be turned off. A few more roll down her cheeks, and she presses her lips together to keep from making a sound.

The main table falls silent as the Leader glances into the audience of believers. He picks us out at once, his icy glare landing right on us.

"Believer Logan, do you and your wife have something to say? Would you like to participate in tonight's dinner?"

I shake my head. "We're watching as requested."

A couple of the Saints hiss their disapproval from the table. They don't like my tone or lack of deference to their master.

The Leader grins. "Interesting you say that, Believer Logan. Because I have an idea how to change that. It is time we have some entertainment for the festivities. What better form of entertainment than to watch the beautiful act that takes place between a loving husband and his bride?"

My jaw clenches and I glare at him, barely holding myself back.

"Believer Logan," he says in his slow, arrogant voice. "Up to the table. You and your lovely, tearful wife. Bend her over and then take her."

4

TEYSHA

ALL SOUND BECOMES AN ECHO IN MY EARS.

Everyone in the room turns their heads for a look at me. The Leader grins wider, pleased by the reluctance he's picked up on.

The man I've married—*Logan*—pauses before giving his reaction. It comes in the form of a resolute nod and slow rise to his feet. He's already disappearing into his head. He's resigned himself to the order he's been given.

Hardly enthusiasm. Thick with unmistakable tension.

Enough insubordination for the Leader to revel in.

This will be a hard lesson that will be learned. I haven't been here long, but I've accepted my captors are the cruelest kind of people. They like establishing how far above they are and how down below we are.

But I can't do this.

Physically, mentally, emotionally. I can't handle what's happening.

Lord, please bring me strength. Please see me through this darkness.

I repeat the prayer over and over again in my head, trying so hard to hold on when it feels like I'm coming apart.

"Teysha," Logan says. He holds out his hand for me to slip mine into.

Each second drags on for its own eternity. In this moment suspended in time, the Leader and the others look on. The guards like Amos inch closer, ready to exert force. Out of the dozens of eyes on me, I find Logan's. I let myself get lost in how vivid they are.

Blue like the Leader's, but a different kind entirely. Peering into his eyes is like swimming deep in the ocean. It's like being carried away by a current, never to return.

The escape I've been praying for.

My hand slips into his and he pulls me to my feet.

He's the only thing I focus on as we do what we've been told. We stop at the table and the Leader instructs him to take me.

I flatten my palms against the tabletop and hold my breath. Logan comes around me, his arms over mine, tucking as much of me inside his arms as he can. I spread my legs and feel him erect, prodding at my entrance.

He squeezes my hips. His lips hover near my ear. "It'll be alright."

He slides into me as slow as he can.

I bite back my sob at the aching discomfort of being penetrated. The table wobbles as he begins to move. The Leader reclines in his chair and sips more of his wine. The others are too enthralled to look away. They watch every drag of Logan's hips and every strangled breath I give.

Entertainment.

Punishment.

Repentance for not falling in line.

I squeeze my eyes shut and listen to the words Logan breathes in my ear.

"It's going to be alright," he says. "Count the days."

My lips move, repeating him, though no sound comes out.

Count the days.

"We'll get out of here."

We'll get out of here.

"You're going to be alright."

I'm going to be alright.

"Harder!" growls the Leader. "Believer Logan, you have more passion for your bride than that. Show us."

I wince as Logan grips me tighter and his thrusts become rougher. I tell myself I'm swimming. I'm making my escape. The fantasy blooms in my imagination and lets me wander away from the moment.

My mind elsewhere, my body responds on its own. I'm hit with a shudder that racks through me, starting in my sex. I've been bent over the table as Logan half collapses on top of me and buries himself deep.

Our heavy breathing fills the room for seconds to come.

Everyone's waiting on the Leader's reaction. His grin has gone nowhere. He's more pleased than ever.

"Bravo, Believer Logan. Guards, take them back to their cabin. They've entertained enough."

Amos and Brody flank us before we've even had a chance to right our clothes. We're escorted out of the dining room in the main house and returned to our cabin.

"That was quite a show you put on, girl," says Amos. "All that panting and shaking."

The insides of my stomach knot up as he bursts into laughter and slams the cabin door shut. His laughter echoes until he's disappeared into the main house.

I feel sick enough to spew what little is in my stomach.

Logan's turned his back on me. He's reached for his workman boots and the rag he shines them with.

I'm a shaky, emotional wreck. I hang by the door wondering if he'll notice. He'll offer the same comfort he did in the dining room as he...

I swallow down more nausea.

My first night as a captive I had my virginity stolen from me. I hadn't consented to being tied down in a bed and taken in front of a room full of people by a man I didn't know. No matter how loud I screamed or desperately I fought, it happened anyway.

I was broken. I was damaged.

As the distraction I found earlier fades away, it's sinking in. I've been broken again, damaged again.

The only solace I can find in a situation so dark and disturbing is that I was with...

"L-Logan," I sputter. I take a couple steps forward.

He doesn't look at me. He scrubs harder into the boot's worn leather. "What?"

"I need..." I choke on the next sob that bubbles up.

"Lay down. Get some rest."

The coldness confuses me. The security I felt earlier, wrapped in his arms, no longer exists.

His only concern is cleaning his boots.

I crawl into my bunk, unsure of what I'm feeling or what's happening and why. I wanted to believe it would be alright, but now I'm not so sure.

When I was a little girl, I saw the princes rescuing princesses in the fairytales and hoped someday I'd experience the same. I've waited my whole life for that kind of fairytale ending. I always assumed it would happen when I married the man I loved.

I imagined he would be everything I ever wanted. He would be the man of my dreams.

I never thought he'd be a man I was forced into making vows with. I never thought I'd be held captive and made to have sex with him for other's entertainment.

And I never thought I'd be finding comfort even in the dark.

More comfort than even my cross brings me. More comfort than the prayers I whisper give me.

Over time it becomes the reality I know. My life from before fades 'til it no longer feels like my own. It's no longer a life I remember.

The days blur together. The warm afternoons collecting fruit. The late nights lying in a bunkbed listening to crickets chirp. Every time we're called upon by the Leader to consummate our marriage.

One night, the lights have already gone out when we're sought out. Xavier comes down to retrieve us. We're brought into the Leader's spacious bedroom where we find him in an armchair, nursing a drink. Mandy's perched on his lap, smoking a cigarette.

I glance up at Logan, seeking reassurance. He's already overtaking me, already easing me against him as if about to wrap me up. He's glaring at the Leader and Mandy.

I can feel the animosity that fills the space between them.

We have sex as they watch. Mandy puts out her cigarette and the Leader pulls down her top to play with her breasts. He barks orders at Logan and applauds when he's pleased by our performance. By the time Logan's spilling himself inside me, the Leader's inside Mandy.

We're not dismissed until after they're done with each other.

The second we're cleared to go, Logan's gripping my elbow. He keeps me pinned to his side the entire walk to our cabin.

We rarely talk when alone. I suspect it's because he knows I'll seek comfort. The same words he whispers when he's taking me. Maybe some affection. Some bonding.

Instead, once it's over, he's distant. He won't look at me, and he refuses to talk. He's my husband only when we're called upon and he's inside me. Yet these dark moments still become some of my most comforting.

Torture and solace wrapped together in moments that change me forever.

I'm still broken. Still damaged.

But I can hang on with Logan's touch. His fingers bruising my skin and his rough breaths in my ear. The little shudder he makes me feel when I fall apart.

They're not much, but they're all I have.

Logan will never be the man I thought I'd marry, but he's enough for a place like this. I count the days with him and admire how he remains strong at all times. He never cracks and never lets them get to him.

It would be great to be that unshakable.

No wonder he's able to comfort me in the darkest moments of our lives. He's so strong, he can withstand anything. I doubt I'll ever be that strong, but if I can hang on for another day, then I'll make it.

Count the days.

It's drizzling out as the evening fades into night, and

we're called upon. Logan grabs my hand, and we cross the field leading up to the house.

"Walk faster," Brody snaps, poking the barrel of his rifle into my spine. "He wants you in his bedroom."

Logan taps his knuckles on the door. We enter expecting to be greeted by a familiar sight.

The Leader in his armchair, clutching his drink. Mandy on his knee, puffing on a cigarette.

But tonight, things are different. Mandy's gone.

It's just the Leader waiting for us.

"Close the door," he says.

I can feel how tense Logan is as he grips the brass handle and snicks it shut. His restraint is held by a thin, invisible string.

"Come here. Both of you."

Logan keeps half a pace ahead of me as we step toward him. The mood couldn't feel more tenuous and unpredictable. I'm holding my breath, unsure what to expect.

"Strip," the Leader says. "Then join me on the bed."

Logan's left arm darts out to keep me from moving. "Join *you* on the bed?"

"You heard me. Tonight it will be the three of us."

5

LOGAN

"SHE'S MY WIFE," I GRIT OUT, CRACKLING LIKE A LIVE wire on the inside.

"She is your wife," the Leader says. He stands up from the armchair and unties his robe to reveal he's got nothing else on. "But what do we believe about those that lead us?"

I refuse to answer, too busy glaring at him. I'm fighting the urge to smash my fist into his pale, smug face, and contemplating my punishment if I did. Would it be worth it?

Only if I break his fucking jaw.

"They are all my wives," he reminds in his cocky tone. He reaches out to stroke Teysha's cheek. "I can have them whenever I want. Surely you remember that from Grace."

My fists shake at my side. "She's never... she's only been with me."

"Excellent. That is why she was chosen after all. For her to be shared among our family."

Teysha grabs my arm and shifts behind me. She's communicating what I already know. The only way she's made it through what she has is because she's been mine. She's found comfort in the fact that I'm the only one.

No one else touches her.

"Come here, my beautiful believer," the Leader says.

"We'll perform for you," I snap. "We'll do what we've been doing. You said it was entertaining."

"I did. Which is why I want to experience the same. Are you disobeying me, Believer Logan?"

My fist tightens. I'm unable to keep the violence from my glare. I'm unable to stop gritting my teeth and imagining his skull cracking clean open.

"Take off our wife's dress," he orders. "Now... or the guards will be called in here."

Every movement becomes stiff and unnatural.

I hold in the explosion and fumble with fingers shaking from rage. Teysha's tattered dress is pulled over her head. I turn her toward me to keep her hidden.

...as much of her as I can when she's wearing nothing.

The Leader's grin widens. "Lay down on the bed, sweetheart."

I grip her arms tighter. "That's not necess—"

"I believe I am speaking to our wife, Believer Logan. Go on, sweetheart. Get on the bed. On your back."

The little control I have over the situation slips out of my grasp. *Teysha* slips out of my fingers, tears shining in her eyes, as she obeys what the Leader says. She crawls onto the bed with shaky breaths and lays down on her back.

"Open those legs, sweetheart."

The moment feels surreal in the most fucked up way. Even more fucked up than things usually feel in captivity by the Chosen Saints. A ringing starts up in my ears, my skin running cold, as the sense of helplessness intensifies. It suffocates the air and takes away any light in the room.

I can barely talk, barely think, so on edge I might jump out of my skin.

"That's right," the Leader coos, stepping to the bed and petting Teysha's hair. "Open them right up. Soon you'll be taking us both, sweetheart."

"She doesn't want to," I choke out, my airway constricted.

The Leader arches a white-blond brow. "Are you challenging me, Believer Logan?"

I glare back at him. "There's no point to it—"

"We do as I say, do we not?" he asks, almost in a laugh. "I ask again, do we need to call in the guards to remind you what happens when we disobey?"

"I'll... I'll do it," I say tensely. "Just me."

The Leader glances down at my crotch. "It doesn't seem like you're up to the task, Believer Logan. But I'll allow you to go first... if you think it will be easier."

My heart's jackhammering in my chest. The ringing has only grown louder. I'm lightheaded as I drop my workman pants and force my mind to slip away. Force myself to compartmentalize like I've learned to do—check out enough to get hard.

Get an erection so I can do this and get us the fuck out of this room.

Teysha lays motionless, or as still as she can given the sobs that sputter out of her. It's almost clinical how she's spread her legs and pinned her arms to her sides. You'd think this was a dreaded medical procedure and not an act between a husband and his wife.

I can't blame her when I stroke my dick and find myself flaccid. The Leader's watchful gaze weighs down on us. The depravity of the moment inescapable.

"It's going to be alright," I mutter under my breath.

Then I stroke my dick, aware I'm not just speaking to Teysha anymore. I'm telling myself too. "I'm going to be alright."

"Hurry up, Believer Logan," the Leader says, impatience sharpening his tone.

"I'm doing it," I growl through gritted teeth. "Give me a moment."

He sneers and drops his robe to the ground, his pale, untoned body frail, in direct contrast to the powerful position he holds. "This is the stallion Mandy's bragged about? It seems I'll need to show you a thing or two."

I run my enclosed fist over my dick a few more times and settle between Teysha's splayed thighs. Cold sweat clings to my brow as I let myself take in the quaking sight of her nude body. Anything to get myself going. Get aroused like I need to be.

But even Teysha's curves aren't enough. Not this time.

The situation's too fucked up. The pressure's unbearable and the repercussions traumatic. I can't compartmentalize this. I can't check out when the Leader climbs onto the bed and kneels at Teysha's head. He presents her his dick and I blink, realizing my eyes are moist.

Desperation claws away at me from the inside. It punctures my lungs and makes it impossible to breathe.

I've never felt so fucking helpless. So fucking... hopeless.

"Take me in your mouth, sweetheart," the Leader coos. "That's right. With those pretty lips. Suck on the head."

A sputtered sob leaves Teysha before she's silenced by his member. Her wide, glossy eyes flick to mine, and I see the pain shining up at me. The damage being done.

The last little piece of herself fracturing.

And I've let it happen.

I can't... I can't let him... I have to...

I release a howl like I've been stabbed in the chest and launch myself across the bed. I spear into the Leader with a fist that smashes his nose. We sail backward off the bed and crash onto the floor. I've slammed my fist into his face a couple more times before the door flings open and the guards flood the room.

I'm wrenched off him, then tossed aside to the floor. Amos points a rifle in my face while the other two help the Leader up.

The commotion's so loud, all the sounds blend together.

Teysha's terrified screams. The pounding on the ground from the guards' boots. The ragged breaths and storm of expletives I've released. The Leader's eerily calm laugh as he spits out blood and grins down at me.

"I believe it is clear what needs to happen," he says, standing naked with a level of cockiness only a man who thinks he's god could have. "It seems Believer Logan needs a friendly reminder of his place."

"NO!" I roar. "DON'T FUCKING—"

A boot to the face shuts me up, pain exploding from my nose, across my cheeks. It's the first hit of many. Amos and the other two guards surround me and begin doling out the friendly reminder. Punches, kicks, the butt of the rifle coming down hard against my skull and then my ribs.

"FUCK OFF!" I yell, twisting on the floor, throwing blind punches.

Soon all I can see are the legs of the men blocking off the rest of the room. All I can hear are my own grunts of pain and the crack of whatever bone's being fractured.

Except for the Leader's voice in the background.

"Now," he says, "to enjoy my wife."

"NO!" I yell before I'm pummeled again. "I TOLD YOU SHE DOESN'T WANT—"

The rifle collides with my mouth and pain vibrates through my teeth. I'm swallowing blood as I weave in and out of consciousness. I come to in time for another punch. Another kick. Another jam of the rifle against some part of my bruised, broken body.

Soon I stop responding. My eye's swollen shut and the pain's throbbing everywhere.

There's no escaping it... or anything else about the moment. I black out several times, then return to the squeaking of the mattress springs. Teysha's choked sobs. The Leader's groans of pleasure.

Until consciousness floats away again before I can even process it.

The fucked up cycle begins again. For hours that seem endless throughout the hellish night 'til morning bleeds across the sky...

6

TEYSHA

THE LEADER EXPECTS TO BE WOKEN UP BY HIS WIFE pleasuring him. Accustomed to the routine, I do as requested. He rips the sheet from over my head and grins down at me.

"You have such a talented tongue, sweetheart," he says. His hand finds my knotted hair and he strokes me like you'd pet a kitten. "No wonder you have become my favorite."

The door springs open, and in breezes Mandy, swathed in a silky floral robe. She's in the middle of braiding her long, flaming hair. Sun wrinkles crease onto her face when she lays eyes on the bed and realizes what she's walked in on.

"I always love coming across a wife pleasing my husband. Is this why you haven't requested me in almost a week, Leader?"

He chuckles, caressing my hair.

I'm supposed to keep pleasuring him. I'm supposed to pretend I'm not being talked about in the most degrading ways. My eyes squeeze shut and I fill my mouth with him, squashing down the nausea that rises up.

Recent times have made me learn how.

I've had to adapt in order to keep going. Keep counting the days.

I'm able to close my eyes and disappear into my head long enough for it to be over, repeating prayers to God. I'm still able to feel what's being done to my body and the velvety texture of the Leader's penis or taste the salty, slimy flavor of his seed.

But none of it registers.

Except when *his* name's spoken.

"You sound jealous, my lovely wife."

"I'm bitter you took away my stallion."

"Believer Logan required disciplinary action," the Leader says. His hand's stilled on the back of my head.

"But a week in the infirmary? I'm sure he wasn't that insolent."

"What warning have I given about questioning your husband?"

"Of course, Leader. I didn't mean—"

"Perhaps," he snaps, "you would be requested more often if your countenance was pleasant. Believer Teysha knows how to be pleasant, don't you, sweetheart?"

My eyes roll open to his twisted grin, and I breathe through the sickness. I give him the pleasantness he's asking for, nodding in obedience, then I finish him off. His fingers screw shut in my knotted hair, and he spills in my mouth.

Mandy's dropped into the cushiony chair by the bed and propped her legs up on the armrests. "I can be pleasant too," she coos. "When I am pleasured. Come here, sweetheart."

I have barely recovered from my nausea after swallowing the Leader's release. He nudges me toward her.

"Go on, sweetheart. Give her what she asks."

I wish I could say it's the first time they've requested me together. It's only once that Mandy demands I perform on her because her 'stallion's' not around.

But the Leader meant what he said when he told me I'm the new favorite. I'm the latest toy they've decided to play with 'til they grow bored or break me and then move onto something else.

Like they broke Logan. Mandy's stallion.

My husband.

I sigh as I kneel before Mandy and count the days 'til I see him again.

───────

Once the Leader learns he can use me to make Mandy jealous, it's a trick he pulls often. He doesn't let me return to the cabin. He demands I sleep in his bed. He keeps me at his side like an obedient pet while he sits at the dining room table and feasts on the meals the believers prepare for him.

Rarely am I fortunate enough to be given even a crumb of what he eats. In his view, the privilege is in the fact that I'm allowed to be in his presence for so long.

"You are my most special believer, sweetheart," he tells me. "Better than all the rest. The most beautiful and loyal. So obedient."

My skin crawls listening to him, though I keep my true feelings from showing on my face.

I busy myself instead with staring around the dining room, taking in the antiquated striped wallpaper and the portraits nailed to the wall. Many are generic art pieces of landscapes painted in watercolors. But there's one framed photograph in particular that stands out to me.

"Boulder," I blurt out. "The church in Boulder."

The Leader's lip quirks slightly. He sips from his goblet, then gives a nod. "That is right. It is a very special place. Tell me, Believer Teysha. How do you recognize it?"

I'm about to answer earnestly when I clamp my mouth shut. The less he and the rest of the Chosen Saints know about me, the better. They don't need to know that my family once attended that church before it closed down several years ago. They don't need any information that could lead them back to Mama, Papa and Grandma Renae...

I glance one last time at the photograph taken of the church, showcasing its gorgeous spire roof and large cross on the front. Then I put on a fake smile that feigns innocence.

"I've seen it in pictures before," I say. "It's a beautiful church."

"Yes, it is. As beautiful as you are, sweetheart."

He holds my gaze for a beat that becomes uncomfortable and makes my stomach churn. We're interrupted only by a shriek coming from the hall. Mandy has knocked a bowl out of a believer's hands and begun screaming in their face.

"When I ask for a bowl of nuts, I expect no peanuts, you insolent sack of bones!" she screeches. She smacks the woman hard enough to leave a red imprint on her cheek. "Do you realize what you could've done? I'm deathly allergic! Try that again and I will cut off those clumsy fingers of yours!"

I sit, silently unnerved by what I'm hearing. The Leader listens as though bored by what he hears. He reaches over to stroke my hair, his long, spindly fingers slipping down to grip my chin.

"She is angry," he explains. "I have not called upon her in days. She feels threatened."

"T-threatened," I eke out. "By... by who?"

"*You*, Believer Teysha. I am sure she will find an excuse to punish you. Which is why you must behave yourself. Continue to be obedient and please me... and she may meet her end before you do."

I rack my brain for how I'm supposed to respond to such a grim warning. He seems to think it's supposed to make me feel better. Instead, I'm simply reminded of how horrible these people are. The Leader and his Saints. Mandy.

It's as this fear threads through me that I make a mistake I shouldn't.

"Believer Logan... will he be returning?" I murmur. "Mandy called upon him regularly. Maybe that is—"

"If you should ever ask about him again, you will come to regret it," the Leader snaps, grimacing. "Do not concern yourself with what happened to him. Concern yourself with pleasuring your leader. *Me*."

The nod I give is a defeated one, my heart dying a little bit more inside my chest. I sit at his side for the rest of his meal, returning to my head, where I can search for comfort. In my prayers. In old memories.

But most of all, in the man who is my husband, who I hope comes back to me soon...

Logan's still bruised and swollen when he returns from his stay at the infirmary. The others in the cabin avert their eyes so as not to be accused of staring. He's hardened and grizzled when he steps through the door, more closed off than ever before. He strides to his bunkbed, picks up his rag and pair of workman boots, and he sets to cleaning.

No one dares address him.

I'm the only one who doesn't resume what they were doing. I've sat up in my bunk, a breathlessness in my lungs.

He looks the same but so different.

Logan... but half shattered in pieces.

Blood-red and plum-purple bruises decorate his face. His lips haven't finished closing up. The gash above his left eye still partially obstructs his vision.

Wounds he received after he took a beating trying to protect me.

An ache ebbs away inside my chest. I'm drawn to him and his pain. I'm consumed by a need to somehow ease it.

Logan scrubs harder at his cracked leather boots as if he doesn't hear me walk up.

"Thank god you're alright," I mutter. "I was wor—"

"Yeah, thank god. It might've turned out bad."

His biting sarcasm makes me frown. "I didn't mean to offend—"

"The only thing that offended me was you thinking I wanted you to come over here."

"Oh... I... okay..." I stammer out, completely confused. My skin prickles like I've been struck as I turn toward my bunk.

He's... angry with me. He must blame me for what happened to him.

Over the next few days, every time I approach Logan, I'm met with scorn. I'm dismissed with hardly a glance. He sends me away like I hadn't once sought safety in him. As if his words whispered into my ear hadn't gotten me through things that would've otherwise broke me.

I'm a stranger to him. Worse than a stranger. Some kind of enemy.

"Logan, will you please look at me?"

I sound pitiful as I find him one evening behind the

cabin. He's filling up his canteen at the spigot. We're far away from anyone else who might intervene.

He snaps the cap back onto his canteen and steps around me. His gaze falls anywhere but on me. I'm invisible as he pushes past and starts for the cabin.

"Why are you doing this to me?" I croak, following after him.

We round the corner of the cabin and almost collide with Xavier. He holds out a warning hand, his other clutching the rifle against his shoulder.

"The Leader has requested your presence, Believer Teysha."

Tension pulses in the silence. It's palpable as Logan squares his jaw and turns his back to enter the cabin, checking out of the situation. I'm confused and aching, pulled away by Xavier a second later.

"You'll be spending the night," he says, squeezing my arm tight. "And if he dismisses you, you'll be in my quarters."

I twist in his grasp, checking over my shoulder.

Logan never looks back.

I'm hot and exhausted, laying in the grass. My empty fruit basket sits beside me. The others browse the fruit bushels in search of good pieces they can fill their baskets with. Should the guards return from their break, I'll take my punishment.

I've learned that there's nothing I can do to prevent it from happening. It doesn't matter if I behave myself or if I act out, because the result is the same. I'm called upon and used in ways that have broken my spirit.

By the Leader. By Mandy. By the guards.

There's no escaping the depravity they inflict upon me and the others.

I pray and pray and it makes no difference. I've cried and gotten down on my knees to beg, only to be beaten or struck with a cane.

How do you keep faith when evil continues to win?

I'm not sure of the answer anymore. I'm barely even sure of my existence. After months of captivity, the life I once lived feels so far away...

"Get up," snarls Xavier. He's strode up, and I hardly flinched.

I wasn't present enough to see him.

He kicks at my side. "I said get the hell up. You're coming with me."

The others watch on as I'm marched out of sight. We leave the field, and he takes me behind one of the cabins. He's rutting away, his breath hot against my skin and hands bruising my breasts, when the commotion erupts. There's a harrowing scream that booms across the flat land. Then the rumble of an engine and screech of tires doing overtime.

Is someone fleeing the property?

Xavier shoves me away in his haste to fasten his pants. I've wandered in his wake, hoping to catch a glimpse of what's going on. A second longer and I would've missed what I do see—the rundown Chevy pickup truck that's used for the laundry rams into the wired fence and speeds off to freedom.

Logan.

7

LOGAN

Have you ever imagined what hell on earth would be like?

I never needed to... 'til I had to live it.

For the first two days I'm in the infirmary, I'm out cold. I don't know up from down, down from up. You could've asked me my government name and I couldn't tell you. I'm somewhere in limbo being tortured by the last things I saw. The last things I heard.

A squeak of mattress springs.

Groans of pleasure.

Desperate sobs for mercy.

I wake with pressure welled up in my chest. I'm unable to speak, my throat swollen and thick. My vision clears, at least partially, to a face smirking down at me.

The Leader's clothed again. His white-blond hair hangs over the shoulders of his robes. His lips spread as soon as he sees I'm up. "Believer Logan, I'm pleased to see you've regained consciousness after all."

I bare my teeth, overcome by hatred.

"You made things more difficult than they needed to be.

You refuse to accept there is nothing that is yours. Everything that is yours is mine. I will use these things when the urge strikes me. That includes your wife. There is nothing you can do to stop me. You are better off obeying.

"Besides, I wonder what you would think if you knew," he says, bowing closer. His calm voice lightens into a silvery whisper, "our wife loves being my favorite. She performs so well every time. Perhaps that's why you wanted her all to yourself. She was born to be a little whore."

He knows to step back as I spring up in the bed and realize I'm tied down by leather straps. Seconds pass where I buck against the binds and roar from the deepest part of my chest. He chuckles and turns to go.

"Well wishes, Believer Logan. Get better so you can be Saint Mandy's stallion again. Somebody needs to fuck her. Better you than me."

His laughter fades as he walks away, but it lives in my head for hours to come.

The believer that works in the infirmary gives me more pain meds. They drag me under where I'm stuck in dreamless sleep. It's a cycle that repeats for the next several days.

I was beaten bloody. I was beaten so badly I had a shoulder dislocated and my eye socket cracked. For all anybody knows, my vision might never be the same.

It doesn't matter either way.

My life's been stolen from me. Years have been taken that I'll never get back.

Even if, by some miracle, this hell came to an end, I could never be the same. I could never be the man I was before this happened.

I'm a different person now. Damaged in too many ways to count.

Whenever we fought growing up, Mace and I accused

each other of being more fucked up. He said Ma's death messed me up. I told him he had daddy issues.

Both true if we were ever honest with ourselves.

But I can't imagine returning to that life after what I've been through. I can't even process how I'll carry on here.

In this fucking hell.

How can I keep counting the days when the depressing truth has been staring me in the face?

There's only one escape from this place. Only one kind of ticket out of here. It's that or devote myself to a lifetime of believing.

I don't have a lifetime of serving the fucking Leader in me. I won't ever be in his presence without wanting to tear his throat open. This place isn't big enough for the two of us.

One of us has to go.

The man I was would've seen this realization as a rallying point. He would've been determined and made it his mission to take out the Leader; he would've seen it as a challenge to kill him and be the survivor.

The swollen man lying in the infirmary sees the realization as a final nail being hammered into his coffin. There's no fight in his broken body. Just... acceptance.

Teysha needs you.

I grit my teeth, shutting out the echo of her cries. It's a sound that's torture. That'll live with me.

She needs me... but I can't live with that. I can't pretend I'm some savior anymore. How can I when I can't even save myself?

The day I'm released from the infirmary, I'm at war in my head. Dark forces try to take over my thoughts. Poisonous thoughts I've never considered a day in my life.

'Til now.

'Til I finally feel it deep in my gut. An emptiness about where this is headed. The only way this will end.

The only option I've got left 'cuz I can't bear it anymore. I can't live knowing what I've allowed to happen. How I've failed her... and myself.

I pick up my workman boots and the rag I clean them with, and I begin plotting. I map out how I'm going to do it. When, where, what time of day.

Teysha comes around, and I almost crack. She's seeking me out, but I focus on the boots. Scrubbing the leather harder, I shut her out and make her walk away.

Over the days to come, I take notice of when the guards take their breaks. After my infirmary stay, they confiscated the dull-bladed knife I had, but I find a small block of wood in the grass, which I slip into my pocket. It can be whittled down to a sharp point with some work.

Teysha catches me by the spigot, filling up my canteen. My thoughts are on how late into the night the guards stay on patrol and hers are on the pleas she's making.

Begging me to look at her.

In tears over how distant I've been.

Then Xavier shows up and deals the final blow.

"The Leader's requested your presence. You'll be spending the night."

The breath's taken out of my lungs better than any punch to the gut could have.

I can't bring myself to do anything but sink into the pain. Let the sick reality take form. There's no fighting, no escaping except...

It's this endless hell on earth or the hell in the afterlife—if one exists.

The latter seems like it'd be more bearable each day that goes by.

I turn my back on Teysha and let Xavier drag her away, knowing what she'll be subjected to, hating myself for being so fucking weak I can't put a stop to it.

Hating myself so much I feel like I can't survive in my own skin.

The disgust rises up 'til it's overtaken me, a self-loathing that runs so deep it's become an inescapable part of myself.

So has the rage.

The sheer, unparalleled rage that I've failed. I'm useless.

As illogical as it sounds, I become angry with her too. Angry she's become his favorite. Angry that she's given into him and I thought I could get us out.

Suddenly, maybe with more clarity than I've ever had, I *get* Grace.

I understand what she did and why. Teysha might come to get it too someday.

I always thought it was pussies who did it. Failures who couldn't hang. Weak people seeking the easy way out.

I was too unbreakable. There was nothing I feared and nobody who could have that power over me.

But as the afternoon hits and I overhear Brody telling Amos about tonight's ceremony where Teysha will be initiated from believer to saint, my mind's made up. It turns out I'm not as unbreakable as I thought. I'm running scared. Giving up and tapping out.

I can't live with it anymore.

Amos and Brody are the ones guarding me at the back house. I take my time stuffing the linens into the washing machines and pouring the detergent. I'm waiting for their break. Just a few minutes unsupervised so I can get it done.

The shaved down hunk of wood rests in my pocket.

They step out for a smoke at half past the hour.

I glance around, digging the sharp hunk of wood out. It comes up against my throat, my pulse racing.

On the count of three.

Gritting my teeth, I prepare myself to rip the Band-Aid off and do it. I press the wooden shiv harder 'til it's piercing my skin and the first bead of blood oozes out.

All I've got to do is push a little more. Jam the shiv into my throat and slice away. I'll bleed out in minutes.

Three.

My eyes remain on the window, watching Brody and Amos blow smoke. The final moment of my life. By the time they find me, I'll be in a gory puddle on the floor.

Two.

The laundry truck sits outside the open door, the engine running. Its hum will be the last sound I'll hear other than my pounding heart.

One.

The path ahead is clear. There's no one standing in my way.

I dig the wood in deeper 'til I've punctured my skin. One more push will really do it.

Now's my chance.

My mind flips on a dime. I make a snap decision that's unexpected even to myself. But my body rushes into motion of its own accord. I sprint toward the door, diving into the pickup truck. Behind the steering wheel, I shift gears and slam on the gas.

Brody and Amos look like they're about to shit themselves when they realize what I've done. The cigarettes tumble out of their mouths. They scream at me and open fire. Shots that land nowhere as I speed away, crashing through the wired fencing.

By the time any of the guards are able to hop in another truck and hit the roads, I'm long gone.

I haven't had a single thought or drawn a breath.

I'm blacked out, operating in a trance. It hasn't even registered—I'm *free*.

Miles turn into hours turn into a plum sky and then twittering morning birds. I drive 'til I recognize the highway and the cities on the signs. Pulsboro comes up, letting me know another fifty miles. The truck's running on fumes when I click my turn signal and cross through familiar roads.

I find the saloon. The house out back where the patio's full of club members, new and old.

I approach as everybody's busy celebrating. People take notice as I pass them up and they look like they've seen a ghost.

Mace is chatting up some girl when he finally sees me. The color drains from his face. Then it hits him.

I'm back from the dead.

8

LOGAN

Returning to the real world is a mindfuck after you've been in captivity for years. The slightest sounds and movements set you off. Everybody everywhere feels like a threat. You no longer trust your own judgment or perception of reality.

It all feels like some sort of simulation.

I don't adjust well. I'm aware of this from the moment I first set foot on club property and dozens of eyes flick toward me.

The dead man walking back into normal life.

So many things have changed since I was gone. So much that it's damn near impossible to process. Instead of trying to, I retreat to what I know, focusing on the only purpose my broken life has left: revenge.

The destruction of the man and his followers who did this to me.

The same people who still have captives they use and abuse... including the woman I promised would escape with me.

Everybody thinks I'm insane for how hard I push to put

together a mission. They thirst for revenge after what's been done to me, but want to go about it smartly, strategically. Take their time so they can figure out who and what they're dealing with.

I allow for none of that, making it clear if they don't come along, I'm going alone. I'm taking out Abraham and the Chosen Saints as an army of one.

"We need time," my younger brother Mace says. "A plan to map out."

"We need to act," I snap. "Now."

"We'll send guys for recon—"

"Now," I repeat coldly, sparing him no glance. "Tomorrow night or I go at it alone."

He scrubs at his jaw as if thinking of a new approach. "You just got back from an ordeal that would break most people—"

"Save the psychobabble shit for somebody else. Either you come with me or you don't. Makes no difference to me. But they've got my wife—and a whole lot of other people captive—and I ain't moving on 'til the score's settled."

If there's one thing about the Steel Kings that hasn't changed since I've been gone, it's that we operate as a pack. If one of us has a battle to fight, the rest of us do too.

The next night as I gear up to return to hell, they're falling in line for the mission. They're revving up their engines and riding out alongside me despite the fact that the general consensus is the opposite—they want to wait, but they know there's no talking me out of it.

I've got nothing else to lose. Nothing left to live for. Why not go in guns blazing?

Mace leads the operation. Cash and Silver serve as his right and left hands.

I'm like a ghost as we go in. I'm no longer my father's

heir. I'm not the guy that leads. The future president of the club. That was me once, but not anymore.

The family is in the middle of a dinner when we barge through. We shout at them to put their hands in the air and lay down on the ground. It'll allow us to sort everybody out between believers and saints. I've made it clear to Mace and the others a lot of these people are captives just like me. Kidnapped and brought into this hell hole.

Some of the guards refuse to put down their rifles. Brody fires on us. Ozzie and Silver are ready and put a bullet in him first. The other guards retaliate, and soon the crack of gunfire fills the air.

Believers run, afraid for their lives. Some saints manage to escape, but others aren't so lucky, knocked down and run through by Cash or Big Eddie.

I move through the scene searching for two things.

Two people.

As we barged into the main house, the Leader fled the room. I've run up the stairs after him. I make it onto the second floor landing as he rounds the corner, clutching someone with him.

"Teysha!" I growl, following him into his bedroom.

"Come closer if you want me to slit her throat."

He's got Teysha in front of him like a shield. He backs up toward the balcony doors, pressing a steak knife to her throat.

"Real brave using her as a shield, you fucking coward."

"And you are so brave when you have a cadre of men backing you up, Believer Logan," he sneers.

"And you think you're so powerful when you've got brainwashed believers following you."

"That is because I am powerful, Believer Logan. I broke you, did I not?"

"You broke me. I kill you."

I raise my assault rifle to take aim, lining him up in my scope. A shot that's beyond risky with Teysha in his arms. One wrong move and she could be hit. One wrong move and he could slit her throat open. She recognizes this, quivering in his hold, her teary eyes pleading silently with me.

My chest pulls tight as my finger hovers over the trigger.

"Make your decision, Believer Logan. Quickly now," he taunts, grinning broadly. He takes a step back toward the balcony. "What is more important? An innocent life or your ego?"

"I could ask you the same thing."

He laughs. "You continue to prove why you will never prevail. You have no respect for those more powerful than you. Tonight may be a small win in your eyes, but you have no idea the extent of my wrath. You will soon find out!"

Teysha screams as he swipes at her neck with the knife, then quickly shoves her toward me.

For a wild second, panic detonates and I catch her in my arms convinced he's slit her throat. My gaze falls to the area, heart beating fast, to find no slash mark. No injury or damage at all except to the gold cross around his neck.

He was creating a distraction.

My head snaps up to find Abraham's used the last few seconds to hurl himself over the edge of the balcony. I rush toward the railing to locate him.

He's a blip in the dark, running straight for the tree line.

I open fire on him anyway before he disappears altogether into the night.

He's not the only one who gets away.

When it's all said and done, there's a handful of others like Mandy and Xavier that escaped. The majority were not so lucky, slaughtered on the spot like they deserved.

The believers we've rescued we drop off at the nearest hospital.

"What about her?" asks Ozzie, jutting his chin at Teysha. "We had her checked out at the hospital, but she didn't stay with the others. Is she coming with us?"

Teysha's passed out in the back of Silver's truck. At some point while waiting, she nodded off. I take a moment to realize I never considered what would come after. I never thought about what would happen once we made it out.

Opening the door to nudge her awake, I ask her what she wants. If she'd like to remain at the hospital where the other captives are being treated or if she wants to stay in the truck and come the rest of the way with us.

She blinks blearily at me, barely conscious. "I'll come with you... please..."

I give a tight nod and then shut the door to let her fall back asleep.

"She'll come with us to Pulsboro," I say. "For now. 'Til we get everything sorted."

"Makes sense. Isn't she Syd's friend too?"

I have no idea.

I don't know a thing about the woman other than her name and the gold cross she wears around her neck. The same gold cross Abraham slashed. But as I climb back onto the bike I'm riding on and take a look at her through the truck window, I spot the telltale signs of captivity. Even after her doctor's checkup. The vague bruises and nails caked with dirt. Worn clothes that you once filled out more.

Tonight's not the night to have all the answers. It's time to rest.

9

TEYSHA

"They're called the Chosen Saints and they're one of the most dangerous cults in the country," says the five o'clock news anchor. On the screen next to her is a photograph of the Chosen Saints's logo: a large cross covered in vines and flowers. "They are believed to operate in the states of Oklahoma, Louisiana, and Texas. Investigators believe they have several factions in Ludic county alone."

The anchor proceeds to brief her captive audience at home on all the warning signs that the Chosen Saints are in the area. She cautions against walking alone at night and giving personal information to solicitors.

"Keep doors and windows locked," she says definitively.

Frustrated by the generic advice, I change the channel with the TV remote. "I'm sure everybody that's been taken left the front door open, Barbara."

"Who're you talking to?"

The gruff voice comes from the hall. Logan appears a second later on his way to the kitchen. He's leather and denim from the torn jeans he wears to the motorcycle boots that clack on the floor tiles.

My gaze drifts from the TV screen for the first time since the last commercial break.

Logan geared up and ready to walk out the door isn't unusual. I quickly learned this only days into living under his roof. He stays on the move, barely ever home.

But the sight of him isn't any less affecting. Logan wears it well. Over six feet, ropey muscles, blue eyes, rough beard. What's not to find visually appealing?

"The TV," I answer, blinking out of my thoughts. I press the mute button on the remote. "Where are you headed?"

"The saloon."

"Can I come?"

"No."

"Why not?"

He pops the tab on a can of beer and swallows his first mouthful. "'Cuz you're supposed to be recovering."

"I'm recovered."

"You're not a member."

"I need fresh air," I say, sitting up. "Don't the others bring their girlfriends?"

"You're not my girlfriend."

"Wives—"

"The answer is no." He sets the beer can down and snatches his keys and wallet off the counter. "I'm out. Don't wait up for me."

The door thuds shut behind him. A couple seconds later, his motorcycle rumbles awake. I listen as he rides off and the thunderous sound fades out.

The silence that follows makes the loneliness ten times worse.

I unmute the TV and turn up the volume.

It's said that some people are sensitive to loud noises

after a traumatic ordeal. I'm a week off my captivity and I'm the opposite—loud noises provide comfort.

The voices from the TV are another presence when I've spent so many hours alone.

When Logan escaped the compound, I never expected him to return days later. The men he showed up with were even less expected. They called themselves the Steel Kings, a motorcycle club I had heard about in passing from living in the nearby town Boulder. By all accounts, they were supposed to be dangerous, violent, bad men.

But while they were violent—taking out many of the Chosen Saints in bloody fashion—they weren't the kind of bad men I had imagined them to be.

They set what believers they could *free*.

They took them to the hospital for treatment and so they could eventually be reunited with their loved ones.

I was taken to the hospital, too. A full checkup confirmed I wasn't seriously injured—just malnourished—and I wasn't pregnant or infected with an STD either. After my exam as I returned to the truck outside, I saw the conflict etched on Logan's face.

He was wondering what I was. What the heck was he going to do with me?

I was his wife. The woman he promised he would help escape with him.

Now here I was, a living, breathing inconvenience he was legally attached to.

He rubbed the back of his neck and asked me what I wanted to do. If I wanted him to take me home to Boulder or if I wanted to come stay with him for a few days while we sorted things out.

In a daze from everything that had happened, I chose the second option.

Logan and his group drove me to Pulsboro and dumped in the apartment his younger brother had never stopped paying rent on in the vain hope he'd someday come back. I've been in a new kind of captivity ever since.

Alone with thoughts I haven't faced and feelings I'm not sure what to make of.

Grandma Renae always said prayer would give me the clarity I need in dark times. She said God would hear me and grant me strength. I would persevere and carry on.

Prayer would heal me.

A part of me still reverts to that belief. I still delude myself into thinking if I read the Bible enough times and say enough prayers, it'll be like it never happened.

They never hurt me or took away pieces of myself. I'd be whole again.

The problem is, every time I close my eyes, I'm inundated with bad memories. The living nightmare I endured being held captive by the Chosen Saints. I see the exorbitant dinners with the Leader at the head of the table and the times one of the guards took me when we were alone.

I taste the seed I've been made to swallow.

I can't sleep and food no longer seems appetizing.

The few minutes Logan's around, I'm hoping for a crumb of affection. Some comfort or reassurance. When I receive nothing, I'm crumpling into a ball of anxiety and stress 'til it starts over again.

Nothing really has changed.

I'm in the same spot on the sofa when Logan returns hours later. He reeks of cigarette smoke and his beard looks like it's grown an inch thicker in the time he's been gone. He scrubs a hand over the wiry hairs and pretends he doesn't have a captive audience. That I'm not watching every step he takes.

He picks up the beer can he'd left hours ago.

"I told you not to wait up."

"I couldn't sleep…"

"It's not resting if you don't get any shuteye."

"I'm more interested in what you were out doing." I climb off the sofa with arms and legs that feel stiff from lack of use. "Did you enjoy yourself?"

"I've told you not to ask about club business."

"I'm trying to make conversation."

He drains the beer can, tossing it in the kitchen garbage. He hasn't looked at me once as he moves from the kitchen into the hall. I become his shadow, following after him.

"What do you do at the saloon?" I ask nosily. I turn into his bedroom like it's my space too. "Do you drink and watch sports?"

"You want to make conversation? Let's talk about our visit to the clerk's office."

My brows knit in confusion. "Why would we go to the clerk's office?"

"We need to get this undone." He shrugs off his leather vest and toes out of his boots. He crosses the room bare chested, more weight and muscle returning by the day. Captivity will leave even tough guys like Logan malnourished.

At the most random times, I'm transfixed by him. A deep-rooted longing pulls at me and warms my skin. I'm left feeling strong urges I've never made sense of before. It's like hunger but the craving for something other than food.

The craving to touch and be touched.

Only by him.

It started when we were still part of the Chosen Saints.

Logan and I were married and made to consummate our union. We were forced to do it so many times, it became a familiar part of my existence. I began to find a kernel of good in what was otherwise dark and ugly roots spreading through me.

I was Logan's wife, and he was my husband.

We didn't choose each other, but we would survive it together.

The vow had been made, and in the eyes of God, it was solidified.

But now that we've left the Chosen Saints, I've realized I might be wrong. While I'm transfixed by Logan, drifting after him, he won't even glance at me.

A habit of his that started during our captivity and continues today now that we've regained our freedom.

He steps into the ensuite bathroom and flicks on the light. His reflection in the mirror shows the inverse of every tattoo inking his chest. It does the same to the tight-lipped expression etched onto his face.

He's agitated.

"The annulment," I say.

"That's right. We agreed, didn't we? It'll be the quickest way for this to be over."

"This...?"

"This situation," he answers, his muscular back turned to me. He twists on the shower, pretending as if I'm not standing a few feet away.

"Our marriage," I say slowly.

"That's what the clerk is for. We've come full circle."

A sharp bout of nerves pricks at me. "Then what?"

"Then it's over." His fingers undo the button on his denim jeans, and he raises his brows at me before he continues undressing. "You mind?"

I'm rocked to my core as I step out of the way in time for the bathroom door to slam shut. There's so much to work through processing the annulment. What direction do I even go in?

The knowledge the vows I took meant nothing. My once-in-a-lifetime marriage has been reduced to a blemish on my record. My virginity has been stolen when I'd only ever saved myself for my future husband. I'm unwanted and used and lost in every way. How can I ever return to my old life when that version of myself is gone?

Everything is ruined.

Logan and my friend Sydney, who happens to be dating Logan's brother, have both asked me about my family. They've made it clear they'll reach out to them the moment I'm ready. Sydney seems lost about my reluctance while Logan's growing impatient by it.

Neither understand why I've stalled as long as I can.

The thought of being bombarded by Mama and Grandma Renae feels like it'll be its own traumatic experience. They'll have a thousand questions and a thousand more judgments. There'll be lectures and prayers and unsolicited advice. I'll be under their microscope and married off to the first man willing to wife up someone as damaged as I am.

Just so they can preserve my—*their*—reputation around town.

Whereas Logan's apartment has been quiet and lonely, being under my family's roof will be like standing in the middle of the spotlight. I'll be studied, analyzed, broken down a hundred times over. I'll be reprogrammed to be the born again, virtuous, perfectly clean woman.

It'll be like my time with the Chosen Saints never happened.

At least at face value.

They'll never understand the pain that's invisible on the outside but unbearable on the inside.

I return to the safety of the sofa in the living room and fall asleep to the white noise of Logan showering. It's well past four in the morning when I wake up. The TV's still on, lighting the dark room in a bluish white filter.

I move through the apartment on memory, cloaked in shadows. Logan's bedroom door squeaks as I nudge it open and pad gently into the room. He's offered me the spare bedroom as my space, but I've never slept in there. I've spent my time on the couch, unable to rest.

At least when I'm not seeking out my husband.

I peel back his bedsheet and slide in next to him. His body serves as an anchor on the bed, warm and heavy as I scoot closer. I'm drawn to his scent that invades my senses. The natural, clean smell of him after a hot shower. Pressing my face into the knotted muscle of his back, I take a slow inhale.

Logan stirs at once. He jerks awake and his hands fly out fast. They clench shut around my wrists as his eyes open to assess the threat.

...then he realizes it's just me.

He lets go as quickly as he'd grabbed hold. "I've fucking told you about doing that."

"I didn't want to sleep in the living room."

"That's what the other bedroom's for."

"I don't feel comfortable in there."

"Teysha," he says in warning. "You can't sleep in this bed. You sleep in this bed, I sleep somewhere else."

"You're my husband."

"We're getting it annulled."

I rack my brain to understand where his coldness is coming from. Why he's shut me out after he gave me comfort and affection all those times in the past. What have I done wrong to make him want to erase our marriage?

Why won't he even give it a chance?

I can't let this end. I can't let another thing be taken from me.

I've dreamt my whole life for a happy union. I've only got one chance...

"If you don't get out this bed, I will," he says after I stay put. "You make things more difficult than they have to be. You'll go your way. I'll go mine."

I slide out of the bed to give him the space he's demanded. I'm not sure what else to say even if I were stubborn enough to stay. He finds me difficult and wants our marriage to be over.

The vows meant nothing.

The day Logan brings me to the clerk's office, we haven't said a word to each other. Sydney's lent me a sundress that I put on to look presentable. My recent post-captive uniform of tank tops and shorts didn't seem appropriate. Logan's staunchly cold and uncompromising in dark flannel.

We'll get the marriage annulled and then go our separate ways.

That's the plan until we're turned away by the clerk. The dirty blonde glances at the form we've filled out, then arches a brow over her scarlet horn-rimmed glasses. "This doesn't fall under the provisions to qualify as an annulment."

Logan lets out a rare chuckle, then his brow creases when he realizes she's serious. "What d'you mean it doesn't qualify? It's a marriage that we were forced into."

"You signed the license."

"Under extreme duress."

"And proceeded to stay married for five months?" she asks, arching a brow.

"Look, lady," he growls, "it was a forced marriage. We didn't consent to it."

"Your signature is your consent by law."

"Not when we were under duress, you fucking bitch!"

"Logan," I choke out.

The woman behind the glass gasps and eyes Logan like he's a beast about to pounce. "Sir, I'm going to have to ask you to leave. Aggressive behavior directed at staff is not tolerated. I will elevate this case to my supervisor and she will reach out to you in ten to fourteen business days if we're able to proceed."

"I'm not waiting fourteen fucking business days to annul a marriage!"

"Sir," she says, glaring at him behind her horn-rimmed frames. "Please leave or I will call security. I repeat, your temper will not be tolerated."

We're walking out of the clerk's office before I've even processed what's happened. Logan lets out an enraged howl and he kicks at the brass fountain in front of the clerk's building.

"Stop it... or was getting kicked out the office not enough for you? You want to get arrested for destruction of government property?"

"That bitch refused to help on purpose!"

"Maybe so. But getting loud and angry doesn't usually help things."

"We need to have this undone."

"I get it! You've said it a dozen times. You don't need to keep repeating yourself," I snap. "You can't stand being married to me another minute. You'll do anything to be rid of me!"

"Teysha sweetie? Is that you?"

Logan and I look up at the same time.

Mama and Grandma Renae have walked up clutching tissues. They rush toward me once they realize it's me.

"It's our Tey Tey! We've come to take you home."

"THANK GOD OUR BABY'S IN ONE PIECE!" CRIES OUT the older woman of the two. They've both smothered Teysha in tearful hugs and kisses.

I've fallen several steps back to make room. I might as well be invisible as the women dote on Teysha. If I had to guess, I'd say it's her mother and grandmother.

"We didn't know what to think," says her mother, blowing into her tissue. "We heard they had you on drugs and you were pregnant. You didn't know which of the cult members was the father."

"Mama," Teysha breathes, almost flinching.

"Oh, Teysha. What have they done to you, sweetie? The filth they put you through," says her grandmother. "My baby girl lost her spark. Lord, please give her back her light."

My eyes narrow, though I remain in the background. I come from a religious household. My mother had us in church every Sunday, and my father agreed because he loved her. But even at a young age I thought it was a crock of shit.

All of it useless garbage.

The more Teysha's mother and grandmother talk, the quieter Teysha becomes. The more she shrinks into herself. If there was ever any light, they're the ones putting it out. They're the ones making her feel like crap after what she's been through.

She's no less valuable because some sick fuck kidnapped her and brought her into his cult.

"Please stop fussing over me."

"How can I not? I heard all about it on the news. The vile things they expose their hostages to. But it's not over for you, sweetie," her mother says. "You'll still find your way. You'll heal and marry a nice man despite what's happened. Someone out there will be willing to overlook those things."

"She's already married."

The women freeze at the sound of my voice. Even Teysha's surprised by my interruption. Her eyes go wide, the rest of her face slack. She doesn't have a clue how to take me.

But her mother and grandmother do. The women mirror each other, their hands on their hips and brows arched, staring at me like I'm an intruder.

I guess, in a way, I am.

This is a private family moment, and I don't belong to their family any more than they belong to mine.

"And you are?" Teysha's mother asks.

"That's Logan, Mama," Teysha murmurs under her breath.

"Hey," I say, offering my hand to shake, "Logan Cutler."

Mrs. Baxter doesn't shake my hand, ignoring my gesture. "Are you the one she's been staying with?"

"That's right..."

She gives a deep hum of disapproval. "Well, Logan, I'm sure you believe you've done a good deed by giving my daughter a place to lay her head. But I'm afraid all you've really done is make the situation worse. My daughter needs to be returned home where she can begin healing from the damage that's been done to her. The last thing she needs is to be shacked up with some man looking to make trouble."

"Make trouble?" I repeat in a scoff.

"Teysha, what have we told you a thousand times? What does Corinthians 15:33 say? Bad company ruins good morals. We need to get you away from this terrible town right now—"

"Excuse me, ma'am," I interject, taking a step toward her. "But your daughter's my wife. We're legally married."

Her eyes snap shut and her features pull tight. The mere idea causes her distress. It sickens her to know her daughter's married to me.

A biker covered in tattoos. I smell of the cigarettes I've been smoking and haven't trimmed my beard in over a week.

"We will be handling that situation," Mrs. Baxter says. "She can get an annulment from Boulder."

"She can go where she wants to go. And Teysha's said nothing about leaving."

"She doesn't live here," spits her mother. "We're taking her home—"

"That's not your decision to make—"

"Now, now," says her grandmother suddenly. "Let's not raise our voices in public. We can talk through this like civil adults. I hope we can all agree Teysha's best interests are most important."

Teysha's shrunk half a step back. Neither woman notices. They're too focused on me.

My objections have become an immediate inconvenience. They already had the entire situation mapped out.

Show up here and take Teysha away. It didn't even occur to them to ask her what she wanted to do.

But I've got my own plan, and it happens to clash with theirs.

If I have any intention of getting this marriage dissolved as quickly as possible, I need Teysha on hand to do so.

Her family's going to have to wait.

For the time being, all they need to know is Teysha's my wife and we don't need their interference.

"Logan, I thank you for rescuing our baby girl," the elder Baxter says. She's a round woman that's dressed up in a hat and pearls as if on her way to a nice brunch. She aims a polite smile at me like I'm a kid on the block trying to sell her lemonade. "It means so much to us that you have stepped in and helped her. But it's best if she's taken home where we, her family, can be there for her."

"Teysha's a grown woman," I say. "I'm sure she can decide what she wants to do."

All eyes fall on her. Mrs. Baxter and her grandmother glare expectantly. Their brows have arched to new heights.

"Well?" snaps her mother. "Use that mouth of yours. Tell him what you want."

"Mama... we weren't expecting you," Teysha offers weakly. "We were in the middle of... of something."

"Unbelievable. We were beside ourselves when you were missing. We cried tears of joy when we found out you were alive. Do you know we got in the car that instant and drove hours to come get you? What's the matter with you?"

Teysha frowns, a soft wrinkle forming between her brows. "I don't mean to be ungrateful. I've missed you, and I want to come home. But... but I'm not... I don't think I'm ready yet."

Mrs. Baxter's sharp gasp sounds like she's a breath away

from passing out. She clutches at her chest and staggers a step back. It's about as dramatic as the disgusted look on her grandmother's face. You'd think she sucked on a lemon the way her features pucker up.

Teysha seeks out my gaze. Her eyes speak to me.

Big and expressive like I'd noticed the first night we met. We'd stood in front of the Chosen Saints and exchanged I dos. I took a glance at her, and my first thought was about how deep her eyes were. Her every emotion swimming in them. They were like portals to another world.

Teysha's *soul* some philosophical prick would say.

Whether or not they're the windows to her soul or if souls even fucking exist, I get it anyway. I can glance at the woman who is legally my wife and sense how she feels. She's uncomfortable and overwhelmed, *begging* me to step in.

...because she won't stand up to them herself.

I clear my throat and scrub my jaw. "You heard her. She's not ready to go to Boulder."

"It doesn't matter if she's ready—Boulder is where she lives!"

"Just because it's her home address doesn't mean it's where she should be right now," I say in my best attempt at a calm tone. It's still rough and gravelly, but with forced restraint. My hand cups Teysha's elbow to ease her closer. "How about we give you a call when she's ready—"

"I don't think so! Get your hands off my daughter!" Mrs. Baxter screeches. Her hysterical call echoes across the walkway area and earns curious looks from people in the parking lot. She shoves at me to sever my hold on Teysha's elbow. "That's my baby girl, and I'm not letting nobody else take her away! You're not about to sully her again!"

"Mama!" Teysha cries out.

As if shoving me away from her daughter wasn't bad enough, Grandmother Baxter swings her handbag. It collides with my shoulder, then the side of my head.

"Get!" she yells. "Go on and go, or we will call the police!"

How the situation has spiraled to the point I'm being whacked over the head by a mother-grandmother duo, I'll never understand. We sure as hell have drawn the attention of everybody around though.

I throw up an arm to block Mrs. Baxter's next shot. Teysha has inserted herself to pry her grandmother away.

"You two done?" I ask, jutting my chin at them. "Or would you like to cause more of a fucking scene?"

It's hard to say if they're more scandalized by my challenge or the cuss word. They exchange looks, their blinks long and slow like it'll help wake them from some shitty dream.

They'll get over it. They've got no choice but to.

I round on Teysha.

"Ready?"

Teysha's big brown eyes flick up to mine. So many damn emotions welled up in them, it's a wonder how one person can feel so much. She gives a small nod and leans into my side.

Tension clenches from deep within my chest.

I put an arm around her and wave off the Baxter women. "Sounds like it's decided. Teysha stays 'cuz that's what Teysha wants. Don't waste your time coming by again. We'll call you."

"Teysha!"

"Come back here!"

"Lord, why has my daughter been led astray by such wickedness?"

I pull open the truck's passenger's side door and stand back for Teysha to slide in. Her family's cries have followed us every step across the parking lot. The others in the area haven't stopped gawking. I walk around to the driver's side, shooting a glare in Mrs. Baxter and her mother's direction.

My warning is clear: *Teysha has made her choice. Get the fuck over it.*

The truck rumbles to life at the turn of the key in the ignition. I check on her one more time before driving off.

"You alright?"

She's shaken. Eyes wide and misty, her body stiff and uncertain. "Get me out of here."

Teysha only needs to ask once.

The truck gives another deep rumble as we ditch the clerk's office parking lot.

We drive for a while in silence. Just the background noises around town. School-aged children giggling on a sidewalk. Rubber tires on tarmac and the jingle from the local ice cream truck.

I glance at her in between watching the road. "I'm taking you back to my place."

She's turned her head toward the window and gives no sign she's heard me. Is she regretting her decision already?

Around her family, she seemed like a wilting flower. Any personality—or spark as they'd called it—went out. She'd looked over as if pleading with me to help her. Did I misread her reactions? Otherwise, what the hell could be wrong with her?

"You sure you're alright? I can take you back to your mother—"

"I..." she says suddenly, then pauses a second. "I... need a drink."

Ask me what I expected Teysha Baxter to say in this

moment, and I'd tell you I had no fucking clue. But I do know her asking for a *drink* was nowhere on the list. Even if one existed.

My brows lift higher. I barely remember to watch the road. "You mean something with alcohol, or are you asking for apple juice?"

The tension breaks with a soft laugh from Teysha. "A drink with alcohol. Why would I want juice?"

"The same reason your family came by yelling about wickedness. You sure it's allowed?"

I'm giving her a hard time. Pushing her buttons. Working her up.

But my attempt falls flat.

Any humor Teysha's found disappears. Her laugh's long gone. She turns her head back toward the window.

I let it go. That scene with her family obviously messed with her head.

We pull into the nearest gas station. I reup on some gas and then walk Teysha into the convenience store. A week since her rescue, she's still nervous in public. She's never said so, but I've picked up on it.

Once inside, she almost turns down the wrong aisle.

"Beer and liquor's this way."

I grab her hand and head in the opposite direction she was going. As I lead her down the aisle filled with salty snacks like potato chips and popcorn, another hunch takes shape. Teysha's hesitant steps tell me all I need to know.

This is a first-time thing for her.

"You ever drink before?"

"That obvious?"

"How old are you again?"

"Twenty-two."

"Jesus fucking Christ," I swear. "You're almost a damn kid."

"I'll be twenty-three in September. I was supposed to graduate college this past semester, but obviously I... I never got to finish."

"Jesus fucking Christ, it gets worse. You're in *college*?"

"Don't speak the Lord's name in vain," she scolds.

I'm still too stuck on her age to care.

I'd known she was younger than me. But I didn't realize it was by almost a whole decade. I'm thirty years old married to a damn college student barely legal enough to drink.

No wonder she feels so... *inexperienced*. From the moment she was hauled into the Chosen Saints ceremony and deposited in front of me, I picked up on it. That she was green.

I corrupted her that night and I'm about to corrupt her again.

"We'll start you off simple. Some wine coolers. There's barely a drop in those."

Her brows knit. "I want what you drink."

"Trust me when I say you couldn't handle it, babe," I say with a rough laugh.

"Yes, I could. *Babe*."

I open the refrigerator door to grab a case of beer. "Feeling snippety, are you? Where was all that mouth when your family was around?"

"I'll buy my own."

She spins on her heel, her chocolatey hair flipping with her, and sets off toward the bottles of hard liquor. I grit my teeth and shake my head.

There's something about gas station convenience stores that feels dingy.

But Teysha Baxter in a gas station convenience store is its own category—she manages to change the atmosphere in a girl-next-door-picking-flowers-in-a-fucking-meadow kinda way. Her sandals and sundress are practically church clothes, yet the sneak peeks of bare skin hint at the shapely curves hidden underneath. I follow half a pace behind, almost a foot taller, close enough to touch her.

Notes of her perfume sweeten the air.

She even smells like a damn meadow.

Summery and floral, with a woody edge.

When we were with the Chosen Saints, we were so filthy, so beatdown, I had stopped picking up on things like smell and taste.

Since returning to Pulsboro and Teysha's come to stay, it's a scent I've been forced to endure. In the crammed space of the convenience store, it's rewiring my brain. Making me feel even more protective of her. Making me hyperaware of not just our surroundings but *her*.

I'm forced to notice the gentle sway of her dark, shoulder-length hair. From far away, it looks almost black. Up close, there's these chocolatey brown tones that are easy to get lost in.

She stops in front of a shelf stocked with White Oak products. Her eyebrows draw together in scrutiny, a tiny wrinkle on her nose. She leans in as if to read the nutritional label.

I roll my eyes. "It's whiskey, Teysha. Pick one."

"But what's the difference between the Gold White Oak Whiskey and the Silver White Oak?"

"They're just different collections. The gold line's usually the good stuff. That's why it's priced more."

She hums, then almost shyly blinks over at me.

I get it immediately. She wants me to help her choose.

I sigh and jut my chin at the shelf. "Just grab that big one of the gold. The one that looks like a trophy. We'll toss it in with my case of beer. I'm gonna need it with the headaches you give me."

"I'll pay you back—"

"Don't worry, babe. Your payback's coming when you're kneeling by the toilet."

"I can handle it," she mumbles.

For half a second, I consider bursting her bubble. Telling her how Steel Kings like Bush and Ozzie end up puking their guts out by drinking this stuff. Men twice her size. Men with borderline alcoholic drinking habits. Men who might as well have guts made of steel, like our club's named after.

But this seems to be some hill she's hell bent on dying on.

So I let her have it. The whiskey *and* the last word.

Teysha clutches the large bottle like it really is a trophy, holding it close to her chest. I take a second to stand back and watch as she carefully walks it up to the register.

I'm not sure if I'm more amused by the situation or irritated that I'm stuck with her for an extra few weeks.

Her family was overbearing. *The* definition of religious nutjobs. She needed to be bailed out of the situation outside the clerk's office earlier.

But I didn't intervene just for Teysha's benefit.

I intervened because I saw the opportunity to have this marriage dissolved as quickly as possible slipping through my fingers. If her family took her away, it would make it a hell of a lot harder to appeal the clerk's decision in the next few days. Who's to say her nutty family would even let me contact her?

I come up from behind at the checkout stand and heave

the case of Pike beer onto the counter. I toss a hundred dollar bill before the clerk's even finished ringing us up.

He flashes me a toothy grin. "I was about to ask this one for ID. Sweet little thing looks like she's never held a glass of White Oak let alone drank any. But you... I remember you. Tom Cutler's son, ain't ya? Didn't you go away for a while?"

"If being thought dead is going away for a while."

I snatch back my change in cash and gather the rest of our things. We walk out with the case of Pike and a bag of other one-off items I've picked up.

And then there's the bottle of Gold White Oak Whiskey.

Teysha's still holding onto it like a lifeline.

I don't say anything as we make our way back to the pickup truck. Something tells me this is a victory in her eyes; something that's not so common.

She's finally gotten her way for once.

"Go ahead. Take a drink."

I jut my chin at the red Solo cup filled with an ounce of White Oak. The pale brown liquid looks almost gold under the kitchen's fluorescent lighting.

Teysha stands on the other side of the counter, perched on one of the stools. She eyes the Solo cup like it's a dangerous animal liable to bite at any moment. The second thoughts are written all over her pretty face. Her brows have inched closer together and her teeth nibble away on her bottom lip.

"What does it taste like?" she asks.

"Strawberry ice cream."

She goes from nibbling on her lips to pursing them. "I might be inexperienced, Logan Cutler, but I'm not stupid."

"Then go on and try it for yourself. Don't chicken out now. You're the one that made a big stink about having a drink."

"I didn't make a big stink," she says almost defensively. She reaches out and curls hesitant fingers around the plastic red cup.

Then she bows her head and *sniffs* it.

I lose any bearing I have. A raspy laugh cranks out of me.

Fuck.

She really *is* irritating and cute all at once.

"Okay, okay. I'm trying it! No need to laugh."

Teysha tosses the ounce of whiskey back. Her throat muscles work as the liquid makes its way down the slender column. The smoky, spicy taste doesn't hit her 'til a second later. She coughs, her chest jerking forward and eyes squeezing shut.

"You alright?" I slide a cup full of coke across the kitchen counter.

She gratefully accepts, washing away the whiskey taste on her tongue.

The corner of my mouth quirks in half a grin. "Well? What'd you think?"

"You drink that for fun? Why would you do that to yourself?"

"I'm a glutton for punishment." I raise my glass of whiskey and ice and then show her how it's done. I drain the whole fucking thing in one swallow. The glass chinks against the counter when I set it back down. "Are we done? Is that little experiment of yours over?"

"Make me a drink," she says. She points at the two liter

bottle of coke and then the White Oak. "Don't people mix coke with whiskey?"

"I thought you were inexperienced?"

"Do I have to remind you I said inexperienced, not dumb?"

"And again I'm asking where was all that mouth earlier today?"

For a second time, she doesn't answer me. I start fixing her drink request. Another ounce of whiskey and a hell of a lot more coke.

Joke about kneeling by the toilet aside, I'm not spending my night babysitting a lightweight.

"You're gonna have to tell me anyway, you know that, right?"

"Tell you what?"

"About earlier. Your family." I nudge the cup of whiskey and coke toward her. "You didn't seem all that happy to see them."

"Is that why you stepped in?"

"You were begging me to with those puppy dog eyes."

She makes a face and shakes her head. "I've missed them so much. I've prayed I'd be fortunate enough I'd see them again."

"So? Why didn't you want to go with them?"

"I never said that."

"You damn sure did with your behavior. But no need to answer anyway. I know all about what it was." I set to refilling my own glass, pouring whiskey in straight.

Teysha spends a moment taking another sip of hers. A small taste test to see if she can handle any more. Either she decides she can or that she needs to as a distraction.

"How can you know all about it when I didn't tell you?"

"'Cuz I know your type. You think I've never met

anybody like you? My mom was religious. She took us to church every week. I'm more than a little familiar."

Her eyes narrow. "My type?"

"Sheltered. Wholesome. Raised in the church. Formed your whole identity around it. Everything you believe is what they told you to," I say with a shrug. "Your mother's the stereotypical overbearing kind that dictates everything you do. Why would you want to go back to that? Especially after what's happened to you?"

I'm not sure what reaction I expect. Part of me hopes it's more sass. More mouth.

Then at least the tension would ease and I could forget I'm irritable for a couple seconds. I could find amusement in whatever sassy thing she's said and give her more shit about it.

But as I drain my second glass of whiskey, she's stopped touching hers. She won't even look me in the eye. The sweetness about her is gone; the girl-next-door-picking-flowers-in-a-fucking-meadow disappears.

The frigid woman I'd witnessed one too many times with the Saints returns.

"Teysha—"

"Thanks for the drink."

She slips out of the barstool and heads straight for the spare bedroom.

The room I've allocated for her. The room she never spends any time in. She much prefers the couch or, better yet, my bed.

I wait five minutes then go knock on the door. She never answers.

I turn in for the night reminded why I didn't want her around. Why I should be spending my newfound freedom alone rather than babysitting some woman I don't know.

Her issues with her religious-freak family's got nothing to do with me.

I've got no shortage of my own damn problems.

Shit I haven't even begun to sort through.

I go to sleep only to be woken up a couple hours later by my phone vibrating. My hand stretches out to grab hold of it. In the pitch dark my screen practically fries my retinas. The text is simple and short.

To the point.

We've caught one of them.

11

TEYSHA

SYDNEY AND HER FRIEND KORINE MCKIBBENS SHOW UP at ten on the dot like agreed. Korine knocks gently while Sydney sends a text.

We've come to rescue you :)

I look up from my phone to the bathroom mirror. The reflection that stares back at me is a woman with uncertain eyes and a natural frown. I've put effort into looking presentable—the sundress I've borrowed from Sydney accentuates my figure and I've barrel-curled my hair. I swiped on some lip gloss thinking about how Logan seems to like it; he can never stop staring at my mouth whenever I do.

But outside appearances can be deceiving. The most presentable person can be hiding an ugly truth.

It's been two weeks since I was rescued from the

Chosen Saints compound. Yet the thought of going somewhere in public—*so out in the open*—gives me anxiety. My ribcage cinches tighter as I draw in a breath.

It's going to be fine. I've been to the mall dozens of times.

My lips spread enough to lift into a smile. I practice holding it for a few seconds, then decide I've stalled long enough.

Knowing Sydney, she'll find a way into the apartment if I don't answer soon. She's been worried about me from the moment she found out I was missing. It's part of the reason she suggested we spend time together today. She says I've been holed up too much in Logan's apartment.

Logan agreed with her and gave me money to enjoy myself.

They might be right that I've locked myself away in the apartment for too long.

While it may be true, at least it's a safe haven.

Everything smells like Logan and he's the only one that I have to be with.

A trip to the Pulsboro Mall means being open and exposed in public. I was okay when I went to the clerk's office because I was with *Logan*.

Today will be my first time in public without him.

"There she is!" Sydney says when I step out the front door.

"Sorry, I was behind on getting ready."

Korine shrugs from my left side. "No big deal. We have plenty of time. Do we want to eat first or do some shopping?"

We vote on lunch first and wind up at a Tex Mex spot on the other side of town. The ceiling fans spin dizzyingly fast, doing overtime to battle the June heat.

We hear the sizzle before we hear our server's voice.

"Loaded fajitas for the beautiful trio of ladies." Our server carefully sets down the huge platter of steak and chicken fajitas in the center of the table. He stands back, clapping his hands together. "Do we need any more napkins? How about a reup on those chips and salsa?"

"We're good, thank you."

Our server winks after he lets us know to call him if we need anything else.

"This was a really good idea," Korine says, sipping from the straw of her Sprite. "I don't even know where to start with these fajitas."

"Divide and conquer." Sydney passes out the smaller plates so we can load our own. "Mace first brought me here after I said I was craving authentic Tex Mex. None of that franchise stuff."

"Mason has always been a foodie," Korine says, smirking. She's carefully transferred a mix of steak and chicken along with peppers onto her plate. "When we were in high school, he was always dragging us to some hole in the wall spot when class let out."

"It's the same now. Except no class." Sydney looks across the table at me. "You want some, Tey?"

"Hmm? Oh, sure."

"Here, take all this."

Sydney serves me a large heap of the sizzling meat. I smile in gratitude, trying to feel more present in the moment.

The truth is, every time the bell above the door rings as it opens and someone new walks in, I'm tensing up. I'm glancing over with a racing heartbeat, questioning who it is that'll enter. If it'll be a customer looking to grab some Tex Mex or if it'll be...

I close my eyes at the imagery of the Leader walking in.

His pale face gleaming in triumph, his icy gaze set on me. One second, he seems so real, then the next, he's gone. He was never here in the first place.

"Tey?"

I blink to find both Sydney and Korine staring. "Hmmm?"

"Syd asked you how things are with Logan," says Korine. Her tone's gentle, her expression neutral.

Neither of them are judging me. Both have taken me out to spend time together and give me a change of scenery, something that's different from Logan's apartment. I just wish I could be more entertaining.

Sticking my fork in a slice of grilled chicken, I give a smile and shrug. "You know how it goes. We're still getting used to each other. It's a lot all at once."

"So, I'm confused. You're legally married? Did you choose each other at the... place?" Sydney asks.

"We... uh, we didn't get to..." I try to swallow the slice of chicken, but it winds up a lump in my throat. I reach for my glass of iced tea, hoping to force it down. It takes me a few hard swallows to realize it isn't the chicken. I clear my throat and try again. "Logan has been considerate. Comforting. It could've been a lot worse."

Sydney and Korine exchange looks.

"I'm glad it sounds like you've been able to form a real bond," Korine says. "Sometimes you find them when you least expect it."

"You mean like me and Mace?" Sydney laughs. "We couldn't stand each other when we first met."

"Now look at you two. *Engaged*." Korine reaches across the table to hold up Sydney's left hand. "He did pretty good on the ring."

"Please! I know he consulted you. Cash let it slip."

"Blake would do that."

I'm relieved to be more of a listener as Sydney and Korine laugh about their men. My mind wanders to Logan, wondering if he would ever confide in his brother and friend about an engagement ring. If he would ever get down on one knee and propose to a woman he loves.

We're married, yet I'll never know the answer...

"What about you and Cash?" Sydney asks, raising her brows. "Any proposals in the future?"

A small smile creeps onto Korine's face, her short hair a perfect frame for the demure expression. "I *just* got divorced. I told Blake we'll get married after Ken's officially sentenced. He's up for ten max. Five minimum."

"Yesss! That's cause for celebration on multiple levels." Sydney snaps her fingers in approval to more of Korine's laughs. "We'll both be seeking marital advice from Tey."

"Oh," I say with a quick shake of my head, "I don't have any advice to give. I don't know anything about marriage."

"You and Logan have decided to work it out, right?" Korine asks.

It's a simple question I shouldn't think twice of.

If Logan and I were really trying to make things work.

The annulment wouldn't be hanging over my head. I wouldn't have an inevitable bus ticket to Boulder with my name on it. Mama and Grandma Renae have made it clear the clock is ticking.

The marriage I've always dreamed of is fading away more by the day...

My eyes drop to the plain silver band on my hand that symbolizes the union Logan and I have. It was slipped onto my finger as tears rolled down my cheeks and I trembled in fear.

I've continued wearing it because it's *supposed* to mean something.

But the truth is, the ring couldn't be less special; it couldn't be more devoid of real meaning.

All Chosen Saints who were partnered off were forced to wear them.

Only the Leader was allowed to forgo his.

We were his for the taking if he chose to have us. I was the Leader's wife just the same as I was Logan's.

Things are somehow more complicated now. In the real world, we're married but free to do as we please. We don't have to stay together anymore.

Logan wants an annulment.

Heat spreads through my chest and climbs up my throat. It flushes onto my face, rendering the cool air from the ceiling fan useless. But I have to keep my act up; I already decided before I left the house that I would do what Mama and Grandma Renae call 'keeping up appearances'.

"We're trying to work everything out," I say after a pause. "We've decided it's for the best. We've become one flesh."

Korine offers me a kind smile. Sydney's reaction is a lot more cryptic. Her brows furrow, a studious vibe developing about her. Almost as if she senses something off.

I was never the best liar. Mama used to remind me that the Lord detests lying lips. Liars are never rewarded.

...but what if we really did make it? What if I can change his mind?

It started off forced, but what if we give it new meaning? What if we can erase the bad parts and make everything right again?

We finish the rest of our lunch before driving to the

town shopping mall. Sydney and Korine help me pick out a few pieces for my limited wardrobe. Several sundresses, tanks, and denim shorts later, we browse a few other shops. Korine picks out a birthday gift for her mother, Sunny, and Sydney grabs us some frozen yogurt from a stand.

I return to the apartment with bags on my arms and a more genuine smile than I had earlier. Sydney and Korine wave before they drive off, and I head inside.

My spirits are higher. My earlier anxiety is gone.

Hope returns as an excitable beat of my heart.

I'm in such a great mood that I rush into the bedroom and change into one of my new dresses. The sundress Sydney's lent me falls to the floor as I tug the thin-strapped flowery one over my head. I twist and turn in front of the mirror and fix up my hair. Lip gloss is the finishing touch.

After checking the time, I move into the kitchen to start on dinner. If I hurry, I'll be able to have something ready when Logan walks through the door. He's been getting home around six o' clock the past few nights.

It's been over a week since Logan went grocery shopping, so pickings are slim.

I work with what we've got. Thankfully, Mama taught me how to cook from an early age.

I whip up some chicken alfredo using the cutlets we have leftover paired with a hunk of parmesan cheese, heavy cream, and a garlic clove for the sauce.

Pasta is one of Logan's favorites. I've noticed how he always keeps some kind of pasta on hand as one of his go-to meals.

As his wife, I'll learn all of them. I'll happily make them for him.

Six o'clock comes and goes.

The pasta waits on the stove. I've taken out the cutlery and plates.

These days, the sun's staying out later into the evening. It's minutes before eight when it's finally setting.

The living room begins to darken. I slip closed the blinds and twist on the lights.

If he were to come home in the next few minutes, we could still have dinner at a reasonable hour. There's still hope that he'll make it.

After another hour, I resort to texting Logan:

Dinner's waiting :)

And when that goes unanswered:

I hope you'll be home soon. I've missed you. <3

And when that, too, goes unanswered:

Please answer. Will you be home soon??

I set down my phone as I look at the clock on the microwave and my insides knot up at the late hour. The nightly news ends on the local channel and some rerun of an old '90s sitcom comes on. My lip gloss has long ago faded.

Though I'm seated calmly on the sofa, my hands folded in my lap, I'm on the verge of a nervous breakdown.

I'm hanging on by a thread, counting every breath I take. I'm clinging to the thought that Logan will be home any moment and I won't be alone anymore.

Please... hurry...

The night drags on. At some point, I lay down on the sofa and distract myself with the late-night informercials. I fall asleep gripping the remote and throw blanket like they're lifelines.

Logan's key clicking in the lock wakes me up. The door drifts open to make way for Logan to slip inside. He staggers over to the kitchen counter, tossing his wallet and keys. He moves on to the fridge for a can of beer.

I quickly blink away any drowsiness, then leap to my feet. "Where have you been?"

He pops the tab on the beer can and downs a quarter of it. "Why are you still up?"

"I've been waiting for you! Did you see my texts?"

"I haven't checked my phone. There were more important things going on."

He leaves the kitchen for the hall. I follow a couple steps behind, my temper a thin veil for hurt feelings clenched in my chest. How could he dismiss me like he is?

"Were you out drinking? Out partying at the club? Were there other women there?" I ask, firing off questions. "Why won't you ever tell me what you're doing? Why won't you ever take me with you?"

"Teysha, lower your damn voice."

"I've... I've been waiting for you!" I repeat, my throat

aching. I rush to block his path by getting ahead of him. "Why won't you just try?"

Logan's eyes darken when they meet mine. He bares his teeth, leaning closer to growl at me. "I don't have time for this shit! Move out of my way."

I'm moved against my will. Logan grabs me by the upper arm and jerks me to the side. Enough space for him to pass by. I stumble from the forceful tug, almost stepping into the wall. He's already walking through the bedroom doorway.

"You owe me an explanation!"

"I don't owe you shit."

"I'm your wife!"

He barks out a loud, callous laugh. "You ain't my wife, and I ain't your husband. Let's get that straight right now."

Try as I might to hold it together on the outside, on the inside it's like I'm breaking apart. My lungs shatter drawing my next breath. Cracks that form before I can stop them. A wounded cry slips out that sounds pitiful even to my ears.

But it's only a reflection of how I feel. The ache of being unwanted and unloved.

Longing for what we'd had before. Times that were dark but still offered fleeting moments of comfort.

I wipe at my eyes with the back of my hands, rattled to my core. I'm breaking apart before Logan, coming to the realization I've been foolish. I've thought he'd care. I've wondered if he could change his mind and love me...

Irritation and anger greet me instead. His scowl clenches onto his face, no light to be found in his gaze.

I'm wiping away more tears, watching Logan move into the bathroom. He flicks on the bright light and tugs his t-shirt over his head.

It's the first time I'm afforded a clear view of him, bathed in light.

I gasp at the blood and bruises I discover.

Logan's got a bloodied lip. His right cheek's more swollen than usual. A couple bruises color his torso.

He's been in a fight.

12

LOGAN

"IF YOU SHITHEADS DON'T SHUT THE FUCK UP, I'M coming over there to cram my boot up your ass. Got it?" growls Mudd at the barroom full of Steel Kings. When the buzz around the room dies out, he nods at Silver. "All yours, Chief."

Silver can barely keep from grinning. He shakes his head and redirects his attention to the rest of the club.

Today's our first real meeting since our crackdown at the Chosen Saints compound. We've got to plan out our next moves.

There's still business to finish.

Several of the saints escaped that night, including the Leader.

After more recon work, we've learned of another compound in the area that we'll be invading soon. But first we've got to hash out the details.

I sit at the front of the room along with Mace, Cash, and Tito. I've received plenty of curious stares and whispers from members who have been absent the past few weeks. The club hasn't officially been briefed on my story.

I've made it clear to Silver and Mace I want to keep it that way.

It's none of their fucking business where I've been and what I've been up to.

They're not owed the details. That's for me and the Leader to settle when I put him six feet under.

"Where to even start?" Silver asks, peering around the room. "Word travels fast. Contrary to popular belief, bikers are bigger gossip queens than most old ladies. I know most of you have already heard through word of mouth or seen it for yourself. Ghost's back."

Everybody seated in the bar takes the opportunity for a glance at me. Even the barmaids have slowed up delivering pints and peanuts and cast me curious looks.

I ignore them all, staring at an indiscriminate point in the distance.

"Ghost has been to hell and back. Which means he's in no mood to deal with your bullshit. Keep it away from him," Silver explains. His lecturing tone has clearly been perfected over time. Probably all the scolding he's done with his own kids. "We've got no shortage of problems. Which is what today's meetings about."

Johnny Flanagan thrusts his arm in the air. "I've got a question."

I can practically feel Mace's scowl from my right. The two of them have never gotten along. They barely had chin hairs and were going at it as kids. Fast forward almost twenty years later, nothing's changed.

I'm no fan of Flanagan either considering he's a shit stirrer.

"What is your question, Flanagan?" Silver asks.

"If the rumors are true, you raided the compound of that cult. The one that's been in the news."

"I'm not the smartest guy around, but I didn't hear a question, Flanny," Ozzie points out, earning several chuckles around the room.

Flanagan shakes his stringy, shoulder-length hair out of his face. "My question is, what's that got to do with us? Why are we getting involved?"

"If you've heard the rumors," Mace snaps, sitting forward, "then you've heard why. You know exactly what the fuck we were doing raiding them."

"That doesn't answer my question," Flanagan says.

"Interrupt the meeting again with a stupid question like that and I'll answer it with my fist."

"Mace," Silver warns. He looks over at Flanagan, his stare scrutinizing. "It's got to do with us, Flanagan, because they had one of our people. You might remember the oath you took when you became a King. If you don't, I'm inclined to let Mace take you out back and teach you the hard way."

Flanagan falls silent with red blotches coloring his face and neck.

Silver gives it a few seconds, then carries on like he was never interrupted with a stupid question.

"We raided the compound belonging to the religious cult known as the Chosen Saints," Silver explains. "We slaughtered most of the higher-ranking members and set free the captives. But their leader—otherwise known as Abraham James—was able to escape. Ghost, care to offer your two cents? You're heading up this situation."

I stand up from where I'm seated, my arms folded over my chest. I keep it short and sweet. I'm still staring at an indiscriminate point in the distance. Public speaking has never been my thing. Less so after returning from years of captivity.

Crowds put me on guard. Even crowds of my own people.

"Everything he said," I say. "The Chosen Saints are a cult that held people captive. Men and women. All ages, races, it doesn't matter. It's a community based off some bullshit scripture Abraham James invented. They use, abuse, and hurt people, and are out for more power and influence. If what we suspect is true, they've got more than one compound in the area. We destroyed one of them. We'll do the same to the rest.

"We've got one of them in our custody. He's down in the basement. Plan is to interrogate him and get him to crack. Give up the address of their alternate location. Once we get what we can out of him, we'll start mapping out the next mission. Expect to be ready at a moment's notice."

The meeting adjourns how it always does—with another refill of drinks from the barmaids and Mick cutting the music back on from behind the bar counter.

Everyone with real responsibility slips out of the main room and into the back. The door snaps shut behind me, Silver, Mace, Cash, and a couple others.

We're in the basement where our captive is being held.

Xavier's strapped down in a chair by rope, a gag stuffed in his mouth. Dried blood mats his hair and dirt and grime cake his skin. He's seen better days.

Too bad those better days for him were hell for me. Funny how the shoe's on the other foot.

"Who gave him a black eye?" Cash asks.

Ozzie flashes a grin. "We had to subdue him. Fucktard wouldn't stay still."

Silver surveys Xavier for a second longer, then says, "Anybody bring any pliers?"

"Would it be a torture sesh without them? Tito and I put together a whole selection."

"Don't put that on me, *amigo*. That was all you. I supervised."

Ozzie gestures to the assortment of tools he's set down on the table against the wall like some impressive display he couldn't be more excited about. He's brought screwdrivers, wrenches, pliers, a sledgehammer.

"Half of these I stole from the Chop Shop when Korine wasn't looking."

Cash shakes his head. "If she caught you, I'm pretty sure you'd be the one sporting a black eye right now."

"Fuck this."

The two words rumble out of me in an impatient growl.

I stride up to where Xavier's strapped down in the chair and throw a right hook. My fist collides with the side of his head. His neck bends off to the side at the force of the hit. A knot immediately begins to form.

I punch him a second time in the nose. "Remember me?"

"Believer Logan," he croaks. "We meet again."

"You're damn straight we do." Another punch to the face. "Did you think you'd get to flee that night and not be held accountable?"

The others stand back as I unleash a lengthy combination of hits. I hit Xavier so many times, my knuckles crack open. His swollen eye closes the rest of the way up.

"Logan, this is supposed to be an interrogation," Silver says finally.

Mace takes a step toward me. "He's right. We're supposed to be collecting info."

"I'll collect info. *After* I'm done beating the shit out of him."

I reach for the pliers and nod at Ozzie. He understands what I'm asking of him and rushes to prop Xavier's mouth open.

Over the next two minutes, the room fills with Xavier's pained howls as I pry a couple teeth from his gums. The front incisors pop out easily. It's the rear molars that are a bitch.

Xavier has no choice but to bear the excruciating pain. His hands flex open and shut as he seizes up in the chair, and the blood in his mouth muffles his screams.

Mace grabs my shoulder. "Logan, pace yourself. We need him lucid enough to gather info—"

"Back off!" I growl, shrugging him off. When he tries to grab me a second time, I swing on him.

My own brother.

I don't give a shit that I do—we fist fought many times growing up. It was often how Dad had us settle our disputes. He'd clear the coffee table in the living room and let us wrestle and tussle it out. A couple years older, I was always bigger and stronger, but Mace has always loved a challenge.

He usually held his own, even if I more often than not won by the end.

Now's no different as I swing on him. He ducks last second, then locks his arms around me in a submission hold.

The altercation becomes a runaway train from there.

Silver and the others stand back like Dad used to when we fought. They let me break Mace's hold and retaliate with an elbow to his gut. I take a fist in the jaw, and he grunts when I spear into him and we crash against the concrete wall.

I disappear into my pent-up anger.

Mace isn't my enemy—distantly, I can recognize that—

but at the moment, he's a representation of it. He's the guy on the receiving end as I draw back my fist and crush it into his ribs.

The others don't jump in 'til we're on the brink of knocking each other out. Silver and Cash grab hold of Mace while Ozzie and Tito jump on me.

When it's all said and done, the basement looks like a tornado raged through it. Xavier remains in the middle of the room, banded to the chair by the thick rope, dripping blood from his gums. Mace is held back on one side while I'm on the other.

"That's enough," Silver scolds. "Both of you, out. Tito and I will handle the interrogation. And if I find out this happens again, I'll kick both your asses. Or maybe let Tom know what his sons have been up to."

Mace storms out with Cash following to check up on him.

I leave in the same foul mood.

"Ozzie, back the fuck off," I call over my shoulder.

The club's resident joker's on my heels. He must figure since Mace has got Cash, he'll do the same for me. But I don't need anybody to make sure I'm alright.

I'm not alright.

I'm still seething. Rage still pumps through my veins. I cross the covering out front where everybody parks their bikes and mount mine.

"Where you off to?" Ozzie asks. "Break somebody else's face?"

"Maybe. I've only broken two today."

He scoffs. "We've got to get those numbers up. I expect five out of you. Minimum."

"Cut the shit. I told you I don't need anybody checking on me."

"How about a drink? Not here," he adds. He scratches his neck that's covered in tattoos like the rest of him. "You know, blow off some steam."

I pause for half a second, considering his offer. "Where?"

Twenty minutes later, we're two of three inside the Titty Bar. The third guy sits right beside the stage as the early-evening dancers gyrate to "Cherry Pie". He's clearly a regular, peering up at the ladies like they're goddesses on earth, his glasses damn near fogging up.

The place won't be packed for another few hours. That's when the more talented dancers take the stage and the audience fills out.

Ozzie nods his head to the hard rock music and offers dollar bills to any dancer that struts by. He's got no shortage of them, apparently a regular himself.

I'm more distracted by the bottle of beer I'm downing. I've started peeling off the label, my mind miles away.

Things weren't supposed to get so out of hand in the basement. I hadn't intended on exploding like I did.

These days, I've got so much pent-up anger and hatred, I don't know what to do with myself. It can't be healthy, yet it's the only way I know how to cope.

"My girl worked here," Ozzie says over the music. "Her name was Sparkle."

I glance over at him, half exasperated by the fact that he's so damn casual. Like I'm not sporting bloodied knuckles and a busted lip after my fight. But I buy into what he's saying anyway. I figure there's no use not to. He's already dragged me to this bar for drinks.

"What happened to her?"

"She dumped me. Her ex finished his stint in prison."

My eyebrow rises. "And you still come here?"

"She still appreciates the tips," he says, grinning. "So, you going to tell me what the fuck that was about? The way you went off, you blacked out."

I give a shrug.

My phone vibrates in my pocket. I've received a text from Teysha.

Dinner's waiting :)

A deep breath blows out of me. I pocket my phone and pretend I never saw it.

"I don't know what happened," I admit. "That was the first time I've seen one of the pieces of shit from that place. I went into revenge mode."

"You were fucking him up good. Blood everywhere." Ozzie laughs, then catches the eye of another dancer. He waves a wad of dollar bills between his fingers to entice her.

It works. She prances over topless in nothing else but a g-string to pay him a few moments of attention. Sitting in his lap, she smashes his face into her huge tits and then snatches the cash.

"Thank ya, cutie."

Ozzie's grin has only widened. "That was Diamond. Maybe she's the new Sparkle."

My phone has gone off a couple more times. More texts from Teysha.

Over the course of the next two hours, it becomes a running theme. Teysha sending me increasingly upset texts.

I hope you'll be home soon. I've missed you. <3

Please answer. Will you be home soon??

Please don't ignore me. Please come home....

"Who's that? Wifey?" Ozzie asks.

"No," I lie, pocketing my phone. "Somebody unimportant."

Hours go by. The Titty Bar fills up. The music shifts from hard rock from the '80s into more modern songs for the dancers to perform pole tricks to.

I've lost count of what beer I'm on when I finally decide I've had enough.

The lights are still on in the apartment when I make it home. Teysha's waited up for me.

I walk through the door unsure of how I'm going to address the inevitable questions. She's going to want to know what I've been up to, why I didn't answer her texts. I had asked Mace's fiancée Sydney to take her out for the day. Give her something else to do besides mope around my apartment. Even gave her cash to buy herself some things.

But it doesn't seem to have helped. She's as nosy and needy as ever.

I head into the kitchen as she sits up on the couch. "Where have you been?"

"Why are you still up?"

I've popped the tab on a can of beer that I'll be taking with me into my bedroom. Any person with common sense would get the hint that I'm not in the mood for company. Teysha either fails to understand or she doesn't care as she follows me.

"I've been waiting for you! Did you see my texts?"

"I haven't checked my phone. There were more important things going on."

"Were you out drinking? Out partying at the club? Were there other women there?" she asks in a tone that shakes with emotion. "Why won't you ever tell me what you're doing? Why won't you ever take me with you?"

I scowl. "Teysha, lower your damn voice."

"I've... I've been waiting for you!" She rushes ahead of me to block my path. "Why won't you just try?"

In no damn mood to play these games, I grab her by the arm and drag her out of my way. "I don't have time for this shit! Move out of my way."

"You owe me an explanation!"

"I don't owe you shit."

"I'm your wife!"

It's a cold, hollow feeling that pits deep and makes me bark out a loud laugh. I'm about to hurt her, yet I don't give a single fuck that I am.

Just like earlier with Mace.

Teysha's now the stand-in for my anger. My twisted, bitter feelings about all the shit that's happened. It wouldn't be the first time, and since we're stuck together for the time being, it probably won't be the last.

She must know I've got severe mood swings by now.

"You ain't my wife, and I ain't your husband," I snap. "Let's get that straight right now."

I can feel her heart breaking. I can sense the tears welling up in her eyes.

Yet I don't give a damn. I don't have a single fuck to give about what I'm doing.

Maybe she should've done the smart thing and gone home, after all. At least then she wouldn't be subjected to this.

Bringing the beer can to my lips, I down another large mouthful, then head into the bathroom. It's as I flick on the light and tug off my t-shirt that Teysha gasps.

All my scrapes and bruises.

My busted lip and purpled ribs. The tiny cuts up and down my knuckles.

It's been hours and I haven't tended to any of them.

"You got into a fight?" she asks weakly.

"Something like that."

"I wish you'd talk to me."

"I've got nothing to say."

Not to you.

Not after... everything...

Teysha sniffles in the doorway. One second she's there, the next second she's gone. I come up from the sink after rinsing any residual blood out of my mouth.

Nobody's in the doorway. It's empty.

She passes in the hall a second later clutching what looks like an armful of belongings and her duffle bag.

I sigh and go check what fit she's throwing now. I find her in the living room slipping on her pair of sandals and fumbling with the things she's clinging onto. My head slants to the side.

"Going somewhere?"

"Yes," she answers tightly. "Anywhere else but here."

"Teysha—"

"You hate me," she cuts in. "You can't stand being around me. So I'll go."

"It's one in the fucking morning."

"I don't care."

"You've got nowhere else to go."

"I'll find somewhere. The... the bus terminal must be open. And if it isn't..." she pauses to shudder out another upset breath. "I'll wait outside for it to open."

I slam my hand against the front door when she walks over and twists on the knob to pull it open. She tips her head back for a look up at me. Her eyes, so big and expressive, shine with tears. Her whole face wears the emotion she's feeling, from the tremble of her jaw to the way her brows are drawn close.

If it's at all possible, she's pretty when she cries. Something I notice in the brief second our gazes lock.

Then I notice what she has on.

The little flowery blue dress that fits her figure perfectly. She's never worn it before because it's new... and she couldn't look more beautiful.

So damn beautiful it's unreal she's standing before me. That technically she's my *wife*. Somewhere out there, a man better than myself deserves her.

Yet here she is trying to impress me.

I stand back from the door. "Did you just buy that?"

"Dinner is... dinner's on the stove. Good night, Logan."

Teysha wraps her hand on the doorknob a second time to draw it open. I'm quicker, scooping her hand up in mine. I lead her away from the door, unsure if I'm more irritated by her presence or her attempt at leaving.

It doesn't make any sense how I wish I had the place to myself, yet I don't want her gone.

Not yet.

"Put your things down," I say. "You're not going anywhere."

"I'm not staying where I'm not welcome."

My teeth clench together. "Nobody said you're not welcome."

"You didn't need to. Your body language speaks volumes."

"Look," I sigh, scrubbing a hand over my face. "It's been a long day."

"You smell of beer."

"And you smell like fucking flowers. What's your point?"

Her brows scrunch closer, a little line appearing in between. A quirk of hers I've noticed and grown used to. It forms whenever she's thinking.

She's trying to figure out how to take me.

"Sit down," I order. "You said there's dinner? I'll warm it up."

"Are you going to tell me what happened?"

"If you sit down and stop trying to flee in the middle of the fucking night."

"Hasn't anybody ever told you you're not supposed to swear at a lady?"

"I don't follow those rules. Just like I don't follow the rule that says a hysterical woman should go rushing off into the dark because she didn't get enough attention."

She drops to the sofa like a wilted flower, her expression glum, her eyes no less sad and watery.

A kernel of guilt chips away at me. I turn my back and focus on heating up the pasta she's left out on the stove.

Minutes later, I'm walking two large plates into the living room. Hers I set down on the coffee table. Mine stays with me as I claim the loveseat.

More silence stretches on between us.

Teysha picks at the pasta she's prepared. I'm a fast eater, and I drank on an empty stomach. She's barely had a fettuccine noodle by the time I've downed mine like a fucking Hoover vacuum. The pitiful, hunched way she's sitting and picking at her food says enough.

I set down my empty plate and realize I've got to put aside the bitter mood. At least for now if she's going to stop being so damn upset.

"I got into a fight," I admit. "Since you want to know all about it. Me and Mace."

Her eyes widen. "You and Mason? But why?"

"Why not?"

"For starters, he's your brother."

"Which means it's not the first time. Probably won't be the last." I slide fingers through my hair that's grown long up top and then figure I've come this far, might as well keep going. Just for the time being 'til we get this arrangement dissolved. "We found Xavier. We were interrogating him."

She's clearly startled by the news, so much so, she doesn't even answer.

It's as complicated for her as it is for me. Yet our responses couldn't be more different.

"We've learned about another compound we believe belongs to the Saints. We think it's where the Leader—*Abraham* is his name—is hiding out."

"Abraham," she repeats in a whisper. Disbelief's frozen on her face, like she's time-traveling to the past in her head.

"Hey, look at me," I say, reaching over to palm her knee. I wait 'til her big brown eyes flick to me. "I'm going to get him. I'm going to make him pay for everything he did to you, alright?"

I get up and start to walk away but only make it a couple steps.

"Logan?"

"Yeah?"

"Can I..." she murmurs softly, then pauses for a sigh. "Can I please... your bed..."

Fuck. This girl doesn't give up.

"Tonight," I say. "Just tonight."

I don't wait for her reaction before striding the rest of the way out of the room. Teysha's just going to have to understand she's seeking something I can't give her.

13

TEYSHA

Sleep no longer comes easy, but I don't mind when I'm lying in bed beside Logan.

He snores. Not all the time. Only when he rolls onto his back. But it's become a sound that I can listen to for hours. Along with the sound of him breathing.

Comfort noises like when people listen to those sound machines with the ocean waves or pouring rain.

It's not the first time I've listened for them—in our cabin at the Chosen Saints compound, sometimes it would be so quiet at night, I could hear him then too. Sleep was the only time Believer Logan put his guard down, usually so exhausted by a long day of grueling work, his body gave out.

I watch him now like I watched him then.

Before it was from halfway across the cabin. Now it's lying beside him in bed.

One night turns into two and then into three.

On the third night, as I sit on his bed and he approaches, still toweling himself off from his shower, he lets out a deep sigh.

"Teysha, it was one time only."

The three little words he hates almost roll off my tongue —*I'm your wife*. I catch myself this time and ask instead, "But why?"

"You have your own bed."

"But I like this bed."

"Then I'll take the other room."

"I don't want to be in here alone."

He scrubs a hand over his face. "Teysha, nothing's going to happen. The doors are locked. I'm here. I'm strapped. If somebody tries something they'll have a bullet in their skull."

I come up empty on my rebuttal. Instead, the ache I've grown familiar with in recent times returns. A reminder that no matter what I do, it'll never be filled. I might as well be searching the desert for water.

Turning my head so he won't see me blinking away tears, I make a small noise. "*Oh.*"

Part of me hates that I'm so pitiful. Part of me feels manipulative because it always ends the same.

I sniffle despite myself and get up to head for the door. Logan's rubbing his brow like he's pained by a headache. Crying women make him uncomfortable. Another reason why a part of me feels unseemly doing it in front of him.

I know all these things, yet I still let emotion win out. I let tears brim in my eyes, my damaged heart on my sleeve for him to see.

His rejection hurts a little bit more each time.

But then there's the part of me that relishes how he inevitably stops me. As I make for an exit, he reaches for my hand. He *concedes*.

"One more night."

My damaged heart sings.

It beats with hope that it means something. He cares if he's stopped me. If he doesn't let me go when I leave.

...he feels sorry for you. That doesn't mean he cares.

And the toxic cycle begins all over again.

On the fifth night, he stops at the foot of the bed and sighs. "What're you gonna do once it's annulled? Sleep with a teddy bear?"

"Maybe," I answer, smirking. "I could have a life-sized teddy bear of you specially made."

The instant crease in his brow earns a quick giggle out of me.

"Only kidding, Logan Cutler. You can take the stick out of your behind."

"You mean ass?"

"Same thing."

"No drinking. No cursing. Is there *anything* you do for fun?" He pulls back the covers on the bed, his broad, tattooed chest on display. He tends to sleep in his boxers, though he's hinted at sleeping in the buff when I'm not around. "Don't tell me you read the Bible."

"I do," I say, then hurry to clarify. "There's nothing wrong with reading the Bible. It's a perfectly fine past time."

He snorts. "Sure sounds like it."

"I like cooking... and baking... and knitting."

"What are you, sixty-five?"

I realize I've started trailing behind him as he readies the room for bedtime. As he dims the lights and turns up the air conditioning, I'm following, racking my brain for any cool hobbies.

Something that would impress a rebellious biker like him.

"I... uh... I've got nothing. Alright, fine! So I'm a sixty-year-old trapped in the body of a twenty-year-old! I'm not very spontaneous and I don't do crazy things. Don't blame me, blame growing up in a place like Boulder!"

Logan's broken out in gruff laughter. The deepest, longest laugh I've ever heard out of him. It convulses through him 'til he tips his head back in laughter and wipes at his eyes afterward. I'd be more amused if the joke wasn't lost on me.

I stomp my foot. "Are you going to tell me what's so funny?"

"Ain't it obvious? *You.*" His pinches at the apple of my cheek. "I've got to give it to you. You sure know how to be downright fucking adorable. Must be why I also find you so downright fucking irritating."

My hands come to my waist, recognizing his biting humor. "Anyone ever tell you that's not how you compliment a woman?"

"It is in my world." He lays back on his side of the bed, his arm curled under his head. "In my world, a woman's either a groupie or an old lady. There're no candlelit dinners and there damn sure ain't no roses. If you can't cut it, then it's onto the next one. Still want to be married?"

I roll my eyes and then crawl onto the bed beside him. While he's only in his boxer briefs, I'm in a satin negligee. One of my purchases when I went shopping with Sydney and Korine. I bought it because I wanted to be more enticing. I wanted my husband to see me wearing it.

So far, Logan hasn't so much as touched me.

But I've caught his wandering eye. His glances at my chest and thighs when he thinks I'm not paying attention.

Now is one of those times as I climb onto the bed—my negligee rides up and Logan catches a quick peek of my panties. He immediately looks away, his expression tensing up.

I settle in place beside him, pretending not to notice. "I still want to be married."

"Seriously?"

"You're the husband I've been given," I say earnestly, shrugging. "I figure God works in mysterious ways. I'm with you for a reason."

He barks out an incredulous laugh. "Sure you are. You just don't know it yet."

"Maybe not. But soon."

"You shouldn't," he says, reaching for the bedside lamp. "A girl like you should want better."

The light goes out, leaving us in the dark. Logan rolls onto his side so that his back faces me. He'll be out any moment.

I don't bother trying to keep him up.

My head reels with all the thoughts that have formed. I'm caught between wondering how selfish it is that I've guilt-tripped myself into Logan's bed and whether he's right that I should want better.

Mama and Grandma Renae would agree. They've always been perfectly clear they expect me to marry a good man of faith.

Logan Cutler couldn't be more opposite.

Yet here I am. Wanting to stay. Lying in his bed. Hoping and praying he changes his mind.

The rhythm of his breathing becomes the lullaby that eases me off to sleep.

I'm up and moving the next morning. I change into another sundress I bought and head into the kitchen to get started on breakfast. Yesterday I talked Logan into taking me grocery shopping, which means we're stocked up. A smile graces my face as I draw the fridge open and find it so full. I pull out the carton of eggs and packet of bacon.

The eggs finish quick while the bacon's still popping in the pan.

I'm rolling up biscuits I've made using Grandma Renae's secret recipe. The tray goes in the oven to bake a while.

Plates are set out and the coffee's hot by the time Logan appears.

I smile at him. "Good morning. Hungry?"

He's squinting, still half asleep. "What's all this?"

"I made breakfast. Bacon, eggs, some buttery soft biscuits. My grandma's recipe. Everybody loves them. Coffee?"

"Why?"

"I told you I like to cook—"

"You don't have to around here," he interrupts. "I don't need you cooking dinner or getting up early for breakfast. 'Til you showed up, I survived off beer and burritos. You don't need to clean up around here either. Stop trying so damn hard."

I flatten my hands over the skirt portion of my dress and let out a shaky breath. "You know, Logan, you sure try hard at making me feel like a fool. You should take your own advice."

"Teysha, hold up."

Logan catches me on my escape attempt. As I try to flee the kitchen and pass him on my way to the hall, he loops an arm around my waist to hold me.

I twist to free myself. "Don't try to hold me back—"

"Look, it's different, alright? You being here. I'm not used to it." Logan's hands grip my shoulders tightly and he forces me to stand still. I have no choice but to meet his steely blue gaze and feel the funny flip in my stomach. "It's a lot at once. A lot of shit in general. I'm not good with change."

"I *like* cooking. I cooked a few meals. What is there to complain about?" I ask.

Humor flickers in his stare. "Abso-fucking-lutely nothing, baby. Happy?"

"Yes, actually. I'm glad you see things my way."

I duck out of his arms before he can seek revenge. But as I turn back toward the kitchen and he spins around, I sense he wants some. He's tempted to make it happen.

Be playful in return and grab hold of me all over again.

My heart flutters faster at the mere thought. I've been working hard to keep his attention. I've been hoping he would give me the affection he did in the Chosen Saints. Praying he'd change his mind and tell me he wants to be my husband.

I make it across the kitchen untouched.

But I don't let it get me down. Logan drops into one of the chairs and cleans every crumb off his plate when he's done. He goes back for seconds with Grandma's biscuits. By the time the meal's over, he's squeezed my shoulder in thank you.

Later in the evening I'm waiting for him with dinner, and we sit down for another meal. I shower and find his bedroom door cracked open as if just for me. Within minutes of the lights going out, I'm falling asleep to the same lullaby as the previous nights.

It becomes our routine.

Logan letting me sleep with him. My meals waiting for him. Our conversations mundane, like we've accepted our new living arrangement.

Logan leaves the toilet seat up and my hair gets every-where. I put the TV volume on blast while he never tosses any of his clothes in the hamper.

"I have to wonder what you did before me," I confess one morning. Shaking my head, I drop one of his flannels into the dirty clothes pile. "Did you just expect the laundry fairy to sort it all out?"

He cocks a brow at me. "You're one to talk considering you've made a hobby of filling up the drain with clumps of hair."

"I always clean up after myself!"

"Yet more hair keeps popping up. Blows right across the bathroom floor like a tumbleweed."

My jaw drops in offense. "I wouldn't know. I've been too busy wiping down the toilet when you pee all over it."

"You're welcome to use the bathroom in the hall, babe."

"Don't call me babe—"

"What are you going to do about it?"

As I go to shove him in the chest, he catches my hands and links our fingers together. We're locked into an unplanned dance. My steps backward. His, forward.

Tiny little sparks shoot through me at his skin touching mine. He's warm, radiating a raw heat that's energy encir-cling us.

His hand drops to my hip and awakens something deep inside. Something I don't know how to describe but feels like an intense ache.

Logan seems to come to his senses. He lets go of me with a clear of his throat and a mention about heading out.

It's far from the first time I sense it out of him. Desire he's holding back.

I wake a couple mornings later to find the bed empty and Logan in the bathroom. My sleepy mind assumes he's taking a morning shower 'til I hear a grunt from the other side of the door. I stay still and listen for the sound again.

It's the first of several.

I crawl out of bed, tiptoeing over.

Logan groans a final time before he goes silent. I leap back onto the bed, pretending I'm still asleep, just in time for the door to open.

Confusion knots up my insides as I wonder if he was doing what I think he was doing. Yet he's barely laid a finger on his wife...

He hasn't touched me since we were in captivity. The last time was the night Abraham first had me. Is it because he's repulsed by what happened? He doesn't want me now that Abraham's used me in that way?

The rejection takes on a life of its own. It stays on my mind throughout the day. Korine offers to swing by and take me for a mani-pedi, but I decline. I break out the steaks we've bought from our last grocery trip and prepare a big dinner.

I light candles and bake a red velvet cake. I'm in the only dress Logan hasn't seen me in yet—a revealing dress that's tighter than the others.

Mama would claim it's a dress scandalous women wear. The kind of woman with no self-respect for herself who lets too much skin show, but what she thinks doesn't matter anymore. I have a husband to seduce.

The slinky, skintight ensemble stops Logan in his tracks when he walks through the door. His eyes flick up and down, head to toe, and he scrubs his jaw.

"Since when do you dress like that?" he asks.

I pop a hand to my hip. "I don't know what you're talking about."

"Candles?"

"Sit down. I hope you're hungry."

"Yeah... I am..." His gaze wanders over me.

I strut—or do my best interpretation *of* a strut—into the kitchen, trying to be sexy. Desirable.

Both things I've never felt or known how to be.

I've never been the sexy woman. I've always been too intimidated, too fearful and compliant with the beliefs instilled in me.

That was reserved for my husband and my husband only—when I did finally get married. I just never counted on it happening so soon.

Logan sits down at the table, his body language lax. Every move I make is studied. He can't take his eyes off me.

Go for it.

Inhaling a shaky breath, I forget about dinner. I strut toward the dining table with swaying hips and an expression I hope is flirtatious. Logan leans back in his chair as I plant myself in his lap. It's as if he wants to protest but can't bring himself to. I slide onto his lap and come in closer, trailing a finger along his rough beard.

"I've been thinking about you all day," I murmur.

"Yeah?"

"Yeah," I answer, a spark of adrenaline shooting through me. I rock my hips back and forth in his lap. The hem of my dress rides up. "I was thinking about how I wanted you to touch me."

He swallows, his throat tight. "Yeah?" he chokes out again.

"Yeah... all over."

My hips slide back and forth some more. More of my dress bunches up. The strap slips down my shoulder, but I don't fix that either. I tickle my fingers along his jawline and let our lips align in an almost kiss.

So very close.

"I wanted you so bad," I purr, "I didn't put on any panties."

"Fuck... Teysha..."

My skin's flushed, though I don't let myself think too much on it. If I did, I'd lose my nerve. I'd start second-guessing and feeling silly. So far I've managed to block out those thoughts; I've channeled how I imagine a bombshell type of woman would behave.

I press my lips to Logan's while my hands set to work on his belt. "I want to feel you inside me."

It's like once the seal is broken, Logan loses all rational thought.

He growls as he fists my hair and deepens our kiss. I'm barely able to keep up with the intensity that washes over us. His tongue pushes into my mouth, making his dominance known from its first lash.

Heat spreads across my skin as it suddenly occurs to me this is our first *real* kiss. The first real time Logan's unleashing the part of himself I know he's held back.

His lips claim while his tongue plunders. His fist tightens in my hair as he kisses me like he's been waiting a lifetime for the chance and now he can't control himself.

It's a dizzying thought sitting perched in his lap, trying to match his passion. I've never been the girl who impressed guys with my sexual skills. Mostly because I have none. Any kisses I gave were innocent, more like kissing frogs in search of my prince.

But kissing Logan Cutler is like coming alive in a whole new way. It's the instant, intense, spine-tingling epiphany that this is what people mean when they say they felt fireworks.

I feel many of them. Tiny sparks that crackle inside of me.

I'm left hot and dazed as Logan kisses my lips swollen. Then he's peppering them elsewhere, kissing any other parts of me he can, like my throat and shoulders.

He's *hard*. The bulge in his pants feels like steel between my thighs as I sit astride him.

"Oh... oh more... please," I pant, my eyes closing at the feel of his lips on my throat. "Please... Logan, make love to me."

He goes still as if waking from a dream. His fist loosens in my hair. His lips leave my throat, making it feel naked and exposed. He won't look me in the eye.

"We're not doing this. Get up."

I'm nudged out of his lap. I tug on the hem of my dress in confusion.

So lost I'm not even sure what to ask.

Logan strides out of the room. His bedroom door slams shut, sounding twice as loud in the silence.

My phone vibrating does too.

I glance at its lit up screen notifying me that I have a voice message. Still numb with confusion, I reach for it and play the message.

"Hello, Mrs. Cutler? This is Rita Lewis-Castillo with the Pulsboro Clerk's office. I'm calling because I finally got a chance to speak with my supervisor. She believes we may be able to process your annulment after all. If you would like to discuss this matter further, please give me a call back at 391-476-9235. I tried reaching your husband, but his voice mailbox is full. I hope you enjoy your evening."

A beep sounds in my ear before an automated voice comes on asking if I want to repeat the message, save the message, or delete the message. I listen to it a second time with my heart racing and my gaze trained on Logan's closed bedroom door, wondering if I'm ready to give up.

Mind made up, I press option three for delete.

Not yet.

14

TEYSHA

"Tey Tey baby, it's time for you to come home."

I roll my eyes and turn away from the window, my phone to my ear. "Mama, why do you keep bringing this up? I've already told you."

"It can't be good for you there. Cohabitating with that... that man."

"Mama, we're *married*."

"What does God say about mistakes? A person who refuses to admit their mistakes can never be successful. But if they do, another chance is given. There was a mistake made, sweetie. All you need to do is admit the truth and take the time to start over."

"But I didn't make any mistake..."

"Don't act smart. You know what I'm speaking of, Teysha," she scolds. "What you have been through would traumatize anyone. This is why you should be with loved ones."

"I'm with my husband."

"I said loved ones. Come home and allow us to fix the mistake."

"Mama, I'm happy here." I almost wince at the stitch in my ribs. The sharp pain is a dose of reality jabbing into me. I push back against it, stubbornly sticking to my story. "We're working things out. Haven't you always stressed the importance of sickness and health in marriage? Rich times and poor?"

"Sweetie, you know that doesn't apply here—"

"Logan and I might've gotten married under... unusual circumstances, but we've come to care for each other. Respect our union like you would anybody else's."

"Now wait a dang second, Teysha Patrice Baxter—"

"I'm hanging up now, Mama. God bless."

A sense of satisfaction tugs my lips into a smile. If you'd asked me even a year ago if I'd ever hang up on Mama, I would've looked at you like you were crazy.

Because you'd have to be to suggest such a thing.

But things have changed. I've changed.

The girl that was taken from the parking lot of the Sunny Side Up would never be seen from again. What would follow would be months of pain and trauma. The one and only bright spot she found would be in the man she called her husband...

I'll do anything to make it work.

Mama and Grandma Renae will just have to respect my decision. Both mean well, but they've grown so used to being in control that they can't give it up. They refuse to accept I'm a grown woman who is married now. I can find my own way.

With Logan.

"Who was that?" Logan asks, breezing into the kitchen. He's dressed in his dark denim and nothing else. Tattoos cover every inch of skin between his broad chest and corded arms. The muscle he'd lost during our time in captivity has returned in rippling glory. He opens the fridge to grab the carton of orange juice and guzzle some down. "That your mother again?"

"Yes. And remember how we'd agreed we'd drink out of cups? *Not* from cartons?"

"Remember when I said I hated pulp?" He makes a sour face, wiping at his mouth with his forearm.

"I like pulp. Which is why I got the '*some* pulp' version. It's a compromise."

"Your definition needs some work. What'd your mother have to say?"

I swallow against the guilt gnawing at the back of my throat. "She was checking up on me."

"She wants you to come home?"

"She'd prefer if I were closer. But she understands why I'm here."

"It won't be long. Once we get this dissolved, you won't have to be so far away," he says, reaching inside the fridge for the jug of whole milk instead. "Which reminds me, we need to follow up with the clerk's office. The supervisor was supposed to reach out. It's been fourteen business days."

"I'll call," I volunteer, forcing a smile. "You've been so busy with club stuff. Tracking down, um, the Leader. I'll follow up. You shouldn't have to worry about anything else."

Appreciation flickers in his steely blue eyes. He does the thing he's started doing, where he reaches out and pinches the skin on my arm. Not painfully. Not crudely. But in some gesture of affection that feels earned and sends a shiver down my spine.

It's several steps up from where we started since living together.

"Busy day at the club?" I ask.

"You can say that again. We've gotten Xavier to crack about the location of the compound. Now it's all planning."

"For when you go after..."

He nods. "It'll be soon."

"Let's do something special tonight," I blurt out. My smile softens, almost pleadingly. "Sydney asked me if we'd like to go to dinner with her and Mason."

"Teysha—"

"Just a dinner," I say. "It can't hurt. You and your brother have to patch things up eventually. The club won't survive if you don't. And you keep saying you don't want me cooking dinner every night. So give me a break."

His right brow cocks at the same time a crooked grin slashes across his mouth. "Anyone ever tell you you're pretty damn good at sweet-talking?"

"I'm only good if the answer is yes."

"I'll go so long as everybody's clear I'll punch Mace again if he pulls shit."

"At least wait 'til after dinner."

"Tell him that." He gives the flesh on my arm another squeeze before he heads for the door. He snatches a t-shirt hanging over a chair on his way. "I'm out. I'll come back tonight to pick you up."

I wave goodbye feeling a fuzzy warmth spreading in my chest. Validation that I've made the right choice.

We'll get there in time.

———

The Smokin' Pig is one of the most popular spots in Pulsboro on a Friday night. Known for its tangy barbecue sauce and assortment of smoked meats, the restaurant even hosts a karaoke hour. Logan and I enter to find the place packed.

There isn't a single empty table in the house.

Sydney spots us half a second later and thrusts her arm up to flag us down. Logan and I forge a path toward them, dodging servers carrying huge trays of food and a tipsy woman staggering over to the bar area.

It's not until we get closer that we realize our double date is a triple

Blake and Korine have pulled up chairs on the side. Logan slows up as if he's about to make an escape.

My hands slip around his thick forearm to keep him at my side. "Thanks for inviting us."

"We come to the Smokin' Pig every other Friday," Korine says. "It's kind of become a tradition of ours."

"Well, it's a good thing we've been included."

I almost cringe at Logan's curt tone. It drips of sarcasm, his expression disgruntled. If he was ever into the idea of a double dinner date, he's changed his mind. We take the chairs across from Mason and Sydney.

It quickly becomes apparent Logan and his younger brother really haven't patched things up. Whatever truce they've reached is tenuous at best, outright hostile in its worst form. Both men stare off anywhere else but at each other while me, Sydney, Korine, and Blake try to make conversation.

"Do you ever sing karaoke?" I ask.

"Korine's succeeded in getting Blake up there," Sydney giggles.

"You laugh as if you didn't enjoy my rendition of "Sweet Child O' Mine"."

Korine lays her head on his shoulder. "It was cute. Especially when you forgot the lyrics."

"I couldn't read the screen. And watch it—you don't call Kings *cute*. Puppies are cute. Kittens are cute. Kings are—"

"Sexy as hell and I can't wait 'til we get home." Korine drops a kiss on the underside of his jaw.

Blake seems to forget all about what he was saying and is suddenly distracted by Korine. His hand slips under the booth. I have a sneaking suspicion if I looked under there, I'd find his hand on her thigh.

"Someday I'll get Mace drunk enough to do it." Sydney bumps her shoulder into Mason's.

He's in the middle of taking a drink from his beer bottle. He cocks a brow at her, sets down his bottle, and says, "I'll do it if you join the Tits on Heels wet t-shirt contest at the club."

"You already said you'd never let me!"

"There's your answer."

Sydney rolls her eyes and bites back a smile while the others laugh. Everyone except Logan.

A tense beat follows once the laughs die down. I catch Sydney's eye and see her mind hard at work, thinking up a new topic.

"Hey, what's up, fam?!"

We look up at the sound of Ozzie's loud voice. He's walked up alongside a woman I've never seen before. They couldn't seem more different—Ozzie's covered in dozens of tattoos while the woman's pale and unassuming. He's got the kind of energy that draws attention while she's more of a skittish mouse.

"There you are," Blake says. "We were taking bets."

"You kidding? I never miss Smokin' Pig's Friday night specials. Didn't even wear a belt 'cuz I'm about to demolish some ribs."

"Hi, I'm Korine," she says, holding out her hand to greet the woman with Ozzie.

"Oh shit. Where are my manners?" Ozzie snaps his fingers into a finger gun he points at the woman. "Everyone, this is Hope. Hope, everyone. Mace, Cash, Ghost, and their girls Syd, Kori, and Tey."

Everyone murmurs a hello to Hope. Some shuffling is done so the pair can slide into the only empty seats left at the table.

Logan's tensed at my side. First at Ozzie and Hope's appearance, then at Ozzie calling me his girl. His jaw's clenched and his body's hardened. He's pissed; he's regretting ever agreeing to dinner tonight.

I clear my throat. "So, Hope, how did you and Ozzie meet?"

Hope shares a bashful smile with Ozzie. "At the Titty Bar."

Sydney almost chokes on her coke. Blake and Korine turn their heads away to disguise their quiet laughter.

"Sorry," Sydney says, clearing her throat. "It's just... you don't *look* like an exotic dancer."

"I get that a lot. It was my first day on the job when Ozzie came in."

"I took one look at her and knew," Ozzie says, throwing his arm around her shoulders. He leans in close to kiss her on the cheek. "I told her, get off that damn stage right now and put some clothes on."

"And he took me for milkshakes at the Dairy Shack," Hope says brightly.

The rest of us are silent, unsure of how to react to their story. Finally Blake cuts in to give Ozzie a hard time about how he'd said he was swearing off women forever after Sparkle. Ozzie shrugs him off.

"What can I say? Hope is one of a kind."

"Good," Sydney teases, "now you'll stop asking me if I have any single cousins."

The conversation evolves from there as our server finally arrives with our food. Even Mason starts participating as he moves onto his second beer and dines on smoked ribs.

Logan's the only one holding back.

The tension hasn't let up. His muscles feel harder than usual, like he's on guard. He's ready at a moment's notice if something were to pop off.

Every time the restaurant door dings open and people walk in, he's watching. He's tracking everyone's movements around the dining room. Is this what he's always done when out in public or is this a new habit of his?

It's like he won't take his mind off our surroundings long enough to enjoy the moment.

Blake makes an attempt at roping him into the conversation once it turns to bikes and the Chop Shop. He gives a one word answer and goes back to his silent, disgruntled surveillance of the Smokin' Pig.

I'm so tuned into Logan and his reactions that I begin checking out of the conversation too. I try to reach for his hand, but he moves it away before I can. I've tried to catch his eye for a smile, but he's refused to look at me.

The rejection heats up my skin. I roll my lips together, holding it in. Reminding myself patience is key. We've been making progress.

Logan's not *there* yet... but he can be someday.

He cared for me once. He can do it again...

Yet as I tell myself these things, my heart wilts inside my chest. I feel acutely aware of the other three couples seated with us at the table. Blake and Korine can't keep their hands off each other—Blake's stroking her thigh and she's practically propped up against his chest. Mason and Sydney have been flirting with the heated looks they exchange from their verbal sparing, like it's some form of foreplay for them.

And then there's Ozzie and Hope, who seem so smitten with each other it's almost sickening.

Meanwhile, Logan hasn't touched me. He hasn't so much as looked at me.

If we weren't seated together, you'd never know we were a couple at all.

Husband and wife.

A sudden wave of tears emerge from my eyes, and I do my best to ward them off. I blink them away and dab at my eyes with a napkin.

"So when's the wedding?" Ozzie asks Mason and Sydney.

They share a look, then Sydney says, "We're thinking end of summer. On our one year anniversary."

Hope smiles. "That's so sweet."

"How about we make it a double wedding? We drive to Vegas and two for one that shit."

The others laugh. Hope gives Ozzie a kiss on his cheek like he did to her minutes ago.

"We should be taking pointers from these two," Ozzie goes on, jutting his chin at us.

My insides freeze into ice. All while my skin burns.

The attention of the rest of the table shifts to Logan and me, and my voice goes out. I pull my lips into a polite smile and place my hand over Logan's clenched fist on the table.

"We're just... figuring things out."

Logan snatches his hand away and rises to his feet. "Smoke break."

The rejection was bad on its own. It stung enough when Logan's rebuffed me in private. Just between the two of us.

But in a full restaurant? As six other pairs of eyes sit and watch it unfold live?

I feel like I've been slapped across the face. Heat prickles across my cheeks, leaving my skin warm all over again.

After such crippling embarrassment, what else can I do but excuse myself?

I slide out of my chair and ignore everyone who calls my name. Logan went out the side exit. I follow after him, my pulse pounding in my ear.

Humiliation can't begin to compete with the panic that explodes from inside the instant I lose sight of him.

The restaurant's so crowded, so noisy and dizzying, that I breathe harder, trying to find my exit. Trying to find Logan.

How could he leave me like this?

...how could he walk off when I'm alone?

He knows I don't like crowded spaces like this. He knows I freak out easily and get overstimulated.

It's too much after the captivity we've been through.

I'm practically panting for air by the time I make it to the side exit. One of the waitresses coming out of the kitchen asks me if I need help. I merely shake my head and push at the door, praying it'll open.

The night's air caresses my skin, providing much needed relief.

I suck in a deep breath and blink around the dark parking lot, lit up by a few lamp posts.

Logan's not far off. He's leaning against the brick building, a cigarette smoldering between his lips.

The tears I was holding in earlier begin slipping out. I

can't hold them in another second. Not when I'm confronted by the cold reality. The awful truth that I've been hoping against in vain.

I'm such a fool.

He doesn't want me.

He's made it clear. Whatever it is that made him stop showing me kindness and affection can't be undone. He won't ever change his mind.

I choke on the cry that warbles out of me, then promptly turn away before he can notice. I have no real money, nowhere really to go.

But I start walking anyway.

15

LOGAN

"Teysha? Where the hell are you going?!"

I notice her retreating form as I'm blowing out cigarette smoke. I've stepped outside the restaurant to have a moment alone.

All the noises. The lights. The *people*.

The damn door wouldn't stop flying open every other second.

Everybody else at the table sat laughing and chatting like nothing. They were into their stupid date like it was the time of their lives.

Mace and Cash showed their old ladies a good time. Even fucking *Ozzie* was all over his newest girl.

Teysha practically wilted at my side. Her hurt feelings were impossible to miss. I could feel it in the dejected little breaths she shuddered out. She wanted so badly for me to be like them. For me to grab her hand and kiss her brow and make her feel special.

I wanted that for her too.

I'm just not the person who's able to give that to her.

Something she doesn't seem to understand. I've already told her she should want better.

She *deserves* better.

"Teysha."

Her name rumbles out of me as I flick my cigarette butt and start after her.

What the fuck does she think she's doing?

We're on the bad side of town and it's dark out. She's wandering around in tears with a huge ass target on her back. I catch up to her halfway across the backlot, cutting off her next step.

"Where do you think you're going?"

"It's none of your business."

It damn sure is my business.

"You really think it's smart to wander off? Does that sound like it's about to end well?"

She jerks her arm back so I can't grab her. "Better than being rejected over and over again."

"How many times do I have to tell you? I can't—" I stop myself, nostrils flaring, then realize where we are. An argument in the middle of a shoddy backlot after dark isn't the kind of attention we want to be drawing to ourselves. I release a ragged breath and try again. "Back to the apartment."

My reflexes outpace hers. I grab her by the hand before she can rebuff me. As soon as we're inside my pickup truck, I shoot off a text to Mace, letting him know we're bailing.

The entire drive home is full of tense silence.

Teysha's crammed herself into the farthest little corner of the passenger seat, like she can't stand the idea that she's sitting next to me.

That's alright. She can throw as many tantrums as she wants so long as they're at home.

I'm doing what's best for her even if she doesn't like it.

The sooner we're able to get this marriage dissolved, the sooner we'll be able to move on. She'll be able to return to her real home and carve out a new life for herself. A woman like her will be scooped up fast.

Teysha walks ahead of me up to the apartment. I step over the threshold to her dark hair whipping out of view as she rounds the corner into the hall. I toss my keys, phone, and wallet on the end table and twist on the lamp. I'm stalling for time, dragging out every second.

She's hell bent on forcing issues.

I'm fine avoiding all that shit altogether.

But that's not about to happen tonight, because the energy circulating the air predicts what's to come—we're about to have it out.

There's no mistaking where this is headed.

I scrub a hand over my exhausted face, taking a moment to absorb the setting. How different the dark, quiet apartment feels to the noisy, chaotic barbecue restaurant. It eases the sensory overload I'd felt earlier, trapped on a quadruple fucking date I didn't agree to.

Then I head for the second bedroom, where the rustling noises Teysha's making are coming from. I stop in the doorway, unsurprised to find her things being crammed into her duffle bag.

"Are you gonna attempt to leave every other day? 'Cuz this charade is growing old."

"I wouldn't have to attempt it if you'd just let me." She's on her knees, her back to me. Her shoulders droop with the sigh she releases. "Logan, I'm going to call my mama and ask her to come get me."

My insides give an unexpected twist. "Call her now? After avoiding her?"

"It's the only option left. I can't... I can't stay here anymore. I can't do this."

"You're not having to do anything. We're getting it dissolved. That's why you're still here."

She chokes out a laugh that's shaky and dark. Almost like she's laughing at herself. She's the joke. "Please stop reminding me."

"Once we get it annulled—"

"I GET IT!" she screams 'til her voice breaks. She leaps to her feet clutching her duffle bag and rushes past me out of the room, her head bowed. "I get it, okay? I understand. Don't worry."

Thrown by the outburst, I track her down the hall into the living room. "You don't get that I'm only doing what's best for you. The marriage was a mistake. It was never supposed to happen. I've told you I've got no interest in being a husband. Some kind of family man with a wife and kids. I'm too fucked up for that shit. Will you put your bag down? Didn't we already establish you're not going anywhere tonight?"

"You don't want me... but you don't want me to go either!" She throws the bag to the floor and spins around to face me. Anguish rubs her voice raw, her eyes shining enough to show my reflection. "You don't want me to go 'cuz you want to make sure it's done! The mistake's erased from ever existing. I get it!"

"You're confused!" I shout over her. My patience vanishes, my glare narrows. "You think you're supposed to be with me, but you can't see you're wrong! I'm not the kinda guy you should be married to—"

"*You* are who I'm married to!" She raises her voice to match mine, unafraid as tears finally fall free. "You're the man I've exchanged vows with, but you won't take them seriously!"

"Because it wasn't a real ceremony."

"It was under God's view! It was for his eyes to see. It was real to me!"

"You don't believe in divorce, that it?" I ask. "You think 'cuz some freak cult married us off it means we're forever?"

She shakes her head, the pain fresh on her face. "You'll get what you want. You'll be rid of me. You won't ever have to be with me again."

"You'll be better off for it."

"Just let me leave. Just let me go then."

"We've been over this, it's the middle of the—"

"Why does it matter if it is?" she screams in interruption. "You don't want me so what do you care?!"

"I want what's best for you!" I lose all restraint, my hands coming out to grip both of her arms. I've stepped closer, giving her a shake, glaring in her face. "Don't you get it? Don't you see? I want what's fucking best for you! Stop being so damn hardheaded!"

"I know what's best for me! And I know that I wanted to be with you. But you shut me out at every turn. You make it clear you want nothing to do with me. Then you won't let me leave. I have whiplash from it all!"

"It's got nothing to do with wanting you or not—"

"It's got everything to do with it! Because if you did, you would have me! But you don't. You don't want me. So I'll find some man out there who will!"

A trigger inside me is pulled like you would a gun. It goes off with a bang from the deepest, basest part of me and sets off a chain reaction. I growl, gripping her tighter. My pulse has surged, my body crackling from the heat that rushes me.

For a wild, unpredictable moment, I want to break her. Show her how misguided and foolish she is for ever wanting me. For thinking I'm the man she belongs with.

"You want me to have you?" I grit out. "You want me to show you what I'm really like? You think you can handle it?"

"Logan, you're hurting me—" She squirms in my grip.

But I only clench harder, leaning in 'til my face hovers inches from hers. "You want me to hurt you some more? You want me to ruin you? 'Cuz that's what I'm capable of!"

Teysha whimpers as I grab her by the face and force her lips to mine in a rough kiss. I spare no time being gentle. Being considerate like she deserves.

I bite her lip and thrash my tongue against hers. I hold her still, locked within my grip, and kiss her like I'm about to ravage her.

No sweetness, no affection to be found.

Teysha's immediately overwhelmed, shrinking, tugging away. She tries to turn her head but my hand slides into her hair. My fingers twine 'til I'm clutching her strands in a fist.

"Where do you think you're going?" I ask, so close we feel each other's breath on our lips. "You wanted this, right? You wanted me to have you?"

I kiss her again. Just as hard. Just as forcefully.

Teysha makes another strangled noise that's halfway between a whimper and words. Her fingers claw at my forearms and then chest as she struggles with what to do. If she'll fight harder or she'll concede this is what she wants.

This is the lesson she wants me to teach her. The only way she'll learn.

I can taste the salt in her tears, feel the quake of her lips pressed against mine.

The temper I've lost manifests in other ways—blood pumping, adrenaline racing, muscles twitching, I'm a wild animal that can no longer be tamed. I've descended into a headspace I've been avoiding. Dark impulses that haunt me.

I'm going to have Teysha tonight, and tomorrow when the sun comes up, I'll look in the mirror, riddled with shame for the things I've done. Just like I have every other morning she's been under my roof.

For now, I'll let myself enjoy it.

Every detail about her and the moment that's been on my mind nonstop.

Her full, bow-shaped lips that I've stared at a thousand times since I've met her. The way, being so close, her flowery scent permeates the space and makes me borderline feral. How her soft body feels gripped by my calloused hands.

Teysha clenches fingers shut in my t-shirt and twists her hips as if determined to jerk away. But then I realize she's both fighting and giving in at the same time. She's holding onto me the way I'm holding onto her.

She's in tears, then she's letting out a small little moan. I've dragged my mouth from hers and dropped more rough kisses to her throat. I lick up her tears and relish the salt and shove my hand under the hem of her dress.

"Is this how you want it?" I growl into her ear, groping her pussy. "'Cuz this is the only fucking way I give it. Spread your legs."

I kick them apart and tug her panties down her hips. Another little sound comes out of her, one of shock, as she goes still. She's inexperienced, she's only ever experienced what happened in the Chosen Saints, and that's never been more apparent than in this moment.

But I keep going.

I keep giving her what she's asked for.

"I'm going to fuck you," I tell her, sucking on her throat. "See that couch? I'm going to have you with your ass in the air and your pussy clenched around my dick."

Her misty eyes widen.

"Don't look surprised now. You asked for this."

My groping hands and biting kisses are met with a sharp cry. She's got no choice but to bear it as I cage her within my arms and let primal urges take over.

Teysha Baxter is a bright, beautiful woman who probably dreamed of her future husband making love to her in some candlelit bedroom sprinkled with rose petals. She probably expected him to whisper sweet fucking nothings in her ear and hold her afterward.

Her fantasies damn sure never included losing her virginity on some cult's sacrificial altar by a guy like me, made to do it.

Every time after that was no better—performances for Abraham's sick enjoyment 'til he got bored of that and then wanted her for himself.

I failed to stop him.

As rage and lust merge into a single driving force, flashbacks flicker in and out. Images I had hoped I'd scrubbed from memory. But they live on, returning in a flood. I push two fingers into Teysha's tight heat and graze my teeth against the delicate skin of her neck. Then I'm hearing the squeak of the mattress and her sobs as I lay motionless on the floor.

I'm forced to look into her tearful eyes and urge myself to stay hard. Everybody else in the room watches, their attention rapt and unblinking. I thrust into her and feel her body quake in discomfort and pain.

My fingers sink deep in her pussy as I grip her hair and grunt about how I'm about to fuck her hard and fast. I'm going to make her sorry she ever wanted this.

But the memories won't go away. They play one after another as I push her down on the couch and drag her hips back. My hands work to free my cock that's hot, throbbing, and hard. I'm turned on by what's about to happen... while also being sickened by the roiling in my stomach.

Teysha's gone still on the couch. She's right how I positioned her, face buried in the cushions, her curvy ass lifted high in the air. Perfect for me to spear into. For me to slip into the wet heat she offers and rut away.

The animalistic lust and rage claw at me from the inside. Urge me to do it and take what I want. Just like I've done in the past.

Teysha pushed for this. She refused to stop poking the bear when I warned her I wasn't good for her. She wanted to find out the hard way, so who am I to stop now?

I'm all over the fucking place as my rough hands palm her bare ass in between stroking myself. I'm breathing raggedly, barely able to think straight. A fucking angel and demon might as well be on my shoulders the way I'm caught between what to do next.

The bruises still feel too real. Too fresh.

Her tears still shine in her eyes when I remember the recent past. What we'd gone through together and what we'd suffered.

Things that were taken from me.

Her.

A frustrated growl rumbles out of me as I rear back and stick my hands in my hair. My eyes clench shut and will the bad images to go away. All these fucking memories I wish I could forget. That I've wished every night never happened in the first place.

Teysha sniffles and then finally moves from where I've placed her. She sits up on her knees, her brows pinched close to form that soft wrinkle between them, and she reaches a cautious hand for me.

"Logan... are you..."

"Don't touch me," I snarl, heaving breaths beyond my control. "Don't just..."

I can't even finish a damn sentence. Probably because I've got no damn clue what I want to say. What I'm even feeling in this fucked up moment of rage, lust, confusion, and trauma all rolled into one.

But the only certainty that emerges from the hazy cloud surrounding me is hatred. The sheer and utter contempt I've got for Abraham and how I want to fucking annihilate him for what he's done to us.

You'd think Teysha would take a hint. She'd take this last get-out-of-jail free card and run far away from me. Flee into the second bedroom for the night and hope for morning where she could make another escape attempt.

She doesn't do any of those things.

Instead, her gentle hand glides along my forearm in a soothing touch. I open my eyes to her wounded, misty ones. The same that had been so startled minutes ago when I'd told her I'd have my way with her.

"You don't have to if you don't want to," she says. "I know you don't... I know ever since he..."

She trails off there as if she can't bear to finish what's on her mind. The sadness in her tone, the small frown on her face, her dejected body language all speak volumes. They point to the conclusion she's drawn from this confusing moment where we search for what to do.

But she's got the wrong idea and doesn't even realize she does. She couldn't be more wrong.

It's not that I don't want her. Not even close.

...if you knew how much I really wanted you...

"Bed," I husk out. "Time for bed."

I get up off the couch, frustration corded in every tense muscle. I feel her trailing in my wake as I make it to the bedroom and rip my t-shirt over my head. She ambles over to her side of the bed, head bowed, hunks of her dark chocolatey hair blocking her face from view. Though I catch the hitched breaths and quick wipes of her eyes.

She's crying. All because of me.

Fuck.

Why is this shit so complicated? Why can't it be clean and easy? Why can't I make her understand?

"It's not you," I mutter, my back turned on her. "You keep thinking it is. But it's not."

"Thanks... that makes me feel better. It's not me. There's no reason why you don't want me. It just is."

"That's not it either—why won't you drop it?" I spin around, a vexed expression clenched onto my face. "Why do you insist on making it difficult?"

"Because you haven't said an honest thing tonight. You haven't made any sense."

"What have I said that doesn't make sense?" I snap, taking a step toward her.

She holds her ground despite the tremble her jaw gives. "You don't want me staying. You want me to know the marriage will be dissolved. But when I try to leave you don't let—"

"'Cuz you're always trying to run off when you shouldn't! At the worst fucking times," I rant, drowning her out. My pulse gathers speed, seizing the chance to expel some of the pent up energy inside of me. "And you're too damn foolish to realize I'm doing what's best for you. I'm looking out for you. Preventing you from getting hurt by—"

Me.

My mouth clamps shut before the last word barrels out. A word that would reveal too fucking much.

Understanding dawns in her big, expressive eyes. "You think you're protecting me."

"Yeah? From who?"

"You," she says stubbornly. "That's what you really mean, right? That's why you really push me away?"

"Teysha, it's time for bed. Go to fucking bed."

She mulls over the discovery in silence, her thoughts impossible to predict. Times like this I wish I were a mind reader. Her brow's still pinched, her lips still downturned into a frown. A couple runaway tears slide down the swell of her cheeks.

"You have the right to feel how you do. But so do I," she says after the lengthy pause. The anguish has vanished from her voice, replaced by a resoluteness that's sad and earnest. "All I know is that things were taken from me against my will. Many times. More times than I can remember. My whole life changed—not for the better—and I've been left to pick up the fragments and make sense of it all.

"Every time I've... I've been with a man has been forced on me. It was never anything I asked for. But I found comfort in one of the men who I was with. The same man I was married off to," she explains with a hard swallow. "Call it twisted, call it sick, call it wrong. I can't help that I started to feel things for him. For you. And, for the first time in my life—since all of that happened to me—I wanted for it to be *my* choice. I wanted that with you. I hoped... you would give it to me. I'm sorry for being so foolish."

Teysha grabs her Bible and pillow, muttering something about sleeping in the other room tonight. I've fallen quiet hearing her confession and learning what I'd never considered. That she could really want this.

Not because of her religious beliefs. Not because she wanted to play pretend.

Because she wanted something real. She wanted something that was her choice.

I catch her by the arm as she passes me up on her walk toward the door. Holding her where she is, I peer into her face, every beat of my heart harder than the one before it.

"You want me?" I repeat slowly, searching her gaze. "You really want me?"

"I want what you made me feel when you were with me," she answers. "All those times. Except... I want it to be us together because it's what we're choosing."

How the fuck did I ever miss this possibility? How hadn't I considered it before?

This isn't like before, where I was forced to have her for the entertainment of others. This is Teysha making a choice for herself.

...and she chooses me.

At least in this moment. For right now, it doesn't matter if I'm good for her or not. She wants to be with me.

I'd be a liar to say I've got enough willpower to resist.

I take a slow step toward her, eliminating what little space exists between us. Her breath quickens. Mine does too, sounding like crushed gravel. My hand comes up to cup her cheek, cautious and measured as if I'm touching a precious artifact beyond any conceivable value.

She leans into my touch so subtly, you'd think she were afraid of it being real. She's as hesitant as I am to lower her defenses.

An energy ratchets up between us. Heat from tensions boiling over, accompanied by a spine-tingling wave of familiarity.

Maybe, just maybe, we understand each other better than anyone. Nobody else has been through what we have and survived the way we have.

We stand alone on our own island, separate from the rest of humanity.

Still coarching for meaning in what we went through. Still faltering for a recovery that doesn't seem to come soon enough.

My hard gaze anchors to hers, drinking in every beautiful, unique feature. Hers flicks up to mine, just as attuned. Curiosity lives in her eyes, like she's lost in a thousand questions that run through her pretty little head.

I let myself be greedy. Let my gaze dip down the short slope of her button nose 'til I've reached her lips that are full and soft and that she won't stop nibbling on. What would she think if she knew how many times I've imagined pressing mine against them?

All the times I've woken after a night she's spent in my bed and I've barely been able to contain myself. I've rushed off to the bathroom to handle business, my lust-driven fantasies full of the things I wanted to do to her...

We exist in the suspended moment for what almost feels like an eternity. Then restraint snaps like a band pulled too tight, and I can't hold myself back another second. I crush my lips to hers, kissing her like I've done only in my dreams.

Deep. Hungrily.

A man that's got no business experiencing something so soft and sweet, yet I'm claiming it for myself anyway.

The Bible and pillow she's holding onto fall away, crashing to the floor. She arches up into me as my arm curls around her waist and oxygen strangles our lungs. We find a rhythm in the fierce kisses we trade, feeding off each other, fueling the passion that's exploded.

Fire burning out of control.

We melt together, the moment blurring into quick movements toward the bed. She fusses with the buckle on my belt, her hands shaking. I drag the straps of her dress down her shoulders, exposing the swell of her breasts and then taking one peak into my mouth.

She whimpers as my tongue flicks against the hardening bud. I lick and suck away, filling my hands up with her ass and hips. I've got her dress bunched at her waist, savoring how supple and squeezable her bare flesh feels against my rough palms.

My erection hardens to the point of pain, throbbing hard against the constraints of my denim.

How could she ever think I didn't want her?

I've got the opposite problem—I want her too damn much. More than I ever should.

She's got the kind of body you want to feel against you lying in bed and the kind of sweet smile you want to wake up to in the morning.

She smells like fucking flowers and has the purest heart of anybody I've known.

All things that shouldn't be afforded to me. That I'm not good enough for.

We tug off the rest of her dress and finish unbuckling my pants.

I ease her down on the bed without breaking contact. My mouth's traveled from her breasts to her neck, a sensitive spot of hers I quickly discover. Little moans pour out of her, fingers sliding into my hair, her hips canting up toward mine.

My cock's heavy and insistent between her thighs, throbbing away like crazy. Mere inches away from the slick wet heat it craves.

The same wet heat it remembers from the last time I had her. But those times were different. I want to show her it doesn't have to be like that.

It could be good. It could be fucking fantastic. She could feel things she never imagined. Pleasure that could make her see a galaxy of stars. I could be the man who gives that to her.

We lose ourselves in more passionate kisses. Mouths wide open, tongues lash in teasing. My wide hands canvas the curves of her naked body, pausing along the way to knead and squeeze her flesh. She trembles beneath me, fighting to keep up.

Explore.

Feel the muscles that flex and bulge. Trace the tattoos inked on my skin. Take me into her soft grip as her fingers wrap around my girth and I choke out a groan.

Immediately, she goes to let go, probably thinking she's done something wrong. My hand clamps over hers, returning it to my hot, thick cock, guiding her in a slow stroke up and down its length. Showing her how I like it to be done.

Our kisses grow wilder, more urgent, as heat floods me. The primal feeling clawing away only heightens. Teysha doesn't let up, her strokes making my already stiff cock ache that much more. Up and down the silken hard flesh, the pads of her fingers tantalizing against the network of protruding veins.

I rip my mouth away from hers, breathing raggedly, peering down at her. Her lids hang halfway, long eyelashes practically kissing her cheeks. Something tells me I've got the same drunken look about me.

"You really want this?" I ask huskily. "You want to feel this cock inside you?"

Her teeth bite down on her plump bottom lip, and she gives a nod. Her body wriggles, her thighs spreading even wider.

Fuck, once I've caught the scent of her arousal, I can't talk myself out of it. I can't stop myself from gripping my cock and guiding myself to her warm, slick pussy.

We both watch in silent, panting awe as we come together. Teysha's head tips back, her brows knitting at the feel of my thick girth fitting inside. It takes a concerted effort—every cell present in my tense, muscled body—to hold off from sinking any deeper.

I stop at the head and almost go fucking cross-eyed from how good it feels. In all the times we've been together, made to perform for Abraham, I'd never let myself enjoy it. I'd barely felt anything at all, under such duress it was impossible.

But this single moment changes everything.

It's like the glass house I've erected shatters. Walls I've put up to shield not just myself but Teysha.

The vow I made to end our marriage and push her away has been destroyed—how can I ever give this up? Her up?

I pause, sliding in and out a couple more times. Soaking in the warmth of her pussy. Studying how pleasure flickers across her pretty face and she undulates her hips impatiently.

"I'm enjoying you, baby," I growl, kissing her neck. "You

and this sweet fucking pussy already got me in a chokehold."

She arches her back, begging for more. Pleading with me in breathy moans.

I withdraw to rub my cock along her swollen slit, coating myself in her juices. One last moment of teasing for the both of us. Then I slam myself inside, pushing past her tight walls 'til I'm bottoming out.

We release the same strangled breath we've been holding in. The same raw cry of pleasure. Hers, sharper. Mine, grittier and deeper.

The need in me intensifies. Dark, desperate need that unleashes itself and taints my blood. It surges through me as I let go and give into the urges I've fought so damn hard against.

My skin burns hot and sweat slicks itself onto my broad, tattooed chest and arms, down my corded back. I pin Teysha's knees back 'til they're damn near on either side of her head and then natural instincts take course. My hips slip into motion, pounding away.

Her pussy's impossibly tight, fluttering around me. Her walls slick and stretchy, gripping at me to draw me further in.

An invitation I gladly accept. I come in close and capture her lips in a kiss that's feverish and untamed. My hips piston forward, in and then out and then in even deeper.

Our skin slaps, our lungs sputter, our bodies crackle.

We fall into a rhythm that's far from the slow and deliberate exploration we had earlier. We're beyond patience as I grip her knees and drill into her. Teysha touches herself—she gives me the sexiest fucking show I've ever seen as one free hand gropes a breast and the other finds her clit.

I'm afforded a firsthand demonstration as the beautiful woman beneath me explores her own body. She tweaks a nipple and rubs away at her clit, defiantly meeting my gaze, finding a way to drive me even more fucking insane.

A growl revs from my chest. I fist her hair and force her mouth to mine. I pillage her in every way possible, lapping at her mouth, groping her heaving breasts, slamming my hips into hers.

My thrusts come deep and punishing. My kiss equally bruising.

Teysha whimpers and curls her legs around my back, matching my chaotic energy. It's how we race toward the finish line.

I flip her over onto her stomach and sink back into her. More shared groans fill the space of the bedroom. More skin slapping and sweat dripping.

I grip her hips and buck into her. She keens and clenches tight around me. Her hair's a mess, a tangled, dark chocolate whirlwind that's draped across her bare shoulders. That's fallen into her face as she shudders and angles her body 'til it's tilted half upside down. She's buried herself in a pillow to silence her own screams.

Screams I use as fuel. Screams that drive me even harder.

I switch up my stroke, grinding into her, reaching under her to play with her clit. She's soaking wet, so damn swollen and slick.

"Fuck, baby," I groan, "come for me. Be my fucking good girl and come on my cock."

The dirty words do her in. They unlock the final level to her pleasure.

Teysha falls apart before my eyes. The permission I need to do the same. As she writhes underneath me, crying into the pillow, pussy fluttering around my cock, I bury myself deep. The pressure that's built up in my balls releases. I shoot my seed inside her snug, warm hole, feeling like I've fucking died and gone to heaven.

Nothing on this earth has ever felt as good as coming inside Teysha's pussy.

I collapse on top of her, barely able to catch my breath. The aftereffects from my orgasm ping through my body, making my every muscle twitch and spasm. Teysha's no different, giving a shudder underneath me.

Coming down from what just happened takes us a moment.

It leaves me in a surreal state, my mind hazy. I brush aside the damp hair from her bare back and press my lips to her shoulder blade for a kiss.

Unexpected and unplanned.

A need as innate as breathing washes over me. The need to take care of her.

I wrap my arms around her front and nuzzle my face into her. We lay still like this for a while, entangled on the bed 'til our breathing steadies out.

We're silent but acutely aware of the barrier that's been broken. The shield I've put up has crumbled and everything I was trying to keep out is slowly trickling in.

On some level, Teysha knows. Her expressive eyes gleam with hope. "I'm fucked up too."

Fuck sounds so wrong coming from her lips that I let out a chuckle. "What did you just say?"

"I'm fucked up too, like you said you are," she repeats. "I'm not like I was before. I don't know how to be that person anymore."

Though I might get what she means, she needs to know there's still hope for her.

"You're gonna get better," I offer. "You're gonna move on from what happened."

"Maybe we can together. Maybe... maybe we can heal each other."

She sounds so damn sure about it. So damn certain we can.

For the moment, I let myself believe her.

16

LOGAN

Teysha's still sleeping when I leave. I make sure to jot down a note and leave it on the bedside table so she doesn't panic, waking to me gone. It's the first morning since she's moved in that I'm up before she is. She might not realize it, but I'm aware she hasn't been getting a full night's rest.

Just shows how much last night took out of her.

I hop on my Super Glide and ride off down the quiet side street.

The Steel Saloon's about ten minutes away.

When I walk through the doors, a couple Tits on Heels call out to me. They're getting an early start this Saturday. It's not even ten a.m. yet.

Mace catches me on my way to the back office. "There you are. I was about to text you."

"Yeah, about what?"

"Last night. You okay?"

"All things considered." I brush past him entering the room. I head for the desk that's never been cleared off a day I've been alive. Since I was a kid, it's been covered in an assortment of papers, bottles, sometimes stacks of cash. I search for the sheet of paper that has the address scribbled onto it. Silver had jotted it down once Xavier broke down and gave up the info.

"How's Teysha?" he asks.

"Same answer."

Mace leans against the armrest of the well-used suede couch in the room. "You both looked upset."

"Your point?"

"Things are difficult right now." He sighs as if dreading his next words. "Some of us... we've got concerns."

I laugh, throwing a look at him from over my shoulder. "Concerns? Seriously?"

"Sydney and Korine said Teysha seems to tune out often. She seems like she's struggling with something."

"And me?" I straighten up and turn around in a challenge. "What about me?"

"You already know," Mace says tightly. "You've been angry. Easily riled up. Impulsive. All things we can't have with our club business."

"So... what? Where are you going with this?"

"You need some help. Some way to get past what happened."

"How many fucking times do I have to tell you I'm fine?" I snap before I can restrain myself. "I've got a handle on things just fine. But I am gonna find Abraham. Then I'm gonna fucking destroy him."

"Logan, you swung on me."

"Was that the first time? Since when are you a pussy bitch?"

Mace straightens up as if about to prove otherwise. "You're my brother. I'm coming to you man-to-man. Deal with your shit."

My flash of anger fades out like the switch has been turned off. Instead, I jut my chin at him. "You've taken to this fill-in prez thing, haven't you?"

"What else was I supposed to do with you gone, Tom locked up and Silver in the middle of a nasty divorce?"

"My little bro, all grown up."

"You talk to Tom yet?"

"Nah, there's a lot to address. It can wait 'til after Abraham."

"We'll get him," Mace says. "But Silver's right, we've got to have a solid plan."

"The plan is to get in and kill those fuckers."

"What was it like? With them?"

I tense up at the question, playing it off by rolling my shoulders back and cracking my neck. It buys me an extra second or two to figure out a way to answer. So far, every time I've been asked, I've brushed it off. I made vague references to being trapped in hell or cracked a sarcastic comment about it being a walk in the park.

But there's sincerity in Mace's tone. He was serious when he said he was here man-to-man as my brother.

The thing is, I'm not even sure how to process that period.

I've allowed for nothing but rage and the thirst for violent revenge. I've tried my damnedest to block out thoughts about how dehumanizing it was to do what I was made to do. For *years*, day in and day out.

I've been avoiding public spaces—and most people—for a reason.

Being back in regular society fucks with your head after captivity. You have to figure out how to embrace your humanity and be a person again.

Most places, people, sights, and sounds feel threatening. Most situations are a reason to be on guard.

So when I'm asked what it was like, I might as well be describing something only I can see. Something that's invisible to everybody else.

No one that's asked that question's gone through what I have. None of them have known what it was like to live that kind of nightmare.

I stuff my hands in my denim pockets and shrug. "What do you want me to say? Tell you about how you were beat if you so much as spoke your mind? Or about how we survived off half a can of hash a day? Or how about how we were forced to do things—things we'd never choose to do—with whoever they wanted us to?"

"I figured that was what was going on..." Mace wears a heavy expression as he shakes his head to the side. "You and Teysha?"

"They married us off. They made us... do things in front of them... with them..." My throat has gone bone dry. I try and fail to swallow as my thoughts go to last night.

I'd been able to forget our past and focus on the present. Once we gave in to each other, not once did I think about what Teysha and I had done with the Chosen Saints. Yet thinking about it the morning after suddenly feels worse.

How could Teysha ever want it? How could she look past what I did?

I sigh and pinch the bridge of my nose. "The first time I ever had sex with my wife, with *Teysha*, I was doing it against her will."

"After they married you off..." Mace says.

"In front of the entire family as they called it. She was in tears. She couldn't even look at me. That was the first time of many."

"You had about as much of a choice as she did. You realize that, right?"

"She had never been with anybody before me," I snap, suddenly irritated. "I took that from her!"

"Not by choice," Mace says, standing firm. "You're as much of a victim as she is. They used you as much as they did her."

My teeth clench like I'm an animal on the prowl. "I had a choice to listen or not. I listened. I went through with it."

"Look, this is a habit of yours. Blaming yourself for shit you couldn't control. You did the same thing when Mom was murdered. Remember?"

"This is different. I did their bidding."

"Teysha probably sees it differently. You even try talking to her about it?"

I shoot him a skeptical glance. "What do you think?"

"Do you want to work things out? Or are you going through with the annulment?"

...I don't know anymore.

"We're still figuring things out."

"That's what Teysha said last night."

"That's 'cuz it's the truth."

"The clock's ticking," Mace says, moving over to peer out the window. "One thing I've learned from almost losing Sydney is that time... it means a lot. Don't take her for granted. If there's even a chance you want to be with her, you should probably give it a shot. Talk to her. Get on the same page."

He leaves the room on that note.

I can't dispute what he's said, but that doesn't mean it's what'll happen. Teysha and I really do have things we need to sort out. Even after last night, and regardless of what she says, I need to find a way to understand why she'd ever want to stick around. Why in the hell she'd ever want to be with me?

But 'til then, I redirect to the mission I've dedicated myself to—taking out Abraham and the Chosen Saints.

The paper I've been searching for is hidden under a receipt for our latest beer and liquor haul. It's the piece of paper Silver wrote down the address Xavier gave when interrogated. I slip it into my pocket and then head on out.

Mace and Silver think we need some detailed plan to eliminate the Chosen Saints. But that's where I disagree. I'm sick of waiting and doing nothing while Abraham breathes another day. I'll take him out myself, even if I have to do it alone.

The address on the paper leads me to Portales. Beads of sweat slide down the back of my neck by the time I'm turning down one of the last streets approaching the address.

If there's one downside of riding, it's dealing with scorching weather on afternoons like this.

I park my bike a couple blocks away and wipe the sweat from my brow. It's best to keep my bike hidden from view 'til I understand what I'm dealing with. This place could be a false alarm or it could be a full up hornet's nest.

Either way, I'm here to find out.

I'm strapped, my Glock and an assortment of knives a quick draw away if needed.

I'd prefer today stay as a recon mission, but you can never be too safe in situations like this. There's a reason Xavier gave up this address—I just need to figure out why.

The neighborhood seems typical enough. Small single-story houses sit cramped on either side of the street along with plenty of trees, bushes and even a mini market at the corner of the block.

I wander down the sidewalk doing my best to seem inconspicuous. Though if I lived here, I'd be wary of me too.

But the real question is, why would the Chosen Saints have a compound in some nondescript neighborhood in Portales?

I slip between a row of hedges and disappear off the main street. The path leads me between two homes with chain-link fences and clothes hanging out to dry. In heat like this, the t-shirts, shorts and undies are all already stiff cloths of fabric flapping in the hot air.

Pressing on, I come out on the other side, glancing around for the exact address. Where the fuck has Xavier led us, and why does this feel a lot more like a red herring than the real thing?

Maybe Silver and Mace were right that we needed to be careful about following up on what info we were given.

The house belonging to the address resembles many of the others—squat, small, single-story, painted a lemon yellow that's faded and lost its luster over time. The windows are open, the blinds up, affording a decent view inside.

I duck low and creep over toward the house, surveying the area to make sure I'm still alone. Coming up under the open window, I stay crouched and rely on my ears to pick up the sounds from inside.

Some man and a woman are in the middle of a conversation.

But not in English.

In Spanish.

I scowl, wishing I'd either paid attention in high school

Spanish class or I'd brought Tito with me for translation. I'm able to sort out bits and pieces.

"*Por favor, Juan, ¿estarás aquí para la familia?*" the woman asks.

"*Te he dicho. Me han ordenado. No puedo alejarme.*"

"*Pero ¿por qué tú?*"

He slams what sounds like a cabinet before answering. "*Los pedidos son pedidos. No me prejuntes más.*"

His footsteps thud as he leaves the room. The woman remains where she is, sniveling out a soft cry. I chance it by rising up enough that I'm peeking into the window. She doesn't notice as she's wiping her eyes with a tissue.

What the fuck is going on and why do things feel more confusing than when I arrived? Why would Xavier provide this address of all places? Was he fucking with us? But if he was, then why were this guy and his girl talking about orders? Orders from who?

At least, that's if my limited translation skills are correct.

Before I can figure any of this out, the back door slams shut. The man suddenly appears at the side of the house with a bag of trash.

My eyes snap from him to the aluminum bins only a few feet away from where I'm crouched. Caught point blank peering into his window.

His eyes widen and he releases an angry scream. The bag of trash he's holding drops to the ground. He reaches for the piece strapped to his hip.

"Fuck!" I growl, making a split-second decision.

Recon mission over, I break out in a sprint toward the fence. I'm heaving myself over it as he's squeezing the trigger and shooting. I'm able to bolt through more hedges, ducking around a neighbor's home, hoping like hell he doesn't follow.

A couple more gunshots ring out as I'm already a block down, racing toward my Super Glide. I hop on, starting up the engine with a bumbling rev before I take off and don't look back.

I'm still not sure what the fuck Xavier's reason was for giving us this place as the location of Abraham and the Chosen Saints, but it damn sure won't go unaddressed.

Teysha beams when I walk through the door. She's sitting crisscross style on the sofa, a book propped open in her lap. But I'm much more distracted by the fact that she's got no pants on. The door almost slams shut on my fingers, I'm so damn distracted by the sight.

All that silky brown skin on display. I can practically feel the silk clenched in my grip.

Heat rises from the inside, while on the outside, I cock a brow at her.

"Reading the Bible looking like that?"

She giggles. "Not the Bible. A different book."

"You read other books than the Bible?"

"Are you *trying* to frustrate me?"

"Guilty as charged," I admit, tossing my keys down. I walk over to where she's situated and snatch the book out of her lap. "Blazing Passions. Word porn? You?"

"Excuse me!" she cries out with a mortified kind of laugh. She reaches up to steal the book back, but I'm too quick for her. "Give it back!"

"I never would've guessed you're into that. So you really ain't so innocent after all."

"It's *not* pornography!"

"Then why are you all flustered?" I gently tap the book

against the top of her head, then stroll off, reading some of the lines out loud. "Massimo's chest rippled with muscle. He took me in his big, strong arms, making my sex throb. *Seriously?*"

Teysha's leaped off the sofa to launch an attack from behind. She grabs onto my arm to pry it away, surprisingly aggressive. I break out in a laugh, shrugging her off. But it's not so easy when she latches on, tossing one arm over my shoulder and the other around my torso.

The next thing either of us realize, Teysha's strapped to my back. I'm still walking across the apartment with the book held far out of her reach. More thick laughter rolls out of me as I read another few lines from her book.

"He threw me down on the bed and stripped off my panties," I say, speaking louder. "I'm going to have you for dinner, belladonna—"

"Logan!" she screams, desperately swatting at the book.

We're both laughing as I toss the book aside and then reach behind me. I twist her around 'til she's sliding into my arms and I'm setting her down on the closest piece of furniture—which happens to be the kitchen stool. The instant I've set her down, I'm trapping her where she is, coming in close to almost kiss her.

Our noses touch, both of us acutely aware of our mutual attraction.

"Are these things you want done to you?" I ask, sounding huskier than usual. "You want me to have you for dinner?"

I can feel the heat that's flushed all over her brown skin. She can barely meet my eye as she nibbles on her bottom lip. She's so fucking sexy when she gets a little shy like this...

More than ever, it weighs on me how I'm the first man

who's experiencing her like this; I'm the only man whose ever been privileged enough.

My hand ghosts up the side of her bare thigh, and I tug on a crooked grin. "You don't have to say yes, baby. Your silence told me all I needed to know."

She flinches in embarrassment, though she lets out another laugh. "I didn't expect you home so soon."

"So what you're saying is, when I'm not here, you walk around in your undies reading word porn?"

"Logan Cutler, if you don't stop!" She slaps me across the shoulder, then nudges her way to freedom. Hopping off the stool and back onto her feet, she walks into the kitchen. "What do you think about drinking the rest of that bottle of White Oak tonight?"

"I think I'm wondering what happened to the sweet church girl in the sundresses."

"She's still in here. But tonight she's on vacation."

My pulse beats faster at the borderline fucking naughty smirk she shoots me. Forty-five minutes later, we're settled in the living room, the bottle of White Oak sitting in the middle on the coffee table.

Teysha's still got no pants on. I'm still enjoying the view.

I bring my glass of whiskey to my lips, sampling the smoky flavor, my attention on Teysha. She's telling me about the time she was fifteen and her mother caught her with a naughty romance book under the mattress of her bed.

It's amusing in more ways than one.

Teysha's still trying to explain why she was reading the book she was; she's telling me the romance genre is mocked but some of the books are the best she's ever read. I'm nodding along every so often, soaking up the fact that I have her all to myself.

I have her undivided attention and she's comfortable enough to let her passion flow.

It's yet another sexy thing about her—she speaks with conviction as she tells me about the books she likes. Though I don't know a damn thing about romance books or most books in general, if it's important to her, then it's worth listening to.

"How about we head to the bookstore tomorrow and pick you up a couple new books?"

Her eyes widen. "I have Blazing Passions. I'll just reread it."

"Nah, we'll go. It's a different scene for me. Maybe I'll pick up a book too."

"There's always the Bible."

"Don't push it," I warn, the corner of my lip quirking.

"I'm going to get you to read a few passages one of these days." She gets up with her phone in hand, her thumb flicking across the screen as she scrolls. "You know what this occasion calls for? Music!"

I'm a serious man. More serious than most.

I'm not known for my dazzling, panty-dropper smile the way Cash is. I'm not the type to be joking and laughing like Ozzie.

But it's impossible to be serious when Teysha puts on music and begins dancing around like a fucking lunatic. She throws her arms in the air and sways her hips as the bubbly pop song plays. I don't even know what the song is, just that it's got an annoyingly catchy chorus.

"You gonna tell me what you're doing?" I ask.

She picks up her glass of whiskey, still swaying her hips. "Enjoying myself. Is that allowed?"

"It is so long as I get to watch."

Teysha takes me up on the challenge. She tastes some

whiskey and rocks her hips. Her gaze hooks mine as her body moves with the beat drop.

It's the sexiest fucking thing I've ever seen in my life.

It's in how her eyes gleam and she bites away a smile as if daring herself to keep going despite shyness creeping in. She shakes her ass like no one's watching in panties that hug her hips and show off her smooth thighs. Her round ass bobs enticingly in front of me like it's a fucking snack to feast on.

One I can't wait to sink my teeth into.

All the damn sundresses in the world can't disguise a body like that.

But what's really the icing on the cake is how she has fun with it—how she glances over at me and the shine in her gaze sparkles, like she's aware how goofy it is that she's gotten up to start dancing. She keeps going anyway, dancing her heart out to the music.

Both making a moody asshole like me laugh while turning me on all at the same time.

"When was the last time you got up and danced?" she asks breathlessly.

The song changes to something slower, a female voice crooning about heartbreak.

Teysha drops to the sofa cushion, still clutching her glass of whiskey, a light dew about her complexion from dancing so much.

"I don't dance," I say.

"I'll get you to dance," she insists, smiling wide. "One of these days, I'll convince you."

"You think you'll get me to read the Bible. Now you think you'll get me to dance. Keep going and you're gonna end up real disappointed."

"We'll see."

"You want to take that to get fixed? Tomorrow when we

go to the bookstore?" I ask, jutting my chin at the piece of jewelry on the coffee table.

It's Teysha's golden cross. The chain's still broken from when Abraham slashed it the night me and the Kings raided the Chosen Saints compound. Teysha's kept the necklace close at all times even though it's been broken; she's been carrying it in her pocket and fiddling with it whenever anxious.

For a brief second, we both look at the coffee table where the cross lays amid a tangled golden chain.

"I would like that," Teysha says finally, her tone quiet.

The hyperactive energy she had just minutes ago has mellowed out. We sit across from each other sipping our drinks and realizing the silence is a comfortable one.

And when we have something to say, we do.

"You mentioned your mother was religious," Teysha says.

"Yeah, very. She was a good person. A loyal Christian."

"Can I ask why you aren't religious like she was?"

I think about it a second, then shrug. "I've got a hard time believing that there's some guy in the sky that oversees everything. But for some reason he still lets bad things happen to good people. Same question but reversed. Why are you so into it?"

Teysha sets down her glass of whiskey and folds her legs like she had them when I walked through the door. "Because it's nice to know there's a higher power greater than myself. That he sees us all and loves us just the same. That he's there when I need him. Even when times are dark and I have no hope left. He's always there for me."

I spent years sighing and rolling my eyes every time Mom dragged Mace and me to church on Sunday. I slouched in the church pew as the pastor rambled through his sermon and my imagination wandered to sports or what girl I liked in school.

The older I got, the more hostile to it I became. It served as nothing but a reminder of Mom, and how God had allowed her to be so senselessly killed in an act of violence. The very last thing I wanted to think about.

I didn't want to focus on the guilt that I should've known how special Sundays were to Mom before she passed away. I should've been more open, more present for her.

If I shut it off and viewed it in a hostile lens, then I never had to go there.

But hearing Teysha's answer to the question pulls at something deep inside me. It's so earnest and pure, I can only nod in respect. I can't help wondering if I ever could be that damn trusting and hopeful.

Teysha's been through hell, yet somehow she manages to...

In its own way, it's a strength I don't have. The strength to experience adversity—some of the greatest evils this world has to offer—and still somehow have faith in what's good.

"Do you believe in the supernatural? Ghosts? Spirits?" she asks after another few beats of silence.

I'm brought out of my runaway thoughts. I nod, polishing off my whiskey. "I do."

"*You?* Ghosts?"

"Ghosts are different. You ever see one of those candid ghost hunter videos? That shit is real."

Teysha's laugh is so melodic it competes with the music playing from her phone. "Wait a dang second, Logan Cutler. Are you telling me you believe in ghosts but not in God?"

"Not the same. Do I need to pull up YouTube?"

"Ever seen one?" she asks, so amused her eyes sparkle. She reclines on the couch, stretching out those damn shapely legs of hers.

"Why would I tell you? You'll laugh."

"And you say I'm shy!" she teases. "Go on. Tell me."

I blow out a sigh, both irritated but engaged in our conversation. "Alright, fine. If you really wanna know, it happened when I was nine. Mace was seven. We were staying the weekend at our grandparents ranch in West Texas. We loved it 'cuz we got to feed the horses and fuck around on all that acreage. Used to chase each other for hours. Our grandma warned us about going out at night. We were supposed to be in bed by ten."

"But..." Teysha prompts, trialing off.

"But," I continue, "we obviously didn't listen. A cousin of ours, Jimmy, had told us the old barn that was no longer in use was haunted. We wanted to find out for ourselves. So, Mace and me, we waited 'til they went to bed. Then we went exploring in the dark. Just me, him and a lantern."

Her eyes widen. "You went into the old barn?"

"Sure did. We'd only been there a minute when the flame in our lantern suddenly blew out. There was this chill that blew over us. Mace squeaked like a fucking mouse. Pretty sure he covered his eyes and damn near pissed himself. But I kept my eyes open... then I saw her."

"A ghost?!"

"This woman in a ratty old dress—completely see-through—came out of the darkness. She flew straight at us like she was about to hit us over the head for disturbing her."

Teysha's hands come up to her mouth. "What did you do?"

"Got the fuck outta there," I reply with a gruff laugh at

the memory. "Lit a fire right under our little asses. We never ran so fast. We were beside ourselves by the time we made it up the house. Never went back to the barn again."

"And Mace thinks it was a ghost too?"

"He claims he didn't see anything. I always remind him it's 'cuz he covered his eyes like a pussy."

She draws her knees to her chest. "I've never seen one. But I think they could exist. Are you afraid of them?"

"I'm not afraid of anything."

She rolls her eyes. "It's alright to be afraid sometimes, you know that, right?"

"Alright, I wouldn't want to run into one in the middle of the night. But if I did, I'd do what I had to do."

"Logan Cutler, you're afraid of ghosts!" she accuses with a fresh giggle.

"I told you, Steel Kings aren't—"

"I have a phobia of blood. And needles. And the dark and quiet."

Setting down my empty glass, I reach for the bottle of White Oak in the middle of the coffee table. "Is that why you want to sleep in my bed every night?"

"I like being near you," she answers. "It makes me feel better."

...that's 'cuz you've gotten attached when you shouldn't have...

I cut off that negative thought, fighting against its sabotage. I've let thoughts like this rule me, pushing Teysha away, deciding it was best if we separate.

I'm not sure what I think anymore, but I'm trying to be in the moment. Enjoy our time together for what it is.

Teysha's attachment to me will have to be addressed another time.

I point at her half empty glass as I pour thirds for

myself. "I'm impressed you've been handling that so well. You'll build up a tolerance in no time."

"Since I drank whiskey, you should read the Bible."

"I don't remember striking that deal."

"You might enjoy it. It might remind you of your mother."

"I'll pass."

"If you ever want to, you can read mine. If you ever need it."

"I won't. Now how about you turn that Spotify playlist to something good?"

"Only if you dance with me." She grabs at my hand to pull me up off the couch.

I oblige. Briefly.

I don't *really* dance. It's more like she dances around me, grabbing at my hands to pull me into the moment and entice me. My arm hooks around her hips to hold her close, enjoying the way her body sways against mine.

Enjoy the chance to peer down at her smiling face.

It's an hour past midnight by the time we drag ourselves to bed. We've finished the bottle of White Oak and made the most of each other's company, tipsiness and all. We settle in bed like has become our routine—fresh off hot showers, lying close in the dark, the sheet strewn over us.

Teysha yawns as she begins drifting off before me.

I grin as she babbles about romance books as if she's forgotten she already told me all about them. Still a lightweight, the whiskey tends to have that effect on her. She's out in the next few seconds, and I'm left confronting the truth.

Teysha said she likes sleeping in my bed because I make her feel better.

The truth is, I feel the same, listening to her soft breaths and feeling her supple body against mine. I fall asleep looking forward to waking up to her sleepy smile in the morning.

"When I said a couple books, I meant make it quick."

Teysha bows her head and avoids eye contact, though the little curl of her lips tells me she knows what she's doing. She knows she's guilty as charged.

We're at the Book Nook late in the morning. She's circled the shop floor at least three times, stopping at different shelves, pulling out books to flip through them, then sliding them back into place.

I was patient for the first twenty minutes. But as the hand on the clock approaches noon, I'm ready to refuel my tank with some food. She's got five more minutes before I carry her out caveman style.

Because it's Sunday, the store sees steady foot traffic. The little gold bell hanging above the door chimes every time someone wanders in or walks out.

"I can't decide," she says with a book in each hand.

"Then get them both. Toss them in." I gesture to the hand basket I'm holding that already has a modest pile of books in it. "You'll probably read through 'em fast. The more books you get today, the longer it is 'til I have to bring you back."

Teysha snickers as she drops both books in and joins me at my side. We head to the front of the store. The cashier has just finished checking out the redhead in front of us. She shuffles off with a large shopping bag full of books, making way for us to step forward.

Being the bright and sunny woman she is, Teysha

strikes up a conversation with the cashier. I'm busy tapping my card to the card machine and pressing the buttons on the screen.

"All good to go," the cashier says. "I double bagged so your books should be nice and secure."

Teysha's thanking her. I'm cracking open my wallet to put away my card.

The door chimes open and the moment flips on its head.

Time slows to a glacial pace. I look up in time to meet the dark eyes of the man who's walked in and just pointed a gun at us.

17

TEYSHA

It only takes a second.

One second, I'm unable to contain my excitement. I'm so grateful for Logan treating me to a trip to the bookstore, my cheeks hurt from smiling. I'm waiting for the second we step away from the checkout counter so I can throw my arms around him in a hug and press my lips to his cheek for a kiss.

Then another second passes by, and the door's dinging open. Logan's glancing over his shoulder. He grabs me and wrenches me to the ground at the same time the snap of gunfire goes off.

I land on my side, colliding into the ground hard. Pain vibrates through my elbow, the air knocked out of my lungs. I'm left crumpled on the ground as chaos ensues. Logan's drawn his handgun—I didn't even realize he was carrying—and he's fired back at the man.

The front windows shatter and glass sprays everywhere.

Several books fly off shelves. The clerk behind the counter screams, then cowers under the register. The man who's shot at us dives for cover. Logan lands a shot in his chest before he can.

It's only after the gunfire ends and the dust settles that I realize it hasn't even been a minute. All the commotion happened in under thirty seconds. Thirty seconds was all it took to turn our simple morning date to a bookstore upside down.

Logan keeps his gun pointed as he steps toward the man. He's sprawled out on the floor, no longer able to sit up.

The store clerk warbles out something about calling 911. Though, judging from the vague sirens whirring in the background, I'd say somebody else in the shopping mall has already done so. They must've heard the gunshots ring out and called in the moment.

"You follow me from the other day? Who d'you work for, you piece of shit?" Logan asks the man. He punches him in the face when he doesn't answer, then grabs him by the front of his shirt.

The man's eyes hang halfway open, his lips moving soundlessly. His bullet wound resembles a bloodied crater in his chest. He's seconds away from dying.

"Useless fucking garbage." Logan digs around in the man's pocket, retrieving his phone and wallet to check his identification. Then he's turning toward me to pull me onto my feet. "You alright?"

I'm dazed, my blinks quick and fluttery. "Yes... I'm okay... I think..."

"Your elbow's banged up."

"It's okay... really..."

"We'll get it checked out."

The cavalry arrives a minute later. The bookstore goes from a hazy scene riddled with shattered glass and a man bleeding out on the floor to being flooded with police and paramedics.

I put my hands up, dreading the long aftermath to come.

The sky's lit up in hues of orange and gold by the time we make it home.

We spent hours being questioned and interviewed by the Pulsboro PD. Afterward, Logan insisted on taking me to the urgent care. We step through the door, grateful for the day to be over.

Neither of us have eaten anything. We haven't had a moment to rest.

...or process that we were shot at today.

On the drive home, Logan swung us through the Beef & Bunz drive-thru. Their bacon cheeseburgers and garlic fries were obviously not healthy, but neither is being shot at by some stranger in a bookstore.

We kick off our shoes and amble over to the kitchen to unpack the greasy fast food bags.

We've hardly spoken a word to each other, but the silence isn't combative. It's more commiserate, like we're aware of how hard today was and we know the other *needs* the silence. Logan's halfway through his burger when he juts his chin at me.

"How's your elbow?"

"Sore. But the doctor said it should go away in the next couple days."

"I'm surprised the police station released us so easily. From what Mace told me, it sounds like the whole PD has a vendetta against the Kings after what happened with Cash and Korine's ex-husband."

"You were defending yourself! That... that man opened fire at us... and the store clerk!"

"We gave our statements. All we can do now is hope they don't fuck with us."

"But who was he?" I ask. "The man that opened fire—"

"His ID says Juan Cabello. Today wasn't the first time I've seen him before."

"But when? From where?"

"I was at his house... by mistake. His address was the address Xavier gave up when we interrogated him."

I frown. "So, is he connected to the Saints?"

"We've got a guy inside the PD. He'll run the guy's record. Whoever he was, he probably wasn't acting alone."

"Meaning?"

"Meaning he was operating on orders. Somebody *told* him to do what he did."

The fry I'm holding slips through my fingers. "Abraham?!"

"Don't panic," he says knowingly. "That's why I said we'll run his record. It could be Abraham behind what happened. Or it could be somebody else. The club's got no shortage of enemies. Neither do I."

"That's actually worse."

"Point is, it was me he was after. I went to his house. He saw me. Today could've been him settling the score and that's all."

But as Logan reassures me, he doesn't even sound certain. He takes another bite of his burger, then he washes it down with coke.

We return to silence, though it's a different kind. A sense of unease edges through me, tensing up my spine. It feels like being pulled by invisible puppet strings that have me sitting straighter. Less relaxed, more alert.

After the day I've had, it's its own kind of torture.

I prop my elbows on the counter and bring my hands together in a prayer.

My lips mouth the words without realizing they do.

When my prayer ends, I find myself on the receiving end of his probing stare. He's finished his meal from Beef & Bunz and has taken up watching me from across the kitchen counter.

"Does it help you feel better?" he asks. "To pray like that?"

"Yes... usually. Sometimes more than others."

"I figured."

"You think it's silly."

"Didn't say that. Do what you need to to feel better." He digs into his jean pocket to retrieve my broken gold cross necklace. It rests in the middle of his open palm as he holds it out for me to take. "We didn't get a chance to take it for repair."

Warmth invades my chest. It dawns on me why he's handing it back. He's offering it up because he thinks it'll make me feel better. The corner of my lip tips up in a small smile.

"Keep it. Hold onto it."

"You sure?"

"Yes," I answer. "I like the idea of you having it on you."

His thick fingers close over his palm, then he returns the broken chain to his pocket. "I'll get it fixed before I give it back to you."

"My husband's more considerate than he realizes he is."

It's a silly tease that I'm aware could backfire. But I'm clinging to the lighter mood that's developed, hoping we can use it to forget about our terrible day. I'm expecting Logan to shut me down or scold me for daring to use the 'H' word.

Instead, his naturally severe expression twitches—the crease of his brows shift, his jaw losing some of its tension. He flirts with a grin that almost manages to make it onto his face before it's gone entirely in the next blink of an eye. Standing up straighter, he walks around the kitchen counter and grabs my hand.

"It's been a long day. We both need to blow off steam."

Startled by what's happening, I let him lead me into the living room. Logan throws himself onto the sofa, tugging me down with him. We crash down at each other's side as he scoops up the remote and turns the TV on.

He wants to watch TV on the sofa. Just like any other regular couple.

Like any other husband and wife after a long, tiring day.

I try to keep my smile from spreading, but it's useless. A giddy, fluttery feeling invades my belly.

Things could always be like this if we gave ourselves a real shot. If we really tried to make things work.

Logan just needs to see it like I do.

"My beautiful believer is more special than any other."

I turn my head to the side, refusing to meet his icy gaze. His spindly fingers are clenched around my wrists, his pants for air heavy as he exerts himself. His hips work fast, jerking in stabbing motions that feel like torture from the inside.

I'm being torn apart thrust by thrust. Groan by groan. Each second that passes is another second of my destruction, another piece falling away.

"So beautiful," he grunts, gathering speed. "So innocent."

My voice is gone, trapped in my throat. The only sound I'm able to produce is that of a strangled cry.

Pain and panic welled up in my chest that bubbles out of me.

And still it continues. It goes on for hours.

"Look at me!" he hisses, grabbing my face. "Look at your Leader when he graces you with his seed."

He sinks deeper as I cry harder. As my body, my mind, my soul begs for it to end...

A gasp sputters out of me, the sheets soaked in sweat. My body's shaking. My arms and legs thrash. I fight to wake from the dream that felt too real.

I'm in Logan's bedroom. The room's pitch dark and quiet. The other side of the bed's empty.

Logan's gone.

Panic strikes my heart, making it beat faster. Where did he go? How could I sleep through him getting out of bed?

I scramble to get up. The sheet's wrapped around me in a way that's more difficult than it should be to untangle—being half asleep in the dark, struck by panic, makes it feel like an impossible puzzle to solve.

I can't take a full breath. The panic's so clogged up inside that it comes out as a broken sound.

Panic that quickly spirals into outright fear.

Logan's gone and I'm all alone. I'm in a room steeped in darkness, where the shadows feel suffocating and the unknown terrifying. Remnants from the bad dream linger like a ghost intent on haunting me. Abraham's presence that refuses to let me go.

Tears wet my eyes, a pitiful little sob warbling out of me.

Vaguely, I realize it's ridiculous. I'm aware how silly and pathetic it is.

But I can't turn off these emotions rushing me. These intense reactions that almost feel chemically induced.

I bend my knees, drawing them to my chest, burying my head forward.

Barely a second later, the door flings open. Logan strides in, flicking on the light. He scans the room as if in search of the threat he must eliminate.

When he notices it's just me curled up on the bed, he cuts across the room in a couple steps to make it to me.

"What's going on? What's wrong?"

"I had a dream and it felt..." I shake my head, wiping my eyes. "It felt real. Then I woke up and you weren't..."

Here.

Logan understands even though I've trailed off. He sits down on the side of the bed and pulls me toward his chest. His thick, tattooed arms wrap around me, holding me in place. Warmth that feels instantly comforting and secure. I tuck my face into the nook between his bicep and the side of his torso and allow myself a moment to indulge in him.

Inhale his scent. Feel how hard and well-built he is.

For my own selfishness.

So I can calm down.

He's started stroking my hair, rubbing my back. "I had a call come in. Important club business. I went into the living room to take it. Didn't want to wake you."

Suddenly, my memory's not so fuzzy anymore. Our evening plays back to me in a quick reel. We'd cozied up on the sofa and watched a couple hours of TV. Both exhausted and worn out, we turned in for bed early. I must've drifted right off while Logan got up.

"I'm sorry," I whisper. "I don't... I'm really not trying to... you don't like it when I cry..."

"You had a bad dream. Today was a lot." His arms tighten around me, if possible, making me feel even more secure. "Something tells me you're not used to being shot at the way I am."

"Abraham—"

"Is never gonna touch you again," he cuts in. His hand cups the back of my head before he drops a kiss on the top of it. "Just relax. Go back to sleep. I won't leave the room again."

His tender strokes elicit a shiver down my spine. The pattern he's created is slow and soothing as his knowing fingers glide over my back, chasing away the fear and anxiety.

It amazes me how a man like Logan, a rough and tumble biker, can be so gentle sometimes.

As if he senses it's what I need. It's how I should be treated, and though I'm not made of glass by any means, the consideration is nice. It means something to me.

He cares enough to be soft with me when he's vicious with the rest of the world.

"We're going to be raiding the compound that belongs to the Chosen Saints," he says, raking fingers through my straightened strands. "I'll be gone for a couple days."

"But—"

"I already talked about it with Mace and the others. We think it'll be a good idea if you stay with Sydney while I'm gone."

I open my mouth, then shut it again. Inhaling a steadying breath, I give a nod.

Logan's telling me this because we've grown closer. Two weeks ago, he would've barely mentioned a word about leaving. If I had anything to say about it, he would've snapped at me or mentioned he couldn't wait 'til the marriage was dissolved.

He knew I wouldn't want to stay in the apartment alone. He's confiding in me about what the club is up to, hoping I'll support him.

...you're his wife. You should.

"Okay," I answer, then I draw back to meet his eyes in understanding. "Just please promise me you'll be careful."

He cups my face, his thumb swiping the apple of my cheek, then places a kiss on my lips. "Same to you."

18

LOGAN

"Xavier, where're you at?" I growl, barging into the basement. "You've got hell coming your way, dipshit!"

The others flood in behind me as I charge down the stairs. They're already well aware of what I'm about to do. Silver couldn't put his foot down on this even if he wanted to. The piece of shit not only gave us bad information about the Chosen Saints' location, he's the reason the shootout at the bookstore happened.

Had I never gone to Juan Cabello's house, he wouldn't have retaliated by tracking us down that morning. He wouldn't have opened fire on me and Teysha.

I stride across the basement room the second my boot touches the floor. Xavier barely has enough time to look up before my fist connects with his jaw.

It's the first of many as Silver, Mace, Cash, Ozzie, and Tito gather around. Xavier's strapped to the chair as he's forced to endure a barrage from my fists. Left hooks. Right hooks. Jabs and crosses.

I land an uppercut, snapping his jaw together with a

brutal *crunch*. Plenty of blood and two teeth sputter past his lips once I'm through.

Except it's only the beginning. I head over toward the table that has the assortment of instruments. Ozzie takes in an excitable breath, his eyes gleaming at my selection. I've grabbed the power drill, my finger on the trigger to power it on. The basement fills with the motorized whir of the drill, the metal chuck rotating ominously.

I stop in front of Xavier, his face swollen and lumpy from all the hits he's taken.

"You really thought giving bad information would work out in your favor?"

"Bad info? I have no idea what you're talking about," he spits, more blood leaking out his mouth. "I have provided the info you asked for, Believer Logan."

"Don't fucking call me that! You piece of fucking shit, the only reason you're alive is 'cuz the info you've got. If you didn't know Abraham's location, I would've ripped you into pieces myself on day one."

"I have provided the info you asked for," he repeats defiantly. He peers up at me through black and blue eyes that can barely open.

But the challenge is there. It's unmistakable. He's antagonizing me. All of us.

I rev the power drill a second time and assess what body part I want to start with first. The others serve as a silent audience as they watch on, arms folded across their chests.

Xavier no longer serves a purpose for us. Which means he's fair game for revenge—and I've got plenty of reason to exact revenge.

"You had one reason to be kept alive. But now you've made it clear the info you give is no good," I say, stepping closer. "So now you're going to pay for all the shit you've done. All the times you asked how high when Abraham told you to jump. All the times you beat the people you held captive. All those times you took advantage 'cuz you thought you could get away with it."

He's clamped his bloody mouth shut as if refusing to beg for mercy.

But that's alright. Mercy wasn't coming anyway.

"Guess what, dipshit?" I ask. "You thought wrong. This is for Teysha."

Xavier can't hold off his screams anymore. Not when I've jammed the power drill against his crotch and the metal chuck begins boring into him. His jeans dampen with blood as his head falls back and he shakes with agony.

I savor every second, pressing harder the more he screams. Watching the pain clench his swollen face is a one-of-a-kind sight I'll never forget.

Teysha would be horrified if she knew what I'm doing. She'd probably cry and beg me to stop. Even after everything this piece of shit's done to her.

Exactly why I continue. I don't stop 'til his crotch is mangled and the jean fabric is oversaturated with his blood. As he sits slumped in the chair, I move onto other body parts. His thighs and then his chest. Eventually, his cheek.

The torture goes on for over an hour 'til he's barely alive. Then I step back and watch him bleed out.

Silver approaches me first. "I'll have Moses and Big Eddie dispose of him. We've got to move if we're going to follow this other lead."

"And if it's another dead end?" I ask, setting down the power drill. It drips with Xavier's blood. I'm covered in it too, a badge of honor more than anything.

"If it's a dead end, we'll keep looking. But Tate took

photos when he came across it and it looked pretty damn convincing."

We leave the basement to go gear up.

I've got my reservations about this mission. After the shooting, Tate was able to track down an SUV belonging to Juan Cabello and break into it only to discover the vehicle registration didn't match his address. Instead of the address I had followed that led me to Juan's house, the SUV was registered to an abandoned warehouse two hours outside of town.

In the trunk, he found other incriminating evidence like a few duffle bags of cash, weapons, and drugs. But what was most telling of all was the set of robes. The exact kind Abraham and the Chosen Saints wore.

The more we've uncovered, the less things have made sense. If Juan Cabello wasn't a Chosen Saint, then what the hell was he doing with their robes and a truck registered to an abandoned warehouse that could be posing as their new compound?

Why would Xavier give his address when we were interrogating him?

These thoughts and more turn over in my head as we hit the road and I'm steering my bike in formation with the others. We're a pack of rumbling thunder making our way down the highway. Other cars smartly move out of our way and let us pass through.

We're not even sure what we'll encounter when we get there, but we'll handle it like we always do. The others are determined to come out on top. They won't quit 'til we've eliminated the threat.

I'm the same, though magnified by ten. I'll stop at nothing to make Abraham pay. I won't move on no matter how long it takes me to track him down and make sure he suffers for what he's done to us. It's more than personal. It's life or death.

The world can't go on if we're both allowed to live. He's got to go down once and for all.

We slow up, approaching the huge lot that the abandoned warehouse is located on. We've already worked out our plan, splitting up like we always do when conducting raids like this. The first team veers off with Silver as lead.

I'm heading up the second team. My group follows me as we ride along the back of the property and then prepare to breech the fencing. From the reconnaissance Tate did when he checked out the address, we're aware of the security cameras.

We keep to the outskirts, our skull ski masks concealing our faces.

The fence poses no challenge to get over. We pause once we've climbed onto the other side, watchful for any Saints that might be on guard. Though not much has changed since my time held captive by the Chosen Saints— once the sun's down, Abraham and his so-called family are more about their ceremonies and celebrations than they are about security.

Guards like Brody, Amos, and Xavier were more personal security than anything. They were around to make sure the believers kept in line. Quick to slam the butt of their rifles into our guts if we so much as looked at them the wrong way, but they rarely did property checks. One or two a night was the most they bothered.

Little has changed as we jog across the barren land coming up on the warehouse. We're footsteps away from reaching one of the back doors when a gunshot rings out in the night. Several more promptly follow.

"Shit!" Cash grumbles from behind me. "Not what we had planned. Somebody must've been seen!"

"No time like now," I reply, my assault rifle ready as I swing my head at Bush.

He gets what I'm signaling and we tag team the door. Our body weight collides against the barrier and breaks it down.

The night spirals into violence and chaos like the night we invaded the first Chosen Saints compound. From the moment we barge through the door, we're confronted with members of the family. Some of them innocents I recognize, like a gaunt and frightened Isadora who throws her hands up and begs us not to hurt her.

Then there's others like Brody who I shoot point blank in the face. We make it room to room clearing the place, shooting anybody affiliated with Abraham and anybody that's got a weapon who tries to fire on us.

Another man I don't recognize but who dawns the robes of a saint shoots at us from where he's taken cover behind a wall.

"Lay down your weapons and put your fucking hands up," I command. "This is a raid and we're here to shut this shit down. Tell us where Abraham is."

"Or let's skip the words altogether. Smoke bomb!" Ozzie unclips one of the many grenades he's brought with him and tosses it toward the entryway where the guard is taking cover.

The grenade hisses as it rolls onto the ground and explodes into a thick cloud of smoke.

We press forward with our rifles trained to shoot first, ask questions later. The guy who shot at us from behind the wall meets a grisly fate as Cash takes him out with a single bullet. I'm still in the lead, scanning the area for the any sign of Abraham.

"I'll clear the second floor, Cash."

He nods and steps to follow me while the other two finish raiding our half of the first floor.

We dash up the steps and run into more terrified believers who tremble and sob as soon as they see us. I order them to kneel and keep their hands up.

Time is limited and the longer we take parsing through who's a saint and who's a believer, the greater the chance Abraham'll escape or we'll suffer a casualty. We're still on his turf.

My heart pounds faster as I look toward the end of the hall and finally spot him. His white robe flicks out of view as he flees out of sight.

"Motherfucker!" I grunt, springing after him.

Not again.

I won't let him escape a second time.

A couple hurried strides later, I chase him down another hall that's lined with doors on either side. The instant he's back in my line of sight, I'm firing off more bullets, narrowly missing.

He pivots into a room toward the end of the hall with a howl of pain.

Got him!

I close the gap, barreling down the rest of the hall and following him through the doorway.

The room's small and cramped, clearly being used as a bedroom. The living conditions are almost as squalid as the cabins we'd been forced to live in, with a piss bucket in the corner and bedsheets so dirty, streaks of filth cover the fabric.

The window's wide open on the far wall. I rush over to

spot Abraham climbing down the fire escape, clutching at his thigh where I've shot him.

At the bottom, an unmarked SUV waits for him. Their emergency escape vehicle.

"Get the fuck back here!" I roar, squeezing the trigger of my rifle.

My shots land on the iron bars, inches away from Abraham. He glances up at me for a fleeting second, a glimmer in his icy eyes as he reaches the bottom rung and then drops. He lands on the roof of the SUV, rolling down along the front of the vehicle.

I open fire some more, half climbing out the window to leap down and follow.

But it's too late—the SUV floors it as soon as he's thrown himself through the rear passenger door. It blasts off across the barren field 'til it's nothing but a blip on the radar, shrinking smaller and smaller.

"FUCK!"

I slam the rifle against the iron cage that's the fire escape.

The others regroup outside the warehouse when it's all said and done. We've slaughtered most of the saints and released the few believers still captive. I approach Silver and Mace to discover their group fared slightly worse. They've sustained some injuries, including a bullet graze for Tate.

"But we got her this time," Mace says, jerking Mandy toward him. Her wrists are bound, her white robes mucked up. "She tried to make a break for that SUV that got away, but I snatched her up before she could."

Mandy grits her scummy teeth at us, squirming in her binds.

My insides pull tight at the sight of her. Maybe the only

other person beside Abraham I hate most and would love to make pay. For years she made my life a living hell, calling upon me for her every whim.

"It's a start," I say. "We can get info out of her. She's his most loyal follower."

She throws her head back in a cackle. "My stallion, you've come back to me, have you?"

I grip her chin roughly and growl at her, "Careful what you wish for, bitch. You're about to suffer, and I'm about to enjoy every second of it. Take her away."

19

TEYSHA

I'm not sure what to think the first time I set foot inside the Steel Saloon. The bar's dated, with wood-paneled walls and worn down floor boards. Beer posters of scantily clad women are plastered all over and there's a vague smell of cigarette smoke that seems permanent.

But I'm greeted with a huge smile from the white-haired man behind the counter. His bushy brows jump high on his forehead, and he waves me over like we've met before.

"You must be Teysha."

"Hello," I say graciously, shaking his hand. "How did you know my name?"

"Everybody here knows your name. Your Ghost's girl."

My cheeks warm. "I didn't realize Logan told you all about me."

"Of course he did," he says. "He made us promise to take care of you while he's gone. Name's Mick. This is Tito."

"*Hola hermosa esposa de Ghost.*"

My smile's an uncertain one. "Hello, Ghost's beautiful wife?"

"And she knows Spanish!" The man named Tito claps his hands in approval. "You're a keeper."

"I took three years in high school."

"Sit down, Teysha," Mick says, gesturing to the barstools. "Can I fix you a drink?"

I blink at him. "It's... ten a.m."

"Don't let the wall of liquor bottles fool you. We have coffee."

"Burnt coffee," Sydney says from a doorway that leads to the back of the saloon. She starts toward the bar counter, opening her arms up to give me a quick hug.

"Burnt coffee is still coffee," Mick mumbles.

"So glad you could make it. Did you drive yourself?"

"Logan's truck."

"If he's letting you drive his cars, he's got it bad."

I snicker. "I don't think he had any other choice considering he's away."

"Consider it a win anyway. He could've hidden the keys. I'll show you the guest room we've prepped."

I follow Sydney from the barroom to the house that sits behind the Steel Saloon. I'm not sure what I was expecting. It looks surprisingly normal for belonging to the president of a biker club.

"Mace's dad's serving fifteen," Sydney explains, twisting the knob on the front door. "He won't be up for parole for another five."

"I'm surprised Logan doesn't live here too."

"Mace says he's always liked his privacy... and apparently he wasn't Velma's biggest fan."

"Velma?"

"Long story. Maybe over shots of tequila."

I chew on my bottom lip to keep from pointing out that

I've never had tequila before. I've only ever drank whiskey —*with Logan.*

Whiskey that's left me hot and giggly.

The same kind of warmth flushes over me. The little ritual of ours might sound trivial, but it's one I've come to enjoy.

A pang of sadness hits me directly afterward. Logan won't be around for who knows how long.

A couple days at least.

I miss him already. More than he probably realizes I do. More than most would say is appropriate considering he's only been gone a few hours.

Sydney's been talking as she walks me through the house, giving me a tour. Immersed in thoughts about Logan and how I wish I could put my arms around him, I haven't heard a word. She stops abruptly once we're in the kitchen to offer me a drink.

"Grab whatever you want out of the fridge. Mace stocked up for us."

"Oh... that's okay... I don't want to... I'm not here to intrude."

"Girl, stop. You're not bothering anybody. I'm glad you're here. We'll pass the time they're gone together."

For the rest of the morning, Sydney helps me get settled. She updates me about the wedding planning she's in the thick of. They're planning for a small gathering in the meadow on the outskirts of town, but putting together a wedding, no matter how modest, requires a lot of work. I offer my services in whatever she needs.

"You'll be a bridesmaid... if you're up for it," Sydney says.

I smile. "I'd like that."

We move on from the house, returning to the saloon to

help Mick. Only a handful of customers swing by so early in the afternoon. Even with the barroom empty, there's no shortage of work.

I'm happy to slip into my old role as a waitress and take care of the few customers we do have. Two bikers with fuzzy beards named Mudd and Ulysses thank me once I've delivered them their pints and salty pretzels.

"You're a natural," Mick says, whistling. "Sydney, you're fired. I've got Teysha now."

Sydney folds her arms, arching a brow. "Fired? You forget you're speaking to the *head* old lady?"

He scratches the sparse white hairs on his head. "Seems like just yesterday it was you walking through those doors asking about our hiring sign."

I pause from where I am wiping down a table. "I still can't believe you did it. You left Boulder to come work in a biker bar."

"What do you think you're doing right now?" Sydney raises her brows at me.

I laugh as if she's told a joke. "It's not the same thing."

"You're here, aren't you? You're Logan's old lady, right?"

"You left home to be here."

"You didn't?" Sydney asks. "I seem to remember Teysha Baxter was a waitress at the Sunny Side Up, just like me. Born and raised in Boulder. She's got a mama and grandmama who would probably prefer if she returned home. Yet you're here. Doing your own thing."

My bashful smile falters as I give a shake of my head. The feeling inside my chest tightens just at the thought of what's waiting for me at home. Mama and Grandma Renae mean well, but their suffocating love would make anyone feel like a bird trapped in a cage.

I've stayed in Pulsboro so I could breathe for the first time in my adult life.

So I could make things work with my husband.

But I'm nothing like Sydney. She stood on her own. She sought answers. Retribution for what happened to her and her family.

I could never be that brave. I'm practically in hiding, still sweating in my sleep over Abraham and the Chosen Saints. Still losing my voice whenever Mama's near. I'm so weak, Logan had to ask his brother's girlfriend—my old friend from Boulder—to watch after me while he's gone.

Sydney seems to sense I'm getting lost in my thoughts. She taps my wrist for my attention, a sympathetic bend to her mouth. "Tey, the fact that you're still standing after everything you've been through—"

"I'm really tired," I blurt out. The dish rag slips out of my hand. "Mind if I go lay down for a while?"

It's half the truth. I've got aches and pains up and down my body. Almost like my body's acting up in protest of Logan being gone. I've pushed through the morning, but thoughts about home and Abraham and everything else are equally as exhausting.

Sydney shares a look with Mick, then nods. "Go ahead. I'll come get you around dinner."

I'm out of it as I spin on my heel and escape to the house out back. I draw the curtains in the room I'll be staying in, blocking out the bright Texas sun, and collapse into bed. Sleep comes easy. Dreamlessly.

My preference these days.

It means no nightmares about Abraham and what he put me through.

I wrap my arms around a pillow and bury my face in it,

pretending it's not doughy and soft. It's hard and muscled like Logan.

It feels like I'm only out for a couple minutes. The next time I open my eyes and blink blearily around the room, I realize I'm no longer alone. I'm a breath away from screaming 'til I blink again and recognize the face I'm looking up at. The door's cracked open and none other than Korine has wandered in.

She's in coveralls stained with motor oil and grease but when she spots that I'm awake, her smile's never been brighter. She's wearing a ball cap backwards, the short strands of her pixie cut framing her face.

"Sydney asked me to come check on you. How was the nap?"

I sit up, feeling discombobulated. "Quick. What time is it?"

"A few minutes after five."

"I slept for almost four hours?!"

Korine shrugs. "Maybe you needed the rest."

"More like I needed the escape."

"It can be the same thing. I was the same way when I left my husband, Ken." She sits down on the foot on the bed and readjusts her backward ball cap. "It's crazy to think it's already been eight months since I left him."

"I didn't know that you were..."

"Married?" Korine releases a soft, wistful laugh. "Yeah, I was married. Right out of college. So, pretty young like you."

"Then what happened?"

"He beat me. So many times, I couldn't tell you about them all."

Concern pulls my lips into a frown. "That sounds horrific. I'm so sorry."

"The last time it ever happened, he hit my mother. Something inside me snapped. It's like I didn't care about myself enough to leave him. But the moment he tried to hurt Mama... I knew I had to go."

"And Blake?"

"He took us in. He stood by me every moment. He didn't have to. I was so broken, I just wanted to curl up and hide forever."

"But you seem so..." I pause, trying to sort out how to describe her. Korine with her coveralls and ball cap and the bikes in the Chop Shop she loves working on. "You're so cool and laidback. You have it all going for you."

"It took time to put myself back together. I'm just barely now... it's taken work. My ex will be sentenced later this month, and he'll be going away at least for a few years. I'm looking at it as a new beginning."

I'm picking at the loose thread on the bed sheet, considering what she's told me. If I'd been asked to guess Korine's background, I never would've answered with abusive marriage. I would've assumed she was like Sydney, so confident and unshakable.

She stands up from the foot of the bed and slides her hands into the pockets of her coveralls. "The club's a family. We have each other's backs. Sydney told me that when I first left Ken. I found it hard to believe, but it's true—we're all here for you, Teysha. Come out when you're ready."

It takes a lot of nerve and fifteen more minutes to convince myself.

I get up from the bed, fix my hair, and give myself a pep talk in the mirror. My heart still aches being away from Logan and the discomfort in my chest pulls tighter when I think about Abraham and the Chosen Saints. But I push myself to leave the house and seek out the others.

I'm halfway toward the patio when my phone chimes in my hand. It's the clerk's office.

For a second, I consider letting it go to voicemail like the others times. Then I realize it's no use ignoring the calls any longer.

Besides, I did promise Logan I'd contact them.

"I'm so glad you answered, Ms. Baxter," says Rita. "I trust you've heard the voice messages I've left about your case? It seems we'll be able to proceed with the annulment after all. I've been trying to reach your husband, but his voice message box is full."

"Right," I stammer slowly. "Err, about that... we've actually changed our minds."

She pauses. "Changed your minds?"

"About the annulment. We're working things out."

"Oh. Your husband just seemed so sure—"

"We appreciate you reaching out, but it's not necessary," I interrupt sharply, though under a thin layer of politeness. "Have a blessed day."

I'm hanging up in the same moment Sydney spots me approaching and her face lights up.

"Here she is! I was just telling Tito to grill you a burger too."

"One burger for Ghost's girl coming right up."

"Come sit, Teysha." Korine scoots over at the bench. Her smile matches Sydney's.

I return theirs with one of my own, grateful for their friendship.

Hopeful that I've finally found my place with Logan and the Steel Kings and their Queens.

20

TEYSHA

"Baby, you're gonna have to let go so I can unlock the door."

I bite down on a sheepish smile as I loosen my arms from around Logan's torso. He steps forward to the door, twisting the key in the lock, then grabbing my hand to pull me inside with him.

"Are you sure you don't need me to take you to the urgent care?"

"I'll manage. It's just a couple scrapes. Tends to happen when you're caught up in a gunfight."

"It's so dangerous. I wish you wouldn't go." I've tucked myself into his side, laying my head on his chest as if it's too heavy with worry.

Logan curls his arm around me to keep me where I am. He drops a kiss onto my head and takes a second to smell my hair. "I have to. I'm a Steel King."

I take comfort in the tenderness of his rasp. At least he's home now.

"Tell me what happened," I say gently.

I expect a number of different reactions—Logan

reminding me how I'm not supposed to know club business or Logan telling me he's in no mood to talk. But the reaction I expect least is for him to actually answer.

"We found the compound." He drops his arm around me to lurch into the kitchen. It's as he does that my eyes rake over him. The knots in his muscled back, thinly disguised under his torn and mucked white t-shirt. The fresh scrapes and scratches carved into his rough, hairy skin. The heavy clack of his boots, his steps weightier than usual.

He's exhausted and needs to be taken care of.

I dart down the short hall of our apartment into the bathroom. Snatching the first aid kit I've spotted in one of the cabinets, I run back to meet him. I take his hand and bring him to a kitchen barstool, prompting him to slide on.

"Keep going," I say, snapping open the aid kit. "You can tell me these things."

"It's nothing but confrontations and violence."

"I... I can handle it. I want to be here when you need to vent. To take care of you. Please tell me."

He drags a hand over his face, then concedes. "It was like we thought. Another compound of the Saints. We raided the place. They tried to fight back. Things got nasty. Tate was grazed by a bullet. The rest of us scrapped up. But we took most of them out. We took Mandy captive. Maybe she'll be more useful than Xavier was."

My jaw falls open, though I clamp it shut a second later. Instead, I focus on what I'm doing for Logan—I've gently applied the bandage on a nasty scrape he has on his forearm.

It takes more effort to keep my tone even after the name drop.

"Oh... Mandy. I hadn't even thought about what happened to her."

"She had fled with Abraham the first time. But now we know they're separated."

"And, um, what about him?"

Logan shakes his head. It's enough of an answer that I don't press him on it.

Neither of us want to go there. Least of all when we've just been reunited after Logan's mission.

I lift his shirt to assess the bruise on his side. His larger hand catches mine, forcing my gaze to flick up to his.

"I'll get him," he says. "Didn't happen this time. But I'm gonna get him."

My heart thrums faster looking into his rugged face, studying the different shades of blue in his eyes. He's peering at me like he's doing the same, locked into some kind of silent study of me. Being on the receiving end causes a flutter in my belly.

It's intense and scary all at once.

The temperature in the room rises. No longer is the Texas heat confined to outside. It's made its way into the apartment and leaves me flushed and warm.

Logan squeezes my hand and pulls me up higher. He brushes hair away from my face and draws me closer. My thighs part as I slide half into his lap, sitting astride him. We're inches apart, still lost in each other's gaze.

I can feel his pulse beating in his veins. His adrenaline's racing, ready to explode.

His desire for me.

I've never felt more powerful. More valuable.

I've never been more acutely aware of the ache deep inside. The part of me begging to be filled by Logan.

We inch closer at a snail's pace, breathing harder. It's in slow motion that we're pulled together. Then our lips touch and the moment burns hot.

Logan's grip clenches shut. He gropes my hip and palms my backside. His tongue prods insistently at my lips, and I part them to meet him. His kiss makes my head spin faster than I can keep up with.

One second I'm straddling Logan, kissing him. The next second, my feet are off the ground and I'm spinning round and round.

His rough hands feel electric on my skin. Tiny shocks of pleasure hit me as his palm glides up my thigh and my dress rides up.

I shudder, rocking in his lap, pressing my lips to his.

He squeezes my flesh and growls his approval.

His mouth breaks from mine, traveling kiss by kiss across my jaw. Down my throat.

He kisses the corner where it meets my shoulders; the heat he brings flushing over me. I grind my body, riding his thigh, sliding my hand up his neck and into his dark hair. He holds me closer, tighter, in encouragement. Together we create a rocking dance.

"Fuck, you feel so damn good," he groans. His hand comes up to cup my face and he kisses me on the lips. "I'm about to rip these panties off and fuck that tight little pussy."

The dirty word feels wrong, which only makes me shudder. I release a whimper and pick up the pace, gyrating my hips.

"Tell me how you want it, baby." He squeezes my backside as he makes his demand. His mouth covers mine before I can even think about answering.

We trade kisses and heavy breaths. My brain feels scrambled. Basic thought feels impossible. I pant the first words that come to mind.

"I'm so... so..."

"What, baby? Say it."

"So... oh... wet..." I breathe.

"What's wet?"

Logan poses the question as he wedges his hand between my thighs. He nudges my cotton panties to the side, then rubs his fingers over the folds of my labia. The grazing touch is soft but evocative enough to make me throb.

"Oh... my... pussy," I answer as he kisses me with tongue and dips his fingers into me. "My pussy's so wet."

"So fucking wet." He nips at my lips, pumping his digits in and out. My juices coat him, my walls quivering at how good it feels. "You're soaked. You ready for me, baby?"

"Mmm, yes. Yes, please. I want your... oh, put your..." My hips jerk forward in the same thrusting motion as his fingers. I'm practically getting myself off to their every motion. The pleasant tingly feeling washes over me.

It's the same feeling I've felt whenever Logan and I have made love.

It's an ever-heightening sense of pleasure that builds and builds...

Almost at the pinnacle of feel-good chemicals.

I curl my thigh around Logan's waist as he stands up from the barstool. He pins me to the wall and begins undressing me. He sucks on the column of my throat and yanks down the straps of my sundress. A tremor rocks through me trying to keep up, my hand balled up in his shirt. My panties are snatched away, the rip sound loud in the silence of the apartment.

Logan claims my lips the same moment he enters me. My feet disappear from the ground as I'm hoisted up into his arms and my thighs are spread wide. He slides into my pulsing warmth, setting off thousands of tiny nerve endings.

We kiss and slip into a rhythm. His hips work and heat

breaks over our skin. I lose what little breath remains in my lungs. Between his passionate kisses and deep strokes, I'm driven insane from how good it feels. Pleasure courses through me like energy invading my body.

Energy I've traded with Logan and no one else.

It doesn't matter if there have been others. None of those times counted.

I didn't want them, and though I didn't want Logan the first time either, I do now.

I want him every day for the rest of my life.

The pinnacle I've been ascending to finally comes. More pleasure than I've ever imagined erupts from within. The nerve endings send off tingling fireworks that explode at once. Sobs of pleasure tumble out of me one after the other. I cling to Logan's shoulders as if afraid I'll melt to the floor.

He's the pillar I need, pinning me where I am, his hips a drill.

His grunts are raw and uneven. His breath warm and intimate on my skin. I rake fingers through his hair and revel in how deep he goes. How urgent and rough he gets. His final moments are marked by my thighs squeezed tight and the full-body shudder he gives.

He comes as if it pains him. I'm filled with his hot release, the heavy wet feeling its own reward. I don't want him to go, even as I feel him softening. Even as his hips stop moving and he buries his face into my throat.

It's then that I feel something damp. Something cold against my skin.

"Logan," I whisper. "Are you..."

He sighs into me. His heart's hammering inside his chest. Mine beats just as fast.

A strange uncertainty numbs me for a second. I stay

still, questioning how I should respond. Will he be defensive if I ask him? Will he be ashamed if I offer comfort?

I settle on stroking his hair, letting his tears soak into my skin.

Minutes might pass before we move. I'm not paying enough attention to know for sure.

When Logan finally pulls away, he sets me down on my feet and pulls down my dress. His thumb runs the curve of my cheek before he gives me a soft kiss.

"You alright?"

"Yes," I answer, puzzled for half a second. Then I cover his hand with mine when I realize what's going on. "I wanted it. You didn't hurt me."

He nods, the look in his eyes a thousand miles away.

"Did you... want me?" I ask, my tone slightly timid.

The faraway look vanishes for a glint of affection. He thumbs my cheek again and says, "Yeah, I did. Always."

We spend the rest of the night coming down from our lovemaking. We take a shower and settle into bed like I've always imagined doing with my husband. Happiness swells inside my chest curling up against Logan and thanking the Lord for how fortunate I've been.

He's gifted me the husband I never thought I'd have, but that I've come to...

I trail off at that revelation. I'm not sure I'm ready to process it, much less tell Logan.

For now, I enjoy the moment. Logan runs a slow hand up and down my arm as we lay in bed and talk ourselves to sleep. He tells me about earlier; how he'd let his thoughts wander.

"Seeing Mandy again... it made me think about... everything that happened."

I'm silent, letting him get it off his chest. I'm aware

Mandy, Abraham's first wife, used to call upon Logan almost daily. She'd had a fixation with him the same way Abraham seemed to have one for me.

Though I'm not a vengeful person, thinking about how she'd used him makes me hot with fury. It makes me want to do things I've promised God I'd never do. It makes me wish I wasn't so faithful to my beliefs.

"I thought about her... and then I thought about Abraham," he explains. "I thought about all the times we were called upon, and how I used to have to make myself stay hard. It was fucked up... but I had to keep going. I had to trick myself into performing. And with you... I had to do it knowing how you didn't..."

"You were the only thing that kept me going," I say. "Those moments between us. They made me feel safe."

Logan pulls me even closer, 'til I'm half on his chest. I tip my head back in time for the kiss he gives me. One of the last before we eventually drift off.

The Fourth of July bike show is the big event in town that Saturday. Logan and I wake early to head to the Steel Saloon and help set up. Many of the others have arrived to do their part. Ozzie's brought Hope to be his assistant for the day at his fake tattoo booth. Korine's spearheading the bike display. Mick and some of the others carry pounds of meat to the grill under the patio.

In a couple hours, half of Pulsboro will come through.

Logan and I are separated. He goes off with Silver and Mason to iron out the plans for the day. I join Sydney in the kitchen to make sure the rest of the food will be ready on time.

"You're amazing," she says, wiping her brow. "Last year, all we served was burgers and fries. But we just had to get ambitious, offering a bigger menu."

"It's Fourth of July. They'll love some of these sides. I used Grandma Renae's recipe on this mac and cheese."

Sydney samples a spoonful, her eyes lighting up. "No wonder Freddie was so crazy about her when she came around the diner. She can throw down in the kitchen."

"Don't forget she owned her own restaurant once. Her and my grandpa."

"I remember. Renae's Kitchen."

"It only closed 'cuz of his heart attack. They couldn't handle it anymore."

"Maybe we should put you in charge of the club's food," Sydney says. At my scoff, she insists. "You're Logan's old lady, which basically makes you a member of the club. All the old ladies have some role in activities run by the club."

I smirk at her. "I'll think about it."

The crowds arrive within minutes once the event kicks off. People come from every pocket of Pulsboro to browse the booths and check out the sparkling motorcycles put on display.

"Can I interest you ladies in a tattoo?" Ozzie grins at us.

"You mean a *fake* tattoo?" Sydney asks in return.

"Ozzie, didn't you say the ink you brought is real—?" Hope starts only for Ozzie to cough loudly. She realizes a second too late she's supposed to stop talking.

Sydney puts her hands on her hips. "If I find out you're doing real tattoos on people..."

"You'll what, Syd? Tattle on me?"

"That's exactly what I'll do. Then Mace'll kick your ass."

He chuckles, rubbing the back of his neck. "It should be

against the club bylaws for the head old lady to issue threats."

"Then what's the fun in being head old lady?" Sydney asks.

We share our own laugh as we continue navigating the booths. Eventually we stumble on our guys. The brothers have never resembled each other more—an inch separates them in height and though there's differences in their appearance, like Mason's green eyes and Logan's mop of dark hair, you can tell they're brothers. The vague resemblance lives in the dimensions of their face. The general builds of their tall, muscular bodies.

Even how they carry themselves.

Sydney nudges her elbow into my rib. "Do you realize, soon we'll be sisters-in-law?"

A slow smile comes to my face. "I've never thought about that before, but we will."

"I'm glad you're here. I hope you'll stay."

...*I think I will.*

Logan and Mason look up at us at the same time. Mason's gaze lights up for Sydney while Logan's glints for me. Sydney goes to Mason. I step toward Logan almost bashfully before he opens his arms and drags me the rest of the way into him.

"There you are," he says, kissing my cheek. "Thought I was going to have to send out a search party."

"Funny, because I feel the same way about you."

"Hungry? I heard the home-cooked mac and cheese that the club's prepared is the best people have ever had."

My face warms at the subtle-yet-not-so-subtle compliment. "Nobody said it was the best ever."

"You think I'm lying? I overheard two people just now.

Besides, did you forget you've been cooking for me nonstop? Everything you make is too damn good."

I let out a humble laugh as he leads me toward the food booth that's selling our sides. Bush's wife, Lesley, is running it. She beckons us over the second she spots us.

"Here, have some before it's gone. The rate we're selling, we'll be out by mid-afternoon." Scooping a large spoonful of mac and cheese into one of the paper bowls, she hands it over to Logan with two spoons.

Logan offers me the first bite. I shake my head, conscious of the shake in my belly. My appetite hasn't been what it used to be, but that's never been truer than in public settings. I'd be even more anxious if I didn't have Logan at my side.

The more people arrive, the more I'm reminded how I'm still adjusting. Being around strangers still makes me uneasy.

Logan seems to sense I'm overwhelmed. He grabs my hand to lead us farther away from the crowd.

"You sure you don't want any?" he asks. "You skipped breakfast too."

"I'm not hungry. But I am thirsty."

"C'mon, we'll grab some water bottles."

Relief comes over me. The way Logan holds my hand and guides me alongside him feels so natural. It chases away the outside noise and calms the anxiety gnawing at me.

My husband understands me better than anyone, even if he doesn't realize he does.

We approach the stall where people are gathered ordering their beverages. So many people from town have shown up that they've started blending together. All of them except a dirty blonde with scarlet, horn-rimmed glasses.

Rita Lewis-Castillo turns around as though sensing our presence nearby. Her eyes flash in recognition, her mouth forming a smile. "Well, look who it is! I didn't expect to run into you."

I freeze, my insides turning into ice. "Oh... hello. Nice to see you. Logan, it's too crowded here. Maybe we should go—"

"I'm glad you two have decided to work things out."

"We've been waiting for you to return our call," Logan says, his mood instantly souring. "Did you even elevate our case to your supervisor like you said you would?"

"I'm sorry? I was told that was no longer necessary," she says, then she glances at me. "I was told you two had changed your minds."

"Logan, we have to get going," I say, every word rushed. I tug on his arm, but he's immovable. He's not going anywhere 'til he gets answers.

His expression hardens as he looks at me. "You gonna tell me what she's talking about?"

21

TEYSHA

AN ETERNITY MIGHT AS WELL PASS US BY. THAT'S HOW long the moment feels as Logan and Rita turn their attention onto me. I let go of Logan's arm and stitch together the best response I can. It's full of ums and uhs and I settle on coming clean.

Sort of.

"I... I told her we were, um, working things out," I say. "But that's because... I thought... weren't we?"

"We were waiting to hear back from the clerk's office. You said you'd keep reaching out to them for an update."

Rita prods the scarlet frames of her glasses higher up her nose. "That's not what happened. I have called you both several times over the past few weeks. Your voice mailbox needs to be emptied out, Mr. Cutler. Your wife did eventually answer her phone, but it was to tell me the annulment case no longer needed to move forward."

The sticky summer air shifts from uncomfortable to outright unbearable. I wipe my brow, grateful I haven't eaten today as the sick feeling in my stomach intensifies. I'm being put on the spot when I wasn't prepared; it wasn't part of my plan to run into Mrs. Lewis-Castillo.

"I didn't mean to... I was just..." I trail off, unsure of what else to say.

The muscle in Logan's jaw tics. He nods at the clerk and says, "I'll be reaching out on Monday."

Then he's off. He strides away, cutting a forceful path through the bike show crowd. My heart explodes in panicked beats as I rush to go after him. Rita catches me first, stepping in my way. Her lips have thinned, her eyes sharp.

"So you're aware, this will be documented. The court does not look favorably on liars."

I inhale a breath to find panic quickly spreading. "Please... just... move out of my way."

I scurry my way around her, accidentally stepping into another man who happens to be passing by. Murmuring a quick apology to him, I scan the area for the direction Logan went in. The bike show becomes a maze of strangers that block every conceivable path I choose to go down. I squeeze myself between a family of four, finally reaching the parking lot.

Logan's headed for his pickup truck.

"Babe, where are you... wait for me!"

I catch up to him as he's wrenching the driver's side door open. "Teysha, go back to the bike show."

"We should talk. I promise I can explain."

"Who says I want to hear that explanation?" he snaps.

"I really did think... I was hoping..."

"You thought wrong. You hoped wrong. I trusted that you were telling the truth. But apparently it was bullshit."

"Logan, can we please talk about it?"

Stragglers wandering the parking lot take notice. I

fumble with the door handle on the passenger side, desperate to climb inside before he takes off. I make it just as the truck engine roars to life.

But my hope we'll talk fades away.

Logan glares out the windshield, his focus on the road. The truck swings around the street corner in a wild turn that burns rubber and makes a nearby car honk its horn. My pleas fall on deaf ears the entire drive home.

He's retreated into silence, shutting me out. It's like I don't exist. I'm invisible to him.

I can't take a breath. When I go to try, my lungs fail me. I'm fractured on the inside as heartbreak finally bursts free. It cuts deep, rocking me to my core, leaving me breathless and aching.

How do I begin explaining myself? How can I make him understand all I wanted was a chance?

I wasn't trying to deceive him to hurt him. I just wanted to love him...

For him to love me in return.

I'm a wreck by the time we reach the apartment.

Logan spares me no second glance. The driver's side door slams shut as he jumps out and heads up the staircase to an apartment I'd started to think of as home.

I trail behind him, feeling even sicker than before. Once inside, he finally addresses me. His tone is cold and hollow, like I'm a stranger, not his wife.

"I made it clear from the beginning this wasn't permanent. You disrespected that by lying to me," he says from over his shoulder. He's gone straight for the fridge in the kitchen. "I'm guessing you thought I'd never find out."

"You have to understand. It wasn't malicious—"

"I don't have to understand a damn thing. *You* lied to *me*. For weeks!"

I flinch at the volume of his voice, feeling dazed and unprepared for this moment. The moment where I'm forced to face reality.

"Did you think I'd fall in love with you? That what you were hoping for? That we'd live happily ever after like some fucking storybook?" He's opened the fridge to reach for a can of beer, popping the tab as he casts me a look that's so honest and brutal, what's left of my heart shatters. "I've got nows for you, Toysha. Storybooks ain't real. What's real is what I told you from the start—this was never gonna last."

There it is, right there.

The truth of the matter summed up in a single withering look. In five simple words.

The disappointing reality can no longer be bathed in the rosy tint of hopes and dreams. My fantasy was just that —a fantasy where we beat the odds and made this forced arrangement work. We'd fall in love like a real husband and wife love each other, like I've dreamed of since I was a little girl.

We'd give meaning to the vows we took even if they were empty the day we married.

But I've run away with these delusions. I've let them rule me.

I ignored the inescapable reality that my husband wanted the opposite. He wants nothing to do with me.

"I'm... sorry..." I stammer out.

"Look," he sighs, setting the beer can down and planting his hands flat on the kitchen counter. "Wires got crossed somewhere. You got confused and started thinking things you shouldn't've. It's best if you go stay somewhere else. Away from me. I'll call up Mace. He and Syd have that extra room."

"Oh... okay."

"It'll be better this way. Keep things separate. Then when the marriage is dissolved—"

"I'll just go home. Back to Boulder."

"Might not seem like it now, but it'll be easier on you. Give you time and space to move on."

I can barely bring myself to nod as he walks out of the kitchen and disappears into his bedroom. Probably to go make the call he's mentioned. Tell Mason and Sydney all about how I've lied and dreamed up some delusion about our marriage.

I almost wish for his anger to return. For him to show some passion. Some feeling. He can't even bring himself to raise his voice anymore.

It's truly over between us.

My eyes squeeze shut at the emptiness inside me. The hole that's so unfulfilled, so profound, it hurts. I brush more beads of sweat from my brow, feeling sick to my stomach, and walk toward the second bedroom where my things are —the duffle bag I've often packed and unpacked over the past few weeks. Barely bothering to check what's inside, I zip it up and hoist it over my shoulder.

The door to Logan's room is closed. His throaty rasp pierces through the door anyway, traces of a phone conversation reaching me.

I don't let myself listen in.

Logan was right when he said it'll be easier if I have time and space. But, for once, I'm going to find my own way.

I'm going to finally accept what I've fought against. Everything I've ever believed was a lie.

Tᴇʏꜱʜᴀ ʟᴇꜰᴛ ᴛʜᴇ ᴀᴘᴀʀᴛᴍᴇɴᴛ ʙᴇꜰᴏʀᴇ I ᴡᴀꜱ ᴇᴠᴇɴ ᴏꜰꜰ the phone with Mace. I didn't have to search far for her whereabouts. The bus terminal in town confirms she came by and bought a ticket to Boulder. She was finally going home.

We'll have to dissolve the marriage at a distance.

It's not what I preferred, but considering the mix-up of the last few weeks, I'll take it.

Teysha got her wires crossed. She let herself believe what was going on between us was real.

We were really married.

She chose to lie when we talked about updates on the annulment. I was furious with her when the clerk told me the truth. I didn't even want to look at her 'til I calmed down and realized I was at fault too. I had let her believe the things she had.

What else did I expect when I was letting her sleep in my bed every night and having sex with her?

A woman like Teysha was bound to get confused. She thought things meant more than they do.

I care about her... a lot.

I wouldn't have entertained having her around if I didn't. I wouldn't have done half the shit I've done if I didn't care about her.

But she still doesn't get that I'm not the man for her. The husband she's searching for is still out there. He'll give her things I never could.

The kind of happy ending she deserves.

The first night she's gone, the bed feels strangely... empty. She's on my mind as I walk out of the bathroom fresh from my hot shower and find the room silent and untouched. Normally, she'd be waiting for me. She'd be perched on the bed reading or watching TV.

If she hadn't showered with me.

Another routine we had formed over time.

My mind's eye projects the memories before me like a movie reel. I can practically see the smile lighting up her pretty face. Her smooth, golden brown skin peeking out from the little nightgowns she often wore. When I peel back the covers and get in bed, I can still feel her soft weight curling up against me.

A funny pang hits my stomach. I might as well have missed a step on the way down the stairs.

Her Bible catches my eye, sitting on the nightstand. She must've forgotten to take it with her. I reach for it, propping it open out of curiosity, right to the last page she'd bookmarked.

> *Love is patient, love is kind. It does not envy,*
> *it does not boast, it is not proud.*
> *It does not dishonor others, it is not self-seek-*

*ing, it is not easily angered, it keeps no
record of wrongs.*
*Love does not delight in evil but rejoices
with the truth.*
*It always protects, always trusts, always
hopes, always perseveres.*

The funny pang intensifies. Morphs into some kind of deep ache. The kind of feeling you get when you're missing something... or *someone*.

I put the Bible back and twist off the bedroom light under the assumption it'll go away once I fall asleep.

Hours later, as dawn chases off the dark and brightens the world outside, I'm wide awake. I'm sitting up in bed after tossing and turning for most of the night. It comes to me what's bothering me and why I couldn't sleep.

I reach for my phone and send off a text.

> checking in on u. how's boulder? U make it ok?

The message shows sent, though it'll probably be a couple more hours before Teysha reads it. She was probably tired by the time she finally reached her mother's house. If how they behaved when I met them is any indication, I'd be surprised if they even gave her enough breathing room to check her text messages so soon after returning home.

Filing the situation away, I get out of bed.

Mornings have never been my thing, but what else can you do when you're up early?

I start off my day focusing on what's most important—the revenge I'm seeking against Abraham and the Chosen Saints.

Sydney frowns at the sight of me when I walk through the Steel Saloon's doors. She's obviously heard from Mason about Teysha and I going our separate ways. As her closest friend, it's no wonder she disagrees.

"Have you talked to Teysha yet?" she asks without a good morning.

"It's barely eight a.m."

"I called her last night, and she didn't answer."

"Why would she? She's just made it home. Give it time."

I might not know my brother's fiancée well, but if there's one thing I've learned about her, it's that Sydney's not one to mince words or hide her feelings. Her eyes shrink into a narrow-eyed glare as she watches me cross the barroom floor.

"You really don't give a damn, do you?"

I stop mid stride, cocking a brow at her. "You better have a good reason to make that accusation."

Sydney rises from the barstool she's seated on to place her hands on her hips. "I wouldn't if I didn't."

"Then are you gonna elaborate or am I supposed to be a fucking mind reader?"

"Your wife," she grinds out, standing tall on tiptoe. "Or have you already forgotten her?"

It's no wonder Sydney's Mace's old lady.

She's exactly the kinda woman he's attracted to—someone with guts. Someone who can challenge him when he needs it. But while Mace might find her attitude sexy, I find it annoying as hell. Especially when she's insinuating what she is.

"How could I forget her?" I ask. "I'm the one who's been looking after her. I'm the one who went back to the compound just to rescue her. And I'm the one who's gonna slit Abraham's throat for what he did to her. So, no, I ain't fucking forgotten about her. Everything I've been doing has been *for* her. You got any other questions or are you done speaking on shit you don't understand?"

Sydney's nostrils flare, her glare no less fierce. "So you *do* care about her."

"Teysha's a good woman. She didn't deserve what's happened to her."

"We can agree on that." Sydney drops her hands from her hips and blows out a sigh. "I just want to make sure she's alright."

"She is. She bought a ticket to Boulder and got on the bus."

"How do you—"

"I spoke to the clerk at the bus terminal. Her bus arrived on time at seven p.m. last night."

"That's good to know. But I'd still like to speak to her."

"Give it a couple hours. She's probably still asleep."

Sydney nods, though her expression's still worried. "She *is* a good person, Logan. You might've been frustrated by her, but she only ever means well."

It bothers me Sydney's assuming I care so little about Teysha. She's under the impression I don't give a damn when it couldn't be more different. The truth is, Teysha's been on my mind nonstop. I've even got her broken cross necklace on me.

A bad idea considering it reminds me of her every second it's in my pocket.

I've been thinking about her so much that I'm seeking any distraction I can.

Something to get her out of my head.

But voicing this is another matter altogether. While Sydney's assumptions piss me off, I'm not equipped to explain how. I'm not even sure myself.

Why the hell does it bother me that she thinks I don't care about Teysha? What does it matter if she's aware how I feel about her?

I swallow down these questions, rejecting any possible answers. Knowing wouldn't change anything.

Teysha's already gone. It might not seem like it right now, but it's for the best.

She'll be able to move on the way she should.

"Tell me if you talk to her," Sydney says.

I nod. "You'll be the first to know."

"Thanks. I guess you're not so bad."

"You make a habit of busting men's balls?"

"Ask Mace."

"That answer told me all I need to know."

I leave the barroom behind, taking the staircase that leads into the basement. Moses is on shift guarding Mandy. He takes the head nod I give him as a cue to go on a break. The door thuds shut after him.

I give it another second before I step toward Mandy. She's withered and unwashed, connected to a wooden beam by chains. At the sight of me, she perks up, shaking back her scraggly red hair.

"My favorite boy. Finally come for more? It's been so long."

I curl my fists at my sides, wound tight enough to snap. "You're gonna give me answers or you're in for a bad time."

"You're so aggressive. I knew you had it in you. No

wonder the Leader was so threatened." A maniacal giggle bubbles out of her, flashing scum-riddled teeth. "But I wasn't intimidated, boy. I was turned on. I saw that dick on you when they first brought you in and stripped you bare. I knew I had to have a taste—*AGH!*"

I've gripped her by the throat and slammed her into the wall. The chain cuffed around her wrist rattles. She sucks in a sharp breath. I squeeze tighter against the pulse beating in her neck. We're inches apart, peering into each other's eyes.

Surprise lives in hers. She wasn't expecting me to put my hands on her.

As if I don't hate her fucking guts for everything she's done.

"Where is he?" I ask through bared teeth.

"Why would I know?"

"You know more about him than anyone."

She squirms against me, clawing at my clenched hands. "I don't know what you're blathering about."

A second passes. A single drumbeat.

Then I act. I rip Mandy away from the wall and drag her toward the interrogation chair in the middle of the room. She's dropped down into it before she can protest. I twist her arms behind the back of the chair and lock the chains in place. A howl of outrage wavers out of her.

"How dare you, boy?! BOY!"

I've turned my back on her. I'm cutting across the basement floor to pick up one of the water jugs in the corner. It's overstock Mick puts down here when he's out of room everywhere else. On my way, I snatch an old dishrag from the sink.

Mandy's cussing me out as I return. Her eyes bulge from their sockets, the gleam in them wild. It's the same look I've seen her get when one of her demands are not met.

It usually proceeded whatever believer pissed her off being whipped or beaten.

I was on the receiving end more than once. I toss the dirty dish rag over her hideous face and uncap the water jug in my left hand.

"What are you—*gulg-gulg-gulg!*"

She jerks in place as I wrench her head back and pour the water over her face. Her body twitches like an insect sprayed with Raid while water drowns her out. I empty the jug onto her, then twist my fingers tighter in her thinning strands.

"Tell me where the fuck he is or you're about to suffer."

"Don't you dare use that tongue to threaten me!"

"Have it your way."

I'm husking out ragged breaths as I stride over to the rest of the water jugs. I lug several across the room, setting them down like ammunition where Mandy's chained to the chair. A shrill screech rattles out of her as I fist more of her hair and pour another round of water.

The towel's soaked, so drenched the terry fabric has molded to every contour of her face. As gallons of water flood her, it recreates the feeling of being drowned. She's suffocating under the water cascading over her like a waterfall.

Her legs kick out in protest. Her tortured screams garbled.

Halfway through the third jug, I stop again to ask the same question. "Tell me where the fuck he is."

"HOW... DARE... YO—*ARGHHH!*"

I drench her in the rest of the jug. Then a fourth jug 'til she's so overcome, she can't even make any sounds. She's forced to sit in the chair and take it.

A sick, twisted satisfaction pushes me on. I grit my

teeth, relishing the torture I'm putting her through. The pain and discomfort of feeling like she's drowning again and again. She chokes and coughs and twitches and I only pour more water.

It's what she deserves.

It's what she gets for doing what she did. For using me so many fucking times, I've blacked them out. For wielding the power she had to ensure any time I stepped out of line I was beat down. I was broken 'til I was just some thing she called upon like a pet.

This bitch deserves what Abraham deserves—to suffer every moment she's alive. Then to die a death that's a thousand times more painful.

As adrenaline pulses through me, I'm driven crazy with thoughts of revenge. Brutal barbaric methods I could use to carry it out. I could make her garbled screams seem like a child's laughter. I could really have her hurting.

My hand slips into my pocket for my Swiss knife.

"Ghost!"

The drum of madness beating inside me comes to a halt. I look up feeling like I've woken from a dream. I'm no longer alone.

Mace and Sydney are standing at the foot of the staircase leading into the basement.

"What?" I spit, agitated. "What is it?"

"It's Teysha," Sydney answers. "I just got off the phone with her grandmother. She never made it to Boulder."

23

LOGAN

I TURN UP TO THE TOWN BUS TERMINAL READY TO fracture skulls. Ozzie wanders behind me, something of a chaperone to ensure I don't do anything too homicidal. Mace's idea after I found out that Teysha never made it home.

I announced I was headed to the source. The bus terminal that saw her off.

The fucking place where I'd spoken to a clerk who claimed she bought a ticket to Boulder and boarded the bus.

A pimply-faced college kid sits in boredom behind the plexiglass. He's flipping through a comic book, his situational awareness zero. Otherwise he'd see me striding toward him. I slip my arm through the cutout in the glass and grab the front of his polo shirt. A hard tug later, his face smashes into the see-through barrier between us.

"Ugh... hey man, wha..."

"You told me you sold a ticket to Teysha Baxter for Boulder yesterday."

"So what?"

"So you gave me wrong fucking info. Which means you

better start giving the right fucking info or I'm gonna break your face."

"She did buy a... a ticket... lemme go!"

"To Boulder?!"

"Yes... and no."

"You better be fucking kidding!"

"Ghost!" Ozzie yells.

I slam his head into the plexiglass hard enough to chatter his nose. Blood spurts out as he grunts in pain. The two other travelers in the terminal scream and run off. I couldn't give less of a shit who does and doesn't see. Or how much blood I draw from this asshole.

"Where did she buy a ticket to?"

"She did buy a ticket to Boulder!" he screams, blood spewing from his nostrils. "S-she was waiting for it at first... but then she got on a different bus."

"TO WHERE?!"

"I think it was... it-it must've been Jefferson!"

"You fucking shithead! You better pray I find her in one piece!"

I beat his head several more times 'til he's unconscious and his blood decorates the plexiglass. Ozzie nudges me away, throwing glances over his left and right shoulder.

"You trying to catch a case? Let's get the fuck out of here."

We mount our bikes, already on the same wavelength about where we're headed. No questions necessary.

If Teysha went to Jefferson, then that's where I'll be.

Jefferson exists as an even smaller blip on the state map than shitholes like Portales and Wheaton. It's a single stoplight sorta town with one of everything and dust storms as entertainment. From Pulsboro, it's an almost four hour bike ride.

We hit up the likely places. The motels in town. The diner on the edge of town. Jefferson's bus terminal that's more like a garage housing the occasional bus that passes through.

Teysha's nowhere to be found.

Dusk fades along the horizon, the sky purpling. It'll be dark in another hour.

"Where the fuck is she?"

The words husk out of me in a throaty growl. They're underpinned by frustration and rage. Tension knots every muscle I have, putting me on edge.

Right on the cusp of losing my shit.

I peer down the dim road as the streetlights blink on. Ozzie sighs from my side, sitting back on the seat of his sleek Softail Deluxe. He's been patient through our search, though he's growing frustrated too.

"Ghost, brother, it's time to admit the obvious."

"Don't fucking say it," I snap. "Don't fucking think for one second I'm giving up."

"You kidding? Fuck that. We're not leaving without her. But I mean... the obvious place she must be."

"What the hell are you talking about!?"

"We've checked everywhere in town. Motels, diners, stores. The dang bus terminal."

"And?"

"You forget what else is in Jefferson?"

Recognition narrows my eyes, my chest clenching. "You mean the Zapote bar?"

"Where else could she be? If she's still in town."

"That's the Barrera's spot."

"I'm aware. Cash and me met up there for a deal

months ago. It's a shithole but has lots of stragglers. Perfect place to get lost in."

What the fuck would ever drive Teysha to go to a bar that's associated with the local cartel? What could ever fucking possess her to put herself in such a dangerous environment?

A fresh wave of rage surges through me.

I rev my engine, then take off down the dusty road. Ozzie's not far behind.

Jefferson's such a little stain on the map that we're arriving within five minutes. We pull up to the deafening sounds of Spanish music blasting at full volume. The establishment looks more like an outhouse than a legit bar.

A nasty enough wind could blow right through and knock it to pieces.

Ozzie and I park our bikes in the dirt parking lot and approach the door. We earn stares the entire walk up. Our leather Steel King rockers give us away.

But it doesn't fucking matter. We're here for one purpose and one purpose only.

The inside of the bar's tinted blue, a haze of smoke thick in the air.

My eyes scan the space. I've stopped breathing without realizing it. I've stopped thinking 'til I find her.

Nothing else in the world holds any significance 'til I do.

Ozzie elbows me in the rib. "Ghost, the far corner."

It's the moment I've been waiting for. The moment I see her again.

I'm supposed to be relieved.

But instead, it's the opposite—ice-cold dread fills my veins. I come face to face with a scene that rocks through me like no other.

Teysha's slumped over a table, barely sitting up, nursing an empty shot glass. She's seated with two men I've never seen before, both leaned toward her like vultures ready to feed.

I don't think. I act.

"Teysha? Teysha!" I yell.

I charge forward, shoving aside anybody in my way. Me calling her name barely seems to register with her. She glances up with heavy-lidded eyes, a slack expression on her face.

It's been twenty-four hours and she hasn't changed—she's still in the dress she was wearing yesterday, the left strap halfway down her shoulder, her hair messier than she usually likes it.

A man I've only seen before in passing steps in front of me. Average height and build, with dark, wavy hair, he's dressed like he's about to attend a business meeting not hang around some crumby dive bar.

Miguel Barrera has done business with the Steel Kings throughout the years. From what Ozzie's been telling me, the partnership was going well until recent times where it's started to sour.

He smiles wide, his polite air nothing but a smoke-screen. "I'm surprised to see some Steel Kings in our midst. Can I help you gentlemen?"

"I'm here for my wife."

"Wife?" Miguel chuckles, glancing over either shoulder. "I don't see a wife here. Maybe you're confused, *primo*. How about some drinks?"

"That's my wife right there—TEYSHA!"

She perks up as if zapped by electricity. Her gaze pans across the bar 'til she spots me and recognition dawns on her face. "Logan?"

"If you insist on causing a disruption, then I'm going to have to ask you to leave," Miguel says.

"I'm here to pick up my wife and take her home." I move to go around him, but he steps to the side to block me. "Move the fuck out of my way before I drop you."

"That's not going to happen. We have an agreement with your club that you show up to our territory by invite only. Unless you are here at the behest of the Barreras, then you do not belong here," he explains in his fake polite tone. He gestures to the door. "I was willing to offer you a complimentary beverage since your club is a business partner, but I can't let you interfere in the festivities."

"My wife won't be partaking in those festivities, dipshit!"

"I'm afraid the lady is here of her own free will. She has opted to stay with my men. As have the other women being initiated here tonight."

"You fucking prick!"

I knot my fist in the front of his button-up shirt and wrench him toward me. Several men seated around the bar leap to their feet and reach for their weapons. Ozzie throws himself between me and Miguel to play mediator.

"Whoa, fellas, turn the heat down!" He tries to break my hold on the Barreras leader to no luck. "Ghost, let him go, man. Now's not the time."

"Teysha leaves with me."

"Teysha will be enjoying herself in our company." The smile slides off Miguel's face. The courteous tone he's been putting up vanishes for his deeper native tongue. "*Soldados vienen a eliminar esta molestia de nuestro club. Él está acquí para causar problemas.*"

"You touch me, I'm breaking it!" I roar.

His men have closed in on us, pointing guns and grappling to get hold of us. Ozzie groans in regret while I push back and swing on two of them.

Things quickly spiral into a brawl.

Miguel's men attack us. Guns are pointed at our heads, and we're jostled toward the door. The few bystanders in the place crane their necks to watch the commotion. The two guys crowded around Teysha get up and lead her to the back of the bar.

I scream her name some more. I throw another fist. A couple of my punches hit the mark, but it's no use when we're two against twenty. We're tossed through the front door, into the dirt lot that's reserved for parking.

The music blasting from the bar grows even louder, like they've turned it up in celebration.

Ozzie spits out blood from the right hook he took. "That escalated fast. Maybe next time don't start a bar fight?"

"I'm going back in."

"Do you got a death wish? That was a warning. We go back in there—"

"They've got Teysha."

"So we leave and come back with backup—"

"You heard what's going down tonight! Right fucking now. An initiation? There's no time!"

"Ghost, you go back in there and they *will* shoot your ass—"

"I'VE GOT NO CHOICE!"

The words ring out across the dusty lot, echoing in the night.

My stride starts off strong and domineering, then thaws into fitful steps the harder it becomes to breathe. A familiar feeling latches onto me, taking control of all movement. Within seconds, it's like my lungs are collapsing as they sputter for air, and my knees give out. I crash to the dirt, rocked by violent tremors from the inside.

Not again...

Memories crash down. Flashbacks I've fought against.

Everything uproots itself. The past blurs with the present.

I'm on my hands and knees, in the middle of losing my mind. I'm drowning in horror, sick to my stomach at what's happening. I go from the dusty lot behind the dive bar to the rooms filling the big house that was my hell for years. The rocks and grainy dirt digging into my knees morph into carpet burning my skin. The music blasting fades for the squeal of mattress springs. Wounded cries pitted against groans of pleasure.

It's happening again. All over again.

And I can't do anything about it.

Anguish spills out of me in more desperate, rabid breaths. A sense of helplessness that's its own form of torture.

I can't fucking breathe no matter how hard I try.

"Ghost... Ghost... can you hear me!?"

The voice sounds distant 'til it's not. 'Til I blink and look up to find Ozzie kneeling at my side, his face twisted in deep concern.

"Bro, you've got to calm the fuck down. I think you're having a panic attack." He reaches for my arm to help me up, but I smack it away. "You've got to get it together. We've got to get the hell out of here."

Ozzie's interrupted by a woman's bone-chilling scream. The terrified sound pierces the night air louder than the music.

Teysha.

24

LOGAN

DEATH MIGHT BE WAITING FOR ME INSIDE ZAPOTE. I rush toward the bar's rear door anyway.

Locked.

The knob jiggles when I grapple with it, refusing me entry. I back up several feet to gather momentum, then throw my whole body weight at the door. The wooden barrier shakes against its frame, almost budging under the force I'm using.

I repeat the collision two more times, slamming my shoulder into it. If it's painful, I don't feel it—adrenaline buzzes through me. I'm one-track minded. My only purpose in life has become breaking this fucking door down and getting to Teysha.

Summoning what strength I've got left, I crash into the door again, finally cracking it open. Before even giving a thought to what could be waiting for me, I bolt inside. Opting for the more silent and stealthy weapon, my hand fumbles for the hunting knife strapped to my side. I keep my eyes peeled for the first sign of her.

...or the scumbags who she was with.

A guy coming out of the restroom almost walks right into me. He stumbles back, his eyes going wide with surprise as I rush past him.

The back half of Zapote feels like a funhouse with its tight turns and smaller rooms. I shove aside a curtain cordoning off one of these rooms only to find some brunette on her knees, sucking somebody off.

Miguel was vague describing tonight's festivities, but I knew exactly what was going on.

Initiations are infamous in motorcycle clubs and other gangs for a reason.

The Barreras cartel is no different.

The women that drop by bars on nights like tonight are around for one purpose only.

Panic screams from the inside. Silent torment on the outside. The only sound I'm capable of are the labored breaths I take and the throaty grunts I give. Sweat drips down the side of my face as I come up on the last room.

A stockroom not unlike ours at the Steel Saloon.

Cases of beer and alcohol are stacked six feet high, along with other unneeded things stowed away. I almost turn back 'til I catch scraps of dialogue.

"Hold her down."

"Hurry up."

"You'll get your turn."

It's the last words either of them ever speak. The last fucking breath they take as I storm inside and jam the blade of my knife into them. The first piece of shit gets stabbed in the back of the head. I'm able to pry the knife out of his skull in time to slit the other one's throat.

Teysha's been pushed up against a table, her dress bunched at her waist. Her eyes are wide with fear, the rest of her trembling.

She's in one piece.

I made it in time. I stopped it from happening.

The relief's so powerful it makes me lightheaded.

"We should get the hell out of here," Ozzie says from somewhere behind me.

It's enough of a wakeup call to pull me back to the present moment.

I hadn't even realized he'd followed me inside. Giving a nod, I grab hold of Teysha by the hand and sprint for the door. We make it all the way onto the dusty lot before Miguel or any of the Barreras catch on to what's happened.

Our engines rumble starting them up. We blast off into the night without looking back.

The next time we stop we're in Portales. We come up on some truck stop diner and motel that we decide to rest up at. Teysha's sick and out of it and could barely manage on the back of my bike. Whatever the hell she drank at Zapote fucked her up big time.

Ozzie tosses a key at me. "Adjoining rooms. Figured three's a crowd."

"You figured right."

"How's she doing?" He juts his chin at her.

We're in the parking lot of the Lone Star Motel. Teysha's slumped over the back of my bike, her tangled hair half covering her face. All the wind from the ride has messed it up even more than it already was.

"Not too good," I sigh.

"A couple hours of rest will do wonders. Sunup?"

"Sunup."

We part ways outside our respective motel room doors. Ozzie steps into room 310 while I guide Teysha into 311.

You've been to one fleabag truck stop motel off the highway, you've been to them all. The place reeks of cigarettes, and the box AC unit in the window kicks out hot air instead of cold. There're four channels available on the TV and dust and grime wherever you look.

Far from the best accommodations but good enough for a couple hours of rest.

I glance at the dusty clock radio perched on the nightstand.

It'll be another five hours before sunrise. That should be decent time to recover.

"You alright?" I ask.

Teysha's plodded a couple steps into the room, then collapsed on the closest piece of furniture. It just so happens to be the desk chair with a broken wheel at the bottom.

She shakes her head, her expression unreadable. Beads of sweat shine on her brown complexion as if she's been running a few miles. Considering it's seventy-five degrees out and she was on the back of my motorcycle, braving the wind, it doesn't make sense.

...unless she's sick.

All the pieces click together when they need to. Another second, and she'll spew everywhere. I hook an arm around her waist and walk her into the bathroom.

Nobody likes throwing up.

Not the person throwing up. Not the other person standing by watching.

Damn sure not me.

But there's no other option as we make it to the bathroom and Teysha rushes for the toilet. We get the lid up a split second before the toxic contents come sputtering out. The room fills with the thick sounds of retches and gags as she kneels beside the toilet and spits up what's making her ill.

I'm no caretaker. I'm not the thoughtful kind of guy that's cared for family or girlfriends while they were sick. Mostly because I've never been around when they have been. Nobody's ever been sick with the flu and thought I was the person they wanted to look after them.

Why would they when I prefer to be far removed from most people?

I'm more of the loner type for a reason.

My nature emerges as I stand idly by and listen to the soundtrack of Teysha's retching.

Her whole body quivers. She clings to the toilet bowl like it's a lifeline, sweaty and tearful all at once.

Fuck.

Do something.

Unsure how I can even make a difference, I approach slowly and then kneel beside her. My hand comes to her back, feeling how her very spine vibrates. Whatever it is that's got her this sick is bone deep. It's got her spitting up her insides 'til nothing's left but bile.

"Hey, it's alright," I say. "Just get it all out."

"My... hair..." she croaks.

It takes me another half a second to get what she means. I cup her dark chocolate strands away from her face like my hands are a ponytail holder. She bows forward again to yak up more bile. Yellowish green liquid that makes my own stomach churn.

I shove aside any beginnings of nausea and focus on getting Teysha through the moment.

"Here," I say, getting up to grab one of the motel's

complimentary little paper cups. I fill it with water from the sink and then bring it to her chapped lips. "Drink. Rinse. Seems you've got the worst of it out."

"Th-tha..."

"Shhh, just drink."

Another few minutes pass like this. With me kneeling beside her at the toilet as she comes down from the sickness. Then I ease her to her feet and mention the shower.

"At least none of it got on your dress."

The corner of her lip quirks. "Hooray."

"I'm being serious. You're a pretty neat vomiter, all things considered."

The slow blink she gives, her long lashes fluttering, almost makes me laugh.

"My compliments need some work. Alright, let's get you in the shower."

Teysha's obedient as I unzip her sundress. The fabric falls to a heap at her ankles. I help her step out of it and into the bathtub.

Concerned she's so dizzy and sick that she'll slip and fall, I wait on standby every second she's under the shower-head. As soon as she's reaching to twist it off, I'm ready to wrap her up in the biggest bath towel available. She shudders stepping into it, giving me a grateful nod.

"You want to wear my shirt to sleep in?" I offer. "Considering we've got nothing else."

"I want some toothpaste and a toothbrush."

"That might be out of our scope for now. But I've got some gum."

"Anything to take away this vomit breath. I can *taste* it."

My thumb strokes her cheek before I catch myself and drop my hand. "Yeah, alright. Take what's left of the pack."

It quickly becomes undeniable that I'm all over the place.

I'm caught between the urge to take care of her and the anger and frustration at what's happened tonight. The fucked-up shit that could've happened had I not shown up when I did.

The relief it didn't runs so deep I'm lightheaded. Then the next second comes and my temper reemerges.

How could she be so reckless? How could she put herself in that situation? Does she realize I was just about to lose my fucking mind over her missing?

These are the questions I'm asking myself, bitterness materializing.

Finally, she swivels away from the bathroom mirror and pads back into the rest of the motel room. I'm still perched by the window. I cock a brow at her.

"Rinse your mouth out enough times?"

"I think so... for now."

"Feeling better?"

She releases a deep sigh. "For now. My stomach still feels queasy."

"Hopefully it'll pass. We'll grab some food at the diner next door before we take off."

"About tonight... Logan..." She pads over to the edge of the bed to sit down, her bare feet so damn slender and feminine looking against the grungy, decades-old carpet. When she sits down, her knees touch, her hands in her lap like she's in fucking etiquette school.

It couldn't be more obvious this girl's too good for the Lone Star Motel. She's too good to be caught up in... *this*.

She shouldn't be in shitty motels or smoky bars. She shouldn't even be married to me in the first place.

These are my thoughts as she pauses collecting hers.

She braves a look up at me. "I didn't expect you to show up. But thank you for rescuing me."

"Seems to be a theme."

It's the first brutal cut of the bitterness I've been holding in. Anger and frustration have been boiling under the surface for hours now.

More proof that this girl has gotten to me.

I wouldn't be so pissed otherwise. She put herself in such a dangerous situation. She might as well have strolled into a fucking lion's den...

All because she refused to return home. All because she wanted to go off wandering where she should've never gone.

She flinches as if struck. "I'm sorry."

"That also seems to be a theme."

"It's not what you're thinking."

"Then tell me, Teysha, what the fuck is it? 'Cuz from where I'm standing, it looks a lot like what I'm thinking."

"If you're going to raise your voice—"

"Do you understand what you did? How damn lucky you were I came by when I did? You get what was gonna happen at that bar? You know what an initiation into a gang means? You know what women have to do to get in?"

"You don't even know my side of the story!"

"I don't need to know it to know it was a fucking stupid decision!" I'm up on my feet, the veins throbbing in my neck. My pulse kicks up all over again like we're back at Zapote.

I'm an intimidating man. Six-two, two-ten pounds of muscle.

When I'm angry, everybody knows about it. They hear it in my booming voice and feel the hot pulse in the air.

For someone as sheltered and naive as Teysha, I might as well be some barbarian from another world.

She shrinks like a violet where she's seated on the edge of the bed, blinking at me with those damn big, expressive eyes of hers. Eyes the color of coffee. Eyes that carry a shine in them like no other when she's happy and content.

Things she deserves. Things she'll never have if she keeps fucking around where she shouldn't be...

"Don't you get it?" I growl, throwing my hands up. "Don't you see how I'm trying to protect you from all the shit out there? But you can't do what I tell you to do—you've gotta run off and make trouble and then expect me to bail you out. I didn't sign up for this. I didn't ask for you or your baggage!

"You think you can play house and expect me to just go along with it! You've got no damn clue what it means to be married... let alone married to a guy like me! Why can't you just listen and do what's best for yourself? Why can't you go home and heal so you can find somebody who can give you the things you want!?"

By the time the last word in my rant rumbles across the room, I'm breathing hard. I've taken several steps toward the bed where she's seated. I've waved my arms in sharp, aggressive movements like I'm at my wit's end.

And I am.

I don't know how else to get her to understand.

I'm not the man for her.

I'm not the knight in shining armor she's looking for. Why can't she want better for herself?

Teysha's fallen quiet, though her misty eyes and trembling chin speak for her. She's doing her best to hold in her cry. She's succeeding at making me feel like an even bigger piece of shit the second silence fills the void and I realize I didn't listen to a word she had to say.

Instead I yelled at her. I ranted and told her she was *baggage*.

The girl's still clammy from her bout of sickness. She doesn't feel well, yet I'm being an asshole.

Guilt saws through me to the bone. I bite down on my jaw, closing my eyes and counting backward from ten.

This girl will be the death of me. This girl means... something.

Something I'm not sure I'm ready to face.

"Tell me," I grind out seconds later, coming to my senses. "Tell me your side of the story."

She shakes her head, looking anywhere but at me. I cross the room and drop down next to her, scooping her hand up 'til it's in my lap and not her own.

"Tell me, baby," I say in that damn tone. That damn rasp that's gentler just for her. "What happened? Did they..."

I can't even get the fucking words out.

I don't even fucking know what I'd do if they did—I already killed the bastards.

But if they did... I'll hunt down their dead bodies and figure out how to slaughter them all over again.

"You interrupted before they could," she answers. "And I didn't go there by choice. I *did* buy a ticket to Boulder."

"They take you from the terminal?"

Slowly, she nods. "They grabbed me and told me if I screamed they'd kill me and my family. They flashed a gun and told me to act calm. We got on the bus to Jefferson and that's when they brought me to the bar. They were waiting on someone."

Abraham.

"But he didn't show up," she continues, wiping a puffy eye with the back of her hand. "Then they started feeding me drinks. But it wasn't like the drinks you've made me..."

The guilt I was already feeling magnifies by one hundred. Can I really be pissed with her? She told me she was leaving. She went to the bus terminal to go home.

I'm the one who didn't take her; *I'm* the fucktard who didn't check up on her to make sure she made it. Instead, I counted on the unreliable account of some clerk.

I waited hours before I even sent her a text. Ignored Sydney when she expressed concern.

This is on me.

We sit in uncertain silence for another minute. Teysha's busy studying the ugly shag carpet beneath her feet. I'm processing how wrong I've been.

I'm questioning what it means that I've gone off the way I have.

These feelings invading my chest can't be ignored. They can't be pushed aside or denied. They're quickly becoming an issue.

I can't walk away from Teysha; I can't even fucking stop caring for her the second she needs it.

She shivers from beside me and I put an arm around her in hopes I'll warm her up.

"Cold?"

"Just a fever... I think..."

"Probably whatever the hell they gave you. C'mere."

I wrap my other arm around her, half dragging her into my lap. She rests her head against my chest, her long lashes touching her cheeks as she closes her eyes. My nose winds up in her hair, greedily inhaling the flowery scent of whatever product she's put in. It's a scent that's come to ease any stress in my body. It's come to signify peace and calm.

It makes my heart feel like it's skipping a damn beat.

I swallow against the rush of emotion that threatens to take over.

Now is not the time to go there.

"Let's get you in bed. You should get a couple hours of rest. It'll help."

"Will you..." she trails off, seemingly deciding against whatever she was about to say.

But I already know. Because I've started to memorize every little thing about her —including her quirks.

"I'll lay with you," I say, stroking her hair. "I won't go anywhere."

25

TEYSHA

I'm like a new woman come morning. The fever I was running has broken, and my stomach's as settled as it can be after spewing up its contents. I open my groggy eyes to Logan asleep at my side, our legs intertwined. The sight makes my heart thrum an extra beat.

For a few seconds, I don't move at all, savoring the moment. How peaceful and at ease he looks, his muscled chest rising and falling with every breath. His expression's vacant, like he's entrenched in faraway dreams. His features look no less strong—his nose a large, straight slope, his chin prominent and defined, but it's his mouth I'm stuck on. Lips that are soft and commanding, wielding the power to make my head spin. That feel so good on me, it's unreal.

I stretch out my hand and touch his cheek like he's done to me so many times.

Even now, it's crazy to think how much my life has changed in such a short period of time. This man lying beside me is my husband, who I've made a union with under the eyes of God, and who I've come to care about.

Just the feel of his warm flesh reminds me I'm safe. I've

found the person I've spent my lifetime wondering if I ever would.

It happened under dark and disturbing circumstances I never imagined possible, but sometimes life is a contradiction in that way. Sometimes, the most beautiful bond can emerge from the ugliest trauma.

Logan might not see it yet, but I do. He's fought it every step of the way, but on some level, he senses the truth. We're meant to be together.

His breaths deepen. His head jerks to the side, his steely blue eyes opening at once. I don't shy away from smiling good morning at him, my hand still resting on his cheek.

"Sleep well?"

He blinks a couple times, coming out of his sleepy state. Then rasps out, "I should be asking you that question. Feel better?"

"I do. Thanks for being there."

He grabs hold of my hand that's on his cheek, tucking it inside his own. "It never should've happened in the first place."

"I didn't choose—"

"What I mean is," he chimes in, cutting me off, "I never should've let you leave. What happened—what *almost* happened—it's all on me."

"I don't blame you."

"That's the problem. You're too good. Too damn pure-hearted, baby."

A pleasant warmth spreads over me at his rasp, his words. It's like being wrapped up in a blanket of love and comfort, even if he's unaware the effect he has on me. I soften against him, scooting closer, wanting to be as close as someone can be to another human being.

For a while we lay silent and still, both aware it's the

final moment we'll have for a while. The entire day's ahead of us, and we've got to make our journey back to Pulsboro.

Logan strokes his thumb over each small swell of my knuckles as if he's counting them up. He's really in deep thought. Probably thinking the same thing I am.

This feels nice. It feels safe lying together like this.

Intimate.

We've often shared in these moments at the apartment. Late nights and slow mornings.

Something tells me Logan secretly treasures them as much as I do.

He finally brings my knuckles to his lips for a kiss of the back of my hand. His last second indulging in the quiet moment before moving on. He gets up to check the time and use the bathroom.

I do the same, sitting up, realizing I'm still in his shirt. He'd offered it to me to sleep in. *After* I'd shed my dress during my vomiting marathon. I've changed back into my dress when the toilet whooshes and he emerges from the bathroom.

"Where's Ozzie?"

"You don't remember much from last night, do you?"

"Sort of happens when you're running a fever and about to cough up your insides."

"He's in the adjoining room."

Logan walks over to the door linking our room with Ozzie's and pounds a fist to it. Ozzie's answer sounds garbled through the door.

"I'm up! I'm up!"

"Meet us downstairs in five," Logan says.

We grab food from the diner like Logan promised last night. We're heading out to where the bikes are parked when it occurs to me how we'll be getting home.

It should've been obvious considering I rode on the back of one to get to the Lone Star Motel.

But I'd been so out of it, I hadn't given the ride much thought. I'd clung to Logan like I'd turned into a backpack strapped to him.

I slow up as we reach the polished blood-red paint job and chrome that sparkles under the morning sun. Logan kneels beside the saddlebag, placing our few belongings inside. He juts his chin up at me.

"You good?"

"Your bike," I say, swallowing. "It's how we're getting home?"

"We're damn sure not walking."

Ozzie's already mounted his bike, a chrome beast just as big as Logan's. "Teysha, tell me you're not about to yak again."

"How did you know?"

"I heard you through the motel room wall." Ozzie winks at me, grinning as he squeezes his handlebars and revs his engine. "Glad you're feeling better, by the way."

"Here," Logan says, standing up. He drops a helmet over my head, then checks that it's secure enough. "That feel okay?"

"Yes... but..."

"Baby, it's the only way we've got to get home. You'll be safe, alright?"

Hesitantly, I nod. The helmet feels heavy and large, my neck aching. "Alright. But please don't go too fast."

"Move with me and hold on tight. I'll handle the rest. We'll be there in no time."

Logan does that thing again, where he squeezes the skin on my arm in affection. It's become yet another gesture of comfort. The unease pooled inside me recedes even if only slightly. I climb aboard behind Logan, feeling strangely small on such a large, rumbling bike.

He glances over his shoulder at me one last time before we take off. I understand the silent question he's asking and tighten my arms around his stomach, confirming I'm ready.

We're speeding off within the next few seconds. Ozzie goes first, turning out of the parking lot of the Lone Star Motel and the nearby diner. Logan comes up the rear, his bike like thunder as it crashes onto the open roads.

I focus on my breathing. Each breath in and out at a steady pace. My rapid heartbeat gradually slows, returning to normal.

The warm morning air blows past us, surprisingly refreshing on the parts of my skin that are exposed.

We remain behind Ozzie, a wide berth between his bike and ours. Logan's measured in every move he makes, demonstrating what a skilled rider he is. I've placed my hands on his chest, the muscled wall its own form of comfort. He's firm and invincible.

He's showing me there's nothing to worry about.

I relax into the ride. The scenery whizzes by. Along the way, we encounter other trucks and cars. We heat up under the blaze of the summer sun and rising temperatures.

Natural instincts take over my body. I learn exactly what Logan meant by move with him. My body leans in tune with his, my thighs secure astride the back of the bike. Eventually, I'm comfortable enough to let my hands slip to his waist.

I let myself glance at the brown landscape we're crossing over. The faraway towns we're passing by. The patches of dead grass and wildflowers and deep valleys that lead out of sight. I'm inundated with the sensory details like the sticky air and the vibration the bike gives.

I'm enjoying the moment for what it is. A couple hours on the back of a Steel King's bike.

The helmet I'm wearing serves as a disguise for the bright smile that comes to my face.

I wouldn't mind going on more rides like this. Just the two of us.

Before I know it, the 'Welcome to Pulsboro' sign pops up on the shoulder of the road.

We're home.

Ozzie parts ways with us, turning down a different street to head to the trailer park where I'm told he lives.

I feel dizzy by the time my feet touch solid ground. Logan turns to wrench off my helmet, grinning as soon as our gazes link up.

"All good?"

I smirk myself. "All good."

"What would your mama and grandmama have to say? If they could see you now, what would they think? Riding on the back of a dangerous biker's motorcycle?"

He's teasing me. I giggle as he scoops my hand in his, and we walk up the steps to the apartment. I can't even pretend Mama and Grandma Renae wouldn't be mortified. They'd probably pass out. Mama would probably wind up in tears, crying about how she raised her daughter better than to do these kinds of things.

But I've been coming to the conclusion that not everything I was taught was right.

Not for me.

Growing up, I learned from an early age I was supposed to follow what Mama and Papa told me to do. I read the Bible every day and behaved myself at all times. I crossed my t's and dotted my i's. I did all the things they said a good girl—*an honorable Christian woman*—should do.

And, in the end, I discovered none of it mattered. I was punished anyway.

I was taken because of it.

One evening, I found myself kidnapped. Tied up in the back of a truck, transported to some place where I was made to do vile things that almost destroyed me.

But I've survived. I've made it out alive, and I've fallen for the man that helped me through the darkest time of my life.

He's showing me how to live. Day by day. Moment to moment.

He's shown me there's a whole world to explore. Other ways of life to experience. All of it I'm doing by his side.

I squeeze his hand, laughter threaded in my tone. "If my mama saw me on the back of your bike, Logan Cutler, I think she'd melt into a puddle of tears."

"Yeah? And you don't care?"

"I don't give a damn."

It's his turn to laugh as we step through the door. "Fuck, it's so sexy when you swear."

"Then maybe you should join me in the shower. Maybe you can fuck me."

His thick brows raise in immediate interest. His expression goes slack, like he's so thrown by my suggestion it'll take him a second to catch up.

Five minutes later, we make it a reality.

I'm pressed up against the tile wall as Logan claims my mouth. His hands grope my breasts and hips and thighs. He fondles my pussy—a word he forces out of me as he bites my lip and orders me to tell him what he's doing to me.

I shudder, so delirious from the pleasure thrumming through me that it's a challenge. Basic speech feels like an accomplishment.

"My p-pussy," I stammer out with another shudder. "Oh, please... touch it some more..."

"Touch what, baby?" he growls.

"My pussy!" I squeak, and he laughs, rubbing me some more. "Yes, touch my pussy. Fuck my pussy. I want to feel you."

"Yeah?"

"Mhmmm."

He slips his fingers inside me, pumping them in and out. He sucks on my neck, his large body like a wall that keeps me trapped against the bathroom tiles. The shower sprays hot water on us, wetting my already slippery pussy.

I find his heavy erection and begin returning the favor. My hand feels small in comparison, wrapped around his veiny, velvety girth.

We come almost at the same time, with Logan's fingers deep inside me and mine encircled around him. He makes no attempt to free me, keeping me pinned against the shower tiles, smashing his lips to mine in another heated kiss.

"You are so god damn sexy."

"Even with my shower cap on?"

"Especially with your fucking shower cap on. Sexiest fucking shower cap I've ever seen," he grunts, teasing me like only he can. He can barely keep from grinning as he nips at my neck, and I giggle.

It's one of many showers.

A new ritual of ours, we make lengthy, X-rated showers a thing more often than not. We mark a lot of other places in the apartment as X-rated too—Logan's insatiable appetite becomes a regular occurrence where sometimes he must have me then and there.

Against the kitchen counter. Bent over the living room

sofa. In the hallway on our way to the bedroom. Once on the balcony late at night when we're certain everybody's asleep.

The intensity of his desires is startling at first.

I've never been in a relationship that's sexual before. The few guys I've dated have never gotten more than a handhold and a few kisses out of me. I'm not prepared for what the libido of a healthy, testosterone-riddled adult male entails.

But I quickly discover I love it. My appetite for him is equally as insatiable.

I learn all the different ways to feel pleasure. My body awakens to the many good feelings Logan can draw out of me.

The pussy throbbing. Heart pounding. Deep shudders and curled toes.

I'm a tingling, dripping, writhing mess whenever he's through with me.

I'm speechless the first time he buries his head between my thighs and his mouth does things to my pussy I've only ever read about.

"My fucking gorgeous wife and her gorgeous fucking pussy. I want a taste."

I can only moan for the next few minutes to come. His warm tongue traces every fold, every inch of flesh. It pushes into me and makes me arch against his face. My thighs squeeze together, instinctively trying to trap him where he is, where he's bringing me a level of pleasure that feels unreal.

He responds by nibbling on the inside of my thighs. His beard's rough and coarse on the sensitive skin. His breath so heavy and ragged, it's yet another way he's driving me closer to the edge.

I fall apart like I've got no bones. My body goes limp, and I scream his name for the neighbors to hear. He comes up, his lips slick with evidence of me, and kisses me to silence. He thrusts his tongue into my mouth and then tells me how good I tasted.

A shiver racks through me at my scent on his breath. At the way he's made me feel so womanly and desired.

We settle into bed, already on the cusp of sleep. I'm feeling loose and lazy, the orgasm Logan's given me better than any sleeping pill. He pulls me closer, his arm slung over my hips, and brushes his lips to my brow.

"I might need to go away again."

Seven words that do the opposite of the orgasm—they jolt me all the way awake.

I tip my head up for a glance at him, my eyes going wide. Familiar worry churns in my stomach, queasy sensations I've hoped wouldn't return.

"Go away?" I choke out.

"We've got trouble brewing. Abraham's still out there."

"But maybe you can just... leave him out there. So long as he stays away."

"It's more complicated than that, baby. We know he's got ties to the Barreras."

"The men who had me at Zapote?"

Logan nods, squeezing my fleshy hip. "They were selling you to him."

"*Selling* me!?"

"They're in the flesh trade. Almost all cartels are."

A feeling I can't place worms through me. Some kind of combination of disgust and terror. I process it for a second—or do my best to—and then murmur the only question that seems to make sense.

"Then does that mean I was... the first time?"

"It's possible," he answers. "It's possible that's what happened to the both of us."

"*Oh.*"

The word puffs out of me in a breath that makes my lungs feel like they're on the brink of collapse. I'm not sure why I've never thought more about why I was selected when I was. I haven't let myself think much on that evening where I'd wandered onto the parking lot of the Sunny Side Up like I'd done dozens of times before.

I'd wait a few minutes for Grandma Renae to drive by and pick me up.

Instead, somebody else altogether showed up. A white van crashed onto the scene and men jumped out to grab me. I couldn't fight them off. I could barely scream before I was being smacked hard enough to see stars and then dragged away.

The traumatic scene fades before my eyes with my next blink.

Logan squeezes me closer against him, sensing I'm upset. "It makes sense that's what Abraham and the Saints have been doing—they've got to get their people from somewhere. You remember that wine they used to make us drink?"

"That tasted funny..."

"It was spiked with something. Probably courtesy of the cartel too."

"It made it so hard to... to stay awake. So hard sometimes to... move." A ticklish sensation hits my throat, making swallowing difficult. "Sometimes I'd wake in Abraham's bed and... and... I couldn't do anything but lay there... as he..."

A sob cuts me off. I bury my face in him, my tears hot. Logan's muscles clench against me. Otherwise, he's gone still. He's peering up at the ceiling fan as it whirs around. The steely blue shade of his eyes has darkened.

He lets me grieve what's happened, taking however long I need.

Then he does something he's rarely done. He tells me what it was like for him.

"The same thing happened to me," he says, his tone lacking feeling, like he's forced it away. "The wine made it hard to think. I had to do much. When I did fight back, I paid the price for it. I refused to give in for a long time. Then... then eventually... I realized I had to. I had to do it. I did whatever Mandy wanted me to do to her. I did whatever Abraham told me to do to others."

"You were there for years. You did what you had to to survive," I sniffle. "I don't know how you lasted. I couldn't have."

"I almost didn't. More than once. Including the afternoon I escaped. I was about to end it... end my life. Then I saw the truck unattended and I went for it."

The blood chills in my veins. "I didn't know that."

He points at a scar on his throat, half obscured by the stubble that's grown in. "I tried to slit my throat."

"Logan," I croak, tears rushing to my eyes. "Why would you ever... why would you do that?!"

"'Cuz I was a fucking coward taking the easy way out," he answers, his dark expression reflecting his internal conflict. "I couldn't handle knowing I'd failed... that he was doing what he was and there was nothing I could do. So I was giving up."

I can't even speak. My voice has gone out to make way for the cry that bubbles out of me. Thinking back to that point in time, I'd never guessed what he was going through. I had no clue what he was about to do...

"I made a shiv from a hunk of wood I found. I sharpened it to a point. All I needed was a moment alone."

"You wouldn't speak to me," I whisper, vision blurred from tears. My throat's gone tight, my heart aching. "You wouldn't even look at me."

"I was ashamed," he admits, scrubbing a hand over his face. "I had failed you, Teysha. I promised you'd escape with me. I told you it was gonna be alright. But it wasn't alright. I couldn't protect you. And I couldn't compartmentalize anymore. I couldn't be there knowing what they were doing. Truth be told, I don't even fucking get why you're here. How you don't hate my guts."

Suddenly, it all makes sense. His detached behavior and hostile mood swings. He'd tried his best to push me away, not because he was disgusted and angry with me. But because he was disgusted and angry with himself. This entire time he's blamed himself for what happened.

I throw my arms around him and bury my face in his chest. The sob bursts free, trembling out of me as I spend a second reminding myself, he's real. He didn't go through with it. He's lying with me in bed and we've been given a second chance at life.

"I never," I murmur between breaths, "Logan, I never blamed you. Not once. You kept me going. Don't you see how you've saved me? Don't you know that you were my only comfort?"

"Shhh... don't work yourself up, baby." His palm glides along the swell of my hip as though he's not only reassuring me. He's doing the same for himself. "It's alright. I didn't tell you that to make you upset."

"But you need to know. You need to understand why I... why I..."

...*love you.*

I lose my voice a second time as the realization seizes me up. It brings even more tears, the gravity of it almost too much to comprehend.

"Don't cry, baby," he coos, holding me close. "I didn't do it. I couldn't. 'Cuz I've got to make sure he'll never come back. I've got to destroy him for good. That's why I might have to go away again."

My lungs twinge from the cries I've let out. "I wish there was another way."

"There is no other way. I've got to destroy him. Him and the rest of the Chosen Saints. I'll do anything to make it happen. Even if I don't make it out this time."

"But..." I pause to force a breath, trying to keep calm. "But... you have to make it out."

I don't know what I'd do if you didn't...

"The club will make sure you're taken care of," he says. "Mace knows. Silver too. Everybody will look after you. Or you can return to Boulder. Make a new life for yourself there."

"My life is with you. My future is with you. We'll survive it together."

The corner of his mouth twitches like he's endeared by my commitment. "I love that about you, you know that, right? Your hope. Your fucking never ending optimism. Even if it also drives me batshit sometimes that you are."

"Then you should be more like me. More optimistic."

He laughs, the sound rough and hoarse. "Maybe that's what you're for. Maybe that's why you've been brought into my life. To make a grouchy SOB like me a little bit less angry."

"You make me braver. You make me feel..."

Safe.

Seen.

Loved.

Logan lets me trail off. The silence does our work for us, communicating things we're not ready to voice aloud. My epiphany about my feelings and possibly his too.

I distract myself with his tattoos. The many shades of ink marring his skin and their different meanings. He's still studying the ceiling fan as it spins so fast it's a blur.

"You ever gonna go back to school?"

"Hmmm?"

"You were taking classes, weren't you?"

"Oh," I say softly. "Yes, before that happened."

"You should start them up again. Next semester."

"I don't know about that."

"It'll be good for you. You should finish your education. It's important."

I scrunch my nose at him. "You've never taken any classes."

"So? I'm a Steel King. We're not the studious type. But you... it'd be good. What were you majoring in anyway?"

"Don't laugh."

"Now I'll be sure to." He squeezes my hip in warning.

I curl into him, stretching my arm over his stomach. "Biblical studies."

"Why am I not surprised?" he laughs.

But it's not a mocking laugh. It's a laugh born of affection. It's a laugh that makes me laugh too.

"You know I read some of your Bible. While you were gone. I saw it on the nightstand, so I cracked it open."

"You did!?" I squeak, more excited than I probably should be.

"Yeah, a whole passage. It only made me think about you more. Which is the worst thing you can do when you're already missing somebody."

"You missed me?"

"What did you think would happen when you're so damn gorgeous and perfect and sleeping in my bed every night?"

"Then I should be here every night from here on out."

His eyes gleam as they meet mine. "After Abraham's gone. Then... maybe we can figure out a future for us."

It might sound uncertain, but coming from a brooding loner like Logan, it feels like confirmation of what I've sensed is happening. He's falling for me in the same way I've fallen for him; he's *already* fallen for me in that way.

He just won't let himself admit it and be happy 'til the threat's eliminated...

26

LOGAN

"Wanna go for a ride?" I ask.

It's late in the evening when I've come home to find Teysha in the kitchen. She's doing what she's often doing— she's whipping up some home-cooked meal so it'll be ready by the time I make it home.

Her cooking's some of the best I've ever had. It's damn sure better than what I used to scarf down before she came into my life. I survived on a diet of frozen pizzas and bologna sandwiches. The fanciest I ever got was whipping up some pasta. The box stuff you grab off the shelves at the store.

Compare that to Teysha's borderline chef-level dishes she puts together that feel straight out of some gourmet restaurant.

I'm grateful for the effort she makes. But it also makes me question if she feels like it's something she *has* to do for me. Second-guessing I've done plenty of times before.

Our relationship—*our entire marriage*—began off a forced encounter. Though she insists she wants me, sometimes it's difficult to wrap my head around the fact that she does. That she really wants to be with a man like me.

Some renegade who's devoted his life to bikes and lawlessness. Some guy who couldn't be less marriage material if he tried.

I shake these thoughts off as I enter the apartment and she beams at me from the stove.

"A ride?" she asks, stirring the pot that's on the burner in front of her. "What do you mean?"

"A ride around the area."

"On your bike?"

"Who else's?" I answer, grinning back at her. "Damn sure ain't letting you ride on Ozzie's. You're *my* old lady."

She blushes—her brown complexion makes it hard to tell, but I know the look. I can read it on her. Her skin's warming up, more golden and radiant if possible.

We head out with dinner still waiting in the kitchen. We'll only be gone an hour, and I argue it'll be better before a heavy meal.

Teysha's face lights up in surprise when she sees what's sitting on the backseat of my Super Glide. "You got me a helmet?"

"One fitted for you," I answer with a nod. "It won't be so heavy for your neck."

Teysha's a lot more comfortable the second time on my bike. I check on her before we set off to her eager squeeze of my midsection.

I don't take her far. Just a few miles outside of Pulsboro.

Our ride's not about going far or fast. It's about taking her out for some alone time between us. Something we get at the apartment, but she needs fresh air. She needs to get out more. Being cooped up in the apartment almost all day isn't good for her.

I've started encouraging her to be more involved at the club. The other old ladies, Sydney and Korine in particular, have happily taken her under their wing.

But I still worry about her. She's still not sleeping as well as she should. If I leave the room, she wakes in a panic.

Maybe if I weren't so fucked up myself, I'd know how to help her. I could do something other than what I'm doing, fixating on destroying Abraham and the Chosen Saints.

It's a situation of the blind leading the blind.

For a second time this evening, I force aside these destructive thoughts. These thoughts that have driven me to push Teysha away in the past. I divert my attention to the present.

As dusk hits, the sky explodes in hues of gold. The heat cools a couple degrees. Insects that go into hiding during daylight hours start coming alive again, buzzing and clicking their wings.

I pull off the road to a patch of land that hasn't been claimed in years. Maybe decades.

Teysha's glancing around with a curious knit of her brows as I grab her hand and lead her across the tall, uncut grass.

"What are we... *beer*?"

She comes to a halt even as I try to pull her along. She's spotted the beer cans lined up on the top of a wooden fence. I let go of her hand and lift up the hem of my V-neck shirt. A sharp gasp leaves her as she takes a step back.

"Logan, why are you showing me your gun?"

"You know I carry."

Her throat works in a slow swallow. "Yes... but... why are you..."

"I'm going to teach you how to shoot. You need to

learn," I explain, gesturing to the beer cans. "I want you to start carrying."

"Me? Carry a gun?!"

"Plenty of women do. It's for protection."

"Against what?"

The expression that curls onto her face is so perplexed, it's like she's questioning my sanity. I step toward her and cup her by the elbows.

"You know what," I say. "Against him. If anyone tries to take you and I'm not around."

"I couldn't ever shoot him... or anyone."

I hate that I believe her. I can peer into her wide, expressive eyes and see she couldn't bring herself to do something like that. It's not in her nature.

But I need her to be prepared. We don't know what Abraham has up his sleeve, including his alliance with the Barreras. I can't be around every minute of every hour. I'd rather she have the ability to do something should the worst case scenario arise...

"Listen to me, baby. You don't like violence. You don't believe in it. I get it. I respect it. Not everybody does. But when it comes to survival, sometimes you've got to protect yourself. Just let me teach you, alright?"

"It'll only be the beer cans?"

"Only the beer cans. Nobody's around for miles. I'll be here making sure nothing goes wrong."

We spend a few minutes going over the Glock 48 I've selected just for her. It fits her hands and she's able to grip it properly. I brief her about the different parts of the Glock and the basics of handling one.

Teysha's attentive, if not palpably nervous with the occasional shake she gives. But she tries... she presses on even as it's clear she's uncertain about the lesson. I stand behind her and guide her hands around the grip, making sure her trigger finger's positioned where it needs to be.

"Now, you want to line up the front sight in clear focus," I explain, my hands still covering hers. "You want your breathing to be steady. Take a breath, exhale, hold, shoot, then repeat. There's gonna be some recoil. Keep your elbows slightly loose, your wrists locked. Ready?"

"I... I think so."

"I'm right here," I rasp into her ear, so close I can smell flowers. I'd let it distract me if it were any other situation. Instead, I lower my hands from hers but remain where I am. Close enough for support if she needs it. "Go ahead. Make sure you're in position and your front sight is good. Make sure your breathing's steady. Make sure you're ready. Then pull the trigger."

Teysha replicates what I've advised... or does her best to.

The Glock 48 sits in the palm of her hands, her arms straight out, her posture tense. She lets out a soft breath, taking seconds in between. After the slight pause, she goes for it. She pulls the trigger, aiming for the line of beer cans.

None of them budge an inch.

Her shot's gone astray, the bullet whizzing into the distance.

"It's okay," I reassure right away. "It takes practice. That's what this evening's for. Let's correct some of your technique."

My hands fall to her hips to draw them back, then I reposition the Glock in her hands. It's sitting too high against her palm and needs to be more secure within her grip. I remind her about using her front sight before telling her to try again when she's ready.

"You got this, baby. Just remember to brace for the recoil."

Teysha shudders out another breath, gathering up more nerve, and then she pulls the trigger a second time. The bang rings out across the barren land, missing the beer cans by a couple inches.

"Better. That's all that matters. Improvement."

We work on it.

By her fifth shot, I've got her technique markedly better. I've got her wrist holding straight when the recoil kicks in, though her breathing still needs work. The bullet chinks the side of the farthest beer can, nudging it enough that it wobbles like a bowling pin.

"Good," I say. "That's good. Your aim is almost there. Let's see you do it again."

For the next hour, we practice shooting at the row of cans. The first time she hits one, her mouth drops open in shocked delight. She glances over her shoulder at me with twinkling eyes, like she's checking if I just saw what happened.

I can't help disguising my chuckle with a scrub of my jaw.

I'm not sure how it's possible this woman found a way to be even more damn adorable than she already is, but she's done it. The first beer can with a bullet hole starts a pattern of others. After a couple more shots, half the beer cans are knocked off the ledge. They fall to the grass, shriveled up hunks of aluminum.

Teysha flings her arms around me as soon as we're done. Her body collides with mine and forces me half a step back as I catch her.

Our mouths lock in a kiss born of celebration. I hold her up as she clings to me, wrapping those silky, shapely legs of hers around my waist. We trade smiles in between small kisses, parting long enough to tease each other in the lead up to the next time our lips meet. Each time they do, the passion grows.

The heat rises as I suck on her bottom lip and she cards her fingers through my hair.

We're forgetting about our surroundings. The deserted field we're in slips away. The beer cans littering the dry grass are no more. Neither is the rest of the world as the sun fades and twilight scatters across the sky.

I grip her by the thighs, her ankles crisscrossed at my back, and I walk us toward the nearest pillar we have—the wooden fence we've used as a prop for the beer cans. I set her down on the top beam that happens to stop at my waist, just as our kisses pick up steam.

She's clutching at the tuft of hair on my nape, her soft lips so damn delicious against mine. I'm barely containing myself, wedged between her parted thighs. My hands begin wandering as soon as she's perched on the top beam.

Taking all the time in the world to enjoy her curves.

Her hips and thighs. Her breasts and stomach. Her ass as I palm the round shape of it, sliding my hand down the back of her denim jeans.

She gasps into my mouth at the feel of my rough touch. Our tongues tangle, our kisses fueled by passion.

There's no stopping once we get going. Once we're so damn turned on we've got to have each other right here and now.

I help slide Teysha's jean shorts down her legs and she pulls out my dick. We're like addicts fiending for another hit in the second leading up to it—the moment I slide myself inside her pussy and we both groan at how incredible it feels.

I'm surrounded by heat. Slicked in her juices. Clenched by walls that pulse and stretch to accommodate me.

"Damn, baby," I grunt, my hand on her tailbone. "Tell me you want it. Tell me how it feels."

"So good," she breathes, kissing my lips. "I'm so full, Logan. You're so big."

"I know, baby. But you can take it, can't you? You can handle it, right?"

Her brows knit as I draw back then slnk back In. She's closed her eyes, every emotion playing across her beautiful face in real time. I watch her closely, stroking into her, kissing her lips, cussing at how fucking good it is.

The moment runs away from us. We're enveloped by the pleasure.

The heat that burns through us. The tingling wave that strikes us down.

All the ways we make each other feel as our bodies lead us and we lose the air in our lungs.

We come so hard, we damn near see shooting stars in the sky. They twinkle before our eyes as I slip deep inside her pussy and she squeezes her thighs around my waist. Our lips crash together amid our heavy pants and we hold onto each other like we're the only thing keeping us grounded to the earth.

We're the only ones living in this intimate moment. No one else knows. No one else bore witness but us.

It's only the beginning to the rest of our night.

We return to the apartment more charged than when we started in the field. We rip off our clothes all over again, with me hoisting Teysha back up into my arms and her clawing at my chest.

In a flash, we're on the bed, bodies slick and limbs tangled. I'm kissing every patch of naked skin within reach, squeezing every curve I can. She writhes under me, so unbelievably sexy, moaning my name a thousand times as I make her come.

I make her whole body seize up, my cock buried deep and my fist in her hair.

Teysha learns yet again the possibilities are limitless—I can satisfy her in so many different ways. So long as we're together, I always will.

"Yes, baby, squeeze my cock," I growl, my thrusts hitting all new angles. We're folded up in another position, her legs thrown over my shoulders. "Squeeze that tight little pussy around my big cock."

Her cries of pleasure become a song that bounces off the walls. She tips her head back, her mouth agape as her orgasm washes over her. I come in close, silencing her cries with a hard kiss, stroking harder and faster as I'm right behind her.

Mine is even more satisfying knowing I've already pleasured her. I've earned my release, planting myself deep, groaning at the soft, hot pussy I spill into.

We're so damn drunk in the aftermath that we can't stop smiling. We can't keep our hands off each other as we lay tangled together, soaking up the post-orgasm high.

But only one thing's on my hazy mind—how unbelievably lucky I am in this moment.

It weighs on me how undeserving I still feel that Teysha wants this; she wants to be with me.

After everything that's happened and all that we've been through, she's chosen to be my wife. She's chosen me as her husband. It didn't start out that way, but what was once forced has become something else altogether.

It's grown into something that's real and deep.

Something I don't think I can ever let go of.

I stroke her cheek and she smiles at me—the most beautiful thing I've ever seen. The dark threads that are her hair spill across my pillowcase, her brown skin radiant and dewy from what we've just finished doing. The rest of her is wrapped up in my bedsheet, the cotton fabric molded to her curves.

This could be the rest of my life. Every morning and night like this, with this woman I don't deserve in my bed.

The question is, can I let myself experience something so good? Can I stop being the miserable, angry asshole long enough to give her what she needs?

"Logan," Teysha murmurs almost sleepily. Her eyes twinkle looking up at me. "Why are you staring like that?"

"Nothing," I answer. "Just thinking."

"About what?"

"The future."

The twinkle in her eye brightens even more. "Us?"

"Yeah. Us. I like the sound of that."

"Me too."

I lean forward and kiss her brow, stroking her cheek then pulling her closer. It's not long before we slip off to sleep and I'm left dreaming about the same things.

Us.

And our future together.

"We're on high alert," Silver says the next morning in the club office. He's called the rest of us higher ranking members in for a meeting. Folding his arms across his chest, he leans back against the edge of the desk, his expression solemn. "Last night, Tito saw some guys in a Camaro a block down from the saloon, watching us."

"Probably plotting their next move," Cash says.

Mace nods from where he stands beside his best friend. "The question is, what would that be?"

"Likely revenge, *hermano*," answers Tito. "They're out for blood."

"Ozzie and I did what we had to do," I say unapologetically. My scowl matches my tone. "They had Teysha, and they weren't gonna give her back."

"We understand why you did what you did, Ghost," says Silver. "You did what any of us would've done for one of our own. Let alone your wife. But we know what it means."

"Retaliation," pipes up Ozzie.

Silver releases a sigh, then stands up straighter. "That's right. We need to be prepared for anything they might pull."

"But I don't understand," Tito says, "why would they be working with the cult you were taken by, Ghost?"

I take my time providing an answer. I'm thinking on what I know about the cartel and the pieces of shit who took me and Teysha captive. After suffering at their hands for years, the reason doesn't even matter. Revenge is the only thing on the menu.

"Simple," I answer finally. "Money. The Barreras are in the flesh trade. The Chosen Saints needed flesh."

"The Barreras weren't in the area when you had your accident. It was Madrigal."

"Who says they're not one and the same? What do we know about Miguel Barrera and his background?"

My question leads to a beat of silence among the others. Mace and Cash exchange looks while Tito's brow creases in thought. Silver remains where he is, studying me under his dark gaze; the sunlight that pours in from the window makes his shock of whitish gray hair stand out even more than usual.

"We'll get to the bottom of it," he replies finally. "But 'til then, high alert."

"Then no use for the parties we're throwing. Not when we've got real shit going down," Mace says.

Cash raises a brow, his face relaxing in humor. "Your bachelor party? We're not letting you off that easily."

"Cash is right. We're getting you shitfaced by the end of the night. And remaining on high alert. We can multitask."

The others laugh at Ozzie's comment, even Mace. The moment changes from the severe edge it's held to something lighter, more like solidarity. We've established we'll fight the threat the Chosen Saints and the Barreras pose, and we'll come out on top like we always do.

We'll find a way to make it happen.

The meeting ends with us going our separate ways. Cash and Ozzie return to the Chop Shop. Silver announces he's got to go pick up his kids; it's his weekend for custody. Tito leaves a few steps behind him with a similar obligation —his missus demands he go to some family function with her.

The next thing I know, it's me and Mace on the barroom floor. For being brothers, the two of us haven't spent much time alone since I've returned. I stop him halfway across the bar, clamping my hand down on his shoulder.

"They had a point. You know that, right?"

"About what? The Barreras and Madrigal being connected to the Saints?"

The left side of my mouth cants upward. "About your bachelor party. We're throwing you one."

"We never threw you one."

"That's 'cuz I got married under different circumstances. But you... we're gonna make that night a damn good night."

"How? Invite the Tits on Heels? I've got Syd for that."

I rasp out a laugh. "You're really in love, ain't you?"

"Why're you asking?"

"'Cuz I know my baby brother. And he's fucked his share of club girls."

"So have you."

"Point is," I go on, "you're committed. You've got eyes for nobody else."

"You don't see how the same applies, do you?"

I'd be lying if I said a flicker of shock doesn't strike me. My own words easily being used against me. I scrub my hand to my jaw, the realization trickling in. Every accusation—as joking as I was—applies to myself.

No other woman holds my attention like Teysha does. No other woman's on my mind.

I can't even imagine anybody else. There's nobody else that comes close.

Mace's grin spreads slowly. His laugh sounds like mine only seconds ago. "It's a mindfuck, right? When you first realize you've got 'em? Those things called feelings."

"I'm not... I don't... I ain't ever..."

"Yeah, yeah. I said the same thing. Look at me now. About to get married. And I want to." Mace throws a fist at my arm, the jab a brotherly tap more than anything. "It might as well be *our* bachelor party."

I don't get the chance to answer him. Natural light pours in by way of the saloon doors opening. We both glance over at the same time to find we've got company. Two of the dressiest people to ever enter our territory—a man and a woman in tailored slacks and crisp white shirts.

They walk through like they're aware of what they're getting themselves into.

They've been plotting this visit for a while.

The man's a couple inches under six feet with hair spiky and gelled. The woman's a dark brown complexion with huge sunglasses blocking her eyes from view. Both look like official business. More like they belong in some fucking office somewhere.

I jut my chin at them. "Can we help you?"

"Yes, we're here to collect some pertinent information," answers the woman. She flashes a badge at us. "Zoe Strauss. This is my partner, Eduardo Rodriguez. FBI."

27

TEYSHA

Sydney groans when she finds out what we have planned. Honestly, Korine's the brains behind the operation. Hope and I are more so her accomplices.

We're taking her on an all-day spa experience, and then we'll be doing wine-tasting at a local winery. All things Sydney will enjoy as one of her last days as a bachelorette.

She folds her arms on the Steel Saloon's bar counter and puts her head down. "I should've known when you asked me to wait on you."

"Don't make things difficult," Korine says. "We're prepared to kidnap you."

"The trunk space in my Camry is surprisingly roomy. Pretty sure I've got some rope too." Hope winks at the rest of us.

"You hear this? Come willingly or we will snatch you up."

Sydney groans again at Korine's threat. "I said I didn't want a bachelorette party."

"It'll be fun! You'll have a good time."

"Don't be a spoil sport."

I stand by as the other two badger the bride-to-be. Things have been amazing between me and Logan lately, but I'm still stuck between smiling at their light teasing and sinking into my own thoughts about how I'll never experience moments like this. Though I'm married, I never got the chance to be a real bride-to-be, celebrating my oncoming nuptials.

Those things were taken from me.

Marriage proposals. Engagement announcements. Bachelorette parties. A real wedding.

The honeymoon.

None if it will ever be something I've experienced.

My marriage happened much more differently than most people. I didn't get a choice, and it was during the most traumatic period of my life. It was to a man who didn't even want to be married to me once we re-entered the real world...

My smile slips and I glance away from the other ladies and their animated chatter. An itch tickles my throat, a trapped sob trying to make its way out.

Not now. Please not right now.

This is Sydney's moment. Sydney's the one getting married. It's her time to shine.

I'm happy for her. I truly, truly am. She deserves to be celebrated, and I can't wait to be a part of her wedding to Mason.

But I can't pretend I'm not feeling jealous. Seeds of envy plant themselves inside me and begin growing despite how I try to squash them out. I need a moment to collect myself.

Jealousy is one of the most toxic feelings, and I won't allow myself to become *that* woman.

Sydney's my closest friend.

"Excuse me, ladies," I mumble. "I need to grab more White Oak from the back room. Mick says we want to stock up for the fellas and their party."

"Do you need help?" Korine asks. "The bottles are heavy."

"That's alright. I'm just going to grab two."

I leave them staring after me as I cut out from the barroom. The second I'm out of sight, out of earshot, a stifled breath finally finds freedom. I've been holding it in, doing my best to present as excited and upbeat.

A moment alone allows for the truth to spill out.

I make my way to the stockroom only to find the White Oak's gone. The other bottles must be in the basement. In need of an excuse to use the next few minutes to collect myself, I head down the hall where the door is that leads down into the basement.

It doesn't matter that I never got to have the same experiences as Sydney.

Everyone's journey is different. Mine has been dark and painful, but that doesn't make it any less beautiful. Things have begun to take shape, and I'm proud of being able to survive what I've gone through. I'm cautiously optimistic about the fact that my husband is more open now than ever to giving our marriage a real chance.

I can celebrate tonight without focusing on what I don't have. It won't do anything to change the past.

I'm in the middle of talking sense to myself, making it down the stairs that descend into the basement. My hand stretches out for the light switch at the bottom. The space is cool and dank even in the thick of summer, and shadows cloak every inch of the room.

The light flickers on, weak and dim.

My eyebrows jerk together. The draft in the air invades my lungs, making it hard to breathe again.

I'm not alone.

Chained to a chair on the opposite side of the room is none other than Mandy. She's withered and grimy, in torn clothes that hang off her emaciated frame. Her limp fiery red hair drapes her face in thin sheets. She glances up at me with sunken eyes and a snarl of her lip.

"Well, if it isn't my little sweetheart. I didn't expect to see you down here. You've missed me?"

A startled breath bursts out of me as I falter to a stop where I am. I had forgotten what Mick had warned me about—the Kings have been using the basement as an interrogation cell for the Chosen Saints they've captured. It started out with Xavier before he died. Mandy's their latest prisoner.

My heart skips inside my chest, the range of complicated emotions playing from the top. Panic that threatens to take root. Shock that she's greeting me with affection. Unexpected anger that kindles to life. A slow burn that torches the other emotions down.

How dare she?!

"What is it, sweetheart?" she asks, adding a shrill cackle. "You mean you're not happy to see me?"

I'm not sure how to behave. I'm stiff as I step toward the collection of liquor in the corner. My legs feel more like wooden stilts than anything.

Get in. Get out. Don't even acknowledge her.

"I expected him, not you. My stallion boy. Did you know he's been coming down to see me?"

Her cackle fills the room some more, bouncing off the walls. I reach for the bottles of whiskey and notice how my hands shake. From anger? From more panic? I'm not sure.

But I don't think I've ever wished more ill on someone than I do Mandy in this moment.

For what she did to me. For what she did to *Logan*.

"He's pretty rough, my stallion boy. Did you know that?" she asks, her nasty smile widening. "Just the way I like it. But you were a favorite too, sweetheart. So pretty, so untouched. So easy for us to train. That's why the Leader called upon you so many times—"

"Stop it!" I scream. The bottle of whiskey I've grabbed onto slips out of my grasp and shatters onto the floor. I leap back as shards of glass scatter.

Bile rushes me all at once. The nausea an onslaught that doesn't care about time or place.

I scramble for the nearby sink basin and spill my stomach contents inside it.

Mandy laughs. She convulses against her bindings in the chair as her witchy cackle rings out.

I'm stuck retching, my head in the sink, eyes watery and throat sore.

"Teysha? My god, what's going on down here?"

Mick hobbles down the last of the basement stairs and hurries over to help me. He snatches a towel off a shelf and hands it over to me, his hand gentle on my back.

"Let's get you upstairs. Why'd you come down here? I can get the White Oak myself, darling." He slides his arm around me to guide me toward the staircase, throwing a dirty look in Mandy's direction. "I heard the bottle shatter and came rushing down. The girls said you'd gone to the stockroom."

"I couldn't find..." I trail off, the queasy feeling going nowhere. "Please don't tell anyone."

"But—"

"I don't want to worry anyone."

Mick's bushy white brows crease, but he gives a nod. "Alright, head on upstairs. I'll handle this mess."

Korine asks me several times if I'm okay and still up for Sydney's bachelorette party. With my earlier bout of nausea gone, I reassure her that I am.

The spa we're taking Sydney to is an hour outside of Pulsboro. We arrive in two separate vehicles. Korine drives the first while Bush's wife, Lesley, drives the second. For the duration of the afternoon, we're stripped down to comfy robes while we indulge in various spa treatments like facials and massages.

The spa offers unlimited drinks and a delicious food selection like fruit platters, cheeses, pasta salads, and even a chocolate fondue. After her first glass of champagne, Sydney stops complaining. She embraces the idea that today is her day and she's the bride-to-be being pampered and celebrated.

It's impossible not to feel at ease at the spa.

The sensitive reactions I'd been experiencing earlier feel ridiculous as I sit on a reclining lounge chair by the therapeutic whirlpool. It wouldn't be the first time I've had an emotional spell that seemingly came out of nowhere. A rush of hormones that I can't control, spilling out of me like water from a faucet.

I'm not sure what could be the cause other than the trauma I've suffered. The difficulty I've had adjusting to life afterward.

But as I lay on the lounge chair and listen to the trickling water, I let out a slow breath and remind myself it's working out. I just have to believe it will.

My phone vibrates from the pocket of my robe. I smile realizing who it's from.

> How's it going, baby? Mick told me u got sick...

I shouldn't even be surprised he would. Mick was worried and he's aware Logan expects to be told anything important about me. He must be with the rest of the guys who are getting ready to celebrate Mason for the night. Yet he's texting me. He's thinking about me.

Warmth spreads in my belly. I quickly respond.

> I'm feeling better. Thanks for thinking about me. :)

His reply comes not even five seconds after.

> Always. Behave urself.

I pocket my phone still smiling. Still with the warmth glowing inside me.

"The hubby checking in on you?" Sydney asks,

wandering over. She's sporting the same soft lavender robe I am, her face painted in a minty green mask.

"He is. Just making sure I'm okay. I was a little sick earlier."

"I heard. Mick told me."

"Apparently Mick told everyone."

"Don't take it personally. Consider him something like the grandpa of the saloon. He looks out for all of us."

"I'm not. But I don't want anyone worrying about me when it's your day."

Sydney snorts, dropping into the lounge chair next to mine. "It's not my day, Tey. It's *our* day. I'm not about that the-bride-is-special nonsense. So what if I'm getting married? We're all celebrating each other. Not just me."

"How do you feel? Nervous?"

"About being a married woman?" Sydney lets out a small laugh. "Nervous would be an understatement. But... I can't wait. This past year with Mace has been the best of my life. I can't wait to live out the rest of them with him."

"I'm happy for you. Both of you."

"What about you and Logan? You're doing better, right?"

I nod, the warmth expanding, flushing onto my skin. "Much better."

"It's going to work out for all of us. Once the guys handle the latest threat, we'll be good."

"Has Mace told you much about it?"

"Not really. I'm head old lady, but club business is club business. I like not knowing too much anyway. The last time I got involved, I was buried alive."

"I don't blame you."

"But," she goes on, "I think Mace wants me to learn how to shoot. He heard about how Logan's teaching you. Maybe the next lady's night we have, you can show us what you've learned."

I can only laugh in response. I'm in no position to show off my firearm skills, but I take it as a compliment anyway.

Come evening, we end our time at the spa and move on to wine tasting. Half of the ladies are already tipsy from sipping on mimosas, belinis, and champagne throughout the day. I've barely had a drop. I'm used to whiskey the few times I have drank. Always with Logan in our apartment.

...except for the time at Zapote with the two men from the Barreras and the times with the Chosen Saints, which I don't count.

My first taste of wine disagrees with my stomach. It churns mere seconds after I've tasted some cabernet.

Hope gives me a sympathetic frown. "I'm not much of a cabernet fan either. It tastes like medicine to me. Try some pinot."

I know before even taking a sip the pinot noir won't be any better. From the moment it slides down my throat, my belly quakes. My hand claps over my mouth.

Korine notices as she's in the middle of sampling wine with some of the other ladies. She breaks away to check on me, concern etched on her face.

"I'm fine... really..." I mumble. "I'm just..."

"Nauseous?" Hope supplies. Then she glances at Korine.

"We should probably go. You should lie down."

"I don't want to ruin Sydney's party."

"Girl, stop it," Sydney says, moving closer. She's taken notice the way the others have. She sets down the wine glass she was sipping from. "You're more important than some wine-tasting event. We can go wine tasting any time. Time to go."

Any protests fall on deaf ears. The women pile into the cars we've driven over in. I'm in the backseat, my brow pressed into the glass window of the rear passenger seat. The constant motion of the ride does nothing to settle my stomach.

I distract myself by texting Logan. Unlike a few hours ago, he doesn't respond right away.

The bachelor party probably has him distracted.

We pull up outside the apartment I share with him. Korine parks against the curb. The ladies insist on helping me up to the second floor despite more of my protests. As we approach, we gradually slow down, then stop altogether.

The front door hangs open.

Someone has been here... and they wanted us to know they have.

28

LOGAN

FBI AGENTS ZOE STRAUSS AND EDUARDO RODRIGUEZ requested any information we had on the Chosen Saints. We met their request with hostile silence. We exchanged looks, communicating without words, then gave them an answer they wouldn't like.

"We don't talk to feds," Mace said.

Tepid humor flickered in Strauss's hazel eyes. "I expected that answer. However, I'm afraid if you decline to provide us the information now, we'll simply find workarounds to make you later. Cooperate with our investigation or be prepared to face the consequences."

"Is that a threat?" Mace snapped.

"Take it however you would like to take it, Mr. Cutler."

Mace's top lip curled. "You know my name."

"I believe in doing research before walking into hostile environments."

"Then you should know you'll never get anywhere here, so no use in asking."

"That brings us back to the workarounds we're prepared to utilize."

He took a step forward. "I'd like to see you try."

"Maybe we've gotten off on the wrong foot," interrupted her partner, Agent Rodriguez. He held up his hands as if it'd fix the tension circulating in the room. "We've come to your club because we're aware that you've become involved with the Chosen Saints. Our investigation into them is a nationwide endeavor. Texas is not the only location where they have been active."

"Cut the bullshit," I grunted. "You know it was me. I'm the connection."

Agent Strauss expelled a sigh that was condescending and exasperated all in one breath. She barely refrained from rolling her eyes as she said, "Yes, Mr. Cutler. We are aware you were in captivity at the hands of the Chosen Saints. However, we have reason to believe the cult has been targeting more than just you. Regardless, it would be in your best interest if you—"

"We're not interested," I said. "Now get the fuck out of our bar."

"Suit yourself. But be aware, should you interfere with our investigation in any way, you will be held criminally responsible. Rodriguez." She nodded at him, signaling it was time to go.

The male agent gave us a judgy look of his own—the kind of disappointed shake of his head you'd receive from a parent growing up when you got a bad grade. He turned to follow her out of the club.

As they walked out, Ozzie was wandering in. Over the past fifteen minutes he had been at the Chop Shop with Cash, he'd managed to get himself covered in grease and motor oil. That didn't stop him from grinning and eye-fucking Agent Strauss as they passed each other up.

"Hey, beautiful. What are you doing all dressed up in a biker bar?" he whistled.

She arched a brow at him. "Move out of my way."

Ozzie being Ozzie, *laughed*. "Kidding. I'm a taken man. You're not my type anyway."

"That goes for both of us. Good day."

The agents left as abruptly as they'd shown up. The hostile energy they'd brought with them remained.

Ozzie scratched his shaved, tattooed head and shot a clueless look over at us. "What was that all about?"

Fast forward a few hours later, I stop by the apartment to find it empty. No surprise considering Teysha and the girls have their bachelorette party today. Unlike Mace and the guys, they had turned the occasion into an all-day, all-night event. Spa during daylight hours. Wine tasting in the evening and into the night.

I had encouraged Teysha to go. Getting out and spending time with the other ladies in the club was good for her. But damn if I don't miss her when coming home to an empty apartment.

I toss my keys on the kitchen counter and then open the fridge. Out of habit, my hand reaches for the can of Texas Brew before I stop myself then go for the jug of sweet tea instead.

Teysha prefers it when I don't drink much during the day and she likes that I've stopped smoking altogether. I've started taking into consideration these kinda things. I've begun thinking about how to make her happy. I've slowly come to realize that much of what she wants is good for me.

An improvement to my life.

She makes me a better person. A better *man*.

Not 'cuz she's trying to change me. Not 'cuz she doesn't like who I am. For some reason I still can't figure out, she does.

But being with her, around her, does the trick. It makes me want to live up to being the husband she deserves.

I swallow a couple gulps of sweet tea, then drop to the couch. I've got a missed voice message from Mick that I listen to.

"Not to alarm you, Ghost, but the girls were just at the bar getting ready to head out to their bachelorette thingamajigger, and I thought you'd want to know Teysha was a little under the weather. I found her in the basement throwing up a bit. Mandy was down there cackling like a loon so that might have something to do with it. Anyhow, figured you'd want to know about it. See ya tonight for Mace's get-together."

My jaw hardened with tension before I tamped down on my urge to go rushing off. I could track Teysha and the ladies down and demand she come home to recover.

I come to my senses a split second later. Another sign I'm changing. *Growing.*

Instead, I breathe out a steadying breath and send her a text to let her know she's on my mind. Her quick response confirms I've made the right decision. She's fine. She's with the other ladies, enjoying their bachelorette activities.

The same way I'll be with Mace and the others in a couple hours. We're throwing a party at the saloon to celebrate one of his last nights as a single man. He's requested no Tits on Heels, but I overheard Ozzie and Tito plotting earlier. The club girls will be there and likely causing a scene like they always do.

I drift off on the couch. My eyes close when it's about half past two in the afternoon and they don't open 'til it's well after five. Jerking awake, it takes a few drowsy seconds to understand what's happened. I dozed off.

I've got a crick in my neck and sleep lines on my face. If Teysha were here, she'd have giggled at the sight.

I get up off the sofa and go splash water on my face in the bathroom to finish waking myself up. Thankfully, there's leftovers from last night—she made some kind of creamy chicken casserole that's got green bits of vegetables in it but tastes fucking amazing. Even better when I warm it up in the oven.

To think I survived as long as I did off frozen burritos. I survived as long as I did off the slop I'd been force fed at the Chosen Saints compound for years.

Gruel and flimsy slices of bologna and whatever cheese they had on hand. More than once that cheese had mold on it. As desperate as many of us were, our stomachs aching from hunger, we'd scraped it off and ate it anyway.

People don't think about the kind of things they'd do in the most inhumane situations.

I finish up the meal courtesy of Teysha with a head full of thoughts about her. How much I'd rather be spending a cozy night at home watching TV with her than about to head out to this bachelor party.

I take my truck to the saloon just as the festivities are underway. The music's already booming a block away, and the Tits on Heels are offering body shots out of their belly buttons. Bush and Mudd are four beers deep. Johnny Flanagan's as sour faced as ever, bitching and moaning at the bar counter to Mick, the only person patient enough to listen.

Mace is at a table with Cash and Silver, babysitting a bottle of beer that he's hardly touched.

"Look who finally shows up," Silver says.

I pull out a chair to crash down in. "You asshats are lucky I showed up at all."

Silver chuckles. "I told Mace the same thing. When you hit forty, you don't party like you used to."

"I seem to remember you and Tom would go all night," Cash says.

"That was years ago. Before the gray. Before the divorce."

"How's that working out?"

Silver busies himself with watching two club girls climb on top of a table to writhe to the hard rock music playing. "Better now. Not so good at first. The kids are adjusting."

"I meant you," Cash says. "How're you holding up?"

"You sure you want to talk about my divorce when Mace is getting married? It's his night."

Mace shrugs off the comment, finally drinking from his beer. He's been people-watching too, scanning the bar to take in the scene. "You know better than anyone, Silver, I don't give a fuck. I never needed some party to marry Syd."

"We really should be talking about Ghost."

The conversation swings in my direction. The others look over at me expectantly, like they're waiting on some sage words of wisdom or some shit. Some game changing piece of advice for Mace and Cash. I'm the only married man at the table.

My shoulders lift up in a half-interested shrug. "What the fuck do you expect me to say?"

"Tell us what you've learned." Cash smirks.

I think on it for a second, stroking my beard. I go with what first comes to mind. In a roundabout way, it's advice Mace gave that I've discovered firsthand to be true. "Make sure she understands she's wanted. That she's valued. Make her feel that way."

"Smart man," Silver adds. "Too bad Rachel and I stopped wanting each other."

More beers are passed around the table—Cash orders another coke instead—and, if possible, the music's dialed up even louder.

The party *really* kicks off.

The club girls dance on the bar counter. Different club members toss back shots and play rounds of poker. Cigarette and cigar smoke haze the air. A fight almost breaks out between Tate and Johnny Flanagan. Tate's got him by the front of his shirt before Silver gets in and talks him off the ledge like the fatherly figure he is for the club.

Ozzie shows up, announcing his arrival. "Who's ready to get this party crackin'?!"

Cash tries to hold off his laugh, but it winds up spilling out anyway. "Look around you, Oz. Everything's already in full swing."

"It ain't a party 'til DJ Ozzie Oz is in the house. What's this old school shit we've got playing? Time for something from the twenty-first century."

Mace and I share a he's incorrigible kind of shake of our heads, but neither of us expect anything different from Ozzie. He's the class clown of the MC for a reason.

A club girl wanders over to our table and yanks her top down to shake her titties. Her attention is solely on Mace, trying to draw his interest.

Ozzie slaps a hand to his back. "That's a nice rack."

"Syd's is better."

"Damn. Hear that, gents? The man is a goner. He can't be tempted."

"You heard him," Mace snaps at the club girl. "I'm not interested. Get going."

Her bottom lip pokes out in a pout 'til Mudd swaggers over from behind, now on his eighth or ninth beer. He throws an arm around her and says, "Don't worry, darling. One man's trash is another man's treasure. Come on over to our table. We'll have some fun."

Cash laughs as they wander off. "At least it's not Sandy. She would've burst into tears."

Mace is far from amused. "Don't mention that chick around me. She was more than enough trouble."

"Last I heard, she is with the Hellrazors now."

"Good riddance."

I check my phone, barely listening to the commotion around me. The loud music and stench of liquor and smoke in the air only make me miss Teysha more. It's fucking pathetic in a way, but I can't deny how I'm feeling. I'd much rather be home with her right now.

The bachelor party drags on for another few hours. By midnight, I'm throwing in the towel. A few others are as well. Cash, Silver, and Big Eddie are with me as we cross the parking lot. Silver and Big Eddie reminisce about the past, where they'd once partied 'til dawn.

Cash is yawning, talking about how he's got to check in on Korine's mother.

None of us are ready for the gunfire that breaks out.

It drowns out the music booming from the saloon and upends everything about the night.

The revenge we've been waiting for is finally underway.

29

LOGAN

By the time we're drawing our weapons, it's too late. The SUV that's opened fire on us speeds away, tires screeching in the night. I shoot at them anyway, chasing in their wake on foot. I keep up for the first block and a half before they outpace me.

None of my shots land, but I get a look at the license plate.

My heart thumps hard against my ribs, the air I husk out coming fast. For a wild half second, I consider pressing on, going after them. If not on foot, then by smashing the windows of the nearest car and hot-wiring it in hopes I'll catch them in time.

I shove a hand through my hair that's grown long up top and then turn back toward the saloon.

In my rush to go after the SUV and return fire, I hadn't grasped what else had happened. We'd all taken cover the instant they sprayed bullets in our direction. Silver had taken refuge by the bikes parked under the carport. Mace and I managed to duck behind my truck.

Cash wasn't so lucky.

I return to the lot in front of the Steel Saloon to the jarring sight of him on the ground. A pool of blood surrounds him.

Chills wash over me. I sprint toward him and the others, my pulse racing all over again.

"What the fuck happened!?"

"They got him. In the chest," Silver answers. He's kneeling beside a blanching Cash, pressing a torn piece of cloth to the wound.

"FUCK!" I roar, swinging my arms in the air.

"911's on their way," Mick says. He's come out of the saloon's front doors clutching his phone, as pale as Cash has become. Everybody else inside the saloon rushed out with him, everybody on guard, weapons drawn.

I look over at Mace, who's gone borderline catatonic at his best friend's side.

I'm not sure if he's about to break down from the prospect of losing him or go on a murderous rampage. Knowing my baby brother, probably both.

The moment becomes a whirlwind. Police and para-medics flood the scene within minutes.

Cash is transported to the local hospital. We're left to loiter in the waiting room while he goes into emergency surgery to remove the bullet lodged in his chest.

Mace won't stop pacing the area, swearing under his breath. I step up to the plate, trying to be the support he needs.

"He'll be alright," I say. "You heard the ER nurse. It didn't pierce any major organs. Once they remove it and he's out of surgery, he'll be in the green."

"It never should've happened in the first place!" Mace spits. Veins dilate in his neck, his fists clenched. He paces another leg around the room. "It's those fucking Saints! This shit's over! We fucking annihilate them. No mercy."

Silver rises from the waiting room chair he's been seated in. He grips Mace by the shoulder in the same vain effort to calm him down. "How about some fresh air?"

Mace shrugs him off. "Don't fucking touch me! This isn't a joke!"

"Nobody said it was. But what use is exploding in the middle of an ER waiting room?" Silver asks.

"You might be acting prez, Silv, but you damn sure ain't Tom."

I scrub a hand over my face and turn my back to the rising tensions. I can't think straight with so much racket, so much fucking chaos around me. Cash was shot but *I'm* the reason they were targeting the Steel Kings in the first place.

It was Abraham seeking revenge. Possibly the Barreras. Maybe both.

They're not gonna let up 'til one of us comes out on top. 'Til I crush every last one of them.

I step outside for the fresh air Silver had suggested. Pulling my phone out of my pocket, I discover I've got six missed calls and fifteen text messages.

Almost all from Teysha.

"Shit," I mutter under my breath.

Everything's happened so fast over the last twenty minutes there's hardly been time to process it all.

Teysha answers before the first ring's even over. "Logan," she gasps, "Logan, someone broke into the apartment!"

"*What*?!"

"The door was open and... and the place was trashed inside. Everything turned over. Furniture broken. Things ripped off the walls."

"Teysha, get the fuck out of there!" I yell, charging forward. "I'm coming to get you!"

"We left. We went to Korine's place... but Ozzie just called her. Cash was shot?"

My muscles ache, contracting tight. I close my eyes. "Yeah, he's in surgery."

"Korine's in hysterics. Her mother too. We're on our way."

I hang up to the rustling noise of Teysha and the others piling into the car. I'm halfway convinced they need to stay where they are and half certain they should be with us. But there's no telling them to stay put. Not when Cash has been shot.

"This is a fucking mess," I swear under my breath.

It's early morning by the time Cash is out of surgery. The ER nurse emerges from flapping doors to let us know he's in stable condition. Two of us are allowed to see him. Mace and Korine make the most sense. The rest of us hang back and breathe for the first time in what feels like hours.

Exhaustion sets in. We look around the room and come to the same silent conclusion—it's been a long fucking night and we're all spent.

Teysha and I head home in strained silence. She's nodding off in the passenger seat. I'm caught between the fatigue that weighs down my eyelids and the rage that's bubbling under the surface. How can I rest when the Chosen Saints have once again come after somebody I care about? How the hell can I take a breather when Abraham's still out there?

He trashed our apartment.

Our home.

Teysha could've come home earlier, and he could've been there. Then what?

What the fuck could've happened if she'd walked through the door and he and his followers had been around?

The disturbing thoughts make me grit my teeth. My grip on the wheel tightens and every breath I draw feels labored.

It's happening all over again. It's spiraling like it has before.

Everything's beyond my control.

No matter what I do, no matter how hard I try, it's never good enough. He persists. He remains an unstoppable force that'll do whatever it takes to crush me. Take everything from me. Hurt me.

Hurt Teysha.

I can see it coming. Predict where this is headed.

Abraham's playing a game. He's taunting me, letting me know he has easy access to my home whenever he wants it, and he can just as easily bring her harm again. He *will* if I'm foolish enough to give him the opportunity.

He'll do what he's always done. He'll take. He'll use and abuse.

I'm supposed to stop him. I'm supposed to be strong and capable enough to.

Yet here I am, fucking failing all over again.

I rush ahead of her on our way inside the apartment. There's a persistent throb in my skull, making it more difficult to think by the second. I've succumbed to the fury. The unhealthy blend of anger and anxiety that's got me feeling like a grenade about to explode.

The wreckage sprawls out in front of me. Teysha hadn't

done the destruction justice—just about everything I own has been shattered and smashed.

All of it destroyed as a clear and unmistakable message.

This is not over. Far from it.

My hands clamp shut into tight fists. I stride through the carnage on a fresh pulse of anger, vaguely aware Teysha's my shadow. Though she hasn't uttered a peep, I know she's worried about me. Her energy's almost as tangible as mine. She's afraid I'll do something dumb.

She's right.

Thinking rationally has never been my thing during fits of rage.

"You've got to return to Boulder," I grunt from over my shoulder. "It's the only place you'll be safe. You'll be far away from... this."

"But we agreed I'd—"

"I know what we agreed. Plans have changed. You've got to go."

"I want to stay here with—"

"You can't," I snap, my tone harsher than I normally use with her. I spin around, the same rage throbbing inside me now clenching up my face. "Don't you get it? This is bigger than you and me. Lives are at stake, and I've got to handle this."

"What are you going to do?"

"What do you think I'm going to do? I'm going to fucking kill him! I'm going to massacre him and everybody else around him! All of them will be in pieces in a fucking grave by the time I'm through!"

She flinches at the raise of my voice. "But can't we... earlier I heard Silver mention the FBI's involved. Maybe they can handle it?"

"You've got to be kidding me! You can't be serious!"

"If they handle it, you won't have to risk yourself," she says, her eyes large and expressive. *Imploring.* She takes a cautious step toward me. "If you just calm down—"

"You should want him fucking dead! You should want him to pay for what he did to you! What's the matter with you? You repeat these stupid fucking flowery words about forgiveness and healing, and you don't realize how weak and pathetic it sounds!" I rage at her, exploding at once. Heat floods me. My heart pounds in my ears. "Do you realize how pathetic it is that this piece of shit did what he did to you, and you still don't want him dead?!"

Her first couple tears roll free. "I can't... I can't wish that on him. Or anyone. It's not my place to—"

"YOU'RE WEAK!" I roar in her face. "You're fucking weak! And he knows it—and that's why he did what he did!"

Teysha flinches a second time, this time like I've struck her. I might as well have. My words are that cruel. That low, cutting deep.

As soon as they leave me, I see my reflection in her dark, glassy eyes. I see an angry, vicious man raging at her like she's a stand-in for the person I'm really pissed with. The person I'm really speaking to right now.

Myself.

I was weak. I was pathetic. I was unable to protect myself—and Teysha—and Abraham knew that. He used it to hurt us over and over again. He's still doing it today.

Right now.

I have to live the rest of my life with the knowledge that I've failed. It's part of who I am. The blood circulating in my veins. The very oxygen I breathe into my lungs. I can never rid myself of the truth. That I'm some shell of a man, too weak to put up a real fight.

The ire inside me surges all over again, so damn unbearable I can't stand it. I can't live like this. I let out a roar that thunders around the room. Fists clenched, I spin around, itching to destroy the first thing within reach.

Whatever's left in my apartment that hasn't already been destroyed by Abraham and his Saints.

I rush into the bathroom and smash my fist into the mirror. The damage webs out across the glass. My knuckles split open, dripping blood.

Teysha screams in horror.

"Get away from me," I grunt, my breaths ugly and ragged. "You need to leave. You need to get away from me 'cuz you're not safe here. GO!"

I return for a second strike at the cracked bathroom mirror. More blood pours down my clenched fist. More shards of glass crack.

"Logan, please stop!" Teysha cries. "You're hurting yourself. You're getting glass everywhere."

"LEAVE!"

"NO!"

I slam into the broken glass a third time, savoring the sharp sting. Shards of all sizes peel away from the mirror's frame. A satisfying sight.

...until I draw back and discover a piece sticking out of my hand.

Blood's everywhere.

My blood.

All over the counter. Splattered in the sink basin. Trickling down the inside of my forearm then dripping to the tiled floor.

I deserve it.

I go to pry the piece of glass from where it's lodged in my palm. The stabbing pain intensifies, forcing a grunt out of me. I can't get it out without risking slicing up my hand even more.

"Logan... please... let me see..." Teysha begs, her voice shaky. "Please... this is so much blood... please... Logan..."

She sounds on the verge of her own breakdown. I've driven her to it. Her tears and hoarse cries.

I blink, a woozy filter washing over me. Effects from losing so much blood so quickly. Leaning against the bathroom counter, I prick myself with other broken pieces of glass and growl at her to leave. For her to get the hell out and save herself.

Sweat clings to my brow. My hair's damp and limp.

I'm a fucking mess.

"Leave," I choke out.

"There is no fear in love. But perfect love drives out fear. Because fear has to do with punishment," Teysha warbles out the bible verse, sniffling. She cautiously steps over the shattered glass and reaches for me. Her hand's soft touching my blood-smeared arm.

I shrug her off at first, but she doesn't give up. Her fingertips slide across the throbbing veins in my forearm in a soothing motion. The touch is gentle and considerate, like she's aware she must go slow or else I'll explode again.

But not because she's scared of me—because she's scared *for* me.

I realize this as she links my uninjured hand with hers. I look over at her. Pity's nowhere to be found. Neither is judgment or disappointment.

Just concern. Just... *love.*

"Fuck," I mutter as it hits me what I've done. The rage has been like alcohol that's intoxicated me. Now I've sobered up and seen the situation for what it is. My eyes clench shut, and I hang my head back. "FUCK!"

"It's okay," she says softly. "It's going to be okay, Logan. We just need to... we need to take you to the ER."

I don't put up a fight. I let Teysha hold my uninjured hand and walk me to the truck parked outside. She slides behind the steering wheel, adjusting the seat for our height difference. I'm in the passenger seat, weighed down by exhaustion. Still clammy and bloody.

The adrenaline that surged through me minutes ago is long gone. It's left me depleted, feeling like the energy's been zapped out of me.

I rest my head against the headrest of the seat. "Thanks. For putting up with me."

"We took vows. This is as much my fight as it is yours."

"But... I... the things I said... I was lashing out. I didn't mean to hurt you."

She glances at me before setting the car in reverse, a glimmer in her beautiful, expressive brown eyes. "Sometimes when you love each other, you hurt each other. Even when you don't really mean to. But that doesn't make me love you any less. We don't quit on each other, Logan. Ever. That's what marriage means."

I fall silent at the gravity of the words she's used. Words that ring as true for me as they are for her.

Love.

***

I need nineteen stitches to patch up the damage I've done to my right hand. The ER docs give me painkillers and release me on my way when it's all said and done. Teysha waits for me like the patient, kind, loving woman she is. She doesn't scold me, doesn't rub it in, doesn't say, "I told you so."

More than anything, she's relieved I'm alright.

We visit Cash in his hospital room, checking in on him before we head home. For the rest of the morning we're like zombies. We call an emergency locksmith and clean up what we can around the apartment before we tap out. Exhaustion sets in as we curl up in bed and take the time to recover.

But as spent as my body is, my mind's a nonstop machine. It churns out thought after thought that keeps me awake late into the morning, even as Teysha slips off.

I've checked and rechecked the last-minute locks that have been replaced on the doors and windows. I've strained my ears to pick up on the slightest sound, hyperaware of the possibility that Abraham could be out there at any moment.

At any time, he could be watching us. He could be waiting for the opportunity.

My gun's in the drawer of my bedside table. I've got a hunting knife under my pillow. There's a baseball bat in the far corner of the room, by the door.

The afternoon sun bursts through the curtains a couple hours later like a lifeline. It chases away the remaining shadows and unknown that looms around us. I convince Teysha to spend the rest of the day with Sydney, and Korine, driving her over to Mace's house.

I've got business to handle.

At least if she's with Mace and the others, I can be assured Abraham won't come across her should he return to our apartment.

I slide on my shades and mount my Super Glide. The engine warms up with a thunderous rumble. The sleek body vibrates underneath me. My grip squeezes down on the throttle and I'm off in a cloud of dust.

I have the Pulsboro roads to myself.

Sunday afternoon, everybody's either still at church or at home doing chores or spending time with family.

I cut across town 'til I'm on the highway.

The warm air runs through my hair. The sun beats down on me as it rises higher into the sky. There'll be no escaping its rays on a hot afternoon in July.

I ride the eighty-four miles outside Pulsboro 'til I'm coming up on Jefferson.

Sweat sticks my shirt to my back by the time I'm braking outside the Zapote bar. My leather boot crushes the gravel under me as I step off my bike and stride toward the entrance. There're a couple stragglers hanging around outside who look me up and down like they're on the verge of stepping in.

None of them do.

I shove open the doors to the dive bar, ready to accept what comes of this. I could be walking into another trap; I could live to regret returning to the place affiliated with my worst enemy.

But it's worth it, all things considered. If it means I'm closer to destroying Abraham, I'll do anything.

The hum of conversation drops off once everybody inside recognizes me. Members of the Barreras can only gape across the room then check for their leader's reaction. His is a lot more interesting.

Miguel Barrera quirks a brow, his lip curling. *"Mira lo que arrastró el gato. ¿A qué le debemos el honor?"*

30

LOGAN

"How about we talk?" I ask. "Man-to-man. Nobody else."

Miguel scratches under his chin, tilting his head back. His gaze never leaves mine, eyes darker than coal as he sizes me up. He's younger, inexperienced despite the show he puts on. Like Mace, he took over an organization prematurely. Before he ever thought he would.

A few beats of us glaring at each other, and I've got him figured out. His whole story unfolds in his behavior and body language.

He tips his head at the others, signaling for them to leave. The hulking guy on his left with the tear tattoo on his face is the only one who hangs back.

"Go ahead, *jefe*. I have this."

The guy takes his leader's command, but not before he warns me with a murderous look. He's made his intention clear—if I fuck with Miguel, he'll be coming for me.

I remain unfazed. I've got more important shit to focus on.

"Have a seat," Miguel says, gesturing to the chair opposite him. "Would you like some tequila?"

"Depends. Is it really tequila?"

His laugh is short and brittle. "If this is about the situation the last time you were here, I'm not sure what you're expecting. If you'd like an apology, maybe you're in the wrong place."

"An apology," I repeat. My large hand curls around the glass of tequila he's poured. "You mean for what you pulled with my wife?"

"I had no hand in your wife visiting our bar."

"Cut the shit. She told me what happened."

"I had no hand in the situation. If that's what you have come to discuss, then we are done here." He half rises out of his chair.

"That's not what I came to discuss," I grit out. "But let's get one thing straight. I don't like you. I don't like your group. Matter of fact, I might make it my mission after this is all said and done to come for you. It'd damn sure be deserved. Lucky for you, I've got bigger fish to fry. More important enemies to go after."

Miguel doesn't sit back down. His fingertips graze the tabletop as he leans closer. "Then what are you here for? *Rápido. Mi paciencia se está acabando.*"

"I've got a proposition for you. It'll be in your best interest to accept."

"And what is this proposition?"

"Cards on the table. We both know you haven't been open with us about your affiliations."

"I owe the Steel Kings no loyalty. Our arrangement was business only."

"Maybe. But you knew we'd never do business with you if we knew the truth. You didn't want us knowing who else you entertain." I fold my arms behind my head and lean back in my chair. "Can't say I blame you, all things considered. You're about your money and your standing. Fuck everybody else."

Miguel narrows his eyes. "Where is this going?"

"Sit down and find out," I urge. "I'm sure you're aware our business partnership is over. Trying to kidnap and then initiate my wife into your gang will do that. But I've got a final proposition for you that'll work in your favor."

Distrust encircles the air between us. Miguel scratches his chin as he thinks on what I've said. His poker face needs some work; I see straight through him. He's interested, even if he wants to play hard to get.

Fine with me. I can work with that.

Slowly, he lowers himself back into his seat across from me. Taking a sip from his glass of tequila, he says, "*Apresúrate. Dime.*"

"You know the whereabouts of the Chosen Saints," I say, then quickly add, "Don't tell me you don't. I already know you do. I already know you've been doing their bidding. Matter of fact, I'm pretty damn sure you've been the ones taking people captive then selling them off. That correct?"

Miguel's lips pull back for a dark smile. "We work for who pays us. You know our policy."

"That's a yes. Fair enough. Well, consider this your latest payment. Not monetary. Something more beneficial. *If* you give up their location."

"Our interest is money only—"

"You'll want this information," I interrupt. "Important info for your survival."

"How do I know this is real? How do I know I can trust this info?"

"You're just gonna have to take a chance. Just like I'm gonna have to take a chance you'll give me their accurate location."

He polishes off his tequila, then slams down his empty glass. *"Dime."*

"We had a visit by some federal agents not very long ago. Your name came up."

"Federal agents? FBI?" he repeats. His disdain flashes in and out of his expression before he can catch himself. "What did they say? What do they know?"

"Gimme the location of Abraham and the Chosen Saints, and I'll share."

Miguel bares his teeth at me. The disdain returns, filling out his features, except it's for me this time. He reaches for the bottle of tequila to pour himself another serving. The liquor trickles into the empty glass drop by drop as if it's its own timer.

"Alright," he says after the long pause, "that I can give you."

I emerge from Zapote an hour later with no blood or bullet holes in me, armed with more knowledge than when I came in. A successful mission as far as I'm concerned.

Miguel gave up the location of Abraham's latest hiding spot. He's been operating out of an abandoned church in *Boulder* of all places.

Which means he's been closer than any of us realized.

No wonder he's been able to pull off what he has. He's practically been hiding in plain sight.

I take a quick second to text Mace and the others about what I've discovered.

My Super Glide launches out of the Zapote parking lot. I hit the highway on my ride back, nothing but me and the miles ahead. Plenty of time to mull over what I want to do and where I want to go from here.

I could return to Pulsboro so we can begin plotting the next steps in our revenge against the Saints.

The other option would be to pursue the lead I've got on the spot. Go straight to Boulder and scope out the compound Abraham is operating out of.

The reckless, hotheaded side of me demands the latter. Every minute counts, and I'm done biding time. I'm done being on the defensive when I should be on offense. I should be making Abraham regret the day he took me captive. He should be groveling, sniveling, begging for fucking mercy as I deny him any decency.

The same way he'd done to me and others countless times. The same way he'd done to *Teysha*.

The longer I spend on the road steeped in vengeful thoughts, the more I'm certain what I want to do. A taste for violence has sprung up inside me, uncoiling like a venomous snake. I'm not sure I can spend another night without knowing what it feels like to rip him to shreds...

I'm halfway between Jefferson and Pulsboro when two SUVs speed up from behind. They close in on either side, flanking me left and right. The windows are tinted, concealing their identities from view, but I don't need to see any faces to know what's going on.

Flashbacks of the last time this happened to me filter in and out.

I'd been on the highway riding after the Road Rebels. Our motorcycle clubs had been engaging in a vicious war. My father had sent me as the lead on a mission to retaliate, and I was prepared to stop at nothing to make him proud.

It only took seconds to be run off the road. As my bike spiraled out of my control, I ran right off a nearby cliff. My world blacked out after that.

When I woke up, I was in chains. A *captive* of Abraham and the Saints.

As these SUVs close in now, I clench the handles of my bike and bolt forward. I shoot out ahead of them in a burst of speed. They barrel after me, refusing to give up anytime soon.

That's alright.

We can do things the hard way.

I make them work for it. My expertise comes in handy. I'm skillful, keeping ahead of them, dodging their attempts to box me in. They charge toward me, about to rear end the back of my bike. I swerve left to keep them guessing, then slide across the road to force their hand.

SUVs don't move as deftly as bikes do. They zig and zag, tires squealing, rubber burning.

The one on the right loses control of the wheel and jerks into a wild spin. They don't regain it in time to avoid veering off road, where they crash into wooden fencing.

I toss a look over my shoulder to spot the rubble behind me.

And the other SUV that's still riding my ass.

I can handle one. If I can shake off the first vehicle, I can damn sure make quick work of the second.

Turning back around to reset my gaze on the road, my heart punches against my chest. I slam down on the brakes, but it's already too late.

A third SUV has crashed onto the scene and blocked off the road ahead.

The inevitable finally catches up to me.

Braking means the SUV closes in enough to force my

hand. Their front bumper plows into the back of my bike, and it's over.

My body's ripped from the safety of my Super Glide, sailing through the air, landing in a bone-crushing tumble on the road.

31

TEYSHA

I'M SEATED ON THE CLOSED LID OF THE TOILET WITH my face in my hands. I've come off another spell of nausea that had me throwing up acid because there was nothing else in my stomach. How could there be when I can't keep anything down?

Any time I've tried to eat, my belly roils. The smells alone make me nauseous. The texture of certain foods has the same effect.

A shaky breath puffs out of me as I sit up and wipe my eyes with the back of my hands.

Where do I even go from here? What do I even do now?

None of this was planned.

Yet here I am again, forced into a situation that feels like cruel irony.

Knuckles rap against the closed door. Sydney's voice follows. "Tey, you good? You've been in there a while."

"Oh... err... yes... I'm... just a second!" I scramble to my feet, flushing the toilet and rushing to the sink. I quickly pump soap into my hands and rinse them off. My gaze scans the length of the bathroom counter making sure I haven't left any evidence behind.

Everything's been disposed of, wrapped in tissues and tossed in the trash.

Sydney arches a brow at me when I snatch the door open and we come face to face. "You sure? You seem flustered."

"I was just... thinking."

"Thinking?"

"I do my best thinking on the toilet. TMI. But you're asking, so..."

I brush past her with warm cheeks and a warning quake in my belly. She pads after me, following down the hall of the house she shares with Mason.

There's no escaping her on her turf.

I wander into the den and park myself on the loveseat, hoping for a change of subject. Sydney being Sydney, refuses to drop the matter. I've ignited her sense of curiosity and once that's piqued, there's no slowing her down.

She collapses on the cushiony armchair, drawing her legs up to fold them like a pretzel. "I know what's bothering you."

"You do!?"

"Tey, give me some credit. I've known you for how long? I know all your tells."

"Like what?"

"The stammering. The rushing off. Avoiding eye contact."

"Well... you... I'm not... ugh!" I grumble in sudden frustration, words failing me.

Sydney laughs. "It's okay. I don't blame you."

"You... don't?"

"After everything that's been going on? Why would I?"

she asks, picking at a loose string she finds at the hem of her cutoff denim shorts. "You should know you can always come to me about these things."

A sigh eases out of my lungs. "Of course. Thanks for even having me."

"You're basically family."

"It's been difficult, and I'm trying to be strong. It's not just about me."

"I get it," she says. "I'm feeling the same way."

My brows knit closer. "You... are?"

"Why wouldn't I be? Everything's a mess. I spoke to Kori earlier. She's barely left Cash's side. He's doing better. The doctors say he should be released soon. But that doesn't change what's happened—the storm on the horizon. I'm sure it's a lot for you considering your situation."

I'm still lost as to whether she understands me as well as she believes she does. It could go either way. Sydney and I have known each other since we were kids. She was several years older than me, but her family attended the same church as mine. I was more involved, attending Bible Study, behaving myself every step of the way.

As we grew older, Sydney was living life. She was skipping classes and sneaking out for parties. We never hung out together 'til we started working at the Sunny Side Up years later.

After Sydney had gone off to university, then returned to help her sick father out.

In a lot of ways, she's always been the braver, more outspoken person I wondered if I could ever be. The version of myself that had real confidence.

But listening to her now, I'm not sure if we're on the same wavelength at all.

"My situation?"

"Yeah, with Logan. He and the guys are gearing up to take out the Saints."

"You think I'm worried about the MC going up against them?"

Sydney frowns, blinking slowly. "Aren't you?"

"Yes," I sputter. "Very worried. I just... I wasn't sure if you were talking about what I thought you were."

"I keep telling Mace maybe it's time we *do* involve the FBI. You know they're investigating too."

"Right, to prevent any more death. And danger."

Sydney gives a fervent nod. "You get it. Why should our guys put themselves in harm's way when the feds are already on it? But let Mace tell it, it's their score to settle. Fucking male egos."

I can only give off a nervous laugh. Mostly because it's confirmation we're of separate minds. In this moment, while I am worried about the same thing as Sydney, I'm preoccupied by other things too. I'm a wreck piecing together how to move forward. How I can even broach the subject and what to do about it.

My heart aches at the thought it could mean the end of us. It could be a deal breaker for Logan...

"Have you heard from him?" Sydney asks. "Mace mentioned he had some stuff to get done. He didn't tell me what. I'm not even sure if he knew."

I shake my head in answer, too torn up on the inside to say much else.

Sydney suggests we head to the saloon for lunch and to check if Mick needs any help. In need of a distraction, I'm eager to go along with her. Since the shooting, security around the club has been turned up to the maximum degree.

Which is why it comes as no surprise that we enter to a

more crowded bar than usual. Unless there's a club meeting, most afternoons see few visitors. I'm at Sydney's side as we approach Mason and Silver in the middle of a conversation.

"He's supposed to be back now."

"You said he texted you?" Silver asks, his arms bulging out of the short sleeves of his t-shirt. "What did he have to say?"

"Boulder," Mason answers. "He said he's been in Boulder."

"That explains a lot. Including how he and his group have been keeping such a close eye."

"Who's in Boulder and who texted you?" Sydney asks nosily.

Mason gives his fiancée a look that would probably scare most people. But there's a flicker of knowing in his gaze too, as though he's fully aware there's no running Sydney off. She'd only stand her ground, and that's what he loves about her.

"Ghost," he says. "He texted me."

Nerves tickle my already sensitive insides. I inch half a step forward. "Logan texted you? He wouldn't tell me what he was up to today. Is he coming back?"

"This is why we don't tell you," Mason says. "It always leads to trouble. Old ladies aren't supposed to be involved in club business."

"Mace, this is hardly confidential," Silver points out. "Let Teysha know about what Logan said. It'll probably calm her fears."

Mason's jaw clenches, regarding me for a second. "Logan went to the Zapote bar to confront the Barreras. He got some info out of them. The Chosen Saints' where-abouts. Last he texted me, he said he was on his way back here. He said he'd brief us on specifics once he does."

I swallow down the gasp that almost slips out. But it doesn't change the fact that I'm shocked, stricken by a shiver that runs down my back. Taking in what I've heard, my thoughts race trying to piece everything together.

"Logan's on his way back. The Barreras told him where Abraham is," I repeat slowly. "Boulder."

The memory forms before my eyes. Fuzzy at first 'til it clears up and I feel like I've wandered into the past.

"You are my most special believer, sweetheart," he tells me. *"Better than all the rest. The most beautiful and loyal. So obedient."*

My skin crawls listening to him, though I keep my true feelings from showing on my face.

I busy myself instead with staring around the dining room, taking in the antiquated striped wallpaper and the portraits nailed to the wall. Many are generic art pieces of landscapes painted in watercolors. But there's one framed photograph in particular that stands out to me.

"Boulder," I blurt out. "The church in Boulder."

The Leader's lip quirks slightly. He sips from his goblet, then gives a nod. "That is right. It is a very special place. Tell me, Believer Teysha. How do you recognize it?"

I'm about to answer earnestly when I clamp my mouth shut. The less he and the rest of the Chosen Saints know about me, the better. They don't need to know that my family once attended that church before it closed down several years ago. They don't need any information that could lead them back to Mama, Papa and Grandma Renae...

I glance one last time at the photograph taken of the church, showcasing its gorgeous spire roof and large cross on the front. Then I put on a fake smile that feigns innocence.

"I've seen it in pictures before," I say. "It's a beautiful church."

When the present moment returns, the conversation has moved on. Sydney is asking Mason and Silver about what they plan on doing from here. Neither provides many specifics, citing what we already know. Old ladies aren't supposed to be involved in the inner workings of the club.

But I'm hardly listening. The trip down memory lane has set my teeth on edge. I'm breathing fast, a wave of dizziness passing over me.

Sydney notices first. "Hey, don't tell me you're feeling sick again."

I shake my head. "I just... I realized something. Something about Abraham."

Silver's brow furrows. "What is it?"

"I know where he is," I whisper. "Abraham. He told me about it. A long time ago when he..."

I can't bring myself to finish the sentence. As it turns out, Sydney's right. The sick sensation returns with a deep churn that makes me grateful I have nothing else to throw up. I breathe in to fight off the feeling and focus on the matter at hand.

"The old, abandoned church in Boulder," I say, meeting their gazes. "He had a photo of it. That must be where he's been all this time."

32

TEYSHA

"The abandoned church near the town park?" Sydney chokes out. "The one our families used to go to when we were young?"

I shake my head up and down. "He's kept a picture of it from its glory days. He said something about it being a special place."

"Then that's where he'll meet his end," Mason says. He redirects his attention to Silver. "We've got to make a move. There's no more time for planning."

"Call up the rest of the guys. We'll get it going."

Both men forget about Sydney and me as they start for the back office. I'm not willing to be brushed off so easily. Channeling my inner Sydney, I rush after them, throwing myself into their path.

"You're going to Boulder now?"

"Teysha, you and the others will be safe here," Silver says. "Bush and Mudd will be staying behind to—"

"What about Logan?" I interrupt. "Where is he?"

"He said he's on his way back. He's part of this mission. It's going to work itself out. We're going to end this."

Silver palms my shoulder for a reassuring squeeze, though anxiety has pitted in my stomach. I'm not sure if I can let it go. If I can shake the bad feeling that's sunk into me as heavy as stones. Something's missing. Something's off about this moment.

In the coming minutes, I have my answer why.

The saloon doors burst open. Ozzie and Hope spill through with wide-eyed expressions that make several Kings get up out of their seats. Most of them have caught word about what's going on in Boulder. They've split off in groups. Some staying at the saloon to protect our turf. Most about to ride off with Mason and Silver to face the Chosen Saints.

"You look like you've seen Casper the Ghost," Moses says from where he's perched in a stool at the bar counter.

Bush piggybacks off what he said. "Yeah, what in the hell's got you about to piss your pants?"

"You guys haven't heard?" Ozzie says, letting go of Hope's hand. He digs his phone out of his pocket to hold it up. "There's been some huge accident on highway 20. The wreckage was found. Parts of a Super Glide ripped in half."

"A Super Glide?!" Sydney blurts out.

"One that's identical to Ghost's. Look at the story the local news has put up. They've got pictures."

Mason makes it to Ozzie first, snatching his phone away for a look. "Shit. *Shit!*"

I'm frozen in place, ice-cold horror raining down on me. I can barely form a thought let alone speak, except to sputter out his name. "Logan?!"

"But here's the thing," Ozzie continues, "no body's been found. Apparently the bike was run off the road."

"The Saints," Mason grits out.

"Time to roll," Silver calls. "No time to waste. We've got to track them down before they disappear again."

The saloon descends into frenzied chaos. Everywhere around me, Steel Kings grab their gear and rush out to their bikes. Those staying behind start securing the club as if expecting an attack at any moment. Sydney and Mick begin doing what they can—cleaning up the half-drunk bottles of beer and pushing the tables and chairs out of the way.

And then there's me. Still frozen in place. Still trapped in a paralyzing iceberg of shock and horror.

No... not Logan... not again...

But it's a given this is what the war between him and Abraham would lead to. Abraham warned him the night the Steel Kings raided their compound and freed captives like me that he would make Logan regret what he'd done.

Abraham is power hungry. He's unafraid to harm anyone he must in order to stay on top. He wasn't going to go quietly.

The Chosen Saints were an entity bigger than any of us realized. He truly sees himself as God in the flesh. In his eyes, there's no escaping his wrath.

Logan made a mockery of him and everything he stands for when he shattered the illusion. Now Abraham's out to recreate his vision. He's out for blood.

There's only one thing that could stop him....

It's only as Mason and Silver stride past me on their way out that I snap out of my trance. Scrambling in their wake, I call both of their names.

"I need to come with you!"

"Teysha, get back inside the saloon," Mason barks.

"I know him better than any of you!"

"I said get back inside!"

"No! You need me to come with you!" I shout louder

than him. I'm panting, trying to keep up with their lengthy strides. My body's achy and my stomach still hasn't settled, but I press on. "I'm the only one who understands how to get him to give Logan back!"

Silver abruptly stops, almost causing me to run right into him. He attempts a different approach than Mason. Rather than outright refusal and throaty growls, he grips me by the shoulders and puts on a sympathetic frown. We might as well be a father lecturing his daughter.

"I understand this is difficult for you," he says. "But you have to go back inside. You have to let us handle it."

Around us, Steel Kings mount their bikes and rev their engines. The scene feels eerily violent even before the first drop of blood has splattered. Precursors to violence that unfold before my watery eyes. I shake my head and shrug off Silver's touch.

"I can talk some sense into him," I say, my tone breathless and desperate. "I can get him to stop all of this. He'll listen to me. I was his favorite."

"Go back inside."

It's their parting words as they carry on. I'm left behind as they swing their legs over the sides of their bikes and ride off in a long line of exhaust smoke and blinding chrome.

My breathing's spiraled into choppy, panicked air that gusts out of me. The moment feels surreal and nightmarish. Everything's beyond my control.

But what else is new? When have I ever been in the driver's seat? When have I ever had enough agency to decide what happens around me?

The sense of helplessness becomes so suffocating, I choke out a cry and dig fingers into my hair. My vision pans to the remnants the Steel Kings left behind. The empty lot still vibrates from the sheer magnitude of their thunderous bikes. Aftershocks of a man-made earthquake.

...except for the last King that remains behind.

Ozzie and Hope are standing beside a Toyota Camry, sharing in a goodbye kiss. I blink through tears as he promises he'll return soon, then hops on his bike to ride off after the others.

The desperation rising up inside me reaches its fill. Then it bursts free in a flurry of quick steps. I dash over to Hope like a mad woman, vaguely aware of how I must look.

"Teysha?" She frowns, noticing me last second. "What are you—"

"I need your car," I interrupt sharply. "I need to drive somewhere."

"But what are you—"

"Please!" I beg, my voice cracking. "It's life or death, Hope!"

Her frown deepens. "This isn't my car. It's my pa's. He made me promise not to let anybody else drive it."

"I need to get somewhere immediately. He'll never know!"

"The best I can offer is driving you there. Wherever there is..."

My face clenches as if I'm in deep pain—and in a way, I am. I'm tormented by the possibility that Logan could be lying broken and bleeding in Abraham's custody. He could be making him pay right now. I could be the only one who could give him what he wants.

I can make him stop.

"Fine!" I shriek. "Drive me then! Let's go!"

"Hang on, where would we be going?"

"Get in the car." I run over to the passenger side and

yank on the door handle. "If we leave now, we'll get there in no time. I know all the shortcuts. We need to make it to Boulder before it's too late."

33

LOGAN

I'm fucked up good.

I'm aware of it before even opening my eyes and fully regaining consciousness. My body's a single burning, throbbing pulse of pain. Up and down my sides. Burrowed deep from the inside of my chest. Even my skull.

My brain's definitely been knocked around. Rattled like a fucking saltshaker.

Probably a concussion.

It's a hard-earned victory just to open my eyes. If possible, my eye sockets hurt too. They ache and pulsate like they're being stretched past their limits.

It's no wonder—everything surrounding me is a blur of indistinguishable shapes and colors. I shift my body from its twisted position only for a fresh jolt of pain to shoot through me. A hoarse groan creaks from my throat as I let the pain do what it's supposed to do.

Fuck me up. Torture me. Make life hell.

The pain percolates through me like a stream down a river. It ebbs and flows at different strengths and speeds. I'm along for the ride.

What else is there to do but welcome it?

I focus on other things. Details about my surroundings like the weak floorboard beneath me and the smell of dust in the air. Light bleeds in through stained glass windows, tints of sapphire blue, golden orange, and emerald green.

Where the fuck would I be with stained glass?

The last thing I remember is being thrown from my Super Glide, colliding with the gravel on the open road.

Silence meets any question turning over inside my head. An eerie silence that feels foreboding and grim. I might as well be in a fucking graveyard.

...I'm in a church... or chapel of some kind...

I flatten my hands on the floorboard and push myself to sit up. My body screams in protest. The palms of my scraped up hands burn. The ribs on my left side creak like they've been snapped in half. I lift myself into a half upright position, using a podium that's behind me as a prop.

Just that little bit of movement has me panting from exertion.

I'm a bloody, mangled mess.

"Excellent. You're awake."

The voice, cool and aloof, slithers out of the silence like an invisible snake. The man it belongs to emerges from the shadows a second after. Abraham is still the same pallid, icy-eyed man with sheets of white-blond hair that lay flat and lifeless.

But instead of the luxury robes he'd once worn, he's in tattered threads. An old set of robes that're torn and mucked up with mud and dirt.

He's not clean and god-like as he'd once presented himself.

That illusion has melted away for a reality that's less flattering.

I might be lying broken and bruised, but one thing I'll never be again is deferential. Not to a piece of fucking shit like Abraham *or* his Chosen Saints.

"Finally showing your ugly face," I spit out. "You alone or you got minions like the fucking coward you are?"

Abraham starts toward me, a limp in his step. Probably from where I shot him the last time we squared off. His expression's emotionless and calm, a blank slate offering nothing.

Just indifference and loathing.

"Tell me, Believer Logan, how is it possible you're lying on my floor bleeding out, yet still so rebellious? Still so disobedient?"

"Why don't you tell me how you're still a sack of shit first?"

His thin lips stretch into a wry smile. "You really have not learned your lesson. It seems we will have to teach you. Saints, I am in need of your assistance!"

He's calling out to someone unseen. A second drums by before I learn who—two of his guards enter the worship room on cue, clutching rifles, looking as disheveled as Abraham. It's obvious their latest accommodations haven't been as luxurious as the previous compounds were.

The broad-shouldered, twenty-something chickenshit I recognize as Amos. The second guy I recognize too, though he wasn't a saint when I knew him.

"*Hershel*!?"

He ignores me, too locked into Abraham to pay me any mind.

It seems in the time since the Steel Kings raided the original compound and now, he's been promoted. He's gone from believer to saint.

I'd once thought of Hershel as a grandfatherly figure.

That perception disintegrates into nothing. If he wants to side with the tyrannical cult leader, so be it. His blood will be spilled by the end of tonight too.

...assuming I'm able to get the upper hand somehow.

"Yes, Leader?" Amos answers like the obedient fuck he is.

"Pick Believer Logan up and put him on the table. It's time to prepare for our latest ceremony. Sacrifices are to be made. Unfavorable souls must be purged from our midst."

The pair march over to drag me off the floor as instructed. I spit at their feet and curse at them.

"Touch me and be prepared to lose your fucking hands!"

My threats fall on deaf ears.

The pain that'd been agonizing moments ago takes a back burner as my temper snaps. I jerk and twist against their grip, doing what I can to fight them off. A few broken ribs, deep bruising, bleeding cuts and scrapes, and a throbbing skull pose limitations.

I'm in no condition for a physical confrontation. I'm running on fumes after being thrown however many feet off my bike.

Amos and Hershel each take an end and hoist me up on the table. Rope is used to bind me down. The rough texture burns against the many open scrapes I already have. I grunt at the new flavor of pain, refusing to let them know how much it hurts.

Refusing to show any sign of weakness.

"Excellent," Abraham says once they're down. "Have you prepared all the instruments and supplies needed for the dissection?"

"We haven't finished grabbing everything."

His jaw tightens in displeasure. "Then go get it."

The two are like fucking dumb and dumber shuffling off at his command. No sense of individuality. No independent thought or questioning. They're brainwashed like so many others who belong to the Chosen Saints.

Many of them have given their lives for Abraham and his bullshit.

Abraham steps over to the table where I'm strapped down and peers down at me. He might as well be a scientist studying his latest lab experiment. I challenge him with a rage-fueled, hate-filled glare, once again numbed to pain.

Once again more tuned into the temper pulsing in my veins.

He's the man who ruined my life. Made me as good as a slave for years. Took away my freedom and broke me down 'til I almost chose to end it.

He's the reason Teysha wakes up in the middle of the night in a panic if she's alone. He's the reason she'll never get to live the life she was meant to live.

I've never wanted the destruction of something more.

I *will* destroy him if it's the last thing I do. If it means destroying myself in the process.

"This will be a fitting ending, Believer Logan," he says calmly. "Our beliefs state that the wicked must be purged from our company. You are as wicked as they come. It will be cathartic in a way. Sending you off in excruciating pain as is deserved. You will beg. You will cry. You will die a blubbering, bloodied mess on this table before me.

"And I will celebrate with my saints and believers. We will toast to the evil we have defeated," he rambles on. "Then we will continue rebuilding our family. We will grow larger than ever before. I will ensure Believer Teysha is returned where she rightfully belongs. At my side."

"You mean like how you already tried to buy her back?"

I growl, bucking against the rope's binds. "You think I'll ever let you get your hands on her again?"

Abraham smirks. "How will you stop me? You'll be... in the afterlife. Burning in hell."

"Only if I get to take you with me, you pathetic coward!"

"Stop talking! You will talk when you are given permission to do so!"

"What's the matter, Abe?" I taunt, my pulse pounding. I'm still struggling against the rope. Trying to find a subtle way to loosen the knot on my left side. "You mean to tell me it upsets you when I tell you about yourself? You don't want to hear about how much of a fucking loser you are? So damn pale and hideous, you've got to force people to follow you."

"Shut up, Believer Logan!"

"You've got to force women to have sex with you!" I crank out a husky laugh. Colder and crueler than the one he'd released earlier. "It's no wonder with that shrimp dick that could never satisfy a woman. Why do you think Mandy sought me out so often?"

"I said shut up!"

"Why do you think Grace killed herself rather than spend another night in your bed?" I press, reveling in how his pale skin flushes scarlet. "Why do you think you had to force Teysha, tears and all, just to let you lay a finger on her? Do you think she ever wanted you? Do you think for a fucking second she enjoyed even breathing the same air as you? She hates you! They all do! You're nothing without your cult... NOTHING!"

"WHY DO YOU REFUSE TO LISTEN!?" he roars, thrashing his arms. His white-blond hair swings like a curtain. He snatches a knife off the podium that I recognize as my hunting knife and whips around to bring it down on me. Heaving manic breaths, he peers down at me with bulging eyes. The right larger than the left, twitching as if he's on the brink of insanity. "Say another word, Believer Logan, and I will run you straight through with your own knife! I will savor the blood that seeps out of you, and you will stare into my eyes as you die. The last thing you ever see."

"Leader, please, have mercy."

The soft, quiet voice is amplified in the cavernous room of the church. It echoes, sounding five times louder than it is. Enough for both of us to snap our heads toward the side door that's just squeaked open.

Teysha's slipped through, her summer dress wrinkled and hair windswept as if she's spent the afternoon on the go. Her big, brown eyes are as beautiful and expressive as ever.

Abraham forgets all about me. He turns the rest of the way around, his back to me.

"Believer Teysha," he croaks out. "Sweetheart, you have returned."

"Yes," she answers gently, taking a couple steps down the row of pews. Her hands are weaved together in front of her. "I realized this is where you would be."

Abraham smiles proudly. "My most adored believer, I always knew you would come."

"NO!" I yell. "Teysha, get the fuck out of here!"

"I can't," she answers. "I have to stay with him."

"Teysha... run... now!"

My words leave me as a rumble that's straight from the gut. That's deepened by sheer panic at her presence. What the fuck is she thinking!?

"Sweetheart, come here," Abraham commands. "Come to me, and we will be reunited as one."

She remains where she is. "There's something I must tell you first. But only if you release Believer Logan."

"You are in no position to make such demands. You will do as I tell you—"

"I'm pregnant," she blurts out. Her hand comes to her stomach, mapping out the smallest bulge hidden by the fabric of her dress. "I'm having your baby, Abraham."

34

TEYSHA

THE NEWS IS MET WITH STUNNED SILENCE.

It's unclear who's more shocked by the news—Logan or Abraham.

I'm not sure whose reaction makes me shake more. A range of emotions pass in Logan's gaze, from shock to confusion to anger of some kind. His eyes narrow, his jaw so clenched it could be wired shut.

Abraham's shock fades for confusion too, then his pointed features spread in glee. He gains a feverish gleam about him, like he's been told he's won the lottery. In his twisted view, impregnating one of his wives is one and the same.

It's an open secret that he's struggled to spread his seed. None of his wives have produced any heirs that were his. The few pregnancies that have occurred within the Chosen Saints were always the doing of other men in the family.

By virtue of carrying his child, I'm as precious as gold. I've got an upper hand that I'm hoping to use as a bargaining chip.

Me for Logan.

At least in this moment. At least 'til we can figure something else out.

Abraham won't hurt me so long as I'm pregnant... I hope.

It's a wager that could be life or death for Logan and me, but what other choice is there?

I'm finally taking the situation into my own hands. I'm exercising an agency that I haven't otherwise been afforded in what's the most difficult time of my life.

The truth is, I'm not sure *who* the father is. I'm barely even sure I'm pregnant. When he drove me to Mason and Sydney's house, I had asked Logan to stop by the Buy N' Save, pretending I needed more tampons. Instead I snuck off to the female health section and snagged a couple pregnancy tests. While he left to handle his business, I took the tests in the bathroom of Mason and Sydney's house.

All four came back positive.

It made sense given how emotional and sick I've become over recent weeks. It hadn't even been a consideration I'd thought of until Sydney's bachelorette party. As my belly churned at the taste of wine and the smells of the cheeses available, I realized something was up. Something was wrong if I couldn't even handle a tiny bite of brie.

You'd think as a married woman, I'd be over the moon to be expecting. I'd be excited about telling my husband the news and celebrating the life we'd be welcoming in the coming months.

But I'd broken down in tears instead.

How could I be happy when a disturbing possibility hung over my head? What if... what if the baby growing inside me wasn't Logan's? What if I'd been pregnant all along and the test I'd been given when I was freed from captivity had been wrong? What if it had been too early in my pregnancy to tell and now I'm carrying someone else's baby?

Logan and I have struggled to find our footing in our marriage, and that was without the burden of pregnancy.

...without the devastating blow that I could be carrying another man's child.

There's a chance he would probably want nothing to do with the situation. Me and the baby.

My heart shrivels up every time I consider the possibility. It weighs on my mind again as I make my revelation to the two men before me.

Potential heartbreak I shove aside for the time being. Right now, I have to stay strong. I have to find a way out for Logan, distracting Abraham long enough for the Kings to arrive... which should be any minute.

Hope had gunned it down the highway. We'd gotten off early, before we hit the traffic that clogs up the highway come early evening. We took back roads at my direction that led us straight into Boulder, mere miles away from the old, abandoned church.

The MC was nowhere in sight by the time we pulled up. I sucked down some air and put a brave face on, pressing forward alone anyway.

"My sweetheart," Abraham finally says. He opens his arms. "Come to me. Come to me my precious, sweet believer. You have proved your worth to be immeasurable."

I remain where I am, my hand on my belly. "Please agree to what I said. Please... just cut Logan free. Let him walk."

The light dims on Abraham's face. "You know I won't be able to do that."

"He has no bearing on the future of our family. I will give you the heir you've wanted. Isn't that more important?"

"Teysha, what the fuck are you talking about?" Logan growls at me, jerking against his binds. "Are you crazy coming here? What have I told you? Get the hell out of here!"

"Untie him and let him walk free. Be the merciful, loving Leader—the father of my child—that I know you can be," I say gently. "You'll never see him again."

Abraham arches a white-blond brow. "Believer Teysha, you know better than to speak beyond your station. You will be rewarded if you have become pregnant with my heir, yes, but that in no way means you can decide Believer Logan's fate. Come here now. Obey or you will be punished."

"I told you the truth out of love and respect," I fib. "I was hoping you would see it as a gesture of good will."

"The child you carry is mine. Your hopes do not factor in. I will only tell you once more. Come here right now."

"Don't you fucking talk to her!" Logan barks.

I gather up nerve, ignoring how my lungs constrict. It's not easy doing what I am, telling these lies and putting on this charade. The man who really owns my heart is only a few feet away, yet he's not the one I'm about to make these confessions to. He's the one forced to listen as I tell a monster I couldn't want less how I'm here for him.

Though it's a necessary evil, it tears me up from the inside even uttering the words. I close my eyes so I won't have to look at him—either of them—and push the words out.

"I wanted to start over with you. I wanted to raise our child free of what happened in the past. I wanted us to be together without the violence and bloodshed. Does the Lord not say he examines the righteous, but the wicked, who love violence, he hates with a passion? Can you find it in your heart to be the benevolent man I know you are?'

"Believer Teysha—"

"Please," I beg shakily, "I am devoted to you and our Lord and no one else. I... I love you."

Uncertain silence spreads around the large room in the seconds following my confession. Opening my eyes, I try my best to give Abraham a soft smile. It's broken and sad instead, reflecting the distress that's filling me up on the inside.

But Abraham doesn't care about authenticity. He doesn't care about what's real.

So long as you appeal to his ego, you present him an illusion he can buy into, then it's good enough.

He slants his head to the side, wearing suspicion on his pale face. "You are speaking candidly, Believer Teysha?"

"Yes," I gulp down air, "yes, of course."

Abraham takes another moment to consider what I've said. Behind him, Logan wriggles against his binds, creating slack, loosening the rope enough that he's able to move more. I can't see what else he's doing, but his left hand seems to be at work on something.

A knot?

His face is set in concentration, his hard eyes still on me, as if he's communicating wordlessly. He's realized what I'm doing and is telling me to keep going.

Keep Abraham distracted.

It's the encouragement, the strength he offers, that breathes new life into me.

I can do this.

"We can have a ceremony," I say, scanning the room full of antique stained glass windows and wooden pews collecting dust. "We can invite the other believers and make a joyous occasion out of it. Is this church special to you, Leader?"

He follows my gaze, turning his head for a look around. "This place? This beautiful church. It is very... meaningful. It is the place my father once gave sermons. He was a pastor. Pastor William James. A long time ago. Before the church closed its doors."

"My family used to come to this church too. I... I knew your father. He was a very kind man."

The ego-stroking words seem to win him over even more. His expression eases and he takes a step toward me. "Yes, he was, Believer Teysha. I saw you before. Did you know that? At my father's church? I saw you blossoming into a young woman—though you never saw me—but I knew, I knew one day, I would welcome you into our family. The family I created when I decided to continue my father's work. He would be so proud to see you here today."

"I'm sure he would be," I stammer.

Logan's freed his left arm. He wrenches it out of the rope, then goes still as if biding his time. He's waiting to see if Abraham's still distracted and if he can make another move. Once he deems it safe to do so, he reaches across to the other knot that's bound his right arm and begins working on it.

I breathe easier, thinking on what else to say.

But Abraham's noticed the shift of my gaze. He picks up on what it means and whips around to check on Logan.

Logan's as attuned to the situation as he is. He antici- pates what to do next. As Abraham turns toward him, Logan throws a fist that lands in his gut.

Abraham doubles over, curling his arms around his mid- section. Logan uses the momentum he's gathered to strike again. He grips a fistful of Abraham's blond strands and steals the knife he's holding from his grasp.

"SAINTS!" Abraham croaks, coughing. "SAINTS!"

Before I can even react, the main doors fling open, and Amos and Hershel burst inside. They raise their rifles at us.

One aimed at Logan as he slashes himself free then holds the knife to Abraham's throat.

The other rifle's pointed at me. My stomach pits staring at the barrel that could end my life at the quick pull of a trigger.

"SHOOT THEM!" Abraham roars. "SHOOT HIM!"

"But... Leader, I'm not sure I have a clear shot," Amos says.

"Then shoot her! SHOOT HER!"

My eyes widen, and I take an anxious step back. "Please... I'm pregnant. You can't kill an unborn child..."

Hershel wavers. His hesitancy drips from him. He lowers his rifle slightly, then glances at Abraham, silently pleading for more direction.

"DO IT!" Abraham yells, bucking against Logan. The blade against his throat presses against the knob that bounces up and down with each fanatical swallow. "They must learn! They must pay for what they've done!"

Hershel double blinks, his hands shaking. "I don't know if I can, Leader. I don't think... if she's pregnant... what would the Lord say?"

"I SAID DO IT!"

"I can't... I can't... I'm sorry... I can't."

The rifle slips from Hershel's hands and thuds on the floor as he breaks into hysterical sobs, then falls to his knees, his hands covering his face.

Amos looks just as taken aback, lowering his rifle as he glances at me, then Hershel, then over at Logan pressing the blade into Abraham's throat.

"YOU COWARDS!" Abraham barks, his face

reddening with manic fury. "YOU COWARDS WILL DO WHAT I SAY AND SHOOT THE—"

Logan takes what's perhaps the greatest risk of our lives —he slashes Abraham's throat mid-sentence, despite the fact that Amos still holds his rifle and can easily go through with his leader's wishes. Blood gushes out of the slit the blade creates, and Abraham's mouth drops open in a mix of shock and pain.

For a second, he's still alive, blinking and staring, then his face goes blank and his body goes still.

"You gonna shoot me?" Logan challenges, shoving the cult leader to the ground. He beckons at Amos, his jaw clenched in defiance. "Then do it—fucking shoot me! I just killed your leader. What will you do now? Who will you take your marching orders from now?"

Amos's nostrils glare, his grip tightening on the handle of his rifle as though tempted to lift it and aim. Any second, he'll go through with it. He'll pull the trigger and shoot Logan.

A crackling explosion worthy of fireworks rocks the church. The standoff goes from tense silence and challenging glares to the four of us turning our heads in every direction to place the sudden deafening sounds.

It's coming from outside.

Gunfire.

The Steel Kings have arrived, and they're about to make quick work of the few followers Abraham has left.

It only takes Amos a second longer to make up his minds. He bolts for the door to escape.

Logan's not letting him off that easily. Not after what he's done to us and how he's served faithfully as a guard under Abraham. He launches into a sprint, scooping up the rifle that Hershel's dropped as he sobs on the floor.

He takes aim and lands the shot on Amos's retreating form. The bullet hits him in the spine and he drops to the floor in a scream of agony.

Logan turns the rifle on Hershel next, teeth gritted, sweat clinging to his face.

"P-please," Hershel begs. The elderly man holds up trembling hands. "T-they ma-made me... he-he had no other fo-followers left..."

I take a step forward. "Logan, he was a believer like us. We both remember what that was like. He didn't shoot me when he had the chance."

Logan takes another second to make up his mind before he lowers the rifle and then motions for Hershel to get out of his sight. The older man needs no further instruction as he wobbles to his feet and darts for the same side door I'd entered through.

Logan snaps into action too, heading straight for me, the assault rifle still at his side.

"C'mon," he says, scooping my hand up with his free one. "Let's get the hell out of here."

35

TEYSHA

MY MOUTH IS DRY, AND MY THOUGHTS ARE LOST IN A thick fog that won't clear from my head. I kneel on the floor, my thighs pressed together, my knees suffering carpet burn, as I fold the last pair of underwear I have and place it on top.

Just about everything I own lays inside this duffle bag.

All of it packaged and pieced neatly together like a nomadic jigsaw puzzle.

Over the past six months, I've grown used to life this way. Little belongings. Monumental, life-altering events.

I'm not the college girl that once had a room full of pretty things—the tiny porcelain figurines that rested on my desk and the bookshelf crammed with my favorite book series I had read and gone back to numerous times. A stuffed bear sat on my bed among a cascade of pillows, a childhood memento I could never bring myself to get rid of.

That I clung to on difficult days even into early adult-hood. Back then my idea of difficult was a lot different. The guy from school I had feelings for dating a new girl or the family dog Cooper passing away.

I didn't have a concept of what the world was really like.

I thought problems could be solved with flowery language and a bowl of Grandma Renae's home-cooked chicken noodle soup. The future seemed bright. The possibilities limitless. I dreamed of the day I'd walk down the aisle and then ride off into the sunset with the love of my life.

Happily ever afters and fairytale endings.

I never conceived of the darker, crueler truth—that life wasn't always so kind and things didn't always work out how you want them to. Sometimes, it was the exact opposite.

Sometimes, those fairytales weren't fairytales at all. They were tragedies.

I've convinced myself I could pretend otherwise. I could keep dreaming because the dream was easier than the reality.

But I'm awake now. I'm aware of what I need to do.

A hollow sigh finds its way out of me as I tug the zipper along the open seam of the duffle bag.

It's been two days since the events at the old church in Boulder, and I'm more torn up now than I was then.

Probably because I've had time to do nothing but obsess over every small detail. I've felt the awkward pauses and uncertain glances Logan and I have shared. He's been in the hospital the past few days, recovering from his motorcycle accident.

When I've visited him, his eyes have lit up. He's held my hand and told me he's glad I came. I shed tears over the sight of him swollen and scraped up with too many bruises to count marring his skin.

Logan Cutler was a Steel King. He was made of steel

himself. He was unbreakable and powerful, with taut muscles that flexed and strained and an intensity in his stormy gaze that could turn any enemy to dust. He was resilience and strength and wasn't supposed to be laid up in a bed covered in bandages.

We couldn't bring ourselves to address anything beyond the moment.

Beyond his enjoyment at seeing me and my relief that he was alive and breathing.

It was like a stampede of invisible elephants rushed through the room.

We certainly couldn't talk about us. We couldn't address all the things hanging in the air. Things like the future, where our marriage would be going from here, and what I'd confessed to Abraham.

Surprise! I'm pregnant.

I sniffle lifting the duffle bag off the floor and hauling it over to the space by the door. The note I've written Logan gets left on the kitchen counter for him to find. I've already bought my bus ticket out of town and called Mama up to let her know I'll be arriving by eight. She said Papa will be parked outside waiting for me.

I reached out to the Pulsboro clerk's office again, offered several profuse apologies, and requested they start the annulment process like we'd asked so many weeks ago.

Everything's in order.

Logan won't have to worry about a thing when he returns home. It'll all be taken care of for him. He'll be able to move on from this ordeal. I'll be able to... deal with the aftermath of what returning to Boulder entails.

My family won't be happy I'm pregnant. It'll be just another reminder I'm damaged goods. How will they marry me off to some proper Christian man now?

I can hear their voices in my head, suggesting I hide out for the rest of the year 'til I give birth. Then I can give the baby up for adoption and pretend it never happened.

I spend the next couple minutes wandering the apartment, making sure I've packed up what's mine. The Bible I've kept on my bedside table catches my eye. For a moment my hand hovers over it as an internal debate takes place.

Just months ago, I couldn't imagine ever leaving it behind. Now only dull cynicism passes through me when I consider bringing the beloved book with me.

The bolt on the front door snicks as it's unlocked. Heavy boots clack on the tile.

Oh no!

What's he doing home so early?!

I flee the bedroom to meet him in the hall, my heartbeat accelerating like the criminal I am. I've been caught red-handed and my mind's too foggy to think up a story.

Logan stands before me in a plain charcoal t-shirt that clings to his muscles and worn denim that fits him just right. A few bandages and scrapes remain from his collision. He comes to a stop directly in front of me, his eyes charged like a severe storm at sea.

Any lines, any words I have thought up, vanish.

I have no idea what to say. I divert my gaze to the floor where I can study our feet. My sandals that show off my painted toes and his that are almost twice my size, covered in the beaten leather boots the same shade as tobacco.

"I didn't think you'd be home yet."

"They released me early."

"You... you should've called," I say, braving a quick glance up at him. "I would've driven your truck to come get you."

"Didn't need you to. Mace gave me a ride."

"Oh, okay. Excuse me."

I shift to his left to squeeze by him in the narrow hall. He steps to the side to block me. His hand lands on my hip as if to steady me from tipping over. His touch feels so natural, so comforting even now, without him even trying.

I meet his charged gaze and blink to the sudden prick of tears.

Just like that, the emotions I've been bottling up and hoping to hold in 'til I can get out of town threaten to spill out. They're on the precipice of rolling down my cheeks and quivering my lips and making me look like a fool.

I'm not strong enough for any of this.

Why... why, Lord, have you chosen for me to suffer like this? Can't you tell I'm not built for it?

"Teysha," Logan says, his voice husky, "what is it? Did something happen?"

I shake my head, bowing it 'til my chin's tucked to my chest. "Everything's fine. I was just not expecting you."

"Were you going somewhere?"

"Excuse me."

They're the only two words I can warble out as I out-maneuver him this time. I slide past him to the freedom of the open-spaced living room. Plenty of room to roam around and not get caught in the cage Logan seeks to put me in during moments like this.

"Teysha... where do you think you're going?"

"Home," I answer. "I've already got my bus ticket. Papa's going to pick me up. No need to worry."

Logan combs his fingers through his hair as if he can't understand what I've said. I might as well be speaking in a foreign language.

"Is this what you want?" he asks finally. "You want to go back to Boulder?"

"If there's one thing I've figured out over the last six months of my life, it's that I don't get what I want. That couldn't matter less." I cross the room to hoist my duffle bag off the floor and tug it over my shoulder. "Will you give me a ride to the bus terminal?"

"Will you slow the fuck down for a sec and—what's this?"

Logan tears his eyes away from me. His attention travels to the folded up note on the kitchen counter. He walks over to snatch it up. With every clack of his boot, my heart lurches inside my chest.

Panic and dread rolled into one, beating in sync with his grisly curiosity.

"Don't read that right now," I blurt out. "Please wait 'til I've—"

"Is this some kind of fucking Dear John letter?" he asks after skimming the first line or two. His stormy eyes flick up for a vexed look at me. "You wrote me this, and then what? By the time I'd see it you'd be long gone?"

Yes. That's exactly what I hoped for.

"No," I mutter. "It's just easier if I got it down on paper. I'd never be able to tell you face to face."

He reads the letter out loud, repeating back to me the shame, fear, and pain I've poured into every drop of ink. Ugly truths I'd rather cry myself to sleep to than offer up for the inevitable rejection that's to come.

Logan,

Thank you for providing me a roof over my head these past couple months. You have shown me kindness and cared for me when you could've easily turned me away. I'm sorry for all the times I frustrated you and for ever getting things mixed up. I let what I wanted make an already confusing situation worse, but you still never gave up on me.

You made me feel safe and valued, and you should know I'll never forget it. Or any of the times we've had together.

But you were right when you said we couldn't play house forever. Eventually, reality seeps in and you have to face the truth.

We were never meant to be married. You never wanted to be, and you made that clear. You told me you weren't the marrying type and you weren't planning on settling down with a wife and kids. I was forced on you and I refused to let go.

I've realized I have to do that now. I have a lot of things to figure out, and I'm done saddling you with my baggage. Just know I want nothing but the best for you.

Love, Teysha

My pounding heart becomes the only sound in the room. Logan's finished reading the letter, but he hasn't said a word. His thick brows snap together and the tension in his jaw tightens.

I'm not sure whether I'm about to burst into tears, pass out, or spew the contents of my stomach.

He crumples the sheet of paper in his fist and says, "Why do you think you need to leave?"

"It's for the best. You said it yourself, this was never permanent. The marriage would be dissolved."

"We agreed we'd wait 'til everything was over before we decided."

"Everything *is* over. Abraham's dead. The Saints have been eliminated. It's a closed chapter."

"I thought it was clear that 'we decided' meant we'd sit down and talk it out."

I fuss with the strap of the duffle bag and shake my head. "That's alright, I'm done obligating you. I need to go home and heal like you said."

"I'm your home now. We're each other's home now," he snaps. "Isn't that what being married means?"

"I'm pregnant."

"Yeah, I heard you in the church. What's that got to do with what I'm asking? Why are you leaving?"

The question feels so ridiculous, I can't resist laughing. It sputters out of me as a solitary tear leaks out and slips down my cheek. Logan comes out from behind the kitchen counter with the letter still clenched inside his hand.

"Can you stop beating around the bush and tell me what the fuck is going on?" he asks. "You're pregnant so that's why you're leaving? Where'd you get the idea you've got to leave 'cuz you're pregnant?"

"Because I don't know who the father is!" I scream. I *explode*, erupting into the tears that I've fought so hard against. They're hot streaking down my cheeks and salty on my lips. I'm like a hummingbird no longer able to stand still, throwing my arms up, pacing back and forth. Desperate to be heard, the ugly truths claw their way out of me. "I don't know whose baby this is, and I didn't expect for it to happen, and I don't want to put this on you. You can't raise another man's baby—that wouldn't be fair!

"I won't trap you like that, and I won't wait for you to grow bitter. You'll resent me and hate me for it. But I can't handle the rejection. I can't deal with you not wanting me anymore. But I can't get an abortion and just get rid of it. I can't do that either. So I'm leaving before all of that," I ramble in a mess of tears and gasping breaths. "I'm sparing us all the heartbreak and drama, so just let me go!"

"Slow down. You're talking too fast. You're jumping to conclusions. You don't know it's Abraham's—"

"He wasn't the only one!" I sob, my hands covering my mouth in hopes I'll hold in what's spilling out. It's no use. It can't be stopped. "He wasn't the only one who did that to me. The guards... Xavier... a-and Brody... they... oh, god. I'm going to be sick."

"Teysha!"

I scramble through the other half of the apartment in a mad dash for the bathroom. The lid of the toilet's barely flipped up before I'm bent over it, heaving and retching. Like most days when nausea hits, there's little to spit up.

But I have no choice except to ride it out. Let the nausea play out like it demands.

More tears murk my vision, and I curl closer to the ceramic toilet as if I'll be able to hide myself. As if I can shrink somehow so that Logan won't be able to find me. Unfortunately, he's already followed me into the bathroom. He's kneeling at my side, his large palm a comfort on my shivery, feverish skin.

"Hey, it's alright," he rasps. He rubs my back in soft circles. "Just breathe. Baby, just breathe."

Baby.

How is it that one gentle word can bring such warmth to my insides when the rest of me feels so much turmoil?

I cough and drown in tears, fighting my way out of it. Fighting my way back to the moment rather than wallowing in what's taken over.

Sheer grief and devastation at my circumstances.

"I'm sorry," I croak, my throat aching. "I've made a mess..."

"Fuck the mess. C'mere." Logan's arms envelop me in a cocoon of warm comfort and safety. His hand cups the back of my head, stroking my messy hair as I find a nook between his neck and shoulder. "Fuck what some DNA says. I don't give a damn. Don't you get it? I'm in love with you, baby."

"But... but..." Hiccups deter me from finishing my sentence.

"But nothing. I fucking love you, and there's nothing that's gonna keep us apart. We're bound by the vows we took. Vows that meant nothing then but everything now. You said it yourself. Marriage means never quitting on each other."

Any walls left standing come crashing down.

My cries deepen. My body quakes. All the trauma and fear and bad emotions I've shoved down floods out of me 'til I have no more to give.

Logan's there to catch every teardrop that falls. He breathes me in, absorbs my pain 'til it's his. 'Til we're healing together in each other's arms.

Minutes must go by of us huddled on the bathroom floor like this. Neither of us are keeping track.

I'm achy and exhausted by the time it's over.

He helps me off the floor, and we clean up. I chug water

hoping it'll settle my stomach. Logan notices my phone vibrating on the kitchen counter.

"Baby, somebody's calling you."

I look over and frown at the local number. It's only after it goes to voicemail that I decide to answer and listen to the message left for me.

"Hello, Ms. Baxter, I am calling from the lab at Pulsboro General. Your test results for your blood work have come in earlier than expected. You may stop by the lab any time between noon and five p.m. on weekdays and noon and three p.m. on weekends. Thank you."

I'm speechless as the line beeps and I lower the phone from my ear.

Logan turns his head half to the side. "Everything alright?"

"I'm not sure," I whisper, then I meet his concerned gaze with my own puffy eyes. "I... I asked for a blood test the other day when you were admitted to the hospital. It was to determine the paternity. The results have come in early."

36

LOGAN

"You don't have to do this," I say once I've shifted gears into park. We're seated in my pickup truck, parked in the lot of the town hospital. "I told you I don't care what the DNA results say. We're a family. The baby's mine."

"I... I..." she lets out a shaky breath. "I feel like I need to know."

I take her hand, linking our fingers. "I wish you would've told me. You would've come straight to me about the pregnancy."

Teysha's frown fractures my heart... or whatever it is beating inside my chest. I'd never imagined a scenario where I could look at a woman and feel her emotion as my own. Any woman I was ever involved with had never affected me like this. I hadn't allowed myself to be close enough to develop real feelings. Flings and one night stands made up the bulk of my experiences with the opposite sex.

But one sad look from Teysha and I can feel the urgency doubling my heartbeat. I stroke my thumb along the small ridges of her knuckles and wish I could take every lick of pain away. Since it's impossible, I settle on the next best thing.

Reassurance.

"I'm not mad at you. I don't blame you," I go on. "None of it was your fault, and you're doing the best you can. I get that. No matter what, we'll figure it out, alright?"

She inhales a deep breath, then nods, clinging to my hand like it's a lifeline. We walk toward the hospital in sync with each other, a true united front.

"Teysha? Logan?"

We turn at the sound of our names to find Korine and her mother, Sunny. Both women seem to be lacking on rest judging by their fatigued energy.

It's no surprise—Sunny's seriously ill, and Korine has barely left the hospital since Cash was shot. Teysha being the nurturer she is, rushes toward both women for quick hugs.

"What are you two doing here?" Korine asks. "Are you going to visit Cash?"

I glance at Teysha, who gives me a small smile, then answers for me. "We're here for some test results. But we would love to visit him too. Is he still in the same room?"

We end up on a detour, riding the elevator to the fifth floor where Cash's room is located. Mace and Sydney are already there, in the middle of chatting with Cash.

All things considered, Cash looks better than he has in days. The color's returned to his complexion and so has the twinkle to his gaze. Only he could be laid up in the hospital and still look like a fucking GQ model with his shoulder-length golden brown hair framing his face.

I break off with him and Mace while the ladies hover on the other end of the room to mingle.

"Feeling better?" I ask, nudging Cash's blanket-clad foot.

"As good as one can feel when they're shot a centimeter away from their heart," Cash answers. He gestures to Mace on the other side of his hospital bed. "Mace was telling me all about the finale with the Saints."

"You missed out," I say. "Lots of bullets in skulls."

"Probably good I wasn't there. You know." Cash holds a hand to the large bandage taped onto his pectoral.

"We made due without you," Mace says.

"I do hate that I didn't get to see that piece of shit Abraham go down."

I tuck my hands into the front pockets of my jeans. "My only regret is that he didn't bleed out more."

"How're things between you and Teysha?" Cash asks.

Glancing over my shoulder at her, a funny feeling lights me up on the inside. She's currently laughing alongside the others at something Sunny's said.

So damn beautiful and precious even under the hospital's fluorescent lighting. She might as well be a fucking angel.

"Good," I answer slowly, almost in a trance. "Real good."

"Mind if I speak to you outside for a second?" Mace doesn't wait for me to agree before he starts for the hospital room door.

We head halfway down the hall so to stay out of earshot from the others. Mace turns to face me with an expression that's stuck between curiosity and concern. The urge to remind him who's the older brother of the two of us strikes me. He speaks first.

"How're you really?"

"What?"

"You good? A lot's been going on."

I crack out a rare laugh. "You worried about me?"

"Both of you," Mace clarifies. "Syd told me Teysha told her she was leaving town again..."

"She's staying. We're together. We're... we're working things out."

Mace brings his hand up to his scalp, scratching his head as if it'll help him think. "Look, I'm not sure if she told you. But she told Sydney. She's pregnant."

Suddenly, I get where Mace's concern's coming from. He's been around for the past two months and witnessed how we've struggled. We've had plenty of ups and downs wading through dark, uncertain waters.

He wants to make sure we're thinking straight.

"I know," I answer, then I let my mouth cant up in a slight grin. "I'm gonna be a father."

For a second, Mace is thrown. He's clearly more surprised by my excitement than he is by the revelation. It unfolds on his face and through his body language as his eyes widen and his hands come to rest on his waist.

"You're in love with her," he says. "It's a real marriage."

"It was always a real marriage," I answer, clapping my hand to his shoulder. "I was just slow on the uptake."

"It's good for you. Both of you. That you're working things out."

We return to the hospital room where the others are discussing Cash's release and Mason and Sydney's upcoming wedding. I grab Teysha by the hand, and we give our goodbyes on our way out.

"You still alright to know?" I ask as we board the elevator. "Say the word, and we're leaving."

"I'm alright. You're with me."

She smiles sweetly, squeezing my hand that's engulfing

hers. Approaching the front desk for the hospital lab feels surreal. A life-defining moment that neither of us can predict the outcome of.

Teysha explains that while I was admitted to the hospital, the staff collected blood samples and swabs, which the lab has used for the test. Vaguely, I remember being told by the nurse as she stuck the needle in my veins, but I had been in pain and was distracted by everything else going on, I'd hardly put two and two together.

The technician at the front desk beams up at us as we approach.

"Teysha Baxter," she says, her finger scrolling on her computer mouse. "Ah, yes. I see you right here. I'll print your results."

We stand by listening to the jerky crank of the printer as it stamps ink all across the page. The technician scoops up the sheet of paper and skims what it says to make sure it has the correct information before handing it over.

Teysha takes the sheet with shaking hands. Then she gasps and *almost* passes out. I know because she bumps into my side, trembling from head to toe. I tighten my arm around her and glance down at the paper.

"It's a match," she warbles out. "I-it's a match?"

The technician gives her a sympathetic smile. "Yes, that's right. The fetal DNA is in your blood, and we were able to match the DNA profile for the unborn child using Mr. Cutler's sample. You're about six, almost seven, weeks along."

"But I'm showing?" Teysha's hand falls to her stomach like so many pregnant women tend to do, trying to trace the curve of her belly.

"That little pooch?" The technician churns out a laugh. "That's smaller than the food bloat I get."

"But... but if I'm only six weeks along, then that really does mean..." Her watery eyes light up meeting mine. She bursts into happy tears and laughter. "Logan, it really is yours! The baby's yours!"

Before I know it, I'm laughing too. I'm catching her as she throws herself in my arms, and I give her a joyful spin around in a circle. Setting her on her feet, my arms remain swathed over her hips, holding her only inches away.

We're lovestruck fools grinning ear to ear at each other like we've just been told we've won the lottery. For a married couple beginning the rest of our lives, it's one and the same.

And I couldn't be more fucking excited.

"How about we go out tonight?" I ask. "On a date to celebrate."

"A date?" she squeaks before her pretty smile widens. "I would love to."

37

TEYSHA

WE DO SOMETHING WE'VE NEVER DONE BEFORE together—we get a little dressed up. Logan digs a shirt I didn't even know he owned from the bowels of his bedroom closet. It's made of a quality linen fabric and has short sleeves and buttons. When he shrugs it on over his broad, tattooed shoulders, heat floods me.

He's never looked more handsome. The slate gray shade works perfectly against his stormy blue eyes, making them darker, more vivid. His normally stern face relaxes as he looks up and catches sight of me watching him.

"Like what you see?" he drawls.

More heat. More attraction flushes over me. I'm suddenly bashful, tilting my head away as if in hopes I can still pretend I wasn't spying on him.

"I was just checking if you were ready."

"Not sure. My wife looks so fucking good, I just might need a few minutes to have her to myself."

A yelp rolls out of me as I'm snatched by the waist toward him. His lips come down on my throat in the next second, peppering kisses up and down the sensitive column.

A known weakness of mine, I squirm in his arms and break out into laughter, shoving at his chest.

"Logan!" I gasp.

"You smell like fucking flowers. Have I ever told you that?"

"Many times."

"Well, I'm telling you again."

He presses his face into my throat for a long, greedy inhale and even greedier kisses. My hands land on his rock-hard shoulders. Laughter weaves in between my words as I beg him to stop.

"Logan... you said..." I giggle. "You said dinner!"

"Plot twist," he growls, nipping at my jaw like a feral animal. "*You* are what's for dinner."

For five minutes I'm tortured like this, prey to the man who can't keep his hands off me. Logan regains control of himself only when we're kissing and groping each other, pressed against the wall, and his stomach growls in hunger.

We break apart in a fleeting second of surprise, then burst into laughter. The tips of Logan's ears warm to a soft scarlet and he scratches the back of his neck.

"Guess it is time for dinner. But don't think you're off the hook," he warns, dropping a kiss to my lips. "You're still for dessert."

Pulsboro isn't the most romantic setting for a date night, but in the thick of summer, we make do. Dusk lingers late into the evening, painted across the sky in streaks of lavender and periwinkle blue. Far in the distance the sun hangs on, coasting along the horizon, sinking in slow motion.

Main Street brims with life more than any other part of town. Saturdays in the summer tend to draw out the crowds that would otherwise be hibernating at home.

We park a street away and stroll the sidewalks holding hands. Logan's hand is calloused and warm wrapped around mine, a glove of love and safety.

I never want to let go.

After being denied simple things like this for so long, it truly feels special. We've faced the worst things life has to offer, and we've come out on the other side more united than ever.

God is good.

We pass shops and cafés and a duo of musicians playing live music. Joining the modest crowd cheering them on, we share impressed looks.

The pair are crooning a love song, strumming the strings on their guitar.

Logan holds me close as we vibe with the music, swaying on the spot. I soak up the moment for what it is, peace and contentment rolled into one. A joyful evening out with the man who stole my heart even when he wasn't trying to.

"You like Thai food?"

"Hmm?"

I blink and realize the song's ended and the crowd's dispersed. I was so lost in the moment that I tuned out of it. I tapped into the emotions coursing through me.

"Thai food sounds delicious right now."

"There's a good spot up ahead. I used to come here all the time. They've got the best curry."

Logan sets off at a fast pace, towing me along like he's excited to show me the place he's bragged about. I bite away a smile, practically skipping to keep in step with him.

The Thai spot Logan's told me about is tiny but charming, with only three tables and a handful of chairs. We're immediately greeted by a petite woman that I'm certain is someone's grandma. She sets menus down in front of us and explains the specials and promises she'll return with some iced tea.

I savor the many fragrant spices wafting in the air.

"This place already seems amazing."

"Told you." Logan cracks open his menu, then taps his finger at the number six. "My favorite. You want some quality Panang curry? This is it. Fucking delicious."

"Are you prepared to share?"

I put on a pouty face, barely able to hold it together. Logan goes from disgruntled to reaching for my chair to drag me closer. He kisses my cheek and says, "You're the only one I'd let eat off my plate. But you better be prepared to share too. What're you getting?"

"The Pad Thai seems like a safe bet. No bean sprouts. I'm not a fan."

"I'll make a note of that."

"Are you keep record of things like that?"

"Maybe." He gives a shrug. "I've started noticing things about you. The way you sing songs under your breath or pick the crust off your bread. You always put twice the recommended serving of creamer in your coffee. And your birthday that you told me about two months ago is coming up next month. Which means I better start looking for something to get you."

A kernel of fondness trills through me. I hadn't realized he'd been noticing these things. "You sure memorize a lot of things about me."

"It happens when you become obsessed with a woman."

He clasps my hand and I curl into his side again. "Tell me something I don't know about you yet."

He thinks a second and then says, "I used to be in a garage band."

"A garage band?!"

"Hey, cut that judgment outta your tone. We were decent," he says, his jaw clenching in offense. "Well... *I* was decent. Mace and Cash were another story."

"Was this a high school thing?"

"It was. I was a few years older. Me and a buddy of mine—Ethan—needed two more members. Mace and Cash volunteered. I was on guitar. Mace drums. Ethan bass. Cash was our vocals. We played one gig and quit."

"Kori says Cash is great at karaoke."

"Yeah, well, Kori's in love. He could sound like a fucking rooster and she'd sing his praises."

I giggle. "That... sounds exactly like what could happen."

"Can't blame her. Love makes you say and do crazy things."

"Is that so? Tell me more, Mr. Cutler."

"You tell me, *Mrs.* Cutler. Which reminds me," he says, hiking a brow up high, "when are you changing your name?"

Surprise renders me silent for a second. "You... you want me to?"

"Why wouldn't I? You're my wife. You're about to be the mother of my child. And in case you haven't noticed, Teysha Patrice Baxter, I'm fucking in love with you."

The same heat that had flushed over my skin earlier returns in a warm wave. I'm left dizzy and speechless as I process what it's like to be cherished by Logan Cutler. Loved and cared for by him.

It's better than anything I could've ever imagined.

We enjoy every bite of dinner, sampling off each other's plates and chatting about whatever comes to mind. By the time we stroll back onto the sidewalk of Main Street, dusk has finally faded into night.

Residents still wander the long street, though the sounds of music and laughter have died down.

Logan strokes his thumb along the back of my hand in thought. We wander almost lazily 'til he stops us outside a tattoo parlor. "You ever thought about getting a tattoo?"

"Me? A tattoo? Uh, never." I give off a nervous laugh as if I'm sure he's joking.

"I'm gonna get one. Wanna come in with me?"

"Oh? Okay... sure. What are you getting?"

"A cross."

I halt halfway through the door, my brows drawing close in confusion. "A cross? *You?*"

"Yeah, I've thought a lot about it... and I want it. I want it on me. I want it 'cuz it's important to you."

"But you don't have to," I say, shaking my head. "Really, they're my beliefs. Not yours. You don't have to—"

"I want to. 'Cuz I've finally realized God is real."

"You're being serious? How so?"

Logan scrubs his free hand over his jaw, thinking on my question. "I figure he has to be if you are. If he led me to you."

Goosebumps spring onto my arms and tears mist my eyes. I'm rendered speechless not for the first time tonight, but most overwhelmingly of all. How is it possible to be full of so much love you can cry?

One glance up at Logan, and I see the face of my soulmate. The man I've been waiting a lifetime for.

My breath bursts out of me as I impatiently wipe the tears that have fallen and then throw myself in his arms.

We're blocking the doorway of the tattoo parlor, but the artist seated at the work chairs seems to understand. She softens watching us, a blonde with a pixie cut who's covered in artwork head to toe.

"Then... then I want one too. Maybe a small cross on the inside of my wrist." I hold out my arm turned up for his appraisal. Logan bends forward to press a kiss on the spot I'm thinking of.

"Seems like a good place to put it. But remember it might hurt a little."

I'm so lovestruck I can't even visualize a concept like pain. We finally head the rest of the way into the parlor to introduce ourselves to the blonde and explain what we were thinking. Logan wants his cross tattooed on his chest, placed right in the center where it'll be impossible to miss.

The blonde nods along. "Definitely can do that. And you? What were you thinking, doll?"

"My wrist. Just maybe a small one."

"Doable."

"Am I allowed to get one if I'm pregnant?"

"Generally safe, especially one as small as you're getting. Sit down in my chairs. Name's Cassandra, by the way. Cass for short."

Logan goes first. I'm more nervous than he is as he unbuttons his shirt and plops down in the leather chair. The needle buzzes as Cass draws the piece of art on his chest.

It's true that I've never imagined I would ever get a tattoo. Mama and Grandma Renae would probably cry if they ever found out. They feel tattoos are trashy and unnecessary. But I've learned more and more over the past couple months that while I'll always love them, I'm my own person. I'm my own woman, and I need to create the life I want for myself.

There's so much to experience, and I intend on doing that by Logan's side, including small side quests like tonight.

Getting my first tattoo.

When it's my turn, I release a nervous breath and replace Logan in the chair. The stinging pain is barely noticeable as he holds my hand and we kiss. From start to finish, the session lasts under two hours.

We exit high on life, hand in hand again, sharing adoring looks.

The fresh ink gleams on the inside of my wrist, clear film sealed over it for healing.

"Happy?" Logan asks, squeezing my palm in his.

I smile brightly. "You have no idea."

Logan's mouth is on me from the moment we walk through the door. His large, wide palms slip over my hips, and he comes up from behind to press his lips against my throat. The feel of his kiss, warm and tender, on the sensitive patch of skin makes me shudder.

I go still in his hold and sink into the instant chemical pleasure that washes over me.

"Logan..." I mewl.

"Baby, I want you so fucking bad," he rasps, kissing me all over. His mouth travels up, then down the side of my throat. His long fingers clench tighter on my hips, and he braces himself against me from behind, guiding me through the deep shadows of the apartment.

We maneuver the dark space this way, Logan kissing my neck, groping my hips, steering me from behind like an avatar.

Halfway down the hall, I turn in his hold and rise on tiptoe to meet his hungry lips. My hands roam his stubbly cheeks as I grab his face and kiss him just as enthusiastically. Just as urgently, breathlessly, letting him know how badly I need him too.

Every part of him intertwining with every part of me.

He takes my fervor, using it to light his own even more. Using my passion to fuel his to untold levels.

He's a fire that can't be put out. That intends on razing me down with him.

His arms slide under my thighs to hoist me up off the ground. My feet dangle as it's suddenly like I've climbed a great tree—I'm several feet off the ground, instinctually notching my legs around his waist to level us out. Our mouths align as he crushes his lips to mine.

And really does set me aflame.

Need burns through me, flushing onto my brown skin.

I can barely contain myself, barely remember to breathe as Logan's hot kisses unravel me. My undoing happens all at once.

The desperate breaths fighting their way out of my lungs. The way I dig my nails into his forearm as he holds me up and bites at my bottom lip. Even how my body tremors at the feel of his desire.

The knowledge a man could ever want me this much, it's like he's on the brink of losing his mind.

Logan kicks the bedroom door open and flings me to the bed. We both launch into urgent attempts to undress ourselves, fumbling hands and heavy pants in the dimly lit room. He's unhooking his jeans, shoving down his boxers, his erection bobbing free. I'm on my back on the bed, wiggling out of my panties, the spaghetti straps of my dress low on my shoulders.

His patience is lost in a fierce rumble that's louder and deeper than the engine of his bike revving up.

He snatches the pair of panties caught halfway down

my leg and rips the clingy, delicate fabric the rest of the way off before he's on top of me. His heavy, muscled weight presses down over me, my thighs parted wide to make space for him.

"You wet for me, baby?" he asks, his voice like gravel. His hand finds my pussy, and I writhe at the sudden rough touch.

His fingers on my throbbing little clit, rubbing fast circles, making me wetter than I already am.

He peers into my eyes and watches my face as my mouth falls open for a soft moan. I'm hot and needy, squirming under him like a butterfly caught in the cup of a hand. But he only rubs me faster, harder, bringing me closer to release.

I watch him watch me as my brows pinch and pleasure flickers through me, building, growing, expanding 'til I can't take it. I grind my hips against his hand and scratch at his steel-like shoulder, a woman so easily undone and overcome.

"Give it to me, baby. You like when I play with your pussy, don't you?" he asks. "You want me to taste you? You want my tongue to lap up every fucking drop of those juices?"

Yes becomes the only word I know.

I repeat it over and over again like a chant, breathless and feverish as he makes good on his proposal. Logan travels down the length of my body, pressing kisses onto the different parts of me as he goes—my bare stomach and my hipbone and the mound of flesh just above my sex. He nibbles on my thighs and sucks my clit between his lips.

He spreads my pussy lips, then traces his tongue along my folds. His stormy gaze meets mine, darkened by lust and feral need, as he quite literally devours me.

I tip my head back, no longer able to bear it another second. I can't hang on. I can't fight the tingling pleasure that percolates from my pussy and then surges through the rest of me.

My orgasm is a wrecking ball that smashes into me and knocks me asunder.

I break apart with a hoarse cry of pleasure and my body going limp. For a few blissful seconds, I'm lost to the chemicals, lost to the rush of them that floods me all at once.

Logan suckles away. He licks at my pussy and laps up my pearly cum. More kisses. More love bites.

More hungry stares as he returns to his place over me and claims my mouth. I taste myself on his tongue, another tremor rocking through me.

"You taste so fucking good, baby," he praises. "So fucking sweet. All of that's just for me."

"Yes," I babble. "Only for you."

"Are you gonna do what I say? Are you gonna let me fuck that tight little delicious pussy?"

"Oh, yes... please. I... I need it."

"I need it too, baby," he groans, and I feel him at my opening.

The heat he gives off. The steely hardness. The moist crown of his penis.

"But guess what, baby?" he asks. "I want you to fuck me. I want you to ride my fucking cock like a good girl. Can you do that for me?"

My eyes pop open in shock, meeting his. I'm still breathless, my skin warm. My brain's fuzzy from the orgasm I had seconds ago, so much so speech still feels like an impossibility. "F-fuck your cock?" I repeat almost innocently.

He laughs. "That's right, baby. Sink down on this cock and ride me like a fucking bull."

I'm frazzled as he maneuvers us for me. So strong and capable, he pulls me up and lays back, plopping me on top 'til I'm astride him.

His thighs are so thick, so muscled and hairy that it feels difficult just trapping mine over his. His cock stands tall and upright, gleaming from precum.

I lick at my lips, my heart beating fast.

"C'mere," he says, grabbing me by the hips. He drags me the rest of the way, 'til I'm positioned directly over his length. "Do it, baby. Sink down."

"But... but I don't... I've never..." I warble out.

"Be my good girl and try. You can take it. You can ride me, baby."

It's the desire blazing in his dark eyes that does me in. The husky note of his voice. The love that's visceral and makes me feel safe enough to explore.

I'm clumsy getting myself situated. I pull my summer dress the rest of the way over my head and plant my hand on his chest. It looks tiny against the broad expanse of it. Holding his gaze, I nibble on my bottom lip and go for it, sinking down on him.

Logan hisses like he's been burned. His chest constricts, so powerful in the ragged breath he lets out.

"FUCK!" He clenches my thighs on either side of him. Veins throb in his throat as he swallows with difficulty. "Fuck, that's fucking good. So fucking good."

Encouraged by the praise—even the expletives—I do what feels natural.

I rock my hips, slowly, tentatively, testing and exploring.

Reveling in how thick he is and full he makes me. How I can take him deeper or switch up the depth for new angles of pleasure.

Soon, I'm finding a rhythm. I'm riding him, my skin

burning and heart pounding. I'm mesmerized by the ways I can inflict pleasure on him. The ways I can make him groan and snap shut his eyes.

My pussy grips him, my walls fluttering and stretching.

My breasts bounce along with every move.

A whole new version of myself is born. A sensuous seductress who's bold and unafraid, who embraces her sexuality and wields it to bring her husband to climax.

Sex doesn't just happen *to* me, like so many times in the past. I can be in control. I can make him feel so good and make myself feel just as good too.

These moments are hungry and carnal, driven by lust and desire, but they're also beautiful and intimate. Private moments we share in together. Moments where I can unleash a side of myself no one else gets to see.

I shudder as my pace increases and my rock becomes a full on, frantic bounce.

Logan grips my thighs and helps me along.

"That feels so fucking fantastic, baby. Keep going."

And I do—I undulate my hips like I'm fighting a bull, moaning at how his dick reaches a part of me it never has. Some pleasure button that sends hot sparks through me.

"Fuck yes!" Logan growls as I ride him. He's groping my hips and thighs hard enough to bruise, both of us so close to our endings. "You're doing so good, baby. You're so fucking beautiful. Look at you taking my cock like a good girl."

Our eyes lock, our pants chaotic, bodies slick with sweat, as we ride it out together.

We find our pleasure together.

"Tell me you're mine. Tell me you're my good fucking girl," he demands, his face clenched. His muscles strain. He's on the verge of coming.

"I'm your good girl!" I cry out. "I'm yours... I'm yours..."

"You want my cum, baby? You want to be full with me?"

"Yes... please fill me up. I love being full."

My pussy clamps down on him in a choking grip as he loses it. He grunts as he bruises my hips and his jerk up into me. His cock goes so deep, it reaches the back of my pussy, sending me flying into my second orgasm.

All sound goes out. All breath rips from my lungs. Anything and everything else ceases to exist.

For a magical few seconds, we're suspended in pleasure, convulsing and panting.

My bones leave my body. I can no longer hold myself up, flopping to the side, half on top of Logan.

I can feel him even as he slips out of me. The wet evidence between my thighs, gushing from my pussy, the ache that he leaves behind.

He rolls over to kiss me and wrap me up in his arms. "That was fucking amazing," he mumbles, his words slurred like he's drunk. "I love you so damn much."

I burrow deeper into his arms, already drowsy. "I love you so damn much too."

38

TEYSHA

"Morning," Logan drawls, squinting. "You up already?"

"Coffee. Drink."

I prop myself onto the bed on my knees, holding two mugs with little wisps of steam curling out of them. Logan's grin is sleepy and crooked as it slants across his mouth. He pushes himself up into a sitting position against the headboard and carefully accepts my caffeinated offering.

At the first sip, he groans in satisfaction. "That's damn good. Since when did you learn to make my coffee how I like it?"

"Since you learned how I like mine," I retort, wrinkling my nose playfully.

He reaches out to squeeze the area where my shoulder and neck meet. "How'd you sleep?"

"It's about to be nine, and I *just* got up a few minutes ago."

"Compared to you getting up at the ass crack of dawn all those other mornings? Cooking and cleaning like a crazy woman."

"Yet you ate every bite of breakfast I cooked," I mouth off.

His grin ticks wider. "'Cuz it was fucking delicious. And you really wanna be all sassy right now? I've got no problem picking up where we left off last night."

"My thighs are *sore*."

"From squeezing my head so tight when I was dining on that sweet fucking pussy."

I give up trying to resist his rough charm and burst into another giggle. My thighs *are* sore—and I'm already craving him all over again.

"What are you up to today?" I ask moments later, once we've sipped more coffee and finally crawled out of bed.

Logan wanders into the bathroom to pee and I'm surprised by how... normal it feels. The two of us sharing a space like this. We're halves of each other, comfortable and content in our cozy, intimate space no one else is allowed into. He joins me at the sink as I start the faucet and reach for my toothbrush and the toothpaste.

"Tying up some loose ends around the club," he answers, holding out his toothbrush.

I get the hint and squeeze some toothpaste onto his too. "The wedding's almost here."

"That too. Making sure it's all good."

"I'm glad you're able to be his best man."

"Me and Cash."

I smile. "I'm looking forward to seeing you in a tux... or whatever bikers wear to weddings."

"And I'm looking forward to ripping your bridesmaid dress off you after it's all over." Logan rinses his mouth out with water, then grabs me by the hip 'til I'm pressed into his side. "I bet you're going to look so damn gorgeous in it. Most beautiful woman there."

"You're biased."

"So what if I am?"

I shriek as I tilt my head back and he buries his face into my neck. His kisses from last night still burn all over my skin. He only fuels the heat as his lips skim the length of my throat and he palms my backside, squeezing me in his hands.

It's a new and overwhelming experience—a man being unable to keep his hands off me.

He can't seem to fathom going more than a few minutes without touching me in some way. Kissing me. Nuzzling me. Inhaling my scent.

He's *literally* addicted to me.

And I can't say I feel much differently than him.

There's a reason I've never felt happier and more at ease than when he's around. His arms wrapped tightly around me.

We're slow to finish getting ready for the day. We take Logan's pickup truck to the Steel Saloon where we part ways. He goes off with Mason and some of the other guys to handle club business in the back office while I join Sydney, Korine, and Mick at the bar counter.

We have an appointment today at the local bridal boutique to finalize the fit of our dresses.

But it seems to be the last thing on Sydney's mind at the moment—she practically has a vein about to burst in her temple while the others watch on, amused.

"What's going on? Are we ready to head out to this dress fitting?"

"Sydney tried her hand at baking peanut butter cookies," Mick answers. "As you can imagine, it didn't go well."

"I followed the instructions down to the letter!"

Korine giggles. "I told you I'd help. But nooo... you said you had it."

"I thought I did! How hard can baking cookies be?"

"Apparently very hard. These things are like rocks." Mick flicks one of the lumpy cookies, making it clang against the baking pan they're resting on. The others laugh even more while I half smile, half frown.

"Wait, why were you baking cookies?"

"She was trying to surprise Mace," Korine answers. "It's their last night together before the wedding and she wants to prove she can do wifey-type things."

"I *said* it would be a good idea if I learn to cook and bake. You know, for when we have kids."

Mick's thick white brows jump high on his forehead. "Oh, so you two are already planning kids, are you? Guess we know what you'll be up to on the honeymoon!"

My hand instinctually falls to my stomach as I'm reminded I still haven't shared with some of the others that I'm expecting.

Considering Sydney's crisis about her charcoal peanut butter cookies, now isn't a good time.

But something else comes to mind as I glance at the platter of burnt cookies.

Over the past few months Logan and I have experienced some of the darkest things two people can go through together. Though we've survived and come out the other side united and in love, some evils still haven't been vanquished.

Some evils are still alive and breathing.

I'm never one to interfere with God's plan... but what if I helped it along?

What if I've thought of another use for these cookies?

Someone starving might appreciate them...

"These have real peanuts in them?"

"Sure do. They're Mace's favorite. Why?"

"How about I go throw them out back?"

"Oh," Sydney says, shrugging. "Sure. They're not really edible anyway. Only a desperate person would eat them."

A small smirk comes to my face as I collect the baking tray and head for the back of the saloon. For the first few footsteps, I pretend I'm on my way to the trashcans outside. Once I'm sure Sydney, Korine, and Mick haven't followed, I change course for the basement.

Mandy looks up at the sound of my footsteps descending the staircase. She's withered away even more than the last time I saw her, cheeks sunken in and her eyes ringed black and blue.

"It's you," she spits. "What do you want? Come to gloat about the evils you've committed? Murdering our precious, kind, valiant leader?"

For the first time since I've met her, there's sorrow entrenched in her tone. She sniffles as her nostrils gleam from snot.

She's been crying.

I hold up the tray of cookies. "I came to feed you. They're a bit burnt, but still edible."

"Why?"

"Because it's the charitable thing to do," I answer sweetly, walking the tray over. "The guys have been hard on you. But you were just a woman trying to be loyal to the man you love. I understand how you feel. I'm loyal to the man I love too."

"You think I give a damn about what you think? Shut up and gimme what you brought me then get the hell out of here!"

"That's not very godly of you. What would the Lord think?"

Her hollowed-out eyes shrink to slits as she flashes her scummy teeth. "What use is the Lord if he took my beloved?"

"Everything happens for a reason. Luckily for you, I'm in a charitable mood. Would you like some almond cookies?"

Mandy clings to her suspicions, keeping me under her narrow-eyed glare. Then her stomach gurgles and she seems to realize she doesn't have very many options for nourishment.

"Yes," she grumbles.

"Yes, what?"

"Yes, what what?"

"Yes, please?" I say. "Some manners go a long way."

"Oh, for fucking Christ's sake."

"Don't you ever speak the Lord's name in vain."

My sweetness slips for a quick second before it returns with a smile so warm it's the opposite. It's cold and menacing as I step forward and pick up a cookie off the baking tray.

"Open," I order.

Begrudgingly, she obeys. She parts her chapped, blistered lips expecting to be fed.

I shove the cookie into her mouth whole, hardly giving her time to adjust and bite into the treat. She sputters trying to break it down into tolerable pieces. Cookie crumbs spew from her lips as her cheeks swell and her throat works to swallow.

It manages to go down with another choking cough from her.

I set the tray down, standing back in wait. The flavor will hit her palate soon enough.

Her ringed-out, slit-like eyes double in size when it does. She retches like a cat attempting to cough up a hairball and wheezes out, "This isn't...? You didn't...? You fed me *peanut butter*?!"

"Is it peanut butter?"

"Yes," she croaks. "Peanut butter... peanuts... I'm deathly allergic!"

"Are you? Whoops." I fold my arms behind my back and shrug my shoulders innocently, still smiling. "I could've sworn those were almond butter. Oh well, I better get going."

"No... come... come back! PUH... PUH-LEASE!"

She's gagging by the time I reach the bottom stair. Her face has reddened and her eyes bulge in their sockets, her mouth wide and agape. She huffs out air as if trying to regain her breath, but it's too late. Her lungs are closing up.

For the briefest moment, I almost feel terrible for her. I almost rush over to help and call 911.

Then I remember every foul, evil thing she's ever done to me—*and Logan*—and my smile returns.

"God doesn't like ugly, Mandy," I say. "It's a shame you've had to learn the hard way. Goodbye."

The last noise I hear before slamming shut the basement door is her choking gasps. Dusting my hands off with an air of satisfaction, I return to the barroom floor.

The others notice my return at once.

"There she is!" Korine exclaims.

"Took you long enough," says Sydney. "You sure you and Logan didn't go out back for a quickie?"

I laugh. "Nope. Just threw out the cookies like I said. Are we making this dress fitting or what?"

"Oh, Sydney," Korine says with a surprised gasp. "You look amazing!"

"You think? It's not too much?"

I shake my head and step forward to fuss with the hem of her airy chiffon gown. "Not at all. You make for a beautiful bride."

"Are you two trying to make me cry?" Sydney gently fans at her eyes to stave off the emotion building up. "How the hell am I going to make it down the aisle without tearing up?"

Korine closes in on her left to fuss at her in the same way I am. Whereas I'm straightening the skirt portion of her summery wedding dress, Korine's brushing Sydney's side bang out of the way to make her hair look even more perfect.

We eventually move out of the way so she can get a look at herself in the boutique mirror.

"Damn it!" she murmurs, more emotion rising up. She promptly turns away, releasing a laugh that's watery but happy. "I am crying. This is all your fault. Don't tell Mace. He'll tease the fuck out of me."

"In the vault," Korine promises.

"Change of subject," Sydney says. "Let's talk about how both of you are slaying in your dresses."

"You have a point," I say, popping a hand to my hip to pose in the mirror. "The three of us are elevens out of ten. Our guys don't know how lucky they are."

My words are spoken in jest, but the other two give vigorous nods and laughs anyway.

It's true though—we all look wonderful. Sydney in her delicate wedding dress made of lace and chiffon that's perfect for a breezy wedding out in the meadows in a Texas summer. Korine and I wear the sage green gowns that have been picked out for us. The silhouette is decidedly feminine and flattering, showing off our shoulders, cinched waists, and complementing our different complexions.

I'm drifting off in excited thoughts about what Logan will think when he sees me in it when my phone rings from inside my purse.

"I'll be a few minutes."

Sydney and Korine carry on fussing with each other's dresses as I step outside and answer the call. I'm not sure what to expect as I say, "Hello, Mama."

Knowing Mama, it could be anything.

A lecture telling me how sinful I'm living married to a biker. A plea begging me to come home with family who loves me. Scripture she'll quote that's both a plea and a lecture rolled into one. The options are limitless when Mama normally makes it her business to treat me like an unruly child.

"Your father told me the news. You're not coming home."

I wait a second, deciding on a tone. I go with calm and casual. "It wasn't a decision I made lightly. But it's what I believe is right for me."

"You said you wanted to come home. Your father was going to pick you up from the bus station. Grandma Renae made your favorite—brisket and baked mac and cheese. I prepped your bedroom."

Bits of guilt niggle away at me. I let out a tiny sigh. "Mama, can't you try to understand? I'm a grown woman now. A *married* woman now."

"Married?" she scoffs. "You mean to that... that biker man? The one with all the tattoos who's got a record—and don't tell me he doesn't, because I had the local sheriff look him up in the system. He was arrested twice when he was younger. Once for disorderly conduct in public and another for an illegal firearm possession. That's who you're married to?!"

"Look, I get Logan isn't the kind of guy you envisioned me with. But he's a good man, Mama. I swear he is. Don't you trust my judgment?"

"Before this nightmare of a situation, I would've said yes. Because I knew my daughter had more common sense than this," she says. "It seems I was wrong."

"Ever think you're the problem?" I snap, out of patience.

"Teysha Patrice Baxter—"

"It's Cutler," I interject sharply. "Mrs. Cutler. Mama, I love you. I love all of you. You have no idea how much I missed you when I was held captive—how many nights I sobbed myself to sleep just wishing I could see you all one more time. But I've got to move on. I've got to start my own life, and I want to do that with Logan. We really love each other."

"You were *forced* to marry him!"

"So what?" My voice pitches higher from the rush of emotion. My skin's heated up and I've started pacing up and down the sidewalk outside the bridal shop. "Yes, we had an ugly beginning. One of the ugliest beginnings a relationship can have. But through those dark and terrible times, we came to care for each other. We grew together and found a love that's beautiful. That makes me so happy. Don't you want that for me? Don't you want me happy?"

I'm practically on the verge of tears by the time I'm done. My pulse pounds in my veins, like I'm engaged in a high pressure situation.

And I suppose I am.

Telling Mama my final decision is basically cutting the cord. It's setting the tone for my future no matter what she says.

She's quiet for seconds to come. Once or twice I catch a sniffle on the other end. She's sobbing.

"Mama," I say softly, "I'm not trying to hurt you. But this is what's best."

"I just... I worry about you. After everything you've been through..."

"And I appreciate that you care. Believe me, I do. Thank you for always being there."

"Tey Tey, please... take care of yourself. I've only ever wanted what's best for you."

"I know, Mama. But just... trust me. You'll see in time. Maybe we can come for a visit sometime. Maybe you'll come to love Logan like a son. He's your family now too. He's lost his mother. Maybe someday you can be that for him."

Mama still sounds unsure once we're hanging up, but I'm at peace with our conversation. It's as good as it gets for the moment. My hope is that she'll eventually come around.

But what matters most is that I'm doing what's best for me.

I'm beginning a new life with a man that's earned my heart.

Feeling lighter, like a burden's been lifted off my shoulders, I head back inside the boutique.

We have a wedding to finish prepping for.

39

LOGAN

"Mandy's dead."

Silver makes the announcement like he's announcing scores from a sports game.

I'm in the back office with Mace and Cash, shooting the shit. We're making the most of our last chance to give Mace hell about tying himself down.

"No more club girls," I remind. "You're about to have the old ball and chain attached."

He gives me a dubious look. "You mean like you do? You're the married man around these parts or have you forgotten?"

"He's got you there," Cash says.

"You don't need to be talking either. You might as well be married the way you and Kori are shacking up. You two live *and* work together."

Cash can't keep his signature Hollywood actor smile from inching onto his face. "What can I say? She's my best friend. It's been that way since we were six."

Mace scoffs. "Funny, 'cuz I thought I was your best friend."

"You are... except she's a lot prettier than you. So she automatically wins."

We're cracking up in laughter when Silver enters and makes his announcement.

Mandy's dead.

I lose my sense of humor that fast. Standing up from where I'm reclined on the suede couch, I jut my chin at him. "You joking, or you serious?"

"There are three things I don't joke about, Ghost. Money, divorce, and death." Silver scrubs two fingers against his brow like a terrible migraine's paining him. "I went down there to feed her her daily gruel and found her slumped in the chair. Her face and neck were as swollen as a balloon with too much air. Some kind of allergic reaction."

"Allergic reaction?" I repeat.

"The stranger thing was there was a tray of cookies nearby. Burnt ones."

"Peanut butter cookies?" Cash asks.

The three of us all question him with a mere glance. He gives a shrug.

"I overheard Sydney and Kori talking about it earlier. Sydney had baked them to surprise you, Mace. She said they're your favorite."

"You're saying Syd poisoned Mandy?" Mace asks in return, skepticism thick in his voice. "Don't get me wrong. She hates Mandy's fucking guts. But that's 'cuz she's a Steel Queen and she's all in on our club. Our enemies are her enemies. But poisoning Mandy? Not her thing."

"Mandy was allergic to peanuts," I say slowly, searching my memory. "I've overheard it before. Back when I was... you know. One of the captives was once beaten for trying to feed her peanut butter."

Only one other person affiliated with the MC would know that.

I have to contain my real reaction. I let the others speculate for a couple minutes while I'm dragging a hand across my jaw, resisting the pull my mouth gives to grin.

My sweet and innocent little wife ain't as sweet and innocent as she'd have me believe.

It's exactly the type of nonviolent crime she could justify. She could rationalize feeding someone and wiping her hands of the situation if they have some kind of reaction. It's not like she poisoned the cookies herself.

Matter of fact, knowing my baby, she probably rationalized it as feeding a hungry woman.

Charity work in the Lord's name.

In reality, she was eliminating Mandy. She was seeking revenge for me like I'd done for her.

I give up on my poker face and grin to myself.

"I'm guessing you're happy she's gone?" Silver asks, interrupting my inner monologue.

"Hmm? Yeah," I answer, clearing my throat. My grin widens. "Good fucking riddance to that disgusting bitch."

Over the coming days, things stay hectic. Between the wedding prep, concealing our illegal club business, and dealing with the aftermath of what happened with the Chosen Saints, we've got our hands full.

The FBI continues their intense investigation. They pull several of us in for questioning, asking things like why we were present at the church in Boulder at the time of Abraham's death and how we have ties to the Barreras.

We pay the cartel back for their treachery and part in

the flesh trade by sending the feds sniffing their way. I was misleading in what I told Miguel about what the FBI knew, which means it's the fucking shock of a lifetime when their clubhouse Zapote is raided and they're caught in the middle of a massive drug deal.

Satisfying revenge for selling human beings, including Teysha.

Elsewhere, Silver's at the helm making sure our own tracks are covered. Our stories match. All potential evidence is destroyed.

When I'm brought in for questioning, I give the truth— or the sanitized version that leaves out the info that works against the Steel Kings.

I tell them about how the Chosen Saints took dozens captive and held us against our will. I tell them all about Abraham and what a sick, twisted piece of shit he was. How I'd killed him in self-defense to keep me and Teysha alive.

Then I glared up into the scrutinous stares of Agents Strauss and Rodriguez and dared them to arrest me.

Strauss sighed, her mouth bent at a downturn. She shared a look of disappointment with Rodriguez, then waved a hand at the door.

"You're free to go, Mr. Cutler. If we have any further questions, we'll be in contact."

I ran into Ozzie in the hall outside, waiting on his turn to be interrogated. He grinned at me and said, "So how much of a hard ass is she really?"

But as soon as I walked out of the local police station the FBI was working out of, I was wiping my hands of the situation.

Abraham and the Chosen Saints had stolen enough time from me. I had given up years being held captive, mentally enslaved, physically broken in every way, and now all I wanted to do was live my life.

Love the woman I had pledged the rest of it to.

Just a few weeks ago, I would've considered a prospect like that to be laughable. I wasn't the type of man to get married and I damn sure wasn't the kind who wanted to be some family man. Some husband and father who lived that traditional style of life.

I followed in Dad's footsteps and became a Steel King for the exact opposite reason.

Women were supposed to be guests who came and went in my bed. Easily disposable and forgettable by the time the sun rose.

I wasn't supposed to fall for a woman that changed my whole perspective.

When I was ready to live a life full of rage and self-loathing, she showed me optimism was possible. Hope was within reach.

All I had to do was open myself up to it. All I had to do was give it a real chance.

Give our marriage that chance.

As it turns out, it's been the smartest thing I've ever done. Being with Teysha has shown me that things don't always have to be so damn dark and brooding. There's bright spots to life too, like the kind of love that exists between a man and his woman.

I just have to be the man she truly deserves. Something I've promised I'll work at everyday 'til I'm six feet under.

I come home to her curled up on the couch with another one of those books she loves so much. Not the Bible —though she loves that too—but one of those word porn books.

Pantless.

She knows exactly what the fuck she's doing.

I crack a grin and drop down over her 'til my body's covered hers and my lips do the same. It takes no more than five minutes for us to wind up with our clothes on the floor and her bent over the couch, my cock buried deep in her pussy.

It's the kind of marital bliss you can only hope for but that's our reality.

When the day of the wedding arrives, we're lazy in bed, legs entangled in the sheets, snuggling close like she likes— and I do too.

We arrive at the pasture on the outskirts of town where it's being held, in a calm and joyous mood. Teysha keeps tugging at the collar of my button up shirt, and I keep squeezing her hip, unable to stop touching her.

The others arrive in twos and threes. Some men with their old ladies. Others solo, proudly donning their club vests over slightly more formal shirts. Teysha smiles at Ozzie's flannel he's got on under his leather vest.

"That's an interesting fashion choice."

"This? Oh... yeah. Best I can do." His tone lacks his usual humor, and his gaze grows distant, like he's searching the attendees for someone that's not around.

"You alright?" I ask.

"Yeah... you know, same shit. Different day."

"Where's Hope?" Teysha poses the question to be cheerful. To uplift his mood.

Instead, she accidentally makes it worse. Ozzie stops scouring the crowd and returns his eyes to us, like he's just remembered we're in front of him.

"Hope's gone. We, uh, we broke up last night. She says she needs to get outta town and clean up her act. Apparently, all the shit that went down with the Saints was too much. She couldn't handle the craziness. The FBI interrogated her, and she decided she wanted nothing to do with the club... and me."

Teysha gasps, a sympathetic hand touching his arm. "I'm so sorry, Ozzie. I had no idea."

"It's cool. Who needs love anyway when there's always the Titty Bar in town?"

The laugh he gives is hollow, unlike his usual one. He shrugs walking off, headed in the direction of the refreshment table that's been set up.

"What's this I hear about the Titty Bar and love?" Silver asks from behind us.

We turn around to find he's walked up on the tail end of our conversation with Ozzie. Silver being Silver, looks slightly more groomed and dressed up than the rest of us—he's got a real button down shirt on, and he's skipped out on wearing his rocker. With his tattoos covered, he looks more silver fox bachelor than MC acting prez.

"Ozzie and Hope broke up," I say.

He scratches his gray stubble. "So I heard. Looks like only a select few of us have luck in matters of the heart."

"You will too again... someday," Teysha says in hopes she'll do for him what she couldn't for Ozzie.

But Silver only lets a flicker of humor pass in and out on his face. "No need to sell me that fairytale ending. I gave up on that the second my ex turned into a gambling alcoholic. But I'm happy for Mace and Syd. And you two, of course."

We're left alone for the first time since arriving. Teysha being the optimist who's had her sunshine and bright skies ruined by rain, frowns. I pull her toward me for a tender kiss and reassurance.

"They'll be alright," I say, nuzzling my face with hers. "I

was them once. Moody and brooding. Now look at me. What the loving of a good woman has done to me."

Her nose wrinkles just like I like. "You sure fought it hard enough."

"That's 'cuz I thought you were too good for me. I still think you're too good for me. Which is why I'm gonna thank God every fucking day that he blessed me with you."

"Logan Cutler, you might not realize it, but I could say the same about you," she says, tears emerging in her eyes. "You saved not just my life... you saved my soul in the darkest moments of my life."

"Shhh, baby. Don't cry." I capture her lips again, holding her heart-shaped face in my strong hands. "Which reminds me... your cross necklace. Finally had a chance to get it fixed."

Teysha's damn near lost her voice as I ease her around and drape the golden cross necklace along her chest where it belongs. I connect the little clasp and then press a kiss to her nape, drawing in a greedy inhale of her.

Her golden cross necklace at last right where it belongs.

Hanging from her neck as her devotion to her faith and never ending optimism.

Some that's rubbed off on me these days...

We're so enamored with each other that we don't realize the wedding's underway 'til everybody around us takes their place. We share small, secret smiles between us as we move to do the same.

An acoustic version of the traditional ceremonial music starts to play.

The wedding's officially begun.

40

TEYSHA

"MASON THOMAS CUTLER, DO YOU TAKE SYDNEY Singer to be your lawfully wedded wife?" asks Mick, who's serving as officiant. "Will you honor and cherish her; love, trust, and commit to her, through joy and pain, sickness and health, and whatever life may throw at you both, until death do you part?"

Mason's green eyes gleam as he peers at Sydney. "Yeah, I do. Every damn day from here on out."

Sydney's lips spread wider, the same gleam in her gaze as Mick turns to her.

"Sydney Singer, do you take Mason Cutler to be your lawfully wedded husband? Will you honor and cherish him; love, trust and commit to him, through joy and pain, sickness and health, and whatever life may throw at you both, until death do you part?"

"Every day," she says, parroting Mason. Then the smile that had touched her lips spreads. "I do. I can't wait."

I'm standing off on the sidelines next to Korine, doing my best not to let the tears win. I sniffle as they exchange vows and then Mick orders Mason to kiss his bride.

"I now pronounce you husband and wife. Mace, you've got zero-point-five seconds to kiss your dang bride or I'm going to scoop her up for myself!"

His threatening tease is met with a chorus of laughter, jeers, and catcalls. Mason only needs to be told once—he yanks Sydney toward him, crushing his lips to hers in a kiss that's as hot as the summer afternoon.

We clap and whistle and cheer on the happily married couple as they join hands and rush off. Sydney remembers at the last second she's still clutching her bouquet of wild flowers and turns toward the women in attendance.

Shrill screams enter the air as several scramble to catch the airborne flowers. The bouquet smacks into Korine's chest, then rolls to her feet.

As if the crowd couldn't go wilder than they already have. I'm right with them as we break out into an even louder round of applause and Korine smiles shyly, picking up the bouquet. Cash couldn't look more pleased from where he stands on the opposite side with the rest of the groomsmen.

The afternoon morphs into a celebration. The wedding becomes a party as music fills the background and everyone mingles. Mason and Sydney share a dance—or as close to a dance as Mason's ever going to get—to more hoots and hollers.

I watch on with cheeks that ache from smiling so hard. I've given up on pretending that I'll save my eye makeup from running.

The mood is too joyous to care. The future feels bright and hopeful, and I know in my soul I've made the right decision in joining this family. In letting myself fall in love with the rugged, rough-around-the-edges biker that I have.

He comes up the first chance he's able to, grabbing my

hands to lead me toward where everybody else is chatting and dancing. A simple glance around shows we're not alone in our festive mood. Korine and Cash are slow dancing, Korine still clutching the wildflower bouquet as Cash hugs her close.

Meanwhile, Mason and Sydney couldn't be more ready to get going. They've started inching toward his bike as if they've had enough of the wedding ceremony itself and would prefer to move onto their honeymoon vacation.

Two weeks in Hawaii.

My watery gaze drifts away from everyone else and meets Logan. I've twined my arms around his shoulders as we sway in place.

"I would say it's all worked out. Don't you think?"

"Not sure you could say that just yet," he answers. "There's still one matter we've got to handle."

"This better not be about the peanut butter cookies! I have no idea what you're talking about."

He grins. "You definitely know all about those damn peanut butter cookies. But that's not what I meant."

"If this is about the word porn—"

"Baby, this ain't about no fucking word porn," he interrupts with a gruff laugh, squeezing my hips. "This is about you and me and what we need to do."

My brows join together out of puzzled thoughts. "I'm not sure I understand."

"Marry me," he says. "Again. For real this time. On our terms. Let's elope. Right now."

"What? Logan, I don't—"

"Me. You. My Harley. Las Vegas."

I laugh, the proposal's so ridiculous. Then I glance around as if checking for approval. "You're serious? Right now?"

"Right now. You said you were never spontaneous. You never did things you thought you shouldn't. I'm willing to bet you've never been to Vegas," he says, his grin infectious. His steely eyes brighter than usual. "Think of it as an adventure to kick off our lives together. What d'you think?"

My heart pounds faster in exhilaration as I imagine the long ride on the open road, clinging to Logan as we head off to create our own happy ending. As we remake our wedding in our own unique image and go on an adventure I've never imagined.

A nervous giggle bubbles out of me as I lift myself onto tiptoe and cling tighter to him, my arms locked around his neck.

"Yes," I answer breathlessly. "Okay! Let's do it!"

"Right now?"

"Right now!"

We're both laughing as he grabs hold of my hand and we rush off toward his recently repaired Super Glide that sparkles a vivid shade of crimson under the afternoon sun. Several others notice we're running off and call out to us as we do.

"We're out!" Logan yells from over his shoulder. "Off to go get married."

"Again!" I add between a giggle.

Everybody gathered around explodes into the latest round of cheers. Logan mounts his large bike first then waits for me to bunch up the skirt of my dress and climb aboard behind him. I press myself against his back, snuggling closer, one arm banded around his waist while the other waves goodbye.

The engine rumbles its goodbyes too as we blast off toward the future. The new life we're about to embark on.

As we do, I've never been more grateful for the lesson

I've learned—sometimes, the happiest endings really do come from the ugliest beginnings.

THE END... FOR NOW.

KINGS FEAR NO ONE PLAYLIST

Logan:

1. Blackbird Song - Lee Dewyze

2. Lead Me Home - Jamie N Commons

3. The Pay Off - Royal Deluxe

4. Way Down We Go - Kaleo

5. Line of Fire - Junip

6. Let it Burn - Shaboozey

7. You & Me - Lifehouse

Teysha:

1. 16 Carriages - Beyoncé

2. Civilian - Wye Oak

3. Dark Sky Nights - Blue in Tokio

4. Into Dust - Mazzy Star

5. II Most Wanted - Beyoncé featuring Miley Cyrus

6. Breathe Me - SIA

7. Found it in You - Tiera Kennedy

Listen to Logan and Teysha's playlists on Spotify!

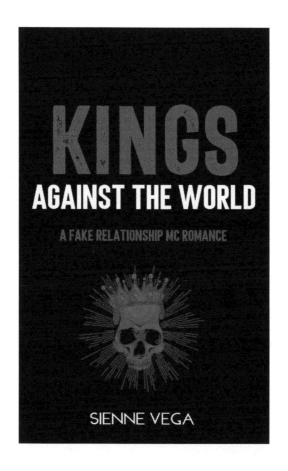

A Dark Fake Relationship MC Romance

COVER, BLURB AND SAMPLE COMING SOON

STAY CONNECTED

Let's keep in touch!

Follow me on social media below. 🤍

ALSO BY SIENNE VEGA

The Capo and the Ballerina

Book 1 - Vicious Impulses

Book 2 - Brutal Impulses

City of Sinners Series

Book 1 - King of Vegas

Book 2 - Queen of Hearts

Book 3 - Kingdom of Sin

Book 4 - Heart of Sin (Louis & Tasha Novella)

City of Sinners Special Edition Boxset

Gangsters & Roses Series

Book 0 - Forbidden Roses

Book 1 - Wicked Roses

Book 2 - Twisted Roses

Book 3 - Savage Roses

Book 4 - Devious Roses

Book 5 - Ruthless Roses

Gangsters & Roses Special Edition Boxset

The Steel Kings MC Series

Book 1 - Kings Have No Mercy

Book 2 - Kings Don't Break

Book 3 - Kings Fear No One

Book 4 - Kings Against the World

The Midnight Society

Book 1 - Cruel Delights

Book 2 - Cruel Pleasures

Book 3 - Cruel Cravings

Seattle Wolves

Book 1 - Break the Ice

Savage Bloodline

Caesar DeLuca

<u>Stand Alones:</u>

Wicked Little Secret

Shared by the Capo

Or scan the QR code below for a direct link to my books!

ABOUT THE AUTHOR

Sienne has a thing for dark and brooding alphas and the women who love them. She enjoys writing stories where lines are blurred, and the romance is dark and delicious. In her spare time, she unwinds with a nice glass of wine and Netflix binge.

Made in the USA
Middletown, DE
09 December 2024

66511616R00253